PENGUIN CLASSICS

COME ALONG WITH ME

SHIRLEY JACKSON was born in San Francisco in 1916. She first received wide critical acclaim for her short story "The Lottery," which was published in *The New Yorker* in 1948. Her novels—which include *The Sundial, The Bird's Nest, Hangsaman, The Road Through the Wall, We Have Always Lived in the Castle,* and *The Haunting of Hill House*—are characterized by her use of realistic settings for tales that often involve elements of horror and the occult. *Raising Demons* and *Life Among the Savages* are her two works of nonfiction. She died in 1965.

STANLEY EDGAR HYMAN was born in Brooklyn in 1919 and married Shirley Jackson in 1940, the year they both graduated from Syracuse University. Hyman was a literary critic, a staff writer for *The New Yorker*, and professor of literature at Bennington College, as well as a noted critic of jazz music. He died in 1970.

LAURA MILLER is a journalist and critic living in New York. She is a cofounder of Salon.com, where she is a senior writer. Her work has appeared in *The New Yorker, Los Angeles Times, Time* magazine, and many other publications. She is the author of *The Magician's Book: A Skeptic's Adventures in Narnia* and *The Salon .com Reader's Guide to Contemporary Authors* (Penguin, 2000). She lives in New York.

SHIRLEY JACKSON

Come Along with Me

CLASSIC SHORT STORIES
AND AN UNFINISHED NOVEL

Edited by
STANLEY EDGAR HYMAN

Foreword by
LAURA MILLER

PENGUIN BOOKS

PENGUIN BOOKS

Published by the Penguin Group
Penguin Group (USA) Inc., 375 Hudson Street, New York, New York 10014, USA
Penguin Group (Canada), 90 Eglinton Avenue East, Suite 700, Toronto,
Ontario M4P 2Y3, Canada (a division of Pearson Penguin Canada Inc.)
Penguin Books Ltd, 80 Strand, London WC2R 0RL, England
Penguin Ireland, 25 St Stephen's Green, Dublin 2, Ireland (a division of Penguin Books Ltd)
Penguin Group (Australia), 707 Collins Street, Melbourne,
Victoria 3008, Australia (a division of Pearson Australia Group Pty Ltd)
Penguin Books India Pvt Ltd, 11 Community Centre, Panchsheel Park, New Delhi–110 017, India
Penguin Group (NZ), 67 Apollo Drive, Rosedale, Auckland 0632,
New Zealand (a division of Pearson New Zealand Ltd)
Penguin Books (South Africa), Rosebank Office Park, 181 Jan Smuts Avenue,
Parktown North 2193, South Africa Penguin China, B7 Jiaming Center,
27 East Third Ring Road North, Chaoyang District, Beijing 100020, China

Penguin Books Ltd, Registered Offices: 80 Strand, London WC2R 0RL, England

First published in the United States of America by The Viking Press, Inc., 1968
Published in Penguin Books 1995
This edition with a new foreword published 2013

"The Lottery" reprinted with permission of Farrar, Straus & Giroux, Inc., from *The Lottery* by
Shirley Jackson; Copyright 1948, 1949 by Shirley Jackson; first published in *The New Yorker*.
"The Summer People" first published in *Charm;* "A Cauliflower in Her Hair" in *Mademoiselle;*
"Pajama Party" in *Vogue*. Other selections have appeared in *Harper's, The Ladies' Home Journal,
New Mexico Quarterly, New World Writing,* and *The Saturday Evening Post.*

PUBLISHER'S NOTE
Some of these selections are works of fiction. Names, characters, places, and incidents either are the
product of the author's imagination or are used fictitiously, and any resemblance to actual persons,
living or dead, events, or locales is entirely coincidental.

ISBN 978-0-14-310711-8 (pbk.)

Set in Sabon

ALWAYS LEARNING   PEARSON

For Carol Brandt

Contents

Foreword

Few women with children and husband and household—however happy they may be with all three—have not fantasized at least once or twice about the sort of radical freedom achieved by Angela Motorman at the beginning of *Come Along with Me*, the novel Shirley Jackson was writing when she died in 1965. Angela has buried her (unmourned) husband, Hughie, sold her house, auctioned off her belongings, and "erased my old name and took my initials off of everything" before leaving town with no particular destination in mind. She arrives in a city, invents a new name for herself, takes a room in a boardinghouse, and begins to give séances. At the age (and dress size) of forty-four, with no connections except to the dead, she is making herself up as she goes along.

Come Along with Me was a late and very welcome literary child for Jackson. She lived with her husband, the critic and academic Stanley Edgar Hyman, and their four children in a big, rambling, book-crammed house in North Bennington, Vermont, and was the commercially and critically successful author of, among other novels, *The Haunting of Hill House* (made into an excellent film in 1963). Her short story "The Lottery" caused a sensation when *The New Yorker* published it in 1948, provoking more letters than the magazine had received about any other piece. She had transformed her children's high jinks into a series of popular, lucrative, and utterly charming humorous essays that appeared in women's magazines and were collected in two books titled *Life Among the Savages* and *Raising Demons*. ("Pajama Party" and "The Night We All Had Grippe" in this volume are examples of these pieces; the child characters are based on and named after Jackson's own kids.) Jackson and Hyman had a lot of fascinating literary friends, including Ralph Ellison, Bernard Malamud, and Dylan Thomas. Their lives, though sometimes disorderly, were also interesting and often fun—anything but the stifling routine associated with housewifery in the 1950s. But to judge from the "fine high gleefulness" with which Angela launches into the unknown, even Shirley Jackson knew what it was like to dream of chucking it all.

Come Along with Me marked a significant point of evolution in Jackson's work. Previously, her main characters tended to be mousy, neurotic young women who hardly anyone noticed: wallflowers, caretaking daughters, fifth wheels. Angela Motorman, however, is more like her creator, a woman of substance, giving as good as she gets. Yet, as the writings collected here illustrate, even this brave new project hewed close to Jackson's long-standing concerns and motifs. The twentieth century's great artist of domesticity and its terrors, her persistent theme was the unspoken and unanticipated prices we pay to belong, whether to a family or to a community.

The fourteen short stories in this volume were selected from Jackson's previously uncollected fiction after her death by Hyman, who felt they were "those best showing the range and variety of her work over three decades." The first, "Janice," may have been a sentimental choice; it was printed in a campus magazine at Syracuse University during Jackson's sophomore year, and Hyman, when he read it, announced that he would marry its author. (At that point they had yet to meet.) The story is very short, almost sketchy, like a collection of notes, but it has many of the stylistic traits that would later become Jackson's signatures: the breathtaking confidence that she can pull off a tragic or mad character in a few strokes; the airy, vernacular dialogue that darts at ominous subtexts, then darts away; the precocious awareness that a suggestion is always more disturbing than a shock.

In part due to "The Lottery," Jackson was and is sometimes referred to as a horror writer. The Shirley Jackson Awards, founded in 2007, honor "outstanding achievement in the literature of psychological suspense, horror, and the dark fantastic" published the preceding year. Stephen King lists Jackson as a major influence on his own work, although their approaches to the supernatural are very different; where King writes epics, Jackson carved exquisite cameos. Jackson, for her part, clearly believed that fear should sneak up on a reader from behind and manifest itself as quietly as a discreet tap on the shoulder. The hauntings in her fiction aren't often recognizable as such until the end, and only after you think about it a bit. In this, she's the link between Henry James, who pioneered the same type of highly psychologized ghost story, and contemporary writers as diverse and unclassifiable as Kelly Link, Jonathan Lethem, and Neil Gaiman. It is her ability to link the homely and the uncanny, the cozy and merciless, that has made her literary vision unforgettable.

Then there are the houses: Jackson's women are always arriving at a big house, or trying to get out of one. Angela Motorman may have jettisoned the place she lived with Hughie, but in no time she's ensconced a new establishment, the boarding-house presided over by the simultaneously hospitable and mercenary Mrs. Faun. Like Louisa in "Louisa, Please Come Home," Angela seems more comfortable with the transactional relationship between landlady and tenant than she is with family ties—those, in Jackson's fiction, always seem to be secured with razor wire.

The impression that menace lurks in life's most familiar precincts, that intimate relations are filled with mortal peril, is the defining mood in the stories collected here. The helpful townfolk of "The Summer People," the nice little old ladies from next door in "The Little House," the upright minister father in "I Know Who I Love"—all are out to get the protagonists. Escape is just another a dangerous illusion, not least because without our old tormentors, identity itself can come unmoored. The housewife in "The Beautiful Stranger" rejoices in the belief that the man who comes home to her one day is not, thank God, the husband "who enjoyed seeing me cry." But if he's not John, then can she be Margaret? Is she really entitled to another, better life? Among the best of the sinister wonders in this collection is "The

Visit," a variation on a romance or fairy tale, in which the big beautiful country house, a catalog of marvel-filled rooms presided over by a handsome prince, is actually a trap. There's a crazy old lady in the tower, and she seems to be you.

Then there's "The Lottery," a story that has been freaking out readers for decades, with its depiction of a folksy New England town (that quintessential touchstone of American values) routinely turning on one of its own. Jackson's amused and amusing account of the initial response to "The Lottery," "Biography of a Story," shows that the letters forwarded to her by *The New Yorker* only confirmed her sardonic view of human nature and social relationships. You might assume that the readers of *The New Yorker* would be cultivated, or at least genteel, she implies, but think again: "What they wanted to know was where these lotteries were held, and whether they could go there and watch." In an era before Internet comments threads, Jackson's correspondents gave her a creepily prescient intimation of just how much of the reading public is "gullible, rude, frequently illiterate, and horribly afraid of being laughed at."

Angela Motorman hasn't freed herself from people like this, but then who could? They are everywhere. She has, however, finally gotten the upper hand. She doesn't care if her neighbors pick over her belongings at auction, give her attitude on a streetcar, charge her for the tea and cookies she assumed were offered in friendship. She has her "fine high gleefulness" and (as she mentions more than once) plenty of money. She knows where she stands. Her voice—jaunty, colloquial, and rich in black humor—is Jackson's. Unlike Flannery O'Connor's (to invoke a writer of similar temperament whom Jackson admired greatly), it is a voice less celebrated today than it ought to be. But its influence has never died out, and a slow-burning Jackson revival—heralded by the recent inclusion of her work in the Library of America series—continues to grow. Where Jackson would have taken that voice next in *Come Along with Me* remains unknowable. Angela Motorman might have pulled a message from her out of the ether, but she too, alas, is gone before her time.

LAURA MILLER

Preface

Come Along with Me is the unfinished novel at which Shirley Jackson, my late wife, was at work at the time of her death in 1965. She rewrote the first three sections; the remaining three sections are in first draft.

The fourteen short stories were chosen from about seventy-five not previously collected, as the best, or those best showing the range and variety of her work over three decades. Most of them have appeared in magazines, in slightly altered versions and in a few cases with different titles suggested by the magazine—thus "A Visit" returns to its original title and dedication. I titled "The Rock," which was found in an early draft, untitled; I cannot imagine why it was discarded, since it seems to me a most impressive story. "Janice" must be one of the shortest short stories on record. Shirley Jackson wrote it as a sophomore at Syracuse University, and it was printed in *Threshold*, the magazine published by her class in creative writing. My admiration for it led to our meeting. I suppose that I reprint it to some degree out of sentiment, although in its economy and power it is surely prophetic of her later mastery.

The three lectures are the lectures that Shirley Jackson delivered at colleges and writers' conferences in her last years. "The Night We All Had Grippe" is printed after the lecture she used to conclude with a reading of it, although it appears as a section of *Life Among the Savages*, since it gets somewhat lost in that book, and I find it the funniest piece since James Thurber's *My Life and Hard Times*. "The Lottery" is printed after the lecture that customarily concluded with *it*, because of the possibility, however remote, that there are readers unfamiliar with it.

The dedication to Carol Brandt, her good friend and agent, was Shirley Jackson's wish.

I most gratefully acknowledge my indebtedness to my children, Barry and Sarah Hyman, and my present wife, Phoebe Pettingell, for help in assembling, selecting, and editing the contents of this book.

STANLEY EDGAR HYMAN
[1968]

COME ALONG
WITH ME

I

I always believe in eating when I can. I had plenty of money and no name when I got off the train and even though I had had lunch in the dining car I liked the idea of stopping off for coffee and a doughnut while I decided exactly which way I intended to go, or which way I was intended to go. I do not believe in turning one way or another without consideration, but then neither do I believe that anything is positively necessary at any given time. I got off the train with plenty of money; I needed a name and a place to go; enjoyment and excitement and a fine high gleefulness I knew I could provide on my own.

A woman said to me in the train station, "My sister might want to rent a room to a nice lady; she's got this little crippled kid."

I could use a little crippled kid, I thought, and so I said, "Where does your sister live, dear?"

A fine high gleefulness; I think you understand me; I have everything I want.

I sold the house at a profit. Once I got Hughie buried—my God, he was a lousy painter—I only had to make a thousand and three trips back and forth from the barn—which was a studio, which was a mess—to the house. At my age and size—both forty-four, in case it's absolutely vital to know—I was carrying those paintings and half-finished canvasses ("This is the one the artist was working on the morning of the day he died," and it was just as lousy as all the rest; not even imminent glowing death could help that Hughie) and books and boxes of letters and more than anything else cartons and cartons of things Hughie saved, his old dance programs and marriage licenses and fans and the like. It was none of it anything I ever wanted to see again, I promise you, but I didn't dare throw any of it away for fear Hughie might turn up someday asking, the way they sometimes do, and knowing Hughie it would be the carbon copy of something back in 1946 he wanted. Everything he might ever possibly come around asking for went into the barn; one thousand and three trips back and forth.

I am not a callous person and no one Hughie ever knew could possibly call me practical, but I had waited long enough. I knew I could sell the house. The furniture went to everyone, and I did think that was funny. They came up to me at the auction, people I had known for years, people who had come to the funeral, people who had sat on the chairs and eaten at the dining-room table and sometimes passed out on the beds, if the truth were known, and they said things like "I bought your little maple desk and anytime you want it back it's waiting for you," and "Listen, we picked up the silver service, but it's nothing personal," and "You know the piano will find a happy home with us," and "We are grieving with you today"—no, that one they said at the funeral. In any case, all the people I had known for years came to the auction and the ones who had the nerve came up and spoke to me, sometimes embarrassed because here they were peeking at the undersprings of my sofa, and sometimes just plain brazen because they had gotten something of mine they wanted. I heard one woman—no names, of course; no one has a name yet—saying to another woman that the dining-room breakfront had always been wasted on me, which was true; I only kept it at all because I was afraid my dead grandmother would come around asking. Actually, almost all of it was wasted on me. It was Hughie's idea. "You come of such a nice family," he used to say to me, "your people were all such cultivated educated people; try to remember."

So that was how I started out. I'd thought about it for a long time of course—not that I positively expected I was going to have to bury Hughie, but he had a good life—and everything went the way I used to figure it would. I sold the house, I auctioned off the furniture, I put all the paintings and boxes in the barn, I erased my old name and took my initials off everything, and I got on the train and left.

I can't say I actually chose the city I was going to; it was actually and truly the only one available at the moment; I hadn't ever been there and it seemed a good size and I had enough in my pocket to pay the fare. When I got off the train I took a deep breath of the dirty city air and carried my suitcase and my pocketbook and my fur stole—Hughie wasn't selfish, I don't want to give a wrong impression; I always had everything I wanted— and stopped at the counter for coffee and doughnuts.

"My sister might want to rent a room to a nice lady," this woman said to me, "she's got this little crippled kid."

So I said, "Where does your sister live, dear?"

That was where I got my first direction, you see. Smith Street. Where I was going to be living for a while.

The city is a pretty city, particularly after living in the country; I have nothing actually against trees and grass, of course, but Hughie always wanted to live in the country. There was a zoo somewhere in this city, and a college, and a few big stores, and streetcars, which I believe you don't often see any more. I knew there was an art gallery—who could be married to Hughie, that painter, and not know about an art gallery?—and a symphony orchestra, and surely a little theater group, mostly wives and fairies; if I liked the city and I stayed I might look up the little theater group; there was an art movie and I hoped at least one good restaurant; I am a first-rate cook.

More than anything else, more than art movies or zoos, I wanted to talk to people; I was starved for strangers. I began with the woman at the counter in the railroad station.

"She has this little crippled kid."

"Where does your sister live, dear?"

"She was married to the same man for twenty-seven years and all he left her was the house and this little kid, he's crippled. Me, I don't like a man like that."

"They don't leave you with much, and that's a fact."

"After twenty-seven years married to the same man she shouldn't have to take in roomers."

"But if one of her roomers turns out to be me it might all have been worthwhile."

"That's where I've been, visiting my sister." She put down her coffee cup. "I come to visit her. And then I take the train back home. You have to take the train to get from my house to hers." She looked at me carefully, as though she might be wondering whether I could remember my own name. "She lives on Smith Street. You'll know the house. It's big. She's got this sign ROOMS."

"At least he left her a big house," I said.

"Up and down stairs all the time, keeping up a big house these days. She's not getting any younger, and the kid."

"Well, we're none of us," I said.

After that I talked to a man on a corner; he was waiting for a streetcar. "Does this streetcar go to Smith Street?" I asked him.

"What streetcar?" He turned and looked down the street.

"The one you're waiting for; this is a car stop, isn't it?"

He looked again, and we marveled together at the delights of the city, where you could stand on a corner and a streetcar would come. "Where you say?" he asked me.

"Smith Street."

"You live there?"

"Yes. I got this little crippled kid. Big house."

"No," he said, "you get that car across the street. Because across the street is going the other way. How long you say you've lived there?"

"Twenty-seven years. With the same man."

"He any better at catching streetcars than you are?"

"He's a motorman," I told him. "I try to avoid his route."

This clearly sounded right to him. "Women always checking up," he said, and turned away from me.

Then I talked to an old lady in a bookshop, who was so very tired that she leaned her elbows on piles of books as we talked; she told me that the city was hell on books, because of the college, and they stole a thousand paperbacks a year. "They can't seem to think of them as books," she said, furious, "books they don't dare steal because of the covers. Also they know I'm watching."

"Do you sell a lot of books?"

"It's the college," she said. "They come here to get an educa-
tion." She laughed, furious. "No one speaks English any more,"
she said. She took her elbows off the pile of books and went
back to sit down on a dirty old chair in the back of the store.
"I'm watching," she called out, "I'm still watching," but I was
leaving.

I went to the correct side of the street and put my suitcase
down and waited carrying my pocketbook and my fur stole
until a streetcar came by reading SMITH STREET and I decided
well this is certainly the streetcar they meant when they said it
went to Smith Street. I swung my suitcase on and climbed up
behind it; you know, *they* know old ladies—not me—and little
crippled kids and pregnant women and maybe sick people
with broken arms are all going to have to ride on those streetcars; you'd think they didn't want passengers, the way they
make those steps. I suppose the salary they pay the motorman
he wouldn't help anyone anyway. He looked at me; he was sitting down driving his streetcar and I was climbing on with my
suitcase and my pocketbook and my fur stole, and I figured if
he wasn't going to help me I wasn't going to help him, so I
said, "Does this streetcar go to Smith Street?"

He looked at me; I must say I like it better when they look at
you; a lot of the time people seem to be scared of finding out
that other people have real faces, as though if you looked at a
stranger clearly and honestly and with both eyes you might
find yourself learning something you didn't actually want to
know. "Lady," he said, "I promise you. This streetcar goes to
Smith Street every trip. That's why," he said, and he was not
smiling, "that's why it says so on the front."

"You're sure?" I was not smiling either and he knew he had
met someone as stubborn as he was, so he quit.

"Yes, lady," he said. "I'm almost positive."

"Thank you," I said. It never pays to let a minute like that
slip by; every word counts. I might never see that motorman
again, but on the other hand, I might be living on Smith Street
and ride home with him every night. He might get to calling
me by whatever name I finally picked out and I might take to

asking him every night how his wife's asthma was today and did his daughter break up with that guy who stole the money and I might take to asking him every night, "Say, driver, does this streetcar go to Smith Street?"

And he might say, every night, not smiling, "Yes, lady, it surely does."

Hughie would not have thought any of that was funny. In case he ever does come back asking I will certainly remember not to tell him.

There is a kind of controlled madness to streetcars; they swing along as though they haven't quite come to terms with tracks yet, and haven't really decided whether tracks are here to stay or streetcars are here to stay on tracks; they swing and tilt and knock people around, especially people who are trying to hold onto a suitcase and a pocketbook and a fur stole. I sat there sliding around on the seat and wondering if anyone was laughing at me and wondering if maybe I was the streetcar type after all, and outside the window the city went by. I saw the biggest store in town and thought that someday very soon I would be in there, and I might say, "Well, if you haven't got this blouse in a size forty-four I'll just run across the street and try there." I would have to have a name before I could open any charge accounts anywhere. "I'd rather you didn't carry money," Hughie used to say, "I want you to go into a store and pick out what you want and tell them your name and walk out; I don't care if it's a thousand dollars, just tell them your name and take what you want." There were hotels; I might come back for a visit someday, and see all my old friends on Smith Street; I might go tea-dancing at the Splendid Hotel, although one letter was missing from its marquee; I might drop into the lobby of the Royal Hotel to hear who was being paged, and pick up a name that way. I saw a drugstore where I might get a prescription filled and buy shampoo, I saw a shop where I might buy records and a place to get my shoes repaired and a laundry and a candy store and a grocery and a leather shop and a pet shop and a toy store. It was a proper little city, correct and complete, set up exactly for my private use, fitted out with quite the right people, waiting for me to come. I slid around on the streetcar seat and thought that they had done it all very well.

I must say that motorman got the last word. I was still looking out the window when he turned around and yelled, "Smith Street." In case there was any doubt about who he was yelling at he pointed his finger at me.

"How is your wife's asthma?" I asked him when I came down the aisle with my suitcase and my pocketbook and my fur stole.

"Better, thank you," he said. "Watch your step."

It was Smith Street all right; no one had lied to me yet. They wanted to make sure I got there as planned; there was a sign on the corner saying SMITH STREET.

I was glad to see that there were trees; far down, at the end, I could see what looked like a little park, and on either side of Smith Street going down to the park there were trees. I thought I would enjoy coming home under the trees, in the rain, perhaps, or in the fall when the leaves were dropping. I thought I would enjoy hearing the sound of the leaves brushing against my window. The houses were the kind no one has built for a good twenty-seven years, big and ample and made for people who liked to sit on their own front porches and watch their neighbors. There were lawns and bushes and garden hoses, there were dogs. The house I wanted was on my right, about halfway down the block; it was a big house with a sign saying ROOMS although I didn't see any little kids looking crippled. I stood across the street from the house for a few minutes; here I am, I thought, here I am.

No one, anywhere, anytime, had given me any word of any other place to go. This was the only objective I had; if I didn't go in here they wouldn't tell me any other place to go. I wondered which room was going to be mine and whether I would look down from its window onto the street and see myself standing there looking up and waiting; by the time I looked out of the window I would have to have a name.

Right then I wished I could sit down for a minute and maybe

have a little something to eat; nothing looks sillier than a
forty-four-year-old woman standing on a sidewalk with a suitcase and a pocketbook and a fur stole trying to think up
a name for herself. Somewhere down the street someone called
a dog, calling "Here, Rover," and I thought that Rover was
probably a good name but it was not actually exactly what I
was looking for; I thought I might stop someone going by and
ask for their name but no one wants to give away a name that
might be terribly important to keep, and even if they did tell it to
me I might not be able to spell it or even pronounce it right and
if you've got a name at all you've got to be able to say it out
loud. I thought of Laura, but Laura was my mother's name. I
didn't want any more of Hughie and his names, and Bertha
was my grandmother and who wants to be named Bertha,
particularly after her grandmother? I thought of Muriel but
that just sounds like someone who gets raped and robbed in an
alley. I once had a cat named Edward, and because he was silver I changed his name to Stargazer and then in the spring to
Robin, and when I got tired, which I did very soon, of a cat
named Robin, I tried to change his name to Edward again and
he got sick and died. You have to be terribly careful with
names; one too many and you lose.

I thought of Jean and Helen and Margaret, but I knew people called by all those names, and perhaps I would not enjoy
answering to them; I thought of Gertrude and Goneril and I
thought of Diana, which was dead wrong and Minerva, which
was closer but silly. I knew I had to think of something right
away, and I got a little chill at the back of my neck; what is
really more frightening than being without a name, nothing to
call yourself, nothing to say when they ask you who you are?
Then it fell on me; I heard it: Angela. It was right, Angela was
the name I had come all this way to find.

The rest of it was easy; I had said it already. Angela Motorman. Mrs. Angela Motorman.

So Mrs. Angela Motorman walked slowly and decently up
the walk to the fine old house with the sign in the window saying ROOMS. She was carrying her suitcase and her pocketbook

and her fur stole, and she stopped for a minute to look the house over very carefully; a lady cannot be too wary of the company she may find herself among, a lady chooses her place of residence with caution. As she set her foot on the steps she put her shoulders back and took a deep breath: Mrs. Angela Motorman, who never walked on earth before.

2

I must say she had the good sense to offer me a cup of tea right away, once she found out I was a friend of her sister's, and in case you are wondering about me having lunch on the train and coffee and a doughnut in the station, and now a cup of tea and cookies, let me just remark that I have plenty of room to put it all.

"And what do you do, Mrs. Motorman?" she asked me.

"I dabble in the supernatural," I told her.

Her name was Mrs. Faun; we both had names. "How is my sister?" she wanted to know.

"Doing well," I said. "Of course, she has her troubles like the rest of us."

I had taken to the house right away; I like most houses, and this was one of the best. The staircase was good, wide and clearly worn by a hundred trips up and down every day, up and down, up and down till your feet could fall off. It was a solid house, a devil to clean, but prepared to stand right where it was forever; enough people had lived here to make the air very alive; I was ready for any number to come around asking, but first I had to deal with Mrs. Faun.

"I've just buried my husband," I said.

"I've just buried mine," she said.

"Isn't it a relief?" I said.

"What?" she said.

"It was a very sad occasion," I said.

"You're right," she said, "it's a relief."

She had a jaw and she served a strong cup of tea and I would not say a bad word against a woman who put out her own homemade sugar cookies for a guest; I am an excellent cook. The tea was served in the kitchen; as soon as I said I was a friend of her sister's she said, quite rightly, "I was just having a cup of tea; come on in the kitchen."

When I tried to say it for the first time I was not actually certain how it was going to sound, because no one had ever said it before in the history of this earth, and I thought to myself, I'm giving birth. "I'm Mrs. Angela Motorman," I said.

"I'm Mrs. Faun," she said right back. "I was just having a cup of tea."

I thought that Mrs. Faun and I were going to be all right together. I didn't know yet whether she had a silly laugh, or went on tapping her fingers on the table, but I liked her kitchen, which had no gadgets, and I liked her stove, which was still warm from making sugar cookies, and I liked her jaw.

"I'm not saying I want a room and I'm not saying I don't," I told her, "but if I did, what would you have to show me?"

"I'm not saying I have a room and I'm not saying I don't," she said right back, "but if you wanted to look I could let you see a very pretty little place."

Oh, I was going to be all right with Mrs. Faun. I liked her jaw and I liked her stove and I liked her house and if she wanted to have a little crippled kid I was certainly not going to stand in her way; "It's hard for a woman alone," I said.

"And what do you do, Mrs. Motorman?"

"I dabble in the supernatural."

"My niece had this meningitis," she said as though I had asked some kind of a question. "Let me fill your cup. She had this meningitis and it got to her heart. They knew it was going to, of course, but they never told her. She had it for years before she found out it got to her heart."

"My cousin had mercury poisoning," I said. "That goes directly to the heart, of course. He only lasted for about three days."

"I had a cousin something like that," she said. "You mentioned what a short time they last. Only in her case it all went to the brain. Reddest face I ever saw and she died not knowing one of us."

"My aunt was the same," I said. "Only she died of pneumonia; that's a very quick one. It catches you without any warning, you swell up, and there you go."

"Bloated," she said, "like my nephew, only his was alcohol."

"And then there was this friend of mine," I said. "She had cirrhosis of the scalp. They don't have a cure yet for any of those things, you know, and they run right through you. I hate to think of the way my friend went right on suffering until the very end."

"Very often the end is the most to be desired," she said. "There was a friend of mine, we all couldn't wait for her to go, but she had cancer. Incurable."

"I had a friend who had cancer," I said, "but they cut off her right leg."

"That's never enough," she said. "Mark me, she'll be back for her other leg. I knew a woman once who lost both arms that way."

"My uncle fell under a truck," I said. I wondered if I should tell her about my great-aunt.

"I'm sorry about your uncle," she said. "Do you want a room or don't you?"

"I do."

"And what do you do, Mrs. Motorman?"

"I dabble in the supernatural. Traffic with spirits. Seances, messages, psychiatric advice, that kind of thing."

"I never had one of those before," Mrs. Faun said. "I'm not saying I haven't had all kinds. You rent out rooms, it's sometimes a surprise what you get."

"I never lived in a room before."

You won't find it terribly difficult," she said, not smiling. "All you have to do is pay for it regularly. I'd be willing to add some meals, but that would be extra."

"Perhaps I could give a hand with the cooking; I'm a fine cook."

"I'm not sure but what that would be extra too," she said. "You may not cook in your room."

"I promise," I said.

"You may not smoke in your bed."

"I promise."

"You may not make noise late at night."

"I promise."

"These are all safety precautions," she explained to me. "Thou shalt not—I mean, you may not keep dirty pets."

"I promise."

"You may not spread any contagious diseases. Although the room I plan to show you has a private bath. Linen provided, we do the heavy cleaning, and anything you raise by way of spirits you have to put back yourself."

Oh, I liked Mrs. Faun. She turned her head suddenly and then she stood up and went over to the back door of the kitchen, the door leading outside, and opened it. "Little early today," she said, and "Must have run all the way," which was clearly some kind of a private joke because there was laughter. I helped myself to another cookie, and then Mrs. Faun came back pushing the wheelchair; there was a ramp built outside the door so she could push it right inside without difficulty. "This is my son Tom," Mrs. Faun said, "Tom, this is Mrs. Motorman." Once again it sounded all right; I was going to learn to answer to it.

"Hi," the boy in the wheelchair said. He seemed to be about twelve years old, although it's hard to tell with a boy sitting down. "Any cookies left?"

"I got my share," I said. "Someday if you want me to I'll make you my special chocolate cake; it's got five layers."

"Okay," he said, and then he laughed. "Motorman's a funny name," he said.

"I just made it up," I told him. "You just home from school?"

"I like school," he said, "but they're always surprised I'm not smarter, because I don't play baseball and stuff, they always think I'm going to be smarter than anyone else. And I'm not."

"Maybe if you practice," I said.

"One kid pushes me down the street every morning and

COME ALONG WITH ME

another kid pushes me back home in the afternoon. They do all the pushing and I ride both ways and it's great, but I'm not as smart as they think I ought to be."

"You're smart enough for your own good," Mrs. Faun said. She brought him a glass of milk and pushed the plate of cookies a little closer to him. "I'll go and check your room," she said to me.

"I'm pretty smart," he said to me anxiously. "I'm not stupid, of course."

"I'm pretty smart, but I never got pushed back and forth to school."

"Well, I'm planning to be a scholar, and I better get started pretty soon. You know any Spanish?"

"No."

"I want to learn Spanish and French and Italian and Russian and then Latin and Greek and be a scholar. So far I only know a little Spanish, but I'm lazy."

"One of these days I might push you to the movies," I said.

"I would like that," he said. "Perhaps a movie in Spanish or French to improve my accent."

We each had another cookie. Then he said, "What do you study, Mrs. Motorman?"

"I was married to a painter."

"Was he any good?"

"He was lousy."

"Is he dead?"

"Yes."

"How long you think I ought to go on studying Spanish before I start French? They're both good languages."

"If you're so lazy why not give up the whole thing?"

"Well," he said, thinking, "I suppose it's because they all keep waiting for me to be so smart. I wouldn't play baseball if I could, you can hurt yourself playing those games. But I don't mind being a scholar."

"Look," I said, "I'm not used to talking to kids."

"Oh, that's all right," he said.

"I don't know why you can't just sit around and read books."

Mrs. Faun came back and said "Drink your milk there," and "Your room is ready." She touched the boy on the head and he said, "Hey, Mrs. Motorman and I are going to the movies someday," and Mrs. Faun looked at me for a minute and then said, "I think you're going to like the room."

3

I brought a couple of cookies upstairs with me, just in case. My room was perfectly square, which was good. My name was Mrs. Angela Motorman and this was where I was going to live, in a square room in Mrs. Faun's house on Smith Street. I did not know as yet what I was going to add to this room; it already held a bed and a dresser and two chairs and a pretty little desk, something like the pretty little desk I had last seen disappearing into the back of a station wagon when I had my auction. There was nothing in these desk drawers; I did not know as yet what I was going to put in them. There was a little bookcase which would hold, I thought, perhaps eleven books; I would have to choose my eleven books very carefully; when I found them I could write "Angela Motorman" on the flyleaves. I put my underwear and stockings into the dresser drawers, and hung my two dresses and my fur stole in the closet; someday I would go to the department stores and buy new clothes; I put my brush and comb on the dresser and put my sleeping pills on the bed-side table and put my reading glasses beside them. I had no pets, no address books, no small effects to set around on tables or pin on walls, I had no lists of friends to keep in touch with and no souvenirs; all I had was myself.

I like people, but I have never needed companions; Hughie was my only mistake.

I set an armchair next to the window of my room, and I was pleased to see that I did indeed look out over the trees and onto the spot on the street where I had stood not long ago wondering over a name; "It's all right, Angela," I said very softly out the window, "it's all right, you made it, you came in and it's all right; you got here after all." And outside the dim nameless creature named herself Mrs. Angela Motorman and came steadily to the door.

4

I have a real feeling for shapes; I like things square, and my room was finely square. Even though I couldn't cook there I thought I could be happy. I wanted the barest rock bottom of a room I could have, I wanted nothing but a place to sleep and a place to sit and a place to put my things; any decorating done to my environment is me.

One reason is, the first time it happened was in a square room, my own room when I was about twelve. Before then, most of it was just whisperings and little half-thoughts, the way a child almost notices something, almost remembers, but this time it was real and I was not dreaming; I know when I'm dreaming. I sat up in bed in the middle of the night, and heard my own voice saying "What? What?" and then I heard another voice, not coming out of my own head—I know what comes out of my own head—saying "Find Rosalind Bleeker. Tell her Sid says hello." Three times I heard that crazy voice say "Tell her Sid says hello."

I knew Rosalind Bleeker—in all the years since I've never forgotten her name—and because she was four or five years older and in high school I had a little trouble finding her the next day, but I caught her when she was walking home. I remember I had trouble getting her attention; I was just a little kid, and she was popular and pretty and always laughing. She was wearing a white blouse and a blue skirt and a charm bracelet. Her hair was curly. She was carrying her biology textbook and a blue-covered notebook. Her shoes were white. Her eyes were blue. She wore a little lipstick. I pulled at her sleeve and said "Rosalind, hey, Rosalind," not very loud because she was a high-school girl. She turned around and looked down at me and frowned, because I was a kid and she was a high-school girl and here I was pulling at her sleeve. "Listen, Rosalind," I said, "listen. I'm supposed to tell you Sid says to say hello." "What?" she said. "Sid says to say hello," I said, and then ran, because I had nothing more to say and I felt silly. I heard later she went home and hanged herself. I don't know.

Anyway, that was the first time. After that there were lots more, some more real than others. There was the time I said to my mother, "Grandma just picked up the phone to call you," and she said, "That's nice," just as the phone rang. She looked at me funny; they always did after a while.

"I dabble in the supernatural," I told Mrs. Faun; she thought I was making some kind of a joke.

I quit when I married Hughie; you'd have to.

I remember another time when I sat by the window and my mother, who ought to have known better by then, said to me, "Why are you always brooding, staring out the window, never doing anything?"

"I'm watching the peacocks walking on the lawn," I said.

"But you ought to be out playing with the other children; why do you suppose we moved here to a nice neighborhood, so you could always sit looking out the window instead of playing with the other kids? Haven't you got any friends? Doesn't anyone like you?"

"I'm watching the peacocks," I tried to tell her. "They're walking on the lawn and I'm watching them."

"You ought to be out with your friends. What are peacocks doing on our lawn, ruining the grass?" and she came over to look out the window; as I say, she ought to have known better.

Sometimes I knew and sometimes I didn't; there would be times when I lay on my stomach on the floor watching creatures playing under the dining-room table, and I knew then of course that my mother wasn't going to see them and was maybe going to put her foot through one when she came by to say why did they move to a nice neighborhood and I wouldn't go out and make friends. Sometimes my good square room would be so full I just lay in bed and laughed. Sometimes weeks would go by and I would be reading some specially interesting book, or painting, or following people every day after school, and nothing would come at all; sometimes they followed me; once an old man followed me, but he turned out to be real. I could see what the cat saw.

When I was about sixteen I began to get self-conscious about all of it; it wasn't that I minded them coming around asking and following me everywhere I went; most sixteen-year-old girls like to be followed, but by then I knew no one else was going to see them and sometimes I felt like a fool; you don't go around staring at empty air all the time, not when you're sixteen years old you don't, not without people beginning to notice. "Do you need glasses?" my mother used to ask me, or "Can't you for heaven's sake stop gawking at nothing and shut your mouth and comb your hair and get out with the other kids?" Then sometimes for weeks at a time I would think that they had gone away, maybe for good, and I'd start taking care of my hair and putting polish on my nails and hanging around the soda shop or going to a football game, and then first thing I knew I'd be talking to someone and a face would come between us and a mouth would open saying some crazy thing, and I'd be watching and listening and whomever I had been talking to would wait for a few minutes and then get edgy and walk away while I was still listening to some other voice. After a while I just stopped talking to anybody.

That's not a good way for a girl to grow up. It's easy to say that if I knew then what I know now I could have handled it better; how can anyone handle things if her head is full of voices and her world is full of things no one else can see? I'm not complaining.

I sat in my pleasant square room at Mrs. Faun's house and thought about it all. Ever since I can remember, I thought as quietly as I could, I have been seeing and hearing things no one else could see and hear. By now I can control the nuisance to some extent. It disappeared entirely when I married Hughie; I have reason to believe now that it is coming back. I sat in Mrs. Faun's house and thought what good did it do to sell the house and find a new name; they don't care what your name is when they come around asking.

At first I tried to point them out to people; I was even foolish enough at first to think other people just hadn't noticed; "Look at that," I would say, "look, right over there, it's a funny man." It didn't take long for my mother to put a stop to that; "There isn't any funny man anywhere," she would say, and jerk on my arm, "what kind of a sewer do you have for a mind?" Once I tried to tell a neighbor about it; it was quite accidental, because I rarely told anyone anything. He was sitting on his front porch one evening in summer and I had been lying on the grass on our lawn, watching small lights go and come among the grass blades, and listening to a kind of singing—sometimes, especially in summer, it was a kind of pleasant world I lived in—and he heard me laughing. He asked me to come and sit on his front porch and he gave me a glass of lemonade, and when he asked me what I had been doing I went ahead and told him. I told him about seeing and hearing, and he listened, which is more than anyone else ever did. "You're clairvoyant," he told me, and I always remembered that; he probably knew less than nothing about it, but he listened and said I was clairvoyant; later he told my mother I ought to be taken to some special clinic and examined, and for about three days she decided I was pregnant. I never talked to him again; I wanted to, once in a while, but he never spoke to me after that.

I knew a lot about people, a lot that they never knew I knew, but I never seemed to have much sense, probably because one thing I never really knew was whether what I was doing was real or not.

The house, I later found out, was almost all square. It had three floors and a basement, and neat trim porches on three sides; whoever built that house had either very little imagination or a mind much like mine, because everything was neatly cornered and as near as possible the same size; that is, one door matched the next almost perfectly and where there were doors they were as often as possible right in the middle of the wall, with an equal space on either side of them. The windows were perfectly correct.

When I asked Mrs. Faun later she told me that there were five people renting rooms in the house; I thought it was wrong that they should be an odd number, but since I was the fifth I could hardly protest, and in any case she had only six rooms to rent. On the top floor were a Mr. Brand who was a bookkeeper, and a Mr. Cabot who was, Mrs. Faun believed, in merchandising. On the second floor were old Mrs. Flanner, who kept a bookshop, Mr. Campbell, who was in transit, and me. Mrs. Faun kept the ground floor for herself. "I always wanted it that way," she told me, "I always used to dream of the time when I could live on the ground floor; I had it planned for years. I always thought the dining room would work out better as a bedroom, and I hated the idea of going upstairs every night and leaving it behind. It's more comfortable, it's more convenient, and it's perfectly safe."

"Safe?"

"In case of fire. I can get out."

I may say that in all the time I was in that house I never met Mr. Campbell, who was in transit.

We were a gay crew, I soon discovered. Here I was, with one suitcase and a fur stole and a pocketbook with plenty of money, but old Mrs. Flanner had had her same room for nine years and she had a television set, all her own furniture, including a Chinese lacquer table, purple drapes on the windows, and a silver tea service. Brand and Cabot on the top floor took cocktails in one another's room every day at six. Mrs. Faun was apt to invite anyone at random to Sunday dinner; she was almost as good a cook as I am. Brand played the cello, and Mrs. Flanner used to sing at one time before her voice cracked. Mrs. Flanner also played the dirtiest game of bridge that Mrs. Faun had ever seen. Brand had a small mustache, Cabot collected Coalport china, Mrs. Faun disliked garlic and consequently never made a decent salad dressing until the day she died; Brand fell over the bottom step of the staircase every night regularly, coming home at five-thirty. He was neither drunk nor clumsy, he never fell over anything else that anyone ever knew of, he never dropped anything or spilled anything, but every night at five-thirty Mr. Brand tripped over the bottom step of the staircase. You could set your clock by Brand falling over the bottom step of the staircase, Mrs. Faun

used to say, if it was important to you to set your clock at
five-thirty. Brand and Cabot and Flanner and I usually took
most of our meals at a little restaurant around the corner, but
every Friday night Brand went to his mother's and every Saturday night Cabot took out a girl; he had been taking her out for
four years now, Mrs. Faun said, but thought marriage was too
confining. I liked Mrs. Faun. I had almost nothing to do, so I
got to helping with the housework and we'd knock off and sit
around the kitchen drinking coffee and eating cookies; Mrs.
Faun baked every second morning, before anyone was up, and
one thing I did like about living in that house was waking up
to the smell of cookies baking.

My room, as I say, was absolutely, perfectly square; I mea-
sured it. I admire a house with a good square room, and when
I unpacked I knew I was going to stay. First I unpacked my picture, my painting; it had been painted with Hughie's paints
but I painted it myself. "Keep it around if you like," Hughie
said, "you're proud of it, all right. Don't think I hate all painting styles but my own." So my own painting went on the wall,
although Mrs. Faun said that it would cost to repair the hole.
Cabot liked my painting, and Brand. Mrs. Flanner poked it with
her finger and said it took her back. Mrs. Faun said it would
cost to repair the hole.

"What do you do, Mrs. Motorman?" Brand asked me.

"A little shoplifting, sometimes," I told him. "Some meddling."

"What brought you to our city?"

"Curiosity," I told him.

Brand and Cabot asked me up for cocktails, and Mrs. Faun
asked me for Sunday dinner, and Mrs. Flanner asked me if I
played bridge and I said no. I walked to the end of Smith Street
and around in the little park, under the trees. One day I went
back to the streetcar and got on and went into the center of
the city, where I went into the first large store and looked at
blouses.

"If you don't have this blouse in a size forty-four," I told the
salesgirl, "I'll just run across the street and look." I didn't go
across the street, actually; I spoke to a lady in a drugstore where
I stopped to have a sandwich and a milk shake. "They're all

chemicals now," she said to me. "You can't even buy pure vanilla. All chemicals."

"In a drugstore you'd expect chemicals."

"Everywhere. You think you're drinking chocolate in that milk shake? Nothing but chemicals."

"I didn't actually come into the city for a milk shake, though; I came to buy a blouse."

"Well, *they*'re chemical. Clothes, food, drink, plants growing in nothing but water, laboratories overcrowded, it's a bad world."

"Bourbon—"

"It's all this mad race into space," she said, and went away.

When I got onto the streetcar to go back, it said SMITH STREET in big letters on the front; "Does this streetcar go to Smith Street?" I asked the motorman, and he looked at me for a minute and then he said very quietly, "Yes, ma'am, it surely does."

"Thank you," I said. "How is your wife's asthma?"

"I am not married," he said, "thank God."

5

When I decided it was time for me to give a seance, I spoke to Mrs. Faun first, of course, since it was her house and I had no idea how she might feel about people coming around asking in her own house; "I thought I might hold a kind of a small seance," I said to her.

"What would that include?" she asked me.

"Well, I sit in the middle, and everyone sits around, and we might have sherry. And then I give messages."

"Who provides the sherry?"

"Everyone has *some* kind of a question they'd like to get answered. Some kind of a question can only be answered from beyond."

I was sure she was going to say "Beyond what?" so I said quickly, "You don't have to believe if you don't want to."

"Thank you," she said. "I'll let you have the cooking sherry."

"May I use the little parlor?"

"That means I'd have to come," Mrs. Faun said. "Unless I choose to sit in the kitchen all the time."

"I'd be honored if you'd come."

"Who else would be here?"

I had made a little sign reading MESSAGES OBTAINED. QUESTIONS ANSWERED. FORTUNES and tacked it up in the bookshop I found my first day. Several people had been interested. The bookshop lady had promised to let them know. So I told Mrs. Faun, "I think there will be several people. And of course anyone from the house."

"Not Tom. I don't allow him seances."

"Has the question ever come up before?"

"Not that I ever thought it would. But he can read all right in his room. He doesn't listen in."

"One reason I want to use the little parlor is that chair."

Mrs. Faun actually laughed. "It used to be my husband's favorite chair," she said. "Night after night."

"Did he ever get any manifestations, sitting there?"

"Not that he thought it worthwhile mentioning. But it's a good chair. I don't much care for it myself, but I could sell it for money."

It was a good chair. It had a back higher than my head, and the arms were solid, and altogether it looked something like a throne of which the seat had been amply seasoned by Mr. Faun's bottom. Whenever the door of the little parlor was open I sneaked in and sat down for a minute; I liked that chair.

"Are you sure," Mrs. Faun asked me, "that you are not tampering with things better left alone? Are you sure that you know what you are doing? Are you sure, Mrs. Motorman, that you are not stirring up some kind of trouble that will hang around my house?"

"It's exactly like taking a long-distance call," I told her. "Once you hang up, it's over."

"I never knew a long-distance call didn't mean trouble for someone."

The little parlor had drapes, which Mrs. Faun never closed,

which is why the dust rose when I closed them, which is why I sneezed and Mrs. Faun scowled; she kept a clean house, generally. I moved the fine chair into the center of the room, and we put a few dining-room chairs around, not too many because I wasn't sure how many would come and I didn't want to look anxious, but enough so no one would stand; no one stood around in Mrs. Faun's house; perhaps because Tom was always sitting down she thought people standing were uncomfortable. Although I have plenty of money I put a large orange bowl, in which Mrs. Faun usually kept apples, on a low table moved just enough out from the wall to be noticeable. "People expect this," I told Mrs. Faun.

"I'll bring the sherry and the glasses," she said, "and you can pay me out of the pot."

"It's really a hobby of mine, mostly. But if it does people good, why keep it to myself?"

"If more people kept more things to themselves this world would be a better place." Mrs. Faun gave the curtain a little shake. "How you can find dust beats me," she said.

I don't know what the bookstore lady could have said around the bookstore, or even what Mrs. Faun might have said around the neighborhood, because when I came to give my seance there were eight people, which made us nine altogether, which is good. I had decided to wear my long dark-blue dress. It doesn't fit as well as it used to, but who says a psychic has to be smart? It has these long sleeves, and I wore my pearls; I will say that for Hughie, he didn't stint me.

All right, I thought, I'll try it once anyway. They all sat there watching me as though they dared me to put something over on them, the watchful, the eager, the perceptive. I realized I was stalling; there were a number of things I wanted to do right now a lot more than lean back and close my eyes in the face of those watching people; I knew they would keep on staring at me after I was gone, and I hated that. I could have said right then that it was a joke, but they would have believed me. "I don't know anything about all this," came to my mind, "please, all of you, go away and don't try to make me do something I hate." But of course I didn't; I looked each of them right in the eye, thinking I hate you I hate you I hope you are brutally disappointed, and I nodded at Mrs. Faun, who at least was almost snarling out loud, and I leaned back and felt the worn velvet of the chair against the back of my neck and wondered who was clamoring around just inside waiting to come around asking, and I closed my eyes. I could hear them breathing. Easy, slow, contemptuous, that would be Mrs. Faun, waiting to be shown. Then the others, quick and eager, a little woman watching, the men aware, alert, dishonest.

I was in a great hall, lofty, pillared, reaching into the distance. There were flowers in great pots, and—the old crystal palace, maybe?—tall glittering walls; there were many people. I waited quietly, not knowing who was going to come around asking, and waited and waited, and then found one man singled out, almost drifting to where I waited, almost moving without movement, surely without sound. "A tall man," I said, and heard my own voice remotely, "a tall man, wanting something. He has gray hair. He is not very old, but he has gray hair."

"My father," someone said.

"*My* brother," someone else said.

"Excuse me. My father."

"He says," and I raised my voice, hearing it speak out there, to them, while I listened inside, "he says to take up the book he left behind, the book that he held in his hands near the end, the book he was holding in his hands. He says to take up the book and turn to page . . . page . . . page . . . it has an eight and a five."

"Dad?"

"I beg your pardon. My brother. I know the very book."

"An eight and a five; find the page and there will be a message—a letter?—a message. He says he left a message."

"Ask him if he is happy. Tell him it's his sister asking."

"Excuse me—"

"He does not know the word happy. He is here, and that is all. He is going now."

"I'm sure it was my father; if I had been given a chance to speak—"

"Someone is here," I said. I heard my voice saying it. "Someone is here asking for Alice? Anna? Angela?" I knew even then there was something wrong with Angela, but I had forgotten what. "Alice?"

"My wife? Her name is Agnes."

"She is ill, is she not? Someone is asking if she is better, if her illness has abated; someone is asking that you tell her the old medicine is better. Someone wants her to know that she is being taken care of, someone is over her now, comforting her."

"But the old medicine didn't—"

"Tell her someone is caring for her. She will be better."

"Will you ask my father to come back again? I must speak to him, really."

"There are many many many here, some of them wanting to speak, some of them moving away. One who wants to speak is asking for a daughter, but it is not a father who wants a daughter; someone is asking for a daughter. Is there a daughter here?"

"My mother? My *mother* wants to talk to me? What for?"

"Are you well? Are you contented? Someone is asking if you are well."

"It's not my mother then, because she—"

"Gone now. Some are pressing close to me, some are far away. Here is someone with a message. Do not forget old Ginger."

"What?"

"Do not forget old Ginger." My Lord, I thought, from somewhere far away, old Ginger was *my* cat. Messages for myself. Better quit soon. "Do not forget old Ginger," I said, as though I ever could. "Here is someone asking, asking; a message for a wife."

"I don't want it," Mrs. Faun said; I could hear her voice thin and annoyed. "Tell him to go away again; I don't want to hear anything he has to say."

"Someone is here, someone who wants to ask about a little child. Was the little child lost? Did it ever come home again? Where is the little child?"

"Get my father back; we don't know any little—"

"Now there is a message here, a message for T. L."

"Me? The first initial's really J., but they always called me Teddy; I guess it's for me."

"Good fortune in store for you, T. L., great good fortune is being warned against; do not be deceived."

So that was my first seance; it couldn't have been a very good one, since no one said anything, and there was only thirty-five cents in the pot; I had to pay fifty cents more out of my own pocket for the sherry.

"All they talk about is death and dying," I said to Mrs. Faun after she had seen them out. "And they are cheap."

"What do you expect?" She opened the drapes, blowing dust off her nose.

"They could take a little bit more interest."

"If they were interested in real life they wouldn't have come to listen to you. You'll find out."

I thought she was being unnecessarily dreary, but that, as it turned out, was going to be Mrs. Faun's way. "They're all crazy," she said, "all they want is to be told what to do. They wait for some crackpot to give them the word."

"If by crackpot you mean—"

"I mean what I mean," Mrs. Faun said. "If the shoe fits, Mrs. Motorman."

6

Well, I don't want you to think that Mrs. Faun and I came right out and quarreled all the time. We kind of sharpened our nails on each other, that was all, and most of the time we finished off our arguments laughing together over a cup of tea, although I must say I was surprised when I began getting a weekly bill from Mrs. Faun, in addition to the rent for the room, for "tea, cookies, etc."

"I thought you invited me," I said to her the first week.

"It won't hurt you," she said. "I get what I can."

I started following people after a day or so in the city; one thing is certain, you can't find your way around a strange city without someone to show you where to go, and when all you know is a Mrs. Faun who won't step out of her front parlor for a bomb explosion on the street outside, you pretty well have to get the way from strangers. The first person I followed was an old fellow I picked up outside a restaurant; he had been eating caviar, and I like to follow someone who is good and full of caviar, although I don't care for it myself; it seemed that he might lead me to a far more interesting place than any I might find by myself, and, in a sense, he did; "Why are you following me?" he asked, turning suddenly on me at a street corner; I was not as good at following people then as I became later.

"Because you were eating caviar," I said. Sometimes the truth doesn't hurt.

"I like caviar."

"I don't."

"Where did you plan to follow me?" He was still bewildered, but I thought amused; I am not very terrifying to look at, I believe. In any case, he was clearly a man without a guilty conscience, or at least no kind of conscience that being followed by me might bother. Perhaps being followed by a lovely young nineteen-year-old boy might have bothered him some.

"Come and have tea with me," he said. I swear, he took out a cardcase and handed me a card; I don't think I have ever known anyone to do that before. "I'd like to," I told him, "it will save me money with Mrs. Faun."

There was the day I tried my hand at shoplifting; it was particularly important because of the weather; it was one of those winter days which suddenly dreams of spring, when the sky is blue and soft and clear, and the wind has dropped its voice and whispers instead of screaming, and the sun is out and the trees look surprised, and over everything there is the faintest, palest tint of green; weather entertains me.

"I'm trying my hand at shoplifting," I told the salesgirl, and we both laughed.

I went to the biggest department store; I had not been there before, but one big department store is much like another. This one was one I might have been in a hundred times before; I knew where things were, and recognized the heavily scented air, so rich after the clean air outside. Sometimes I like big stores, with softness underfoot and pressing against the sides of your head; I like long counters with soft highlights and seductively tumbled scarves and vacant mannequins and the dirty gloves of shoppers; I like everything about big department stores except shopping in them. I do not like salesgirls and their manners, and having to buy my dresses in a special behemoths department, and I do not like the stupid mockery of people who enjoy keeping you waiting; I do not like credit offices, but I enjoy quarreling over a bill. Hughie used to be all lost, really frightened, when I got into a fight with a department store because I never really felt I was fighting with people, and so it was not necessary to observe any of the small delicate graces you use automatically when you are fighting with people; even with the electric company I always knew I was fighting with people, but never with department stores, and of course not with the telephone company. We paid our bills—I don't mean to sound as if I fought with any of them because I wanted to save money—but I could always enjoy a good fight over something. I loved being *in* a department store, and I am only surprised that I had not thought of shoplifting long before. "Shoplifting," I explained to the salesgirl, and touched the little box gently with one finger, and we both laughed.

I had really no good idea how you went about stealing something from a department store, but I thought I could make it up as I went along; that is, you will observe, my way with almost everything. I have always been quite successful at making things up as I went along, and very often surprised at where I led myself. I never thought along the way that I might end up in jail, or hurt, or even embarrassed, because that is simply not the kind of thing that happens to the kind of person I am; I am not above the law, but somehow I make the law, which so many other people do not. This is not arrogance; I first became aware of this when I was a child and always got everything I wanted. Before God, I thought I wanted Hughie. But this is not shoplifting.

For reasons which amused me considerably, and which I do

not care to discuss here, I had decided that what I most wanted to steal was an ornamental candle. I knew that there would probably be a department which sold candles and candlesticks and elaborate boxes of matches, and I thought to steal a candle and take it back to Mrs. Faun to put in the center of her appalling mantelpiece. Moreover, a candle is not too valuable, although perhaps not always easy to hide. Poor Hughie, and he was such a lousy painter.

In any case, I stepped onto the escalator—such a sense of power, such a sense of being carried, of permitting this small service underfoot—and, looking down at the store, let myself be taken to the second floor, where I paused briefly at lingerie; I do like lace; and then on to the third floor and the fourth, where I found a gift shop and, just beyond, the candles I was looking for. Perhaps a black candle for Mrs. Faun's next black mass, perhaps a candle that told time—although I do think that's too much of a good thing; the nicest part of a candle is its inaccuracy—or perhaps a candle topped with flowers, or a candle looking like a cabbage, or a house, or a poodle. I like things made to look like something else, although I draw the line at food. I once had a recipe for imitation potato pancakes made out of ground cauliflower, and they were just as vile as they sound. But an ordinary everyday plain camouflage is quite all right with me.

I saw a candle made of a thousand different colors, and it was very lovely; I quite wanted it. But wanting it and stealing it were two different things; if I started stealing just because I wanted a colored candle the whole point would be lost, and I had already decided that I could not buy it. So, reluctantly, I passed by the lovely candle and found quite a hideous one; it looked rather like Mrs. Faun, I thought, and I put it in my pocket. Then I turned and saw the salesgirl looking at me with an air of complete joy; she had seen me, of course, and she took a step forward and said, "Can I help you?" and waited to see what I would do.

Naturally, I took the candle out of my pocket and said, "No, just trying my hand at shoplifting," and we both laughed. I set the candle back on the counter and turned away, my candle-stealing days over forever. She could have cried, that salesgirl; perhaps she had been waiting all her working life to catch a shoplifter in action; perhaps her big moment tonight at dinner was now hopelessly ruined. After all, "I caught a shop-lifter today," is a much more sensational beginning to a story than just a "I had the craziest old lady in my department today." She must have waited on a good many crazy old ladies, and, understand, I'm not saying I'm old. She just looked like she'd tell it that way. So I had to shoplift something else. I won't go into the number of things I took and had to put back; I don't seem really cut out for the most efficient stealing; but I did manage to pick up a box of birth announcements ("I'm a girl, I'm a girl, I'm a girl") which I though might suit Mrs. Faun. No one seemed to care about those. One of the things I had to put back was a bottle of perfume called Svelte, which was fair anyway since I really wanted that.

Well, I'm not boasting. Some of the things that come to me work out well, and some do not. The seance was pretty good, but I will be the very first to admit that I am not light-fingered.

[1965]

FOURTEEN
STORIES

JANICE

First, to me on the phone, in a half-amused melancholy: "Guess I'm not going back to school . . ."

"Why not, Jan?"

"Oh, my *mother*. She says we can't afford it." How can I reproduce the uncaring inflections of Janice's voice, saying conversationally that what she wanted she could not have? "So I guess I'm not going back."

"I'm so sorry, Jan."

But then, struck by another thought: "Y'know *what*?"

"What?"

"Darn near killed myself this afternoon."

"Jan! How?"

Almost whimsical, indifferent: "Locked myself in the garage and turned on the car motor."

"But why?"

"I dunno. 'Cause I couldn't go back, I suppose."

"What happened?"

"Oh, the fellow that was cutting our lawn heard the motor and came and got me. I was pretty near out."

"But that's terrible, Jan. What ever possessed—"

"Oh, well. Say—" changing again, "—going to Sally's tonight?" . . .

And, later, that night at Sally's where Janice was not the center of the group, but sat talking to me and to Bob: "Nearly killed myself this afternoon, Bob."

"What!"

Lightly: "Nearly killed myself. Locked myself in the garage with the car motor running."

"But why, Jan?"

"I guess because they wouldn't let me go back to school."

"Oh, I'm sorry about that, Jan. But what about this afternoon? What did you do?"

"Man cutting the grass got me out."

Sally coming over: "What's this, Jan?"

"Oh, I'm not going back to school."

Myself, cutting in: "How did it feel to be dying, Jan?"

Laughing "Gee, funny. All black." Then, to Sally's incredulous stare: "Nearly killed myself this afternoon, Sally . . ."

[1938]

TOOTIE IN PEONAGE

I really got the first good look at Tootie Maple, since it fell on to my shoulders to interview her for my friend Julie. Julie had found herself settled in New Hampshire for the summer with her two-year-old son, a husband who only came up from his defense job in Boston for week ends, and a rambling old farmhouse that was lonely enough to make some sort of company a welcome necessity. She had carefully told them in the First National store in town: "I want a girl who can take care of Tommy, who can cook and clean a little, and who isn't scared of the dark. A *nice* girl," she had added hopefully. "The nicer the better."

Tootie was the first and only applicant. She arrived at Julie's house one morning, with a suitcase in her hand, and rang the doorbell emphatically. "You Miz Taylor?" she demanded when I opened the door. I shook my head helplessly. Tootie stood not quite five feet tall in her summer sandals, but she had arranged to add another three inches to her height by a complicated coiffure of curls and hair ribbons which made her look like a badly sketched perfume ad. She was wearing a house dress somehow too small for her, held together loosely with pins at the sides, and her arms dangled down to her knees, with bright red fingernails glittering as she waved her suitcase at me. "I come to stay here," she said. "Like Miz Taylor wanted."

As I stood back for her to come in—there was nothing I could think of to say, with that coiffure catching me somewhere about the chin—I saw that her toenails, too, were bright red. "Tommy will love her," I thought, "just simply love her." "Sit down," I said, and she put down her suitcase and sat down, crossing her legs the way they do in the movies.

"Let's have a cigarette?" she said. I gave her one.

"Mrs. Taylor isn't here right now," I began, "but she ought to be back any minute. Meanwhile suppose you just tell me about yourself and I can probably let you know whether you'll be satisfactory or not."

She looked at me suspiciously. "Miz Taylor say it's all right for you to talk to anyone that comes?" I nodded. "Well," she said, "I got a boy friend. That be all right with Miz Taylor?"

"I should think so, if you didn't want to take too many evenings off. But suppose you tell me your name, first."

"Tootie Maple," she said. "His name's Bud. He works nights, though, so we go for rides in the afternoons. He has a car, a Chevvy, and it'll do fifty if he pushes her up."

"I see. Have you ever had any experience with children? Mrs. Taylor has a two-year-old baby boy you'll have to—"

"That ain't a baby. That's a kid. I took care of m'whole damn family. Guess I can handle this one. He much of a brat?"

I thought of peaceful little Tommy. "Not much," I said.

"Sure," Tootie told me, waving a set of those fingernails, "I can handle him fine. Pot?" she demanded.

"I beg your pardon?"

"I say, does he go on a pot, or—"

"You'll have to ask Mrs. Taylor about all that," I said firmly. "Let me see—can you cook?"

"Never tried," Tootie said.

By the time Julie came home I had discovered that Tootie could not wash clothes ("Never tried"), could not wash dishes ("At least, not a *lot* of dishes all at once"), was not afraid to stay alone with the baby at night ("Me scared? Of the *dark*? Jeez!"), and never bathed during the summertime. All this I told Julie in a sort of hurried whisper in the hall. I will never know how much of it she understood, because the next thing I heard, Tootie was hired, to come to work the following Monday morning.

"It's just got to be *some*body," Julie said weakly after Tootie had left, storing her suitcase suspiciously in Julie's guest room. "Maybe she's sort of wonderful with children."

"She looked a little bit . . . backwoods New Hampshire, don't you think?" I asked, carefully regarding my cigarette.

"Sort of . . . like an ape," Julie said tentatively. "And I got a look at her mate—this Bud. Gargantua."

"Gargantua?"

"And M'Tootie," Julie said. "M'Tootie."

By the following Monday night it had stopped being quite so funny. For some reason, probably because I had seen her first, Julie came to regard M'Tootie as my project, and even after a while became a little bitter toward me. "It's not that I think you could have *warned* me," she kept saying, "But *some*body ought've made me think it *over*."

M'Tootie had arrived Monday morning with Bud, an impressive creature of about sixteen, who stopped the Chevvy that would do fifty in front of Julie's house and disgorged M'Tootie with what looked to Julie, watching from the window, like a sort of desperate relief. M'Tootie shambled in the back door, dropped her jacket on a chair, and said to Julie: "Well, whaddye want me for? Could I have one of them cigarettes?"

Julie gave her a cigarette and told her to wash the dishes, came out into the kitchen an hour later, and found M'Tootie reading a page from *True Confessions* which had been used to pave a closet shelf.

"Aren't the dishes done yet?" Julie asked.

"Just getting to them," M'Tootie said. She flipped the page over. "It don't finish here anyway," she said.

Tommy, as I had suspected, fell madly in love with M'Tootie immediately. He loved her red nail polish, the ribbons in her coiffure, and the shrill version of "I Found a Million Dollar Baby in a Five and Ten Cent Store" with which she used to quiet him when he was nervous. Because of Tommy, Julie was hesitant about attacking the red nail polish, and her first timid attempts at improving M'Tootie were so disastrous that she

was forced to reconcile herself to M'Tootie in an anthropoid
state. "What happens?" Julie wailed to me, "Where do I get? I
give her a bowl of hot water and say, 'While I'm giving Tommy
his bath, Tootie, suppose you wash yourself and then we'll all
go out together, all dressed up—' nice, you know, like a casual
suggestion, and I come upstairs after giving Tommy his bath
and the water's sitting there stone-cold and that damn ape is
lying on the bed reading *Jo's Boys* and when I come in she says
'All ready? Just wait'll I finish this chapter and we'll go,' and
there I am, and so then I figure that if I give her some nice
clothes she might want to be clean and look nice and I say
'Think how much Bud will admire you if you look pretty,' and
she looks at the clothes I have for her and says 'Them? Say, I
got a whole closet-full of them. Look,' and she shows me the
closet and she has ten dresses nicer than any I own, and she
took the ones I gave her and gave them to Bud for his sister to
wear. And all the time if she isn't reading *Jo's Boys* it's *Heidi*,
and she keeps asking me to help her with the long words; while
I'm doing the dishes and taking care of Tommy she's reading
Heidi."

Julie made one attempt on the coiffure, which not only
failed miserably, but brought Bud around to have a talk with
Julie when Tootie was upstairs reading.

"You gotta treat her nice, Miz Taylor," Bud said earnestly.
"She's an independent sort of a kid, like, and you gotta be sure
you're nice to her. All this fooling around trying to get her to
change her ways won't work; she told me about how you come
making her wear other clothes and bothering her hair and all
this talk about washing dishes and stuff . . ."

Julie was dangerously near a stroke, but she said: "Don't you
think Tootie ought to do the work she was hired for, Bud?"

"Sure," Bud said, nodding his head profoundly, "that ain't
right, she shouldn't do her work. But I tell you, Miz Taylor,
Tootie's had a hard time. Her father threw her out of the house
when she was eighteen—"

"When she was *eighteen!*" Julie said. We had estimated
Tootie's age as approximately fourteen.

"Yeah," Bud said, "and she's been living with us ever since, because I'm sort of her boy friend, and she ought to be treated right. So you just be careful of her, Miz Taylor, and she'll turn out fine, I promise you."

"I'd hate to send her back to live with your family, Bud," Julie said, "and I guess I'll have to give her one more chance, except that—"

"You're not going to give her any more chances," Bud said finally. "Tootie *likes* it here, and I guess she won't want to move back with us. She doesn't like my mother, and so I guess she'll sort of figure on staying here, so I guess you'll have to sort of make it up with her."

"I see," Julie said feverishly. "She won't want to leave."

"No'm," Bud said, "she honest to God won't."

As a test Julie put the matter of leaving up to Tootie, as tactfully as possible, and Tootie smiled prettily and shrugged. "The way I see it, Miz Taylor," she said, "you people have been mighty nice to me, and I better stick around."

"But, Tootie," Julie explained, "I may have to get someone else to do your work."

"That's all right," Tootie said, "if you can afford it."

"Your family—" Julie began.

"They don't really mind," Tootie reassured her. "My father says you people are German spies, but I don't much care. Way I see it, it's your business."

"I thought you didn't see your father?" Julie asked. German spies or not, she was thinking, maybe we could give M'Tootie back.

"I see him some," Tootie said. "Bud drives me out there. He thinks you're German spies, too, Bud does, but, like I say, I don't mind."

"Why?" Julie asked. "Why does he think we're German spies?"

"Oh," Tootie waved her hand vaguely. Then she said brightly: "Maybe because you stay up so late, with the lights on, you know, and then you have so much money, and no husband."

"You've met Mr. Taylor," Julie said between her teeth, "he comes up from Boston week ends. You've met him."

Tootie grinned generously. "Yeah," she said. "Sure."

Before Julie had worked up her courage to call in assistance and put Tootie out, Tootie solved the situation in her own peculiar fashion. After she had been with Julie for some three or four weeks, she came down to breakfast one morning just as Julie was finishing the dishes, and indicated by sitting down at the table and lighting a cigarette that she wanted to talk. Julie, who by that time was exerting every ounce of will power she possessed to ignore Tootie and go on about her own business until the happy day when she and Tootie could part company, refused to turn around until Tootie spoke.

"Hey," Tootie said, banging the ash tray on the table to get attention, "hey, Miz Taylor?"

"Yes?"

"Look." Tootie seemed unusually embarrassed. "Tell me this stuff about babies."

Julie half turned. "What about babies?"

"Well . . ." Tootie shuffled her feet. "I mean, about babies, and, like, what you do to get them."

Julie told me later that the only thought in her mind was, "This is what they always told me happened with hired girls, this is what they always told me—but not Tootie; how could it happen to Tootie?" accompanied by a deep unchanging joy which she made no attempt to analyze. She endeavored to answer Tootie in the simplest language possible, "carefully avoiding," she told me, "any moral question, and leaning heavily on the bees and the flowers."

Tootie was delighted. "I guess that's it," she said. "I guess I'm gonna."

Julie clung to the edge of the sink. "Is it Bud?" she asked.

Tootie giggled. "According to the way you tell it," she answered, "I guess it is."

Julie was rehearsing statements which began "Well, I guess I can't let you stay on here, Tootie, after all this . . ." when Tootie went on:

"Told m'father," she said. "I'm going home, Miz Taylor. You can get along."

"What about Bud?"

"Him and me ain't going together no more," Tootie said. "He's got hisself a new car, a Ford, and he's got a girl."

"Better let your father talk to him," Julie said. "After all, if he got you into this . . ."

"M'father don't want no Bud around, him and his cars." Tootie sniffed. "It's the first," she added.

"The first what?"

"First I ever had," Tootie said.

When Tootie had packed all her clothes and the carton of cigarettes Julie gave her, and the bottle of red nail polish, and was standing on the porch waiting for her father to come and get her, Julie had the first feeling of real sympathy she had ever felt for Tootie.

"I hope everything's all right, Tootie," she said graciously. "You must let us know if there is anything we can—"

"Sure," Tootie said. "Y'know what?" she asked.

"Well?"

"I'm going to name it Heidi," Tootie said, "after the nice time I had staying with you folks."

[1942]

A CAULIFLOWER
IN HER HAIR

Mr. and Mrs. Garland and their daughter Virginia lived in a pleasant house in a pretty town and every night at seven they ate the agreeable dinner cooked by Agnes, the maid who cooked well and dusted adequately and made beds abominably. Mr. and Mrs. Garland belonged to two country clubs and Mr. Garland had a mustache; Mrs. Garland had given up evening gowns in favor of dinner dresses and had two fur coats, a leopard and an inferior mink. Virginia was in first year high school and went out with the captain of the basketball team. Every Saturday night Mr. Garland shook hands with this young man and they chatted jovially about the war until Virginia came down the stairs wearing her mother's perfume. Virginia was fifteen years old, Mr. Garland was thirty-nine, and Mrs. Garland was forty-one.

One evening at dinner—it would have been about twenty minutes past seven—Virginia remarked: "Mother, Millie said she'd be around tonight. Can I skip helping Agnes with the dishes?"

"What is Millie?" Mr. Garland inquired, regarding the cauliflower Agnes was offering, "a cow?"

Virginia giggled. "She looks a little bit like one," she said. "Only she isn't. She's Millie, from school. She's coming over and we're going to do algebra."

"Millie can wait while you help Agnes," Mrs. Garland said. She looked at Virginia to make Virginia realize that Agnes must be kept in good humor. "It doesn't take ten minutes, and Millie can wait."

"I'll entertain Millie," Mr. Garland said helpfully, "Millie and I will do all your algebra. Used to be quite a hand at algebra," he told Mrs. Garland solemnly.

"You're still quite a hand at talk," Mrs. Garland said. "Take some cauliflower before it gets too cold. Agnes has to have some too, you know."

"Millie hasn't been in school long," Virginia said. "She didn't come until the second semester and I'm helping her catch up."

"Very kind of you," Mr. Garland said.

The doorbell rang, and Virginia dropped her napkin. "When she says early she means early," she said.

"That would be Millie?" Mr. Garland inquired.

Virginia answered the door and Mr. and Mrs. Garland could hear her voice for a minute in the hall. Then she came back into the dining room, leading Millie. Millie was pretty and stupid-looking, and she had heavy black eyelashes and wore a great deal of lipstick.

"This is my mother and father," Virginia said, sliding into her chair, "this is Millie. Pull up a chair, Millie."

Mrs. Garland frowned slightly. "Have you had your dinner, Millie?"

"Yes," Millie said. She looked at Virginia and giggled. "I ought to wait in the living room," she said, "but Ginny said to come right on in."

"Of course," Mr. Garland said, "have some cauliflower?"

Millie giggled again, staring at Mr. Garland.

"If you don't care to eat it," Mr. Garland said, "you could wear it in your hair."

"My father never takes anything seriously," Virginia said to Millie. "He's like that all the time, don't mind him."

"Maybe you'll have some dessert with us, Millie?" Mrs. Garland said.

"No, thank you," Millie said.

"If you eat anything," Mr. Garland scowled ferociously at Millie, "you'll have to wash dishes. Anyone eats in this house, right after dinner they have to go out in the kitchen and wash dishes."

"Charles!" Mrs. Garland said. "You'll frighten the child."

"Millie isn't scared of anything, Mother," Virginia said, "Millie and I can do anything."

"I'll bet Millie can do anything," Mr. Garland said. Mrs. Garland looked up.

"Virginia," she said finally, "since you and Millie have to do algebra I'll explain to Agnes and she won't mind if you don't help her."

"Hallelujah," Virginia said. "Come on, Millie. Be excused, Mother?"

Mrs. Garland nodded and Virginia slid off her chair and ran out of the dining room, waving Millie to follow her.

Mr. and Mrs. Garland were quiet for a little while after Virginia and Millie had left the room, until finally Mrs. Garland remarked: "She doesn't seem like an awfully *nice* girl, does she, this Millie?"

"I don't know," Mr. Garland said, putting down his coffee cup, "she looked all right to me."

Mr. and Mrs. Garland were sitting quietly in the living room some time later, Mrs. Garland doing needlepoint—she was making a footstool—and Mr. Garland reading the *Saturday Evening Post*, when Virginia and Millie, heralded by a clatter of feet from upstairs, burst into the room.

"Mother," Virginia cried as she came, "Mother, we finished our homework and can we go down and get a soda, Mother?"

Mrs. Garland thought. "I suppose so," she said slowly, "only hurry back."

"Wait," Mr. Garland said reaching into his pocket, "bring back some ice cream and we'll all have some. Mother and I would like some ice cream."

"I don't think . . ." Mrs. Garland said.

Virginia rushed over and grabbed the money from her father's hand. "Back in two seconds," she said, and she and Millie ran out again.

"They do rush around so, don't they," Mrs. Garland said, turning back to her needlework.

"They're young," Mr. Garland said, "let them have their fun."

"I don't think we should encourage Millie as a friend for

Virginia," Mrs. Garland said, "she doesn't seem to be quite a
nice girl."

"She seems all right to me," Mr. Garland said.

Millie and Virginia put the ice cream in dishes and brought
it in to Mr. and Mrs. Garland. Mr. Garland received his with
disgust. "Why should Millie," he inquired, "get away with so
much and only leave this little bit for me?"

Millie giggled. "I don't have one bit more than you do, Mr.
Garland."

"I dished it out myself," Virginia said.

"You certainly do, Millie," Mr. Garland went on, "I got
robbed." He went over to Millie to compare dishes and sat down
next to her on the couch. "Now I'm going to sit right down
here," he said, "and watch every bit you eat, and count how
much you have, and then you'll be sorry you didn't let me have
more."

Millie giggled again. "Stop, Mr. Garland," she said, "I'm
choking."

"Charles," Mrs. Garland said, "you're spoiling the girl's
good time."

"No, Mrs. Garland," Millie said, "I think Mr. Garland's
awfully funny."

"Now I'm funny," Mr. Garland said. "First you rob me of
my ice cream and then you think I'm funny. Just a silly old
man, I guess."

"You're not an old man," Millie said.

"He's old enough not to act like a clown," Mrs. Garland
said sharply.

"I don't think you're old at all," Millie protested, "really, I
think you're young."

Mr. Garland eyed Millie. "How young would you say?" he
demanded.

Millie giggled.

"My father's always like that," Virginia said to Millie. "He's
always fooling people."

"Wouldn't go out with a guy my age, would you, Millie?"
Mr. Garland said.

Millie looked up at him. "I couldn't say," she said.

"Now don't tease me," Mr. Garland said.

Mrs. Garland rose, put down her sewing, and went to the door. In the doorway she stopped for a minute. "Virginia," she said, without turning around, "I want to speak to you for a minute, please."

Virginia got up and followed her mother out of the room. "Be right with you, Millie," she said.

When Virginia was gone Millie turned around to Mr. Garland. "Is Mrs. Garland mad about something I said or something?" she asked.

"Don't pay any attention to her," Mr. Garland said. He touched the flower in Millie's hair. "Pretty flower," he said.

"My boy friend gave it to me," Millie said.

"Got a boy friend?" Mr. Garland said. "Does he take you out and show you a good time?"

Millie giggled. "He sure does," she said.

"Where does he take you?" Mr. Garland asked. "Ever take you to this place downtown, this club they call The Blue Lantern?"

"I've been there," Millie said.

Mr. Garland got up and walked across the room to get a cigarette and, as an afterthought, offered one to Millie.

"*She* coming back?" Millie asked, her hand out.

"Mrs. Garland? Not for a minute or two, probably." Millie took the cigarette and Mr. Garland lit it for her.

"She doesn't like me," Millie said, leaning back.

"I shouldn't think so," Mr. Garland said.

"But Virginia's a swell kid," Millie said. Mr. Garland laughed, and Millie looked up at him. "What did I *say*?" she asked.

Virginia came into the doorway and stopped for a minute. "Millie," she said, and Millie juggled Mr. Garland's hand insistently to make him take her cigarette. "Millie," Virginia said, "Mother wants to know if we will run down and get her a couple of things at the store. Want to go?"

Millie hesitated, and Mrs. Garland came into the doorway behind Virginia. "Charles," she said, "I told Virginia that if she and Millie went down to the store for me like good children you'd give them each a dime."

"We'll get a soda," Virginia said.

"After all that ice cream?" Mrs. Garland asked tolerantly. "You'd like to have a dime, wouldn't you, Millie?"

Millie hesitated. "Come *on*, Millie," Virginia said impatiently. "Daddy, give us a dime."

Mr. Garland looked at his wife, and reached into his pocket and took out a quarter. "Here," he said.

Virginia came over and took the quarter and then grabbed Millie's arm and started her toward the door.

Mrs. Garland sat down and picked up her sewing again. "Charles," she said, "don't you think the children are having too much ice cream?"

[1943]

I KNOW WHO I LOVE

Catharine Vincent began her life in a two-room apartment in New York; she was born in a minister's home in Buffalo; the shift from one to the other might be called her tragedy. When the devil prompted William Vincent to marry he did not prompt William further to inquire if his wife were to bear sons or daughters, or if the daughter were to be Catharine (named after William's mother, finally), thin and frightened, born with a scream and blue eyes.

When Catharine was twenty-three years old she found out that her father would have preferred a son, if he had to have any child at all. At that time she was still thin and noticeably frightened, with blue eyes and a faint talent for painting. She had eventually gone to New York alone; by the time she was self-supporting she had nearly forgotten her father, and her mother was dying.

William Vincent was a short heavy man, who affected a large mustache, which he thought made him look more the master of his house. He had become a minister shortly before his marriage because he had a vague feeling that in that way he was somehow certain of being right, and virtuous, and easily sure of his authority. He was not afraid of his wife, who was the only daughter of a grocer with no money, but he was afraid of the lady next door, and the brisk young man at the bank, and the butcher's delivery boy who made faces over unpaid bills, and asked insolent questions for which he could not be rebuked. William Vincent regarded his daughter as an unnecessary expense, as a trap, and as no true expression of God's will. He thought of his wife as an amiable woman whose place was in the home; practically the only person he felt really close to was God, in the heavy Bibles and the ponderous words, in the shabby church and the cheap hymns. Catharine early grew accustomed to hearing her father say across his small desk, or along the dull dinner table, "Do you think you are satisfactory, in God's sight or mine?"

After Catharine left home, while the train was pulling out of the station, she stopped thinking about her father and mother, except, later, for a weekly letter home. ("I am fine now, my cold is all gone at last. My job is fine, and they said it was all right about my being away three days. I guess I won't be able to leave work again for a while, so cannot expect to come home just yet.") Her father across the desk, her mother's small timid laugh, were emphatically and resolutely put out of her mind, until she was twenty-three and her mother died.

The doctor was there and Catharine waited outside in the apartment-house hall while the doctor and her mother spent the last few minutes together. "She never spoke at all," the doctor said. "She died very peacefully, Miss Vincent."

"Good," Catharine said. Her mother had waited until spring to die; next year she could have a fur coat. "What do I have to do about making arrangements?" she asked the doctor, waving her hand vaguely. "About burying her, and so on?"

The doctor looked at Catharine for a minute. "I'll help you with all that," he said.

Catharine spoke to strange people with soft voices, who told her she was brave, or patted her hand and told her her mother was happier now. "She's with your dear father," the maid in the apartment house said to Catharine, "They're together again at last."

With the funeral over and her mother gone, Catharine put the apartment back the way it had been before her mother came to live with her. The extra bed was moved out and the little table went back by the window. She spent five dollars on a new slip cover for the armchair, and she had the curtains cleaned. The only thing left of her mother was the old trunk full of her mother's memories and hopes. The little money from the sale of the furniture stored in Buffalo had paid for the funeral; Catharine had paid for the doctor and the medicine out of her salary and her fur-coat money. She asked the superintendent to put her mother's trunk in the basement storage room, and the evening before he took it down she opened it, to make sure everything was in moth balls and to take out anything she could use, and, finally, to set her mind dutifully to thinking of her parents.

For a minute or two her parents' memory would be centered in a flood of other memories, the thin teacher who snatched the drawing out of Catharine's hand and snarled, "I should have known better than to assign this to a stupid half-wit." Coming upon a boy named Freddie frantically rubbing out an inscription in chalk on a fence, and, when Freddie ran away, reading with hollow empty sympathy words he had been so anxiously erasing: "Catharine loves Freddie." And then her father: "Catharine, do the girls and boys in your school talk to each other about bad things?" The one or two parties, and the flowered chiffon dress her mother made. Her father sending her next door to get back a nickel she had lent to a school friend. And her mother: "I hardly think, dear, that your father would approve of that little girl. Jane. If I were to speak to her, very tactfully . . ."

And herself, coming back someday, a famous artist with a secretary and gardenias, stepping off the train where they were all waiting for autographs. And there was Freddie, pressing forward, and Catharine, turning slightly aside, said, "I'm afraid you must be mistaken. I never cared for anyone named Freddie." The tallest in the class, and thin, telling the other unpopular girls at recess: "My father doesn't like me to go out with boys. *You* know, the things they do." And finally, after school, staying by the pretty young teacher, saying, "Don't you like Mary Roberts Rinehart, Miss Henwood? I think she's a terribly good author."

The girls in school had called Catharine "Catty," the teachers and her mother and father had called her "Catharine," the girls in her office called her "Katy" or "Kitty," but Aaron had called her "Cara." "Strange Cara," the one note from him began. Catharine had held it in her hands, sitting by an open window at night and looking at the stars, in Buffalo, with her father moving around suspiciously downstairs; in New York, with her mother dead.

"Ratty Catty, sure is batty." Catharine remembered the jingle from the schoolyard and the notes passed from desk to desk, remembered it and turned it over in her mind while she leaned back with her feet on her dead mother's trunk and felt the soft upholstered chair against her shoulders, saw the traffic moving in the street below her apartment window, knew her job and her paycheck were waiting for her the next day. "Ratty Catty, sure is batty." Catharine smiled comfortably. There had been a kissing game at one of the few parties she went to, a grammar-school graduation party, and Catharine, in the background, had unexpectedly had to come forward to kiss a boy (what boy? she wondered now. Freddie again?). And the boy, moving backward, saying, "Hey, listen," while Catharine stood uncertainly. Then someone had shouted, "Catty's father won't ler her kiss a boy," and Catharine, trying to protect her father, had begun a denial before she realized that it was infinitely worse to admit that the boy had turned away from her. Then she told people, the other unpopular girls during recess, "My father won't let me go to the parties where they play that kind of game," or, "If my father ever caught me doing what those other girls do!"

She went to business school, because her father needed someone to help him with his numerous notes and the books of sermons he might write someday, and held the idea of a secretary in his mind as a signal of success. At business school she was no stranger; the pretty girls had all gone on to college, and Catharine was with the other thin dull girls or fat girls who were vivacious and had crushes on the men instructors. The boys in the school were mostly earnest and hard-working, and stopped in the halls to ask Catharine what she thought of the typing test, and whether she had taken down today's assignment. Aaron came to the school in mid-semester, wearing a yellow sweater suddenly into the typing class, standing thin and small and graceful and smiling while the rows of students sat mutely at their typewriters watching him.

"I fell in love with you right away," Catharine told him afterward. "I never knew what hit me."

Once Catharine had asked her mother impulsively and injudiciously, "Mother, did you fall in love with my father?"

"Catharine," her mother said, letting her hands stand quiet in the dishwater, "is there anything wrong, dear?"

High school had been worse for Catharine than any other time in her life. When the other girls wore sweaters or beer jackets and collected autographs, Catharine sat awkwardly under a badly designed wool dress. Once, with money her father borrowed from his brother, her mother bought Catharine a dark-green sweater and skirt, and when Catharine came into school that morning, one girl said, "What'd you do, rob a fire sale?" and another said, "Look at Catty, in the sweater she knit herself." Years later, Catharine told Aaron, leaning forward with her elbows on the table and her cigarette smoke blowing into her eyes, "I don't like clothes, at all. I think everyone makes too much fuss over them. I think the human body is too fine." When the girls with high-heeled shoes and curly hair went to sophomore proms and senior balls, Catharine and her three or four friends gave little hen parties where they served one another cocoa and cake, and said, "You'd be cute, honestly, Catty, if you had a permanent and wore some make-up." And Catharine, blushing, "My father would kill me." "You've got nice skin, though. Mine's always breaking out." "No, it isn't," Catharine said, or, "You're not fat, really. I only wish I looked like you, honestly."

A terrible thing happened to Catharine in her junior year in high school. One of her friends was to usher in a show put on by the local chapter of the American Legion. It was a performance of *The Mikado* and daughters of some of the members were going to usher, in evening gowns, with a chance to help with the make-up. Edna was the name of Catharine's friend, and the third and last night of the performance Edna managed to get Catharine invited to usher in place of another girl who was sick. At seven o'clock Catharine, in a blue crepe dress of her mother's which fitted badly and was cruelly improvised over the shoulders with a white organdy frill, met Edna in the lobby of the auditorium; Mrs. Vincent, who had come over on the streetcar with Catharine, said to Edna, "You'll be sure and see that Catharine gets home all right?"

"My mother and father are going to drive her home," Edna said. Mrs. Vincent kissed Catharine good-by, gave one sweeping suspicious glance over the auditorium, and went out to take the streetcar home. "How do I look?" Edna asked. "Look at me." She held out her skirt and Catharine, horrified, realized that Edna, with her bad complexion and straight hair, looked lovely. "I got a finger wave," Edna said, "and I'm wearing lipstick." Catharine realized even then that once or twice in any girl's life there will be an evening when she looks beautiful; she was not used enough to being ugly to be content to wait until an hour or two of beauty could do her real service. "You look wonderful," Catharine said sickly, "how do I look?" She held her coat open and Edna said, "You look beautiful, listen, we're going to the party for the cast after."

Catharine stayed long enough after the performance to see Edna, with her finger wave uncurling damply and her wide skirts trailing after her, dancing dreamily in the arms of a stout middle-aged man who had been in the chorus; he giggled when he whispered in Edna's ear, and Edna rolled her eyes and slapped his face lightly, while her mother and father, tired and proud, sat at the side of the room and greeted casual acquaintances eagerly.

Catharine walked home, all the way, holding up the blue crepe skirt and not afraid that anyone would notice her. "It's the ugliest thing I ever saw," she was whispering to herself. "Daddy will be furious." Then, only a block from her home, she thought she was a beautiful glorious creature, walking in a garden, her long skirts moving softly over the ground, graceful, with people thronging around her for her autograph. "Please," she said softly, waving a fan, "please don't say I'm beautiful . . . I'm not really, you know," and a chorus of protests drowned out her voice, and she yielded, laughing softly.

Her father forbade her to speak to Edna again, and wrote Edna's father a sharp note, which was ignored. Her mother had to have the blue dress cleaned, because of the dirt on the hem.

"I don't think the ordinary run of person is able to recognize beauty when they see it," Catharine told Aaron later, years later. "I think that your common person tramples on beauty because it is so far above him."

"You always were an ungrateful, spoiled child," her mother said, moving uneasily on the bed.

"You're living off me, aren't you?" Catharine answered indifferently. "You eat, don't you? Doesn't the doctor come twice a week to see you?"

"You never had a spark of affection in you," her mother said.

"*Some*thing must make me take care of you and feed you," Catharine said.

Her mother pulled at the blankets, her hands thin and powerless. "I don't know what I did to deserve a daughter like you."

"You must have taken the Lord's name in vain," Catharine said. She was standing leaning against the doorway to the kitchenette, waiting for her mother's oatmeal to cook. She had had a long and dismal day at the office, it was getting on toward winter (the winter when she could have had a cheap fur coat if her mother had not come) and her mother showed no signs of getting better or worse. She was almost completely careless of everything except that she was twenty-three years old, and still tied down; the romance and glory of her life waiting still.

"If your poor father could hear that."

"My poor father can't hear anything," Catharine said, "and I'm happy about it."

Her mother tried to rise on the bed, tried to soften Catharine with tears in her eyes. "He was a good father to you, Catharine. You shouldn't say evil things like that."

Catharine laughed and went into the kitchenette.

When Catharine was twelve her mother tried to give her a party. She bought little invitation cards at the five and ten, and paper hats and small baskets to hold candies. She bought ice cream and made a cake, and bought a game of pin-the-tail-on-the-donkey. "The whole thing didn't cost but about three dollars," she told Catharine's father. "I took most of the money out of my house money this week."

"There's no reason why Catharine should have expensive entertainments," her father said, frowning. "Her position as my daughter explains the absence of worldly frivolity in her life."

"The child has never had a party before," her mother said firmly.

"I don't want a party," Catharine told herself, alone upstairs in her room, lying on the bed. "I don't want any of the kids to come here." Her mother sent out the little invitations (Catharine Vincent, Thursday, August 24th, 2–5), and almost all of the twelve children invited had come.

The party was a miserable failure. Catharine, in an old dress with new collar and cuffs, and her mother in the dress she wore to church, greeted the guests at the door and sat them down in the living room where the little baskets of candy sat around on tables. The guests took the candy one piece at a time, played pin-the-tail-on-the-donkey as long as Mrs. Vincent wanted them to, and then sat quietly until one of them thought to say she ought to be getting home now. "But you haven't had your ice cream," Catharine's mother cried with bright gaiety, "you *can't* leave before the ice cream." Catharine's memories of that party were of her mother, working furiously, laughing and humming when she walked from place to place, her old dress showing constantly among the party dresses of the children; her mother saying "Well, don't you look pretty!" and "You must be the smartest little girl in Catharine's class."

Afterward, at the dinner table, her mother said encouragingly, "Did you enjoy your party, dear?"

"I told you they'd act like that," Catharine said without emotion. "They don't like me."

"Catharine has no business wanting parties if her friends don't know how to behave to her mother," Mr. Vincent said, devoting himself to a platter of liver and bacon. "You've worn yourself out and spent a lot of money to let the child have something she didn't need to have."

"Remember the party you gave for me?" Catharine said to her mother lying on the bed. "Remember that terrible party you insisted on having?"

"You are an ungrateful daughter," her mother said, moving under the blankets. "You always were a cold thoughtless child."

One day when Catharine was about fourteen her mother came into the bedroom where Catharine was cleaning her dresser drawers. Sitting on the bed, her mother said to Catharine's back, "Your father wants me to talk to you, Catharine."

Catharine, frozen, went on piling handkerchiefs and folding scarves. "What does he want you to talk to me about?"

"He thinks it's time I spoke to you," her mother said unhappily.

All the time her mother talked, apologizing and fumbling, Catharine sat on the floor folding and unfolding a scarf. "Have the girls at school been talking about things like this?" her mother asked once.

"All the time," Catharine said.

"You mustn't listen," her mother said earnestly. "Your father and I are equipped to tell you the truth, the girls at school don't know anything. Catharine, I want you to promise me never to talk to anyone but your mother and father about these things."

"If I have any questions I'll ask Daddy," Catharine said.

"Don't laugh at your mother and father," her mother said.

Catharine turned around to look at her mother. "Are you all finished?" Her mother nodded. "Then please let's never talk about it again," Catharine said. "I don't want to talk about it again, ever."

"Neither do I," her mother said angrily. "It's hard enough to tell you anything at all, young lady, without having to talk about delicate subjects."

"You tell Daddy you told me," Catharine said as her mother went out the door.

"Did you love my father?" Catharine asked her mother lying on the bed, "did you ever love my father, Mother?"

"You never loved him," her mother said, moving against the pillow, "you were an ungrateful child."

"When you married him did you think you were going to be happy?"

"He was a good husband," her mother said, "he tried very hard to be a good father, but you only wanted to make trouble. All your life."

Catharine sat on the edge of the seat; she was nineteen and her hands were neatly on the booth table, her books beside her, her eyes on the door. If only someone comes in, just this once, she was thinking if only one of the girls could see me, just this once.

"You look *très sérieuse*," Aaron said. "Coffee?"

"Yes, please," Catharine said.

"Now listen," Aaron said. "I ask you to come out for coffee with me because I think you're interesting to talk to. You can't just sit there and not say anything." Catharine looked up and saw he was smiling. "Say something witty," he said.

She got a minute to think when the waiter came over and Aaron ordered the coffee, but when the waiter was gone and Aaron turned politely to her, she could only shake her head and smile.

"Let me start a conversation, then," Aaron said. "What was the book you were carrying yesterday?"

"Did you see me?" Catharine asked before she thought.

"Certainly I saw you," Aaron said. "I see you every day. Sometimes you wear a green sweater."

Catharine felt that this had to be said quickly, urgently, before the moment got away from her. "I don't like clothes at all," she said. "I think everyone makes too much fuss over them. I think the human body is too fine."

Aaron stared. "Well!" he said.

Catharine thought back on what she had said and blushed. "I didn't mean to sound so vulgar," she said.

Another time, when Catharine knew how to answer more easily, Aaron asked her, "Why don't we go to the five and ten and buy you a lipstick?"

"My father would kill me," Catharine said.

"You could just wear it in school," Aaron said. "I want my girl to be pretty."

Catharine carried that "my girl" around with her in her mind ever afterward; she bought a lipstick and powder and rouge and nail polish, and put them on inexpertly in the girl's lavatory every morning before classes, and took them off each afternoon after leaving Aaron. Her father never knew; she kept them in a box in her pocketbook, and had a story prepared ("Gerry's family doesn't like her to wear make-up either, but she does anyway, and she asked me if I'd just keep these things—").

Aaron liked to sit with a cigarette hanging out of the corner of his mouth; he kept his eyes narrow when he talked, and the smoke from the cigarette went past his eyebrow. He smiled more than anyone Catharine had ever known, and she thought once that he looked satanic; she told him so and he smiled at her, smoke in his eyes.

"The devil is the only true god," he said.

Once her father frightened Catharine badly by saying to her abruptly at the dinner table "You're not running around with a young man, are you, Catharine?"

"*Catharine?*" her mother said.

"I was speaking to Mr. Blake this afternoon about a matter of business," her father said ponderously, "and he mentioned that he had seen Catharine walking out of her business school with a young man. No one he knew."

"It was probably one of the instructors," Catharine said in a clear voice. "I was probably asking about an assignment."

"I would not like to think that my daughter is associating with young men she is ashamed to introduce to her parents," her father said.

"Mother and Daddy have a great deal of faith in you," her mother said.

"It was probably Mr. Harley, our typing instructor," Catharine said. "I had to ask him about an assignment and we walked down the hall talking and out the door. I did the wrong assignment and had to find out what to make up."

"You should have told him to go to hell," Aaron said later when Catharine told him.

"Someday I will," Catharine said.

"Yes, Daddy dear," Aaron said in a high voice, "I am associating with a young man I am definitely ashamed to introduce to you, because he is a thief and a murderer. And he rapes young women. Even Mother wouldn't be safe with him."

Catharine shook her head helplessly. "He'd die," she said. "He'd just die."

When Aaron met Mr. and Mrs. Vincent he was very agreeable and Catharine was able to feel for a few minutes as though everything were going to pass off well. Aaron had escorted her home from school very properly and she had very properly invited him in. Her mother and father, sitting in the living room, watched Aaron and Catharine come in, and when Catharine said, "Mother and Daddy, this is Aaron, a friend of mine from school," her father came over and took Aaron's hand. "Pleased to meet you, my boy," he said.

"How do you do." Aaron stood next to Catharine, comfortable in his yellow sweater.

"Aaron is in school too," Catharine said to her mother.

"How do you like the school?" Catharine's mother said.

Conversation had continued without silences, they were sitting down, and Catharine met Aaron's eye and he smiled. She smiled back, and then realized that her mother and father were silently waiting. Aaron said smoothly, "Look at Cara's hands, Mrs. Vincent. They're like white waves on a white shore. They touch her face like white moths."

Catharine met her father at the dinner table that night, with a sort of sick resignation that left her unsurprised when he said immediately, "I don't know about that young man." He thought heavily. "Your mother and I have been talking about him."

"It seems like your friends ought to be finer, somehow," her mother said earnestly. "With your background."

"He doesn't seem quite right, to me," her father said. "Not quite right."

"We'll find some money somehow," her mother said, "and see if we can get you another dress. Sensible, but pretty enough to wear to parties."

Sitting by the window with her mother's trunk open on the

floor and her old report card ("English, B–, History, D, Geography, D") in her hand, Catharine, to spite her mother, thought about Aaron. Because the dull eyes of William Vincent and his wife were no longer on her, because she was loose, at least, from their questions ("Catharine, have you been seeing—") and their sudden quiet when she opened the front door, Catharine went to the little cedar box where she kept all her most secret treasures, and always had, and took out Aaron's only letter. In the box were a bright cotton handkerchief, and a tarnished silver charm bracelet. In her years in New York she had collected a match folder from a night club, and a printed note which read "We thank you for submitting the enclosed material and regret that we cannot make use of it." It had come attached to some watercolor impressions Catharine had sent to a magazine; she kept it because of the word "regret" and because it had been addressed to her name and addressed by someone there at the magazine, some bright golden creature who called writers by their first names and sat at chromium bars and walked different streets than Catharine did, from her apartment on West Twentieth Street to her typist's job on Wall Street. And at the chromium bars Aaron was sitting, and he walked quickly past the bright stores, and he might be in any taxi passing, smiling at someone with his quick sudden amusement, saying, "Catharine? I once cared for a girl named Catharine . . ."

[1946]

THE BEAUTIFUL STRANGER

What might be called the first intimation of strangeness occurred at the railroad station. She had come with her children, Smalljohn and her baby girl, to meet her husband when he returned from a business trip to Boston. Because she had been oddly afraid of being late, and perhaps even seeming uneager to encounter her husband after a week's separation, she dressed the children and put them into the car at home a long half hour before the train was due. As a result, of course, they had to wait interminably at the station, and what was to have been a charmingly staged reunion, family embracing husband and father, became at last an ill-timed and awkward performance. Smalljohn's hair was mussed, and he was sticky. The baby was cross, pulling at her pink bonnet and her dainty lace-edged dress, whining. The final arrival of the train caught them in mid-movement, as it were; Margaret was tying the ribbons on the baby's bonnet, Smalljohn was half over the back of the car seat. They scrambled out of the car, cringing from the sound of the train, hopelessly out of sorts.

John Senior waved from the high steps of the train. Unlike his wife and children, he looked utterly prepared for his return, as though he had taken some pains to secure a meeting at least painless, and had, in fact, stood just so, waving cordially from the steps of the train, for perhaps as long as half an hour, ensuring that he should not be caught half-ready, his hand not lifted so far as to overemphasize the extent of his delight in seeing them again.

His wife had an odd sense of lost time. Standing now on the platform with the baby in her arms and Smalljohn beside her, she could not for a minute remember clearly whether he was coming home, or whether they were yet standing here to say good-by to him. They had been quarreling when he left, and she had spent the week of his absence determining to forget that in his presence she had been frightened and hurt. This will be a good time to get things straight, she had been telling herself; while John is gone I can try to get hold of myself again. Now, unsure at last whether this was an arrival or a departure, she felt afraid again, straining to meet an unendurable tension. This will not do, she thought, believing that she was being honest with herself, and as he came down the train steps and walked toward them she smiled, holding the baby tightly against her so that the touch of its small warmth might bring some genuine tenderness into her smile.

This will not do, she thought, and smiled more cordially and told him "hello" as he came to her. Wondering, she kissed him and then when he held his arm around her and the baby for a minute the baby pulled back and struggled, screaming. Everyone moved in anger, and the baby kicked and screamed, "No, no, no."

"What a way to say hello to Daddy," Margaret said, and she shook the baby, half-amused, and yet grateful for the baby's sympathetic support. John turned to Smalljohn and lifted him, Smalljohn kicking and laughing helplessly. "Daddy, Daddy," Smalljohn shouted, and the baby screamed, "No, no."

Helplessly, because no one could talk with the baby screaming so, they turned and went to the car. When the baby was back in her pink basket in the car, and Smalljohn was settled with another lollipop beside her, there was an appalling quiet which would have to be filled as quickly as possible with meaningful words. John had taken the driver's seat in the car while Margaret was quieting the baby, and when Margaret got in beside him she felt a little chill of animosity at the sight of his hands on the wheel; I can't bear to relinquish even this much, she thought; for a week no one has driven the car except me. Because she could see so clearly that this was unreasonable—John owned half the car, after all—she said to him with bright interest, "And how was your trip? The weather?"

"Wonderful," he said, and again she was angered at the warmth in his tone; if she was unreasonable about the car, he was surely unreasonable to have enjoyed himself quite so much. "Everything went very well. I'm pretty sure I got the contract, everyone was very pleasant about it, and I go back in two weeks to settle everything."

The stinger is in the tail, she thought. He wouldn't tell it all so hastily if he didn't want me to miss half of it; I am supposed to be pleased that he got the contract and that everyone was so pleasant, and the part about going back is supposed to slip past me painlessly.

"Maybe I can go with you, then," she said. "Your mother will take the children."

"Fine," he said, but it was much too late; he had hesitated noticeably before he spoke.

"I want to go too," said Smalljohn. "Can I go with Daddy?"

They came into their house, Margaret carrying the baby, and John carrying his suitcase and arguing delightedly with Smalljohn over which of them was carrying the heavier weight of it. The house was ready for them; Margaret had made sure that it was cleaned and emptied of the qualities which attached so surely to her position of wife alone with small children; the toys which Smalljohn had thrown around with unusual freedom were picked up, the baby's clothes (no one, after all, came to call when John was gone) were taken from the kitchen radiator where they had been drying. Aside from the fact that the house gave no impression of waiting for any particular people, but only for anyone well-bred and clean enough to fit within its small trim walls, it could have passed for a home, Margaret thought, even for a home where a happy family lived in domestic peace. She set the baby down in the playpen and turned with the baby's bonnet and jacket in her hand and saw her husband, head bent gravely as he listened to Smalljohn. Who? she wondered suddenly; is he taller? That is not my husband.

She laughed, and they turned to her, Smalljohn curious, and

her husband with a quick bright recognition; she thought, why, it is *not* my husband, and he knows that I have seen it. There was no astonishment in her; she would have thought perhaps thirty seconds before that such a thing was impossible, but since it was now clearly possible, surprise would have been meaningless. Some other emotion was necessary, but she found at first only peripheral manifestations of one. Her heart was beating violently, her hands were shaking, and her fingers were cold. Her legs felt weak and she took hold of the back of a chair to steady herself. She found that she was still laughing, and then her emotion caught up with her and she knew what it was: it was relief.

"I'm glad you came," she said. She went over and put her head against his shoulder. "It was hard to say hello in the station," she said.

Smalljohn looked on for a minute and then wandered off to his toybox. Margaret was thinking, this is not the man who enjoyed seeing me cry; I need not be afraid. She caught her breath and was quiet; there was nothing that needed saying.

For the rest of the day she was happy. There was a constant delight in the relief from her weight of fear and unhappiness, it was pure joy to know that there was no longer any residue of suspicion and hatred; when she called him "John" she did so demurely, knowing that he participated in her secret amusement; when he answered her civilly there was, she thought, an edge of laughter behind his words. They seemed to have agreed soberly that mention of the subject would be in bad taste, might even, in fact, endanger their pleasure.

They were hilarious at dinner. John would not have made her a cocktail, but when she came downstairs from putting the children to bed the stranger met her at the foot of the stairs, smiling up at her, and took her arm to lead her into the living room where the cocktail shaker and glasses stood on the low table before the fire.

"How nice," she said, happy that she had taken a moment to brush her hair and put on fresh lipstick, happy that the coffee table which she had chosen with John and the fireplace which had seen many fires built by John and the low sofa where John had slept sometimes, had all seen fit to welcome the stranger with grace. She sat on the sofa and smiled at him when he handed her a glass; there was an odd illicit excitement in all of it; she was "entertaining" a man. The scene was a little marred by the fact that he had given her a martini with neither olive nor onion; it was the way she preferred her martini, and yet he should not have, strictly, known this, but she reassured herself with the thought that naturally he would have taken some pains to inform himself before coming.

He lifted his glass to her with a smile; he is here only because I am here, she thought.

"It's nice to be here," he said. He had, then, made one attempt to sound like John, in the car coming home. After he knew that she had recognized him for a stranger, he had never made any attempt to say words like "coming home" or "getting back," and of course she could not, not without pointing her lie. She put her hand in his and lay back against the sofa, looking into the fire.

"Being lonely is worse than anything in the world," she said.

"You're not lonely now?"

"Are you going away?"

"Not unless you come too." They laughed at his parody of John.

They sat next to each other at dinner; she and John had always sat at formal opposite ends of the table, asking one another politely to pass the salt and the butter.

"I'm going to put in a little set of shelves over there," he said, nodding toward the corner of the dining room. "It looks empty here, and it needs things. Symbols."

"Like?" She liked to look at him; his hair, she thought, was a little darker than John's, and his hands were stronger; this man would build whatever he decided he wanted built.

"We need things together. Things we like, both of us. Small delicate pretty things. Ivory."

With John she would have felt it necessary to remark at once that they could not afford such delicate pretty things, and put a cold finish to the idea, but with the stranger she said, "We'd have to look for them; not everything would be right."

"I saw a little creature once," he said. "Like a tiny little man, only colored all purple and blue and gold."

She remembered this conversation; it contained the truth like a jewel set in the evening. Much later, she was to tell herself that it was true; John could not have said these things.

She was happy, she was radiant, she had no conscience. He went obediently to his office the next morning, saying good-by at the door with a rueful smile that seemed to mock the present necessity for doing the things that John always did, and as she watched him go down the walk she reflected that this was surely not going to be permanent; she could not endure having him gone for so long every day, although she had felt little about parting from John; moreover, if he kept doing John's things he might grow imperceptibly more like John. We will simply have to go away, she thought. She was pleased, seeing him get into the car; she would gladly share with him—indeed, give him outright—all that had been John's, so long as he stayed her stranger.

She laughed while she did her housework and dressed the baby. She took satisfaction in unpacking his suitcase, which he had abandoned and forgotten in a corner of the bedroom, as though prepared to take it up and leave again if she had not been as he thought her, had not wanted him to stay. She put away his clothes, so disarmingly like John's and wondered for a minute at the closet; would there be a kind of delicacy in him about John's things? Then she told herself no, not so long as he began with John's wife, and laughed again.

The baby was cross all day, but when Smalljohn came home from nursery school his first question was—looking up eagerly—"Where is Daddy?"

"Daddy has gone to the office," and again she laughed, at the moment's quick sly picture of the insult to John.

Half a dozen times during the day she went upstairs, to look at his suitcase and touch the leather softly. She glanced constantly as she passed through the dining room into the corner where the small shelves would be someday, and told herself that they would find a tiny little man, all purple and blue and gold, to stand on the shelves and guard them from intrusion.

When the children awakened from their naps she took them for a walk and then, away from the house and returned violently to her former lonely pattern (walk with the children, talk meaninglessly of Daddy, long for someone to talk to in the evening ahead, restrain herself from hurrying home: he might have telephoned), she began to feel frightened again; suppose she had been wrong? It could not be possible that she was mistaken; it would be unutterably cruel for John to come home tonight.

Then, she heard the car stop and when she opened the door and looked up she thought, no, it is not my husband, with a return of gladness. She was aware from his smile that he had perceived her doubts, and yet he was so clearly a stranger that, seeing him, she had no need of speaking.

She asked him, instead, almost meaningless questions during that evening, and his answers were important only because she was storing them away to reassure herself while he was away. She asked him what was the name of their Shakespeare professor in college, and who was that girl he liked so before he met Margaret. When he smiled and said that he had no idea, that he would not recognize the name if she told him, she was in delight. He had not bothered to master all of the past, then; he had learned enough (the names of the children, the location of the house, how she liked her cocktails) to get to her, and after that, it was not important, because either she would want him to stay, or she would, calling upon John, send him away again.

"What is your favorite food?" she asked him. "Are you fond of fishing? Did you ever have a dog?"

"Someone told me today," he said once, "that he had heard I was back from Boston, and I distinctly thought he said that he heard I was dead in Boston."

He was lonely, too, she thought with sadness, and that is why he came, bringing a destiny with him: now I will see him come every evening through the door and think, this is not my husband, and wait for him remembering that I am waiting for a stranger.

"At any rate," she said, "*you* were not dead in Boston, and nothing else matters."

She saw him leave in the morning with a warm pride, and she did her housework and dressed the baby; when Smalljohn came home from nursery school he did not ask, but looked with quick searching eyes and then sighed. While the children were taking their naps she thought that she might take them to the park this afternoon, and then the thought of another such afternoon, another long afternoon with no one but the children, another afternoon of widowhood, was more than she could submit to; I have done this too much, she thought, I must see something today beyond the faces of my children. No one should be so much alone.

Moving quickly, she dressed and set the house to rights. She called a high-school girl and asked if she would take the children to the park; without guilt, she neglected the thousand small orders regarding the proper jacket for the baby, whether Smalljohn might have popcorn, when to bring them home. She fled, thinking, I must be with people.

She took a taxi into town, because it seemed to her that the only possible thing to do was to seek out a gift for him, her first gift to him, and she thought she would find him, perhaps, a little creature all blue and purple and gold.

She wandered through the strange shops in the town, choosing small lovely things to stand on the new shelves, looking long and critically at ivories, at small statues, at brightly colored meaningless expensive toys, suitable for giving to a stranger.

It was almost dark when she started home, carrying her packages. She looked from the window of the taxi into the dark streets, and thought with pleasure that the stranger would be home before her, and look from the window to see her hurrying to him; he would think, this is a stranger, I am waiting for a stranger, as he saw her coming. "Here," she said, tapping on the glass, "right here, driver." She got out of the taxi and paid the driver, and smiled as he drove away. I must look well, she thought, the driver smiled back at me.

She turned and started for the house, and then hesitated; surely she had come too far? This is not possible, she thought, this cannot be; surely our house was white?

The evening was very dark, and she could see only the houses going in rows, with more rows beyond them and more rows beyond that, and somewhere a house which was hers, with the beautiful stranger inside, and she lost out here.

[c. 1946]

THE SUMMER PEOPLE

The Allisons' country cottage, seven miles from the nearest town, was set prettily on a hill; from three sides it looked down on soft trees and grass that seldom, even at midsummer, lay still and dry. On the fourth side was the lake, which touched against the wooden pier the Allisons had to keep repairing, and which looked equally well from the Allisons' front porch, their side porch or any spot on the wooden staircase leading from the porch down to the water. Although the Allisons loved their summer cottage, looked forward to arriving in the early summer and hated to leave in the fall, they had not troubled themselves to put in any improvements, regarding the cottage itself and the lake as improvement enough for the life left to them. The cottage had no heat, no running water except the precarious supply from the backyard pump, and no electricity. For seventeen summers, Janet Allison had cooked on a kerosene stove, heating all their water; Robert Allison had brought buckets full of water daily from the pump and read his paper by kerosene light in the evenings; and they had both, sanitary city people, become stolid and matter-of-fact about their backhouse. In the first two years they had gone through all the standard vaudeville and magazine jokes about backhouses and by now, when they no longer had frequent guests to impress, they had subsided to a comfortable security which made the backhouse, as well as the pump and the kerosene, an indefinable asset to their summer life.

In themselves, the Allisons were ordinary people. Mrs. Allison was fifty-eight years old and Mr. Allison sixty; they had seen their children outgrow the summer cottage and go on to families of their own and seashore resorts; their friends were either dead or settled in comfortable year-round houses, their nieces and nephews vague. In the winter they told one another they could stand their New York apartment while waiting for the summer; in the summer they told one another that the winter was well worth while, waiting to get to the country.

Since they were old enough not to be ashamed of regular habits, the Allisons invariably left their summer cottage the Tuesday after Labor Day, and were as invariably sorry when the months of September and early October turned out to be pleasant and almost insufferably barren in the city; each year they recognized that there was nothing to bring them back to New York, but it was not until this year that they overcame their traditional inertia enough to decide to stay in the cottage after Labor Day.

"There isn't really anything to take us back to the city," Mrs. Allison told her husband seriously, as though it were a new idea, and he told her, as though neither of them had ever considered it, "We might as well enjoy the country as long as possible."

Consequently, with much pleasure and a slight feeling of adventure, Mrs. Allison went into their village the day after Labor Day and told those natives with whom she had dealings, with a pretty air of breaking away from tradition, that she and her husband had decided to stay at least a month longer at their cottage.

"It isn't as though we had anything to take us back to the city," she said to Mr. Babcock, her grocer. "We might as well enjoy the country while we can."

"Nobody ever stayed at the lake past Labor Day before," Mr. Babcock said. He was putting Mrs. Allison's groceries into a large cardboard carton, and he stopped for a minute to look reflectively into a bag of cookies. "Nobody," he added.

"But the city!" Mrs. Allison always spoke of the city to Mr. Babcock as though it were Mr. Babcock's dream to go there. "It's so hot—you've really no idea. We're always sorry when we leave."

"Hate to leave," Mr. Babcock said. One of the most irritating native tricks Mrs. Allison had noticed was that of taking a trivial statement and rephrasing it downward, into an even more trite statement. "I'd hate to leave myself," Mr. Babcock said, after deliberation, and both he and Mrs. Allison smiled. "But I never heard of anyone ever staying out at the lake after Labor Day before."

"Well, we're going to give it a try," Mrs. Allison said, and Mr. Babcock replied gravely, "Never know till you try."

Physically, Mrs. Allison decided, as she always did when leaving the grocery after one of her inconclusive conversations with Mr. Babcock, physically, Mr. Babcock could model for a statue of Daniel Webster, but mentally . . . it was horrible to think into what old New England Yankee stock had degenerated. She said as much to Mr. Allison when she got into the car, and he said, "It's generations of inbreeding. That and the bad land."

Since this was their big trip into town, which they made only once every two weeks to buy things they could not have delivered, they spent all day at it, stopping to have a sandwich in the newspaper and soda shop, and leaving packages heaped in the back of the car. Although Mrs. Allison was able to order groceries delivered regularly, she was never able to form any accurate idea of Mr. Babcock's current stock by telephone, and her lists of odds and ends that might be procured was always supplemented, almost beyond their need, by the new and fresh local vegetables Mr. Babcock was selling temporarily, or the packaged candy which had just come in. This trip Mrs. Allison was tempted, too, by the set of glass baking dishes that had found themselves completely by chance in the hardware and clothing and general store, and which had seemingly been waiting there for no one but Mrs. Allison, since the country people, with their instinctive distrust of anything that did not look as permanent as trees and rocks and sky, had only recently begun to experiment in aluminum baking dishes instead of ironware, and had, apparently within the memory of local inhabitants, discarded stoneware in favor of iron.

Mrs. Allison had the glass baking dishes carefully wrapped, to endure the uncomfortable ride home over the rocky road

that led up to the Allisons' cottage, and while Mr. Charley
Walpole, who, with his younger brother Albert, ran the
hardware-clothing-general store (the store itself was called
Johnson's because it stood on the site of the old Johnson cabin,
burned fifty years before Charley Walpole was born), laboriously unfolded newspapers to wrap around the dishes, Mrs.
Allison said, informally, "Course, I *could* have waited and
gotten those dishes in New York, but we're not going back so
soon this year."

"Heard you was staying on," Mr. Charley Walpole said. His
old fingers fumbled maddeningly with the thin sheets of newspaper, carefully trying to isolate only one sheet at a time, and
he did not look up at Mrs. Allison as he went on, "Don't know
about staying on up there to the lake. Not after Labor Day."

"Well, you know," Mrs. Allison said, quite as though he
deserved an explanation, "it just seemed to us that we've been
hurrying back to New York every year, and there just wasn't
any need for it. You know what the city's like in the fall." And
she smiled confidingly up at Mr. Charley Walpole.

Rhythmically he wound string around the package. He's
giving me a piece long enough to save, Mrs. Allison thought,
and she looked away quickly to avoid giving any sign of impa-
tience. "I feel sort of like we belong here, more," she said.
"Staying on after everyone else has left." To prove this, she
smiled brightly across the store at a woman with a familiar
face, who might have been the woman who sold berries to the
Allisons one year, or the woman who occasionally helped in
the grocery and was probably Mr. Babcock's aunt.

"Well," Mr. Charley Walpole said. He shoved the package a
little across the counter, to show that it was finished and that
for a sale well made, a package well wrapped, he was willing
to accept pay. "Well," he said again. "Never been summer
people before, at the lake after Labor Day."

Mrs. Allison gave him a five-dollar bill, and he made change
methodically, giving great weight even to the pennies. "Never
after Labor Day," he said, and nodded at Mrs. Allison, and
went soberly along the store to deal with two women who
were looking at cotton house dresses.

As Mrs. Allison passed on her way out she heard one of the women say acutely, "Why is one of them dresses one dollar and thirty-nine cents and this one here is only ninety-eight?"

"They're great people," Mrs. Allison told her husband as they went together down the sidewalk after meeting at the door of the hardware store. "They're so solid, and so reasonable, and so *honest*."

"Makes you feel good, knowing there are still towns like this," Mr. Allison said.

"You know, in New York," Mrs. Allison said, "I might have paid a few cents less for these dishes, but there wouldn't have been anything sort of personal in the transaction."

"Staying on to the lake?" Mrs. Martin, in the newspaper and sandwich shop, asked the Allisons. "Heard you was staying on."

"Thought we'd take advantage of the lovely weather this year," Mr. Allison said.

Mrs. Martin was a comparative newcomer to the town; she had married into the newspaper and sandwich shop from a neighboring farm, and had stayed on after her husband's death. She served bottled soft drinks, and fried egg and onion sandwiches on thick bread, which she made on her own stove at the back of the store. Occasionally when Mrs. Martin served a sandwich it would carry with it the rich fragrance of the stew or the pork chops cooking alongside for Mrs. Martin's dinner.

"I don't guess anyone's ever stayed out there so long before," Mrs. Martin said. "Not after Labor Day, anyway."

"I guess Labor Day is when they usually leave," Mr. Hall, the Allisons' nearest neighbor, told them later, in front of Mr. Babcock's store, where the Allisons were getting into their car to go home. "Surprised you're staying on."

"It seemed a shame to go so soon," Mrs. Allison said. Mr. Hall lived three miles away; he supplied the Allisons with butter and eggs, and occasionally, from the top of their hill, the Allisons could see the lights in his house in the early evening before the Halls went to bed.

"They usually leave Labor Day," Mr. Hall said.

The ride home was long and rough; it was beginning to get

dark, and Mr. Allison had to drive very carefully over the dirt
road by the lake. Mrs. Allison lay back against the seat, pleasantly relaxed after a day of what seemed whirlwind shopping
compared with their day-to-day existence; the new glass baking dishes lurked agreeably in her mind, and the half bushel of
red eating apples, and the package of colored thumbtacks with
which she was going to put up new shelf edging in the kitchen.
"Good to get home," she said softly as they came in sight of
their cottage, silhouetted above them against the sky.

"Glad we decided to stay on," Mr. Allison agreed.

Mrs. Allison spent the next morning lovingly washing her
baking dishes, although in his innocence Charley Walpole had
neglected to notice the chip in the edge of one; she decided,
wastefully, to use some of the red eating apples in a pie for dinner, and, while the pie was in the oven and Mr. Allison was
down getting the mail, she sat out on the little lawn the Allisons had made at the top of the hill, and watched the changing
lights on the lake, alternating gray and blue as clouds moved
quickly across the sun.

Mr. Allison came back a little out of sorts; it always irritated him to walk the mile to the mailbox on the state road
and come back with nothing, even though he assumed that the
walk was good for his health. This morning there was nothing
but a circular from a New York department store, and their
New York paper, which arrived erratically by mail from one to
four days later than it should, so that some days the Allisons
might have three papers and frequently none. Mrs. Allison,
although she shared with her husband the annoyance of not
having mail when they so anticipated it, pored affectionately
over the department store circular, and made a mental note to
drop in at the store when she finally went back to New York,
and check on the sale of wool blankets; it was hard to find
good ones in pretty colors nowadays. She debated saving the
circular to remind herself, but after thinking about getting up
and getting into the cottage to put it away safely somewhere,
she dropped it into the grass beside her chair and lay back, her
eyes half closed.

"Looks like we might have some rain," Mr. Allison said, squinting at the sky.

"Good for the crops," Mrs. Allison said laconically, and they both laughed.

The kerosene man came the next morning while Mr. Allison was down getting the mail; they were getting low on kerosene and Mrs. Allison greeted the man warmly; he sold kerosene and ice, and, during the summer, hauled garbage away for the summer people. A garbage man was only necessary for improvident city folk; country people had no garbage.

"I'm glad to see you," Mrs. Allison told him. "We were getting pretty low."

The kerosene man, whose name Mrs. Allison had never learned, used a hose attachment to fill the twenty-gallon tank which supplied light and heat and cooking facilities for the Allisons; but today, instead of swinging down from his truck and unhooking the hose from where it coiled affectionately around the cab of the truck, the man stared uncomfortably at Mrs. Allison, his truck motor still going.

"Thought you folks'd be leaving," he said.

"We're staying on another month," Mrs. Allison said brightly. "The weather was so nice, and it seemed like—"

"That's what they told me," the man said. "Can't give you no oil, though."

"What do you mean?" Mrs. Allison raised her eyebrows. "We're just going to keep on with our regular—"

"After Labor Day," the man said. "I don't get so much oil myself after Labor Day."

Mrs. Allison reminded herself, as she had frequently to do when in disagreement with her neighbors, that city manners were no good with country people; you could not expect to overrule a country employee as you could a city worker, and Mrs. Allison smiled engagingly as she said, "But can't you get extra oil, at least while we stay?"

"You see," the man said. He tapped his finger exasperatingly against the car wheel as he spoke. "You see," he said slowly, "I order this oil. I order it down from maybe fifty,

fifty-five miles away. I order back in June, how much I'll need for the summer. Then I order again . . . oh, about November. Round about now it's starting to get pretty short." As though the subject were closed, he stopped tapping his finger and tightened his hands on the wheel in preparation for departure.

"But can't you give us *some?*" Mrs. Allison said. "Isn't there anyone else?"

"Don't know as you could get oil anywheres else right now," the man said consideringly. "*I* can't give you none." Before Mrs. Allison could speak, the truck began to move; then it stopped for a minute and he looked at her through the back window of the cab. "Ice?" he called. "I could let you have some ice."

Mrs. Allison shook her head; they were not terribly low on ice, and she was angry. She ran a few steps to catch up with the truck, calling, "Will you try to get us some? Next week?"

"Don't see's I can," the man said. "After Labor Day, it's harder." The truck drove away, and Mrs. Allison, only comforted by the thought that she could probably get kerosene from Mr. Babcock, or, at worst, the Halls, watched it go with anger. "Next summer," she told herself. "Just let *him* try coming around next summer!"

There was no mail again, only the paper, which seemed to be coming doggedly on time, and Mr. Allison was openly cross when he returned. When Mrs. Allison told him about the kerosene man he was not particularly impressed.

"Probably keeping it all for a high price during the winter," he commented. "What's happened to Anne and Jerry, do you think?"

Anne and Jerry were their son and daughter, both married, one living in Chicago, one in the Far West; their dutiful weekly letters were late; so late, in fact, that Mr. Allison's annoyance at the lack of mail was able to settle on a legitimate grievance. "Ought to realize how we wait for their letters," he said. "Thoughtless, selfish children. Ought to know better."

"Well, dear," Mrs. Allison said placatingly. Anger at Anne and Jerry would not relieve her emotions toward the kerosene man. After a few minutes she said, "Wishing won't bring the mail, dear. I'm going to go call Mr. Babcock and tell him to send up some kerosene with my order."

"At least a postcard," Mr. Allison said as she left.

As with most of the cottage's inconveniences, the Allisons no longer noticed the phone particularly, but yielded to its eccentricities without conscious complaint. It was a wall phone, of a type still seen in only few communities; in order to get the operator, Mrs. Allison had first to turn the sidecrank and ring once. Usually it took two or three tries to force the operator to answer, and Mrs. Allison, making any kind of telephone call, approached the phone with resignation and a sort of desperate patience. She had to crank the phone three times this morning before the operator answered, and then it was still longer before Mr. Babcock picked up the receiver at his phone in the corner of the grocery behind the meat table. He said "Store?" with the rising inflection that seemed to indicate suspicion of anyone who tried to communicate with him by means of this unreliable instrument.

"This is Mrs. Allison, Mr. Babcock. I thought I'd give you my order a day early because I wanted to be sure and get some—"

"What say, Mrs. Allison?"

Mrs. Allison raised her voice a little; she saw Mr. Allison, out on the lawn, turn in his chair and regard her sympathetically. "I said, Mr. Babcock, I thought I'd call in my order early so you could send me—"

"Mrs. Allison?" Mr. Babcock said. "You'll come and pick it up?"

"Pick it up?" In her surprise Mrs. Allison let her voice drop back to its normal tone and Mr. Babcock said loudly, "What's that, Mrs. Allison?"

"I thought I'd have you send it out as usual," Mrs. Allison said.

"Well, Mrs. Allison," Mr. Babcock said, and there was a pause while Mrs. Allison waited, staring past the phone over her husband's head out into the sky. "Mrs. Allison," Mr. Babcock went on finally, "I'll tell you, my boy's been working for me went back to school yesterday and now I got no one to deliver. I only got a boy delivering summers, you see."

"I thought you *always* delivered," Mrs. Allison said.

"Not after Labor Day, Mrs. Allison," Mr. Babcock said firmly. "You never been here after Labor Day before, so's you wouldn't know, of course."

"Well," Mrs. Allison said helplessly. Far inside her mind she was saying, over and over, can't use city manners on country folk, no use getting mad.

"Are you *sure*?" she asked finally. "Couldn't you just send out an order today, Mr. Babcock?"

"Matter of fact," Mr. Babcock said, "I guess I couldn't, Mrs. Allison. It wouldn't hardly pay, delivering, with no one else out at the lake."

"What about Mr. Hall?" Mrs. Allison asked suddenly, "the people who live about three miles away from us out here? Mr. Hall could bring it out when he comes."

"Hall?" Mr. Babcock said. "John Hall? They've gone to visit her folks upstate, Mrs. Allison."

"But they bring all our butter and eggs," Mrs. Allison said, appalled.

"Left yesterday," Mr. Babcock said. "Probably didn't think you folks would stay on up there."

"But I told Mr. Hall . . ." Mrs. Allison started to say, and then stopped. "I'll send Mr. Allison in after some groceries tomorrow," she said.

"You got all you need till then," Mr. Babcock said, satisfied; it was not a question, but a confirmation.

After she hung up, Mrs. Allison went slowly out to sit again in her chair next to her husband. "He won't deliver," she said. "You'll have to go in tomorrow. We've got just enough kerosene to last till you get back."

"He should have told us sooner," Mr. Allison said.

It was not possible to remain troubled long in the face of the day; the country had never seemed more inviting, and the lake moved quietly below them, among the trees, with the almost incredible softness of a summer picture. Mrs. Allison sighed deeply, in the pleasure of possessing for themselves that sight of the lake, with the distant green hills beyond, the gentleness of the small wind through the trees.

The weather continued fair; the next morning Mr. Allison, duly armed with a list of groceries, with "kerosene" in large letters at the top, went down the path to the garage, and Mrs. Allison began another pie in her new baking dishes. She had mixed the crust and was starting to pare the apples when Mr. Allison came rapidly up the path and flung open the screen door into the kitchen.

"Damn car won't start," he announced, with the end-of-the-tether voice of a man who depends on a car as he depends on his right arm.

"What's wrong with it?" Mrs. Allison demanded, stopping with the paring knife in one hand and an apple in the other. "It was all right on Tuesday."

"Well," Mr. Allison said between his teeth, "it's not all right on Friday."

"Can you fix it?" Mrs. Allison asked.

"No," Mr. Allison said, "I can not. Got to call someone, I guess."

"Who?" Mrs. Allison asked.

"Man runs the filling station, I guess." Mr. Allison moved purposefully toward the phone. "He fixed it last summer one time."

A little apprehensive, Mrs. Allison went on paring apples absentmindedly, while she listened to Mr. Allison with the phone, ringing, waiting, finally giving the number to the operator, then waiting again and giving the number again, giving the number a third time, and then slamming down the receiver.

"No one there," he announced as he came into the kitchen.

"He's probably gone out for a minute," Mrs. Allison said nervously; she was not quite sure what made her so nervous, unless it was the probability of her husband's losing his temper completely. "He's there alone, I imagine, so if he goes out there's no one to answer the phone."

"That must be it," Mr. Allison said with heavy irony. He

slumped into one of the kitchen chairs and watched Mrs. Allison paring apples. After a minute, Mrs. Allison said soothingly, "Why don't you go down and get the mail and then call him again?"

Mr. Allison debated and then said, "Guess I might as well." He rose heavily and when he got to the kitchen door he turned and said, "But if there's no mail—" and leaving an awful silence behind him, he went off down the path.

Mrs. Allison hurried with her pie. Twice she went to the window to glance at the sky to see if there were clouds coming up. The room seemed unexpectedly dark, and she herself felt in the state of tension that preceded a thunderstorm, but both times when she looked the sky was clear and serene, smiling indifferently down on the Allisons' summer cottage as well as on the rest of the world. When Mrs. Allison, her pie ready for the oven, went a third time to look outside, she saw her husband coming up the path; he seemed more cheerful, and when he saw her, he waved eagerly and held a letter in the air.

"From Jerry," he called as soon as he was close enough for her to hear him, "at last—a letter!" Mrs. Allison noticed with concern that he was no longer able to get up the gentle slope of the path without breathing heavily; but then he was in the doorway, holding out the letter. "I saved it till I got here," he said.

Mrs. Allison looked with an eagerness that surprised her on the familiar handwriting of her son; she could not imagine why the letter excited her so, except that it was the first they had received in so long; it would be a pleasant, dutiful letter, full of the doings of Alice and the children, reporting progress with his job, commenting on the recent weather in Chicago, closing with love from all; both Mr. and Mrs. Allison could, if they wished, recite a pattern letter from either of their children.

Mr. Allison slit the letter open with great deliberation, and then he spread it out on the kitchen table and they leaned down and read it together.

"*Dear Mother and Dad,*" it began, in Jerry's familiar, rather childish, handwriting, "*Am glad this goes to the lake as usual,*

*we always thought you came back too soon and ought to stay
up there as long as you could. Alice says that now that you're
not as young as you used to be and have no demands on your
time, fewer friends, etc., in the city, you ought to get what fun
you can while you can. Since you two are both happy up
there, it's a good idea for you to stay.*"

Uneasily Mrs. Allison glanced sideways at her husband; he
was reading intently, and she reached out and picked up the
empty envelope, not knowing exactly what she wanted from it.
It was addressed quite as usual, in Jerry's handwriting, and
was postmarked "Chicago." Of course it's postmarked Chicago, she thought quickly, why would they want to postmark
it anywhere else? When she looked back down at the letter, her
husband had turned the page, and she read on with him:
"*—and of course if they get measles, etc., now, they will be
better off later. Alice is well, of course; me too. Been playing
a lot of bridge lately with some people you don't know, named
Carruthers. Nice young couple, about our age. Well, will
close now as I guess it bores you to hear about things so far
away. Tell Dad old Dickson, in our Chicago office, died. He
used to ask about Dad a lot. Have a good time up at the lake,
and don't bother about hurrying back. Love from all of us,
Jerry.*"

"Funny," Mr. Allison commented.

"It doesn't sound like Jerry," Mrs. Allison said in a small
voice. "He never wrote anything like . . ." She stopped.

"Like what?" Mr. Allison demanded. "Never wrote anything
like what?"

Mrs. Allison turned the letter over, frowning. It was impossible to find any sentence, any word, even, that did not sound
like Jerry's regular letters. Perhaps it was only that the letter
was so late, or the unusual number of dirty fingerprints on the
envelope.

"I don't *know*," she said impatiently.

"Going to try that phone call again," Mr. Allison said.

Mrs. Allison read the letter twice more, trying to find a
phrase that sounded wrong. Then Mr. Allison came back and
said, very quietly, "Phone's dead."

"What?" Mrs. Allison said, dropping the letter.

"Phone's dead," Mr. Allison said.

The rest of the day went quickly; after a lunch of crackers and milk, the Allisons went to sit outside on the lawn, but their afternoon was cut short by the gradually increasing storm clouds that came up over the lake to the cottage, so that it was as dark as evening by four o'clock. The storm delayed, however, as though in loving anticipation of the moment it would break over the summer cottage, and there was an occasional flash of lightning, but no rain. In the evening Mr. and Mrs. Allison, sitting close together inside their cottage, turned on the battery radio they had brought with them from New York. There were no lamps lighted in the cottage, and the only light came from the lightning outside and the small square glow from the dial of the radio.

The slight framework of the cottage was not strong enough to withstand the city noises, the music and the voices, from the radio, and the Allisons could hear them far off echoing across the lake, the saxophones in the New York dance band wailing over the water, the flat voice of the girl vocalist going inexorably out into the clean country air. Even the announcer, speaking glowingly of the virtues of razor blades, was no more than an inhuman voice sounding out from the Allisons' cottage and echoing back, as though the lake and the hills and the trees were returning it unwanted.

During one pause between commercials, Mrs. Allison turned and smiled weakly at her husband. "I wonder if we're supposed to . . . *do* anything," she said.

"No," Mr. Allison said consideringly. "I don't think so. Just wait."

Mrs. Allison caught her breath quickly, and Mr. Allison said, under the trivial melody of the dance band beginning again, "The car had been tampered with, you know. Even I could see that."

Mrs. Allison hesitated a minute and then said very softly, "I suppose the phone wires were cut."

"I imagine so," Mr. Allison said.

After a while, the dance music stopped and they listened attentively to a news broadcast, the announcer's rich voice telling them breathlessly of a marriage in Hollywood, the latest baseball scores, the estimated rise in food prices during the coming week. He spoke to them, in the summer cottage, quite as though they still deserved to hear news of a world that no longer reached them except through the fallible batteries on the radio, which were already beginning to fade, almost as though they still belonged, however tenuously, to the rest of the world.

Mrs. Allison glanced out the window at the smooth surface of the lake, the black masses of the trees, and the waiting storm, and said conversationally, "I feel better about that letter of Jerry's."

"I knew when I saw the light down at the Hall place last night," Mr. Allison said.

The wind, coming up suddenly over the lake, swept around the summer cottage and slapped hard at the windows. Mr. and Mrs. Allison involuntarily moved closer together, and with the first sudden crash of thunder, Mr. Allison reached out and took his wife's hand. And then, while the lightning flashed outside, and the radio faded and sputtered, the two old people huddled together in their summer cottage and waited.

[1949]

ISLAND

Mrs. Montague's son had been very good to her, with the kind
affection and attention to her well-being that is seldom found
toward mothers in sons with busy wives and growing families
of their own; when Mrs. Montague lost her mind, her son
came into his natural role of guardian. There had always been
a great deal of warm feeling between Mrs. Montague and her
son, and although they lived nearly a thousand miles apart by
now, Henry Paul Montague was careful to see that his mother
was well taken care of; he ascertained, minutely, that the
monthly bills for her apartment, her food, her clothes, and her
companion were large enough to ensure that Mrs. Montague
was getting the best of everything; he wrote to her weekly, tender letters in longhand inquiring about her health; when he
came to New York he visited her promptly, and always left an
extra check for the companion, to make sure that any small
things Mrs. Montague lacked would be given her. The companion, Miss Oakes, had been with Mrs. Montague for six
years, and in that time their invariable quiet routine had been
broken only by the regular visits from Mrs. Montague's son,
and by Miss Oakes's annual six-weeks' leave, during which
Mrs. Montague was cared for no less scrupulously by a carefully chosen substitute.

Between such disturbing occasions, Mrs. Montague lived
quietly and expensively in her handsome apartment, following with Miss Oakes a life of placid regularity, which it required all of Miss Oakes's competence to engineer, and duly
reported on to Mrs. Montague's son. "I *do* think we're very

lucky, dear," was Miss Oakes's frequent comment, "to have a
good son like Mr. Montague to take care of us so well."

To which Mrs. Montague's usual answer was, "Henry Paul
was a good boy."

Mrs. Montague usually spent the morning in bed, and got
up for lunch; after the effort of bathing and dressing and eating she was ready for another rest and then her walk, which
occurred regularly at four o'clock, and which was followed by
dinner sent up from the restaurant downstairs, and, shortly
after, by Mrs. Montague's bedtime. Although Miss Oakes did
not leave the apartment except in an emergency, she had a
great deal of time to herself and her regular duties were not
harsh, although Mrs. Montague was not the best company in
the world. Frequently Miss Oakes would look up from her
magazine to find Mrs. Montague watching her curiously;
sometimes Mrs. Montague, in a spirit of petulant stubborn-
ness, would decline all food under any persuasion until it was
necessary for Miss Oakes to call in Mrs. Montague's doctor
for Mrs. Montague to hear a firm lecture on her duties as a
patient. Once Mrs. Montague had tried to run away, and had
been recaptured by Miss Oakes in the street in front of the
apartment house, going vaguely through the traffic; and
always, constantly, Mrs. Montague was trying to give things
to Miss Oakes, many of which, in absolute frankness, it cost
Miss Oakes a pang to refuse.

Miss Oakes had not been born to the luxury which Mrs.
Montague had known all her life; Miss Oakes had worked
hard and never had a fur coat; no matter how much she tried
Miss Oakes could not disguise the fact that she relished the
food sent up from the restaurant downstairs, delicately cooked
and prettily served; Miss Oakes was persuaded that she dis-
dained jewelry, and she chose her clothes hurriedly and inex-
pensively, under the eye of an impatient, badly dressed salesgirl
in a department store. No matter how agonizingly Miss Oakes
debated under the insinuating lights of the budget dress department, the clothes she carried home with her turned out to be
garish reds and yellows in the daylight, inexactly striped or
dotted, badly cut. Miss Oakes sometimes thought longingly of

the security of her white uniforms, neatly stacked in her dresser drawer, but Mrs. Montague was apt to go into a tantrum at any outward show of Miss Oakes's professional competence, and Miss Oakes dined nightly on the agreeable food from the restaurant downstairs in her red and yellow dresses, with her colorless hair drawn ungracefully to a bun in back, her ringless hands moving appreciatively among the plates. Mrs. Montague, who ordinarily spilled food all over herself, chose her dresses from a selection sent every three or four months from an exclusive dress shop near by; all information as to size and color was predigested in the shop, and the soft-voiced saleslady brought only dresses absolutely right for Mrs. Montague. Mrs. Montague usually chose two dresses each time, and they went, neatly hung on sacheted hangers, to live softly in Mrs. Montague's closet along with other dresses just like them, all in soft blues and grays and mauves.

"We *must* try to be more careful of our pretty clothes," Miss Oakes would say, looking up from her dinner to find Mrs. Montague, almost deliberately, it seemed sometimes, emptying her spoonful of oatmeal down the front of her dress. "Dear, we really *must* try to be more careful; remember what our nice son has to pay for those dresses."

Mrs. Montague stared vaguely sometimes, holding her spoon; sometimes she said, "I want my pudding now; I'll be careful with my pudding." Now and then, usually when the day had gone badly and Mrs. Montague was overtired, or cross for one reason or another, she might turn the dish of oatmeal over onto the tablecloth, and then, frequently, Miss Oakes was angry, and Mrs. Montague was deprived of her pudding and sat blankly while Miss Oakes moved her own dishes to a coffee table and called the waiter to remove the dinner table with its mess of oatmeal.

It was in the late spring that Mrs. Montague was usually at her worst; then, for some reason, it seemed that the stirring of green life, even under the dirty city traffic, communicated a restlessness and longing to her that she felt only spasmodically the rest of the year; around April or May, Miss Oakes began to prepare for trouble, for runnings-away and supreme oatmeal overturnings. In summer, Mrs. Montague seemed happier, because it was possible to walk in the park and feed the squirrels; in the fall, she quieted, in preparation for the long winter when she was almost dormant, like an animal, rarely speaking, and suffering herself to be dressed and undressed without rebellion; it was the winter that Miss Oakes most appreciated, although as the months moved on into spring Miss Oakes began to think more often of giving up her position, her pleasant salary, the odorous meals from the restaurant downstairs.

It was in the spring that Mrs. Montague so often tried to give things to Miss Oakes; one afternoon when their walk was dubious because of the rain, Mrs. Montague had gone as of habit to the hall closet and taken out her coat, and now sat in her armchair with the rich dark mink heaped in her lap, smoothing the fur as though she held a cat. "Pretty," Mrs. Montague was saying, "pretty, pretty."

"We're very lucky to have such lovely things," Miss Oakes said. Because it was her practice to keep busy always, never to let her knowledgeable fingers rest so long as they might be doing something useful, she was knitting a scarf. It was only half-finished, but already Miss Oakes was beginning to despair of it; the yarn, in the store and in the roll, seemed a soft tender green, but knit up into the scarf it assumed a gaudy chartreuse character that made its original purpose—to embrace the firm fleshy neck of Henry Paul Montague—seem faintly improper; when Miss Oakes looked at the scarf impartially it irritated her, as did almost everything she created.

"Think of the money," Miss Oakes said, "that goes into all those beautiful things, just because your son is so generous and kind."

"I will give you this fur," Mrs. Montague said suddenly. "Because you have no beautiful things of your own."

"Thank you, dear," Miss Oakes said. She worked busily at her scarf for a minute and then said, "It's not being very grateful for nice things like that, dear, to want to give them away."

"It wouldn't look nice on you," Mrs. Montague said, "it would look awful. You're not very pretty."

Miss Oakes was silent again for a minute, and then she said,

"Well, dear, shall we see if it's still raining?" With great deliberation she put down the knitting and walked over to the window. When she pulled back the lace curtain and the heavy dark-red drape she did so carefully, because the curtain and the drape were not precisely her own, but were of service to her, and pleasant to her touch, and expensive. "It's almost stopped," she said brightly. She squinted her eyes and looked up at the sky. "I *do* believe it's going to clear up," she went on, as though her brightness might create a sun of reflected brilliance. "In about fifteen minutes . . ." She let her voice trail off, and smiled at Mrs. Montague with vast anticipation.

"I don't want to go for any walk," Mrs. Montague said sullenly. "Once when we were children we used to take off all our clothes and run out in the rain."

Miss Oakes returned to her chair and took up her knitting. "We can start to get ready in a few minutes," she promised.

"I couldn't do that *now*, of course," Mrs. Montague said. "I want to color."

She slid out of her chair, dropping the mink coat into a heap on the floor, and went slowly, with her faltering walk, across the room to the card table where her coloring book and box of crayons lay. Miss Oakes sighed, set her knitting down, and walked over to pick up the mink coat; she draped it tenderly over the back of the chair, and went back and picked up her knitting again.

"Pretty, pretty," Mrs. Montague crooned over her coloring, "Pretty blue, pretty water, pretty, pretty."

Miss Oakes allowed a small smile to touch her face as she regarded the scarf; it was a bright color, perhaps too bright for a man no longer very young, but it was gay and not really *unusually* green. His birthday was three weeks off; the card in the box would say "To remind you of your loyal friend and admirer, Polly Oakes." Miss Oakes sighed quickly.

"I want to go for a *walk*," Mrs. Montague said abruptly.

"Just a minute, dear," Miss Oakes said. She put the knitting down again and smiled at Mrs. Montague. "I'll help you," Miss Oakes said, and went over to assist Mrs. Montague in the slow task that getting out of a straight chair always entailed.

"Why, look at you," Miss Oakes said, regarding the coloring book over Mrs. Montague's head. She laughed. "You've gone and made the whole thing blue, you silly child." She turned back a page. "And here," she said, and laughed again. "Why does the man have a blue face? And the little girl in the picture— she mustn't be blue, dear, her face should be pink and her hair should be—oh, yellow, for instance. Not *blue*."

Mrs. Montague put her hands violently over the picture. "Mine," she said. "Get away, this is mine."

"I'm sorry," Miss Oakes said smoothly, "I wasn't laughing at you, dear. It was just funny to see a man with a blue face." She helped Mrs. Montague out of the chair and escorted her across the room to the mink coat. Mrs. Montague stood stiffly while Miss Oakes put the coat over her shoulders and helped her arms into the sleeves, and when Miss Oakes came around in front of her to button the coat at the neck Mrs. Montague turned down the corners of her mouth and said sullenly into Miss Oakes's face, so close to hers, "You don't know what things *are*, really."

"Perhaps I don't," Miss Oakes said absently. She surveyed Mrs. Montague, neatly buttoned into the mink coat, and then took Mrs. Montague's rose-covered hat from the table in the hall and set it on Mrs. Montague's head, with great regard to the correct angle and the neatness of the roses. "Now we look so pretty," Miss Oakes said. Mrs. Montague stood silently while Miss Oakes went to the hall closet and took out her own serviceable blue coat. She shrugged herself into it, settled it with a brisk tug at the collar, and pulled on her hat with a quick gesture from back to front that landed the hatbrim at exactly the usual angle over her eye. It was not until she was escorting Mrs. Montague to the door that Miss Oakes gave one brief, furtive glance at the hall mirror, as one who does so from a nervous compulsion rather than any real desire for information.

Miss Oakes enjoyed walking down the hall; its carpets were so thick that even the stout shoes of Miss Oakes made no sound. The elevator was self-service, and Miss Oakes, with superhuman control, allowed it to sweep soundlessly down to the main floor, carrying with it Miss Oakes herself, and Mrs. Montague, who sat docilely on the velvet-covered bench and stared at the paneling as though she had never seen it before. When the elevator door opened and they moved out into the lobby Miss Oakes knew that the few people who saw them—the girl at the switchboard, the doorman, another tenant coming to the elevator—recognized Mrs. Montague as the rich old lady who lived high upstairs, and Miss Oakes as the infinitely competent companion, without whose unswerving assistance Mrs. Montague could not live for ten minutes. Miss Oakes walked sturdily and well through the lobby, her firm hand guiding soft little Mrs. Montague; the lobby floor was pale carpeting on which their feet made no sound, and the lobby walls were painted an expensive color so neutral as to be almost invisible; as Miss Oakes went with Mrs. Montague through the lobby it was as though they walked upon clouds, through the noncommittal areas of infinite space. The doorway was their aim, and the doorman, dressed in gray, opened the way for them with a flourish and a "Good afternoon" which began by being directed at Mrs. Montague, as the employer, and ended by addressing Miss Oakes, as the person who would be expected to answer.

"Good afternoon, George," Miss Oakes said, with a stately smile, and passed on through the doorway, leading Mrs. Montague. Once outside on the sidewalk, Miss Oakes steered Mrs. Montague quickly to the left, since, allowed her head, Mrs. Montague might as easily have turned unexpectedly to the right, although they always turned to the left, and so upset Miss Oakes's walk for the day. With slow steps they moved into the current of people walking up the street, Miss Oakes watching ahead to avoid Mrs. Montague's walking into strangers, Mrs. Montague with her face turned up to the gray sky.

"It's a *lovely* day," Miss Oakes said. "Pleasantly cool after the rain."

They had gone perhaps half a block when Mrs. Montague, by a gentle pressure against Miss Oakes's arm, began to direct them toward the inside of the sidewalk and the shop windows;

Miss Oakes, resisting at first, at last allowed herself to be reluctantly influenced and they crossed the sidewalk to stand in front of the window to a stationery store.

They stopped here every day, and, as she said every day, Mrs. Montague murmured softly, "*Look* at all the lovely things." She watched with amusement a plastic bird, colored bright red and yellow, which methodically dipped its beak into a glass of water and withdrew it; while they stood watching the bird lowered its head and touched the water, hesitated, and then rose.

"Does it stop when we're not here?" Mrs. Montague asked, and Miss Oakes laughed, and said, "It never stops. It goes on while we're eating and while we're sleeping and all the time."

Mrs. Montague's attention had wandered to the open pages of a diary, spread nakedly to the pages dated June 14–June 15. Mrs. Montague, looking at the smooth unwritten paper, caught her breath. "I'd like to have *that*," she said, and Miss Oakes, as she answered every day, said, "What would you write in it, dear?"

The thing that always caught Mrs. Montague next was a softly curved blue bowl which stood in the center of the window display; Mrs. Montague pored lovingly and speechlessly over this daily, trying to touch it through the glass of the window.

"Come *on*, dear," Miss Oakes said finally, with an almost-impatient tug at Mrs. Montague's arm. "We'll never get our walk finished if you don't come *on*."

Docilely Mrs. Montague followed. "Pretty," she whispered, "pretty, pretty."

She opened her eyes suddenly and was aware that she saw. The sky was unbelievably, steadily blue, and the sand beneath her feet was hot; she could see the water, colored more deeply than the sky, but faintly greener. Far off was the line where the sky and water met, and it was infinitely pure.

"Pretty," she said inadequately, and was aware that she spoke. She was walking on the sand, and with a sudden impatient gesture she stopped and slipped off her shoes, standing first on one foot and then on the other. This encouraged her to look down at herself; she was very tall, high above her shoes on the sand, and when she moved it was freely and easily except for the cumbering clothes, the heavy coat and the hat, which sat on her head with a tangible, oppressive weight. She threw the hat onto the hot lovely sand, and it looked so offensive, lying with its patently unreal roses against the smooth clarity of the sand, that she bent quickly and covered the hat with handfuls of sand; the coat was more difficult to cover, and the sand ran delicately between the hairs of the short dark fur; before she had half covered the coat she decided to put the rest of her clothes with it, and did so, slipping easily out of the straps and buttons and catches of many garments, which she remembered as difficult to put on. When all her clothes were buried she looked with satisfaction down at her strong white legs, and thought, aware that she was thinking it: they are almost the same color as the sand. She began to run freely, with the blue ocean and the bluer sky on her right, the trees on her left, and the moving sand underfoot; she ran until she came back to the place where a corner of her coat still showed through the sand. When she saw it she stopped again and said, "Pretty, pretty," and leaned over and took a handful of sand and let it run through her fingers.

Far away, somewhere in the grove of trees that centered the island she could hear the parrot calling. "Eat, eat," it shrieked, and then something indistinguishable, and then, "Eat, eat."

An idea came indirectly and subtly to her mind; it was the idea of food, for a minute unpleasant and as though it meant a disagreeable sensation, and then glowingly happy. She turned and ran—it was impossible to move slowly on the island, with the clear hot air all around her, and the ocean stirring constantly, pushing at the island, and the unbelievable blue sky above—and when she came into the sudden warm shade of the trees she ran from one to another, putting her hand for a minute on each.

"Hello," the parrot gabbled, "Hello, who's there, eat?" She could see it flashing among the trees, no more than a sawtoothed voice and a flash of ugly red and yellow.

The grass was green and rich and soft, and she sat down by the little brook where the food was set out. Today there was a great polished wooden bowl, soft to the touch, full of purple grapes; the sun that came unevenly between the trees struck a high shine from the bowl, and lay flatly against the grapes, which were dusty with warmth, and almost black. There was a shimmering glass just full of dark red wine; there was a flat blue plate filled with little cakes; she touched one and it was full of cream, and heavily iced with soft chocolate. There were pomegranates, and cheese, and small, sharp-flavored candies. She lay down beside the food, and closed her eyes against the heavy scent from the grapes.

"Eat, eat," the parrot screamed from somewhere over her head. She opened her eyes lazily and looked up, to see the flash of red and yellow in the trees. "Be still, you noisy beast," she said, and smiled to herself because it was not important, actually, whether the parrot were quiet or not. Later, after she had slept, she ate some of the grapes and the cheese, and several of the rich little cakes. While she ate the parrot came cautiously closer, begging for food, sidling up near to the dish of cakes and then moving quickly away.

"Beast," she said pleasantly to the parrot, "greedy beast."

When she was sure she was quite through with the food, she put one of the cakes on a green leaf and set it a little bit away from her for the parrot. It came up to the cake slowly and fearfully, watching on either side for some sudden prohibitive movement; when it finally reached the cake it hesitated, and then dipped its head down to bury its beak in the soft frosting; it lifted its head, paused to look around, and then lowered its beak to the cake again. The gesture was familiar, and she laughed, not knowing why.

She was faintly aware that she had slept again, and awakened wanting to run, to go out into the hot sand on the beach and run shouting around the island. The parrot was gone, its cake a mess of crumbs and frosting on the ground. She ran out onto the beach, and the water was there, and the sky. For a few minutes she ran, going down to the water and then swiftly

back before it could touch her bare feet, and then she dropped
luxuriously onto the sand and lay there. After a while she
began to draw a picture in the sand; it was a round face with
dots for eyes and nose and a line for a mouth. "Henry Paul,"
she said, touching the face caressingly with her fingers, and
then, laughing, she leaped to her feet and began to run again,
around the island. When she passed the face drawn on the
sand she put one bare foot on it and ground it away. "Eat,
eat," she could hear the parrot calling from the trees; the parrot was afraid of the hot sand and the water and stayed always
in the trees near the food. Far off, across the water, she could
see the sweet, the always comforting, line of the horizon.

When she was tired with running she lay down again on the
sand. For a little while she played idly, writing words on the
sand and then rubbing them out with her hand; once she drew
a crude picture of a doorway and punched her fist through it.

Finally she lay down and put her face down to the sand. It
was hot, hotter than anything else had ever been, and the soft
grits of the sand slipped into her mouth, where she could taste
them, deliciously hard and grainy against her teeth; they were
in her eyes, rich and warm; the sand was covering her face and
the blue sky was gone from above her and the sand was cooler,
then grayer, covering her face, and cold.

"*Nearly* home," Miss Oakes said brightly, as they turned the
last corner of their block. "It's been a *nice* walk, hasn't it?"

She tried, unsuccessfully, to guide Mrs. Montague quickly
past the bakery, but Mrs. Montague's feet, moving against
Miss Oakes's pressure from habit, brought them up to stand in
front of the bakery window.

"I don't know *why* they leave those fly-specked éclairs out
here," Miss Oakes said irritably. "There's nothing *less* appe-
tizing. *Look* at that cake; the cream is positively *curdled*."

She moved her arm insinuatingly within Mrs. Montague's;
"In a few minutes we'll be home," she said softly, "and then
we can have our nice cocktail, and rest for a few minutes, and
then dinner."

"Pretty," Mrs. Montague said at the cakes. "I want some."

Miss Oakes shuddered violently. "Don't even *say* it," she implored. "Just *look* at that stuff. You'd be sick for a week."

She moved Mrs. Montague along, and they came, moving quicker than they had when they started, back to their own doorway where the doorman in gray waited for them. He opened the door and said, beginning with Mrs. Montague and finishing with Miss Oakes, "Have a nice walk?"

"Very pleasant, thank you," Miss Oakes said agreeably. They passed through the doorway and into the lobby where the open doors of the elevator waited for them. "Dinner soon," Miss Oakes said as they went across the lobby.

Miss Oakes was careful, on their own floor, to see that Mrs. Montague found the right doorway; while Miss Oakes put the key in the door Mrs. Montague stood waiting without expression.

Mrs. Montague moved forward automatically when the door was opened, and Miss Oakes caught her arm, saying shrilly, "Don't *step* on it!" Mrs. Montague stopped, and waited, while Miss Oakes picked up the dinner menu from the floor just inside the door; it had been slipped under the door while they were out.

Once inside, Miss Oakes removed Mrs. Montague's rosy hat and the mink coat, and Mrs. Montague took the mink coat in her arms and sat down in her chair with it, smoothing the fur. Miss Oakes slid out of her own coat and hung it neatly in the closet, and then came into the living room, carrying the dinner menu.

"Chicken liver omelette," Miss Oakes read as she walked. "The last time it was a trifle underdone; I could *mention* it, of course, but they never seem to pay much attention. Roast turkey. Filet mignon. I *really* do think a nice little piece of . . ." she looked up at Mrs. Montague and smiled. "Hungry?" she suggested.

"No," Mrs. Montague said. "I've had enough."

"Nice oatmeal?" Miss Oakes said. "If you're *very* good you can have ice cream tonight."

"Don't want ice cream," Mrs. Montague said.

Miss Oakes sighed, and then said "Well . . ." placatingly. She returned to the menu. "French-fried potatoes," she said. "They're *very* heavy on the stomach, but I do have my heart set on a nice little piece of steak and some french-fried potatoes. It sounds just *right*, tonight."

"Shall I give you this coat?" Mrs. Montague asked suddenly.

Miss Oakes stopped on her way to the phone and patted Mrs. Montague lightly on the shoulder. "You're very generous, dear," she said, "but of course you don't really want to give me your beautiful coat. What would your dear son say?"

Mrs. Montague ran her hand over the fur of the coat affectionately. Then she stood up, slowly, and the coat slid to the floor. "I'm going to color," she announced.

Miss Oakes turned back from the phone to pick up the coat and put it over the back of the chair. "All right," she said. She went to the phone, sat so she could keep an eye on Mrs. Montague while she talked, and said into the phone "Room service."

Mrs. Montague moved across the room and sat down at the card table. Reflectively she turned the pages of the coloring book, found a picture that pleased her, and opened the crayon box. Miss Oakes hummed softly into the phone. "Room service?" she said finally. "I want to order dinner sent up to Mrs. Montague's suite, please." She looked over the phone at Mrs. Montague and said, "You all right, dear?"

Without turning, Mrs. Montague moved her shoulders impatiently, and selected a crayon from the box. She examined the point of it with great care while Miss Oakes said, "I want one very sweet martini, please. And Mrs. Montague's prune juice." She picked up the menu and wet her lips, then said, "One crab-meat cocktail. And tonight will you see that Mrs. Montague has milk with her oatmeal; you sent cream last night. Yes, milk, please. You'd think they'd know by *now*," she added to Mrs. Montague over the top of the phone. "Now let me see," she said, into the phone again, her eyes on the menu.

Disregarding Miss Oakes, Mrs. Montague had begun to color. Her shoulders bent low over the book, a vague smile on her old face, she was devoting herself to a picture of a farmyard; a hen and three chickens strutted across the foreground of the picture, a barn surrounded by trees was the background. Mrs. Montague had laboriously colored the hen and the three chickens, the barn and the trees a rich blue, and now, with alternate touches of the crayons, was engaged in putting a red and yellow blot far up in the blue trees.

[1950]

A VISIT

(for Dylan Thomas)

I

The house in itself was, even before anything had happened there, as lovely a thing as she had ever seen. Set among its lavish grounds, with a park and a river and a wooded hill surrounding it, and carefully planned and tended gardens close upon all sides, it lay upon the hills as though it were something too precious to be seen by everyone; Margaret's very coming there had been a product of such elaborate arrangement, and such letters to and fro, and such meetings and hopings and wishings, that when she alighted with Carla Rhodes at the doorway of Carla's home, she felt that she too had come home, to a place striven for and earned. Carla stopped before the doorway and stood for a minute, looking first behind her, at the vast reaching gardens and the green lawn going down to the river, and the soft hills beyond, and then at the perfect grace of the house, showing so clearly the long-boned structure within, the curving staircases and the arched doorways and the tall thin lines of steadying beams, all of it resting back against the hills, and up, past rows of windows and the flying lines of the roof, on, to the tower—Carla stopped, and looked, and smiled, and then turned and said, "Welcome, Margaret."

"It's a lovely house," Margaret said, and felt that she had much better have said nothing.

The doors were opened and Margaret, touching as she went the warm head of a stone faun beside her, passed inside. Carla, following, greeted the servants by name, and was welcomed with reserved pleasure; they stood for a minute on the rose-and-white tiled floor. "Again, welcome, Margaret," Carla said.

Far ahead of them the great stairway soared upward, held to

the hall where they stood by only the slimmest of carved bal-
ustrades; on Margaret's left hand a tapestry moved softly as
the door behind was closed. She could see the fine threads of
the weave, and the light colors, but she could not have told the
picture unless she went far away, perhaps as far away as the
staircase, and looked at it from there; perhaps, she thought,
from halfway up the stairway this great hall, and perhaps the
whole house, is visible, as a complete body of story together,
all joined and in sequence. Or perhaps I shall be allowed to
move slowly from one thing to another, observing each, or
would that take all the time of my visit?

"I never saw anything so lovely," she said to Carla, and
Carla smiled.

"Come and meet my mama," Carla said.

They went through doors at the right, and Margaret, before
she could see the light room she went into, was stricken with
fear at meeting the owners of the house and the park and the
river, and as she went beside Carla she kept her eyes down.

"Mama," said Carla, "This is Margaret, from school."

"Margaret," said Carla's mother, and smiled at Margaret
kindly. "We are very glad you were able to come."

She was a tall lady wearing pale green and pale blue, and
Margaret said as gracefully as she could, "Thank you, Mrs.
Rhodes; I am very grateful for having been invited."

"Surely," said Mrs. Rhodes softly, "surely my daughter's
friend Margaret from school should be welcome here; surely
we should be grateful that she has come."

"Thank you, Mrs. Rhodes," Margaret said, not knowing
how she was answering, but knowing that she was grateful.

When Mrs. Rhodes turned her kind eyes on her daughter,
Margaret was at last able to look at the room where she stood
next to her friend; it was a pale-green and a pale-blue long
room with tall windows that looked out onto the lawn and the
sky, and thin colored china ornaments on the mantel. Mrs.
Rhodes had left her needlepoint when they came in and from
where Margaret stood she could see the pale sweet pattern
from the underside; all soft colors it was, melting into one

another endlessly, and not finished. On the table near by were books, and one large book of sketches that were most certainly Carla's; Carla's harp stood next to the windows, and beyond one window were marble steps outside, going shallowly down to a fountain, where water moved in the sunlight. Margaret thought of her own embroidery—a pair of slippers she was working for her friend—and knew that she should never be able to bring it into this room, where Mrs. Rhodes's long white hands rested on the needlepoint frame, soft as dust on the pale colors.

"Come," said Carla, taking Margaret's hand in her own, "Mama has said that I might show you some of the house."

They went out again into the hall, across the rose and white tiles which made a pattern too large to be seen from the floor, and through a doorway where tiny bronze fauns grinned at them from the carving. The first room that they went into was all gold, with gilt on the window frames and on the legs of the chairs and tables, and the small chairs standing on the yellow carpet were made of gold brocade with small gilded backs, and on the wall were more tapestries showing the house as it looked in the sunlight with even the trees around it shining, and these tapestries were let into the wall and edged with thin gilded frames.

"There is so much tapestry," Margaret said.

"In every room," Carla agreed. "Mama has embroidered all the hangings for her own room, the room where she writes her letters. The other tapestries were done by my grandmamas and my great-grandmamas and my great-great-grandmamas."

The next room was silver, and the small chairs were of silver brocade with narrow silvered backs, and the tapestries on the walls of this room were edged with silver frames and showed the house in moonlight, with the white light shining on the stones and the windows glittering.

"Who uses these rooms?" Margaret asked.

"No one," Carla said.

They passed then into a room where everything grew smaller as they looked at it: the mirrors on both sides of the room showed the door opening and Margaret and Carla coming through, and then, reflected, a smaller door opening and a small Margaret and a smaller Carla coming through, and then, reflected again, a still smaller door and Margaret and Carla, and so on, endlessly, Margaret and Carla diminishing and reflecting. There was a table here and nesting under it another lesser table, and under that another one, and another under that one, and on the greatest table lay a carved wooden bowl holding within it another carved wooden bowl, and another within that, and another within that one. The tapestries in this room were of the house reflected in the lake, and the tapestries themselves were reflected, in and out, among the mirrors on the wall, with the house in the tapestries reflected in the lake.

This room frightened Margaret rather, because it was so difficult for her to tell what was in it and what was not, and how far in any direction she might easily move, and she backed out hastily, pushing Carla behind her. They turned from here into another doorway which led them out again into the great hall under the soaring staircase, and Carla said, "We had better go upstairs and see your room; we can see more of the house another time. We have *plenty* of time, after all," and she squeezed Margaret's hand joyfully.

They climbed the great staircase, and passed, in the hall upstairs, Carla's room, which was like the inside of a shell in pale colors, with lilacs on the table, and the fragrance of the lilacs followed them as they went down the halls.

The sound of their shoes on the polished floor was like rain, but the sun came in on them wherever they went. "Here," Carla said, opening a door, "is where we have breakfast when it is warm; here," opening another door, "is the passage to the room where Mama does her letters. And that—" nodding "—is the stairway to the tower, and *here* is where we shall have dances when my brother comes home."

"A real tower?" Margaret said.

"And *here*," Carla said, "is the old schoolroom, and my brother and I studied here before he went away, and I stayed on alone studying here until it was time for me to come to school and meet *you*."

"Can we go up into the tower?" Margaret asked.

"Down here, at the end of the hall," Carla said, "is where all my grandpapas and my grandmamas and my great-great-grandpapas and grandmamas live." She opened the door to the long gallery, where pictures of tall old people in lace and pale waistcoats leaned down to stare at Margaret and Carla. And then, to a walk at the top of the house, where they leaned over and looked at the ground below and the tower above, and Margaret looked at the gray stone of the tower and wondered who lived there, and Carla pointed out where the river ran far below, far away, and said they should walk there tomorrow.

"When my brother comes," she said, "he will take us boating on the river."

In her room, unpacking her clothes, Margaret realized that her white dress was the only one possible for dinner, and thought that she would have to send home for more things; she had intended to wear her ordinary gray downstairs most evenings before Carla's brother came, but knew she could not when she saw Carla in light blue, with pearls around her neck. When Margaret and Carla came into the drawing room before dinner Mrs. Rhodes greeted them very kindly, and asked had Margaret seen the painted room or the room with the tiles?

"We had no time to go near that part of the house at all," Carla said.

"After dinner, then," Mrs. Rhodes said, putting her arm affectionately around Margaret's shoulders, "we will go and see the painted room and the room with the tiles, because they are particular favorites of mine."

"Come and meet my papa," Carla said.

The door was just opening for Mr. Rhodes, and Margaret, who felt almost at ease now with Mrs. Rhodes, was frightened again of Mr. Rhodes, who spoke loudly and said, "So this is m'girl's friend from school? Lift up your head, girl, and let's have a look at you." When Margaret looked up blindly, and smiled weakly, he patted her cheek and said, "We shall have to make you look bolder before you leave us," and then he tapped his daughter on the shoulder and said she had grown to a monstrous fine girl.

They went in to dinner, and on the walls of the dining room were tapestries of the house in the seasons of the year, and the dinner service was white china with veins of gold running through it, as though it had been mined and not moulded. The fish was one Margaret did not recognize, and Mr. Rhodes very generously insisted upon serving her himself without smiling at her ignorance. Carla and Margaret were each given a glassful of pale spicy wine.

"When my brother comes," Carla said to Margaret, "we will not dare be so quiet at table." She looked across the white cloth to Margaret, and then to her father at the head, to her mother at the foot, with the long table between them, and said, "My brother can make us laugh all the time."

"Your mother will not miss you for these summer months?" Mrs. Rhodes said to Margaret.

"She has my sisters, ma'am," Margaret said, "and I have been away at school for so long that she has learned to do without me."

"We mothers never learn to do without our daughters," Mrs. Rhodes said, and looked fondly at Carla. "Or our sons," she added with a sigh.

"When my brother comes," Carla said, "you will see what this house can be like with life in it."

"When does he come?" Margaret asked.

"One week," Mr. Rhodes said, "three days, and four hours."

When Mrs. Rhodes rose, Margaret and Carla followed her, and Mr. Rhodes rose gallantly to hold the door for them all.

That evening Carla and Margaret played and sang duets, although Carla said that their voices together were too thin to be appealing without a deeper voice accompanying, and that when her brother came they should have some splendid trios. Mrs. Rhodes complimented their singing, and Mr. Rhodes fell asleep in his chair.

Before they went upstairs Mrs. Rhodes reminded herself of

her promise to show Margaret the painted room and the room
with the tiles, and so she and Margaret and Carla, holding
their long dresses up away from the floor in front so that their
skirts whispered behind them, went down a hall and through
a passage and down another hall, and through a room filled
with books and then through a painted door into a tiny octagonal room where each of the sides was paneled and painted,
with pink and blue and green and gold small pictures of shep-
herds and nymphs, lambs and fauns, playing on the broad
green lawns by the river, with the house standing lovely behind
them. There was nothing else in the little room, because seemingly the paintings were furniture enough for one room, and
Margaret felt surely that she could stay happily and watch the
small painted people playing, without ever seeing anything
more of the house. But Mrs. Rhodes led her on, into the room
of the tiles, which was not exactly a room at all, but had one
side all glass window looking out onto the same lawn of the
pictures in the octagonal room. The tiles were set into the
floor of this room, in tiny bright spots of color which showed,
when you stood back and looked at them, that they were again
a picture of the house, only now the same materials that made
the house made the tiles, so that the tiny windows were tiles of
glass, and the stones of the tower were chips of gray stone, and
the bricks of the chimneys were chips of brick.

Beyond the tiles of the house Margaret, lifting her long skirt
as she walked, so that she should not brush a chip of the tower
out of place, stopped and said, "What is *this*?" And stood
back to see, and then knelt down and said, "*What* is this?"

"Isn't she enchanting?" said Mrs. Rhodes, smiling at Margaret, "I've always loved her."

"I was wondering what Margaret would say when she saw
it," said Carla, smiling also.

It was a curiously made picture of a girl's face, with blue-chip
eyes and a red-chip mouth, staring blindly from the floor, with
long light braids made of yellow stone chips going down evenly
on either side of her round cheeks.

"She is pretty," said Margaret, stepping back to see her better. "What does it say underneath?"

She stepped back again, holding her head up and back to read the letters, pieced together with stone chips and set unevenly in the floor. "Here was Margaret," it said, "who died for love."

2

There was, of course, not time to do everything. Before Margaret had seen half the house, Carla's brother came home. Carla came running up the great staircase one afternoon calling "Margaret, Margaret, he's come," and Margaret, running down to meet her, hugged her and said, "I'm so glad."

He had certainly come, and Margaret, entering the drawing room shyly behind Carla, saw Mrs. Rhodes with tears in her eyes and Mr. Rhodes standing straighter and prouder than before, and Carla said, "Brother, here is Margaret."

He was tall and haughty in uniform, and Margaret wished she had met him a little later, when she had perhaps been to her room again, and perhaps tucked up her hair. Next to him stood his friend, a captain, small and dark and bitter, and smiling bleakly upon the family assembled. Margaret smiled back timidly at them both, and stood behind Carla.

Everyone then spoke at once. Mrs. Rhodes said "We've missed you so," and Mr. Rhodes said "Glad to have you back, m'boy," and Carla said "We shall have such times—I've promised Margaret—" and Carla's brother said "So this is Margaret?" and the dark captain said "I've been wanting to come."

It seemed that they all spoke at once, every time; there would be a long waiting silence while all of them looked around with joy at being together, and then suddenly everyone would have found something to say. It was so at dinner: Mrs. Rhodes said "You're not eating enough," and "You used to be more fond of pomegranates," and Carla said "We're to go boating," and "We'll have a dance, won't we?" and "Margaret and I insist upon a picnic," and "I saved the river for my brother to show to Margaret." Mr. Rhodes puffed and laughed and passed the wine, and Margaret hardly dared lift her eyes. The black captain said "Never realized what an attactive old place it could be, after all," and Carla's brother said "There's much about the house I'd like to show Margaret."

After dinner they played charades, and even Mrs. Rhodes did Achilles with Mr. Rhodes, holding his heel and both of them laughing and glancing at Carla and Margaret and the captain. Carla's brother leaned on the back of Margaret's chair and once she looked up at him and said, "No one ever calls you by name. Do you actually have a name?"

"Paul," he said.

The next morning they walked on the lawn, Carla with the captain and Margaret with Paul. They stood by the lake, and Margaret looked at the pure reflection of the house and said, "It almost seems as though we could open a door and go in."

"There," said Paul, and he pointed with his stick at the front entrance, "There is where we shall enter, and it will swing open for us with an underwater crash."

"Margaret," said Carla, laughing, "you say odd things, sometimes. If you tried to go into *that* house, you'd be in the lake."

"Indeed, and not like it much, at all," the captain added.

"Or would you have the side door?" asked Paul, pointing with his stick.

"I think I prefer the front door," said Margaret.

"But you'd be drowned," Carla said. She took Margaret's arm as they started back toward the house, and said, "We'd make a scene for a tapestry right now, on the lawn before the house."

"Another tapestry?" said the captain, and grimaced.

They played croquet, and Paul hit Margaret's ball toward a wicket, and the captain accused her of cheating prettily. And they played word games in the evening, and Margaret and Paul won, and everyone said Margaret was so clever. And they walked endlessly on the lawns before the house, and looked into the still lake, and watched the reflection of the house in the water, and Margaret chose a room in the reflected house for her own, and Paul said she should have it.

"That's the room where Mama writes her letters," said Carla, looking strangely at Margaret.

"Not in our house in the lake," said Paul.

"And I suppose if you like it she would lend it to you while you stay," Carla said.

"Not at all," said Margaret amiably. "I think I should prefer the tower anyway."

"Have you seen the rose garden?" Carla asked.

"Let me take you there," said Paul.

Margaret started across the lawn with him, and Carla called to her, "Where are you off to now, Margaret?"

"Why, to the rose garden," Margaret called back, and Carla said, staring, "You are really very odd, sometimes, Margaret. And it's growing colder, far too cold to linger among the roses," and so Margaret and Paul turned back.

Mrs. Rhodes's needlepoint was coming on well. She had filled in most of the outlines of the house, and was setting in the windows. After the first small shock of surprise, Margaret no longer wondered that Mrs. Rhodes was able to set out the house so well without a pattern or a plan; she did it from memory and Margaret, realizing this for the first time, thought "How amazing," and then "But of course; how else *would* she do it?"

To see a picture of the house, Mrs. Montague needed only to lift her eyes in any direction, but, more than that, she had of course never used any other model for her embroidery; she had of course learned the faces of the house better than the faces of her children. The dreamy life of the Rhodeses in the house was most clearly shown Margaret as she watched Mrs. Rhodes surely and capably building doors and windows, carvings and cornices, in her embroidered house, smiling tenderly across the room to where Carla and the captain bent over a book together, while her fingers almost of themselves turned the edge of a carving Margaret had forgotten or never known about until, leaning over the back of Mrs. Rhodes's chair, she saw it form itself under Mrs. Rhodes's hands.

The small thread of days and sunlight, then, that bound Margaret to the house, was woven here as she watched. And Carla, lifting her head to look over, might say, "Margaret, do come and look, here. Mother is always at her work, but my brother is rarely home."

They went for a picnic, Carla and the captain and Paul and Margaret, and Mrs. Rhodes waved to them from the doorway as they left, and Mr. Rhodes came to his study window and lifted his hand to them. They chose to go to the wooded hill beyond the house, although Carla was timid about going too far away—"I always like to be where I can see the roofs, at least," she said—and sat among the trees, on moss greener than Margaret had ever seen before, and spread out a white cloth and drank red wine.

It was a very proper forest, with neat trees and the green moss, and an occasional purple or yellow flower growing discreetly away from the path. There was no sense of brooding silence, as there sometimes is with trees about, and Margaret realized, looking up to see the sky clearly between the branches, that she had seen this forest in the tapestries in the breakfast room, with the house shining in the sunlight beyond.

"Doesn't the river come through here somewhere?" she asked, hearing, she thought, the sound of it through the trees. "I feel so comfortable here among these trees, so at home."

"It is possible," said Paul, "to take a boat from the lawn in front of the house and move without sound down the river, through the trees, past the fields and then, for some reason, around past the house again. The river, you see, goes almost around the house in a great circle. We are very proud of that."

"The river *is* near by," said Carla. "It goes almost completely around the house."

"Margaret," said the captain. "You must not look rapt on a picnic unless you are contemplating nature."

"I was, as a matter of fact," said Margaret. "I was contemplating a caterpillar approaching Carla's foot."

"Will you come and look at the river?" said Paul, rising and holding his hand out to Margaret. "I think we can see much of its great circle from near here."

"Margaret," said Carla as Margaret stood up. "You are *always* wandering off."

"I'm coming right back," Margaret said, with a laugh. "It's only to look at the river."

"Don't be away long," Carla said. "We must be getting back before dark."

The river as it went through the trees was shadowed and cool, broadening out into pools where only the barest movement disturbed the ferns along its edge, and where small stones made it possible to step out and see the water all around, from a precarious island, and where without sound a leaf might be carried from the limits of sight to the limits of sight, moving swiftly but imperceptibly and turning a little as it went.

"Who lives in the tower, Paul?" asked Margaret, holding a fern and running it softly over the back of her hand. "I know someone lives there, because I saw someone moving at the window once."

"Not *lives* there," said Paul, amused. "Did you think we kept a political prisoner locked away?"

"I thought it might be the birds, at first," Margaret said, glad to be describing this to someone.

"No," said Paul, still amused. "There's an aunt, or a great-aunt, or perhaps even a great-great-great-aunt. She doesn't live there, at all, but goes there because she says she cannot *endure* the sight of tapestry." He laughed. "She has filled the tower with books, and a huge old cat, and she may practice alchemy there, for all anyone knows. The reason you've never seen her would be that she has one of her spells of hiding away. Sometimes she is downstairs daily."

"Will I ever meet her?" Margaret asked wonderingly.

"Perhaps," Paul said. "She might take it into her head to come down formally one night to dinner. Or she might wander carelessly up to you where you sat on the lawn, and introduce herself. Or you might never see her, at that."

"Suppose I went up to the tower?"

Paul glanced at her strangely. "I suppose you could, if you wanted to," he said. "*I've* been there."

"Margaret," Carla called through the woods. "Margaret, we shall be late if you do not give up brooding by the river."

All this time, almost daily, Margaret was seeing new places in the house: the fan room, where the most delicate filigree fans had been set into the walls with their fine ivory sticks

painted in exquisite miniature; the small room where incredibly perfect wooden and glass and metal fruits and flowers and
trees stood on glittering glass shelves, lined up against the
windows. And daily she passed and repassed the door behind
which lay the stairway to the tower, and almost daily she
stepped carefully around the tiles on the floor which read
"Here was Margaret, who died for love."

It was no longer possible, however, to put off going to the
tower. It was no longer possible to pass the doorway several
times a day and do no more than touch her hand secretly to
the panels, or perhaps set her head against and listen, to hear
if there were footsteps going up or down, or a voice calling
her. It was not possible to pass the doorway once more, and so
in the early morning Margaret set her hand firmly to the door
and pulled it open, and it came easily, as though relieved that
at last, after so many hints and insinuations, and so much
waiting and such helpless despair, Margaret had finally come
to open it.

The stairs beyond, gray stone and rough, were, Margaret
thought, steep for an old lady's feet, but Margaret went up
effortlessly, though timidly. The stairway turned around and
around, going up to the tower, and Margaret followed, setting
her feet carefully upon one step after another, and holding her
hands against the warm stone wall on either side, looking forward and up, expecting to be seen or spoken to before she
reached the top; perhaps, she thought once, the walls of the
tower were transparent and she was clearly, ridiculously visible from the outside, and Mrs. Rhodes and Carla, on the
lawn—if indeed they ever looked upward to the tower—might
watch her and turn to one another with smiles, saying "There
is Margaret, going up to the tower at last," and, smiling, nod
to one another.

The stairway ended, as she had not expected it would, in a
heavy wooden door, which made Margaret, standing on the
step below to find room to raise her hand and knock, seem
smaller, and even standing at the top of the tower she felt that
she was not really tall.

"Come in," said the great-aunt's voice, when Margaret had

knocked twice; the first knock had been received with an expectant silence, as though inside someone had said inaudibly, "Is that someone knocking at *this* door?" and then waited to be convinced by a second knock—and Margaret's knuckles hurt from the effort of knocking to be heard through a heavy wooden door. She opened the door awkwardly from below—how much easier this all would be, she thought, if I knew the way—went in, and said politely, before she looked around, "I'm Carla's friend. They said I might come up to the tower to see it, but of course if you would rather I went away I shall." She had planned to say this more gracefully, without such an implication that invitations to the tower were issued by the downstairs Rhodeses, but the long climb and her being out of breath forced her to say everything at once, and she had really no time for the sounding periods she had composed.

In any case the great-aunt said politely—she was sitting at the other side of the round room, against a window, and she was not very clearly visible—"I am amazed that they told you about me at all. However, since you are here I cannot pretend that I really object to having you; you may come in and sit down."

Margaret came obediently into the room and sat down on the stone bench which ran all the way around the tower room, under the windows which of course were on all sides and open to the winds, so that the movement of the air through the tower room was insistent and constant, making talk difficult and even distinguishing objects a matter of some effort.

As though it were necessary to establish her position in the house emphatically and immediatey, the old lady said, with a gesture and a grin, "My tapestries," and waved at the windows. She seemed to be not older than a great-aunt, although perhaps too old for a mere aunt, but her voice was clearly able to carry through the sound of the wind in the tower room and she seemed compact and strong beside the window, not at all as though she might be dizzy from looking out, or tired from the stairs.

"May I look out the window?" Margaret asked, almost of the cat, which sat next to her and regarded her without friendship, but without, as yet, dislike.

"Certainly," said the great-aunt. "Look out the windows, by all means."

Margaret turned on the bench and leaned her arms on the wide stone ledge of the window, but she was disappointed. Although the tops of the trees did not reach halfway up the tower, she could see only branches and leaves below and no sign of the wide lawns or the roofs of the house or the curve of the river.

"I hoped I could see the way the river went, from here."

"The river doesn't *go* from here," said the old lady, and laughed.

"I mean," Margaret said, "they told me that the river went around in a curve, almost surrounding the house."

"Who told you?" said the old lady.

"Paul."

"I see," said the old lady. "*He*'s back, is he?"

"He's been here for several days, but he's going away again soon."

"And what's *your* name?" asked the old lady, leaning forward.

"Margaret."

"I see," said the old lady again. "That's my name, too," she said.

Margaret thought that "How nice" would be an inappropriate reply to this, and something like "Is it?" or "Just imagine" or "What a coincidence" would certainly make her feel more foolish than she believed she really was, so she smiled uncertainly at the old lady and dismissed the notion of saying "What a lovely name."

"He should have come and gone sooner," the old lady went on, as though to herself. "Then we'd have it all behind us."

"Have all *what* behind us?" Margaret asked, although she felt that she was not really being included in the old lady's conversation with herself, a conversation that seemed—and probably was—part of a larger conversation which the old lady had with herself constantly and on larger subjects than the matter of Margaret's name, and which even Margaret, intruder as she was, and young, could not be allowed to interrupt for very long. "Have all *what* behind us?" Margaret asked insistently.

"I say," said the old lady, turning to look at Margaret, "he should have come and gone already, and we'd all be well out of it by now."

"I see," said Margaret. "Well, I don't think he's going to be here much longer. He's talking of going." In spite of herself, her voice trembled a little. In order to prove to the old lady that the trembling in her voice was imaginary, Margaret said almost defiantly, "It will be very lonely here after he has gone."

"We'll be well out of it, Margaret, you and I," the old lady said. "Stand away from the window, child, you'll be wet."

Margaret realized with this that the storm, which had—she knew now—been hanging over the house for long sunny days had broken, suddenly, and that the wind had grown louder and was bringing with it through the windows of the tower long stinging rain. There were drops on the cat's black fur, and Margaret felt the side of her face wet. "Do your windows close?" she asked. "If I could help you—?"

"*I* don't mind the rain," the old lady said. "It wouldn't be the first time it's rained around the tower."

"*I* don't mind it," Margaret said hastily, drawing away from the window. She realized that she was staring back at the cat, and added nervously, "Although, of course, getting wet is—" She hesitated and the cat stared back at her without expression. "I mean," she said apologetically, "some people don't *like* getting wet."

The cat deliberately turned its back on her and put its face closer to the window.

"What were you saying about Paul?" Margaret asked the old lady, feeling somehow that there might be a thin thread of reason tangling the old lady and the cat and the tower and the rain, and even, with abrupt clarity, defining Margaret herself and the strange hesitation which had caught at her here in the tower. "He's going away soon, you know."

"It would have been better if it were over with by now," the old lady said. "These things don't take really long, you know, and the sooner the better, *I* say."

"I suppose *that's* true," Margaret said intelligently.

"After all," said the old lady dreamily, with raindrops in her hair, "we don't always see ahead, into things that are going to happen."

Margaret was wondering how soon she might politely go back downstairs and dry herself off, and she meant to stay politely only so long as the old lady seemed to be talking, however remotely, about Paul. Also, the rain and the wind were coming through the window onto Margaret in great driving gusts, as though Margaret and the old lady and the books and the cat would be washed away, and the top of the tower cleaned of them.

"I *would* help you if I could," the old lady said earnestly to Margaret, raising her voice almost to a scream to be heard over the wind and the rain. She stood up to approach Margaret, and Margaret, thinking she was about to fall, reached out a hand to catch her. The cat stood up and spat, the rain came through the window in a great sweep, and Margaret, holding the old lady's hands, heard through the sounds of the wind the equal sounds of all the voices in the world, and they called to her saying "Good-by, good-by," and "All is lost," and another voice saying "I will always remember you," and still another called, "It is so dark." And, far away from the others, she could hear a voice calling, "Come back, come back." Then the old lady pulled her hands away from Margaret and the voices were gone. The cat shrank back and the old lady looked coldly at Margaret and said, "As I was saying, I would help you if I *could*."

"I'm so sorry," Margaret said weakly. "I thought you were going to fall."

"Good-by," said the old lady.

3

At the ball Margaret wore a gown of thin blue lace that belonged to Carla, and yellow roses in her hair, and she carried one of the fans from the fan room, a daintily painted ivory thing which seemed indestructible, since she dropped it twice, and which had a tiny picture of the house painted on its ivory sticks, so that when the fan was closed the house was gone. Mrs. Rhodes had given it to her to carry, and had given Carla another, so that when Margaret and Carla passed one another dancing, or met by the punch bowl or in the halls, they said happily to one another, "Have you still got your fan? I gave mine to someone to hold for a minute; I showed mine to everyone. Are you still carrying your fan? I've got *mine*."

Margaret danced with strangers and with Paul, and when she danced with Paul they danced away from the others, up and down the long gallery hung with pictures, in and out between the pillars which led to the great hall opening into the room of the tiles. Near them danced ladies in scarlet silk, and green satin, and white velvet, and Mrs. Rhodes, in black with diamonds at her throat and on her hands, stood at the top of the room and smiled at the dancers, or went on Mr. Rhodes's arm to greet guests who came laughingly in between the pillars looking eagerly and already moving in time to the music as they walked. One lady wore white feathers in her hair, curling down against her shoulder; another had a pink scarf over her arms, and it floated behind her as she danced. Paul was in his haughty uniform, and Carla wore red roses in her hair and danced with the captain.

"Are you really going tomorrow?" Margaret asked Paul once during the evening; she knew that he was, but somehow asking the question—which she had done several times before—established a communication between them, of his right to go and her right to wonder, which was sadly sweet to her.

"I *said* you might meet the great-aunt," said Paul, as though in answer; Margaret followed his glance, and saw the old lady of the tower. She was dressed in yellow satin, and looked very regal and proud as she moved through the crowd of dancers, drawing her skirt aside if any of them came too close to her. She was coming toward Margaret and Paul where they sat on small chairs against the wall, and when she came close enough she smiled, looking at Paul, and said to him, holding out her hands, "I am very glad to see you, my dear."

Then she smiled at Margaret and Margaret smiled back, very glad that the old lady held out no hands to her.

"Margaret told me you were here," the old lady said to Paul, "and I came down to see you once more."

"I'm very glad you did," Paul said. "I wanted to see you so much that I almost came to the tower."

They both laughed and Margaret, looking from one to the other of them, wondered at the strong resemblance between them. Margaret sat very straight and stiff on her narrow chair, with her blue lace skirt falling charmingly around her and her hands folded neatly in her lap, and listened to their talk. Paul had found the old lady a chair and they sat with their heads near together, looking at one another as they talked, and smiling.

"You look very fit," the old lady said. "Very fit indeed." She sighed.

"You look wonderfully well," Paul said.

"Oh, well," said the old lady. "I've aged. I've aged, I know it."

"So have I," said Paul.

"Not noticeably," said the old lady, shaking her head and regarding him soberly for a minute. "*You* never will, I suppose."

At that moment the captain came up and bowed in front of Margaret, and Margaret, hoping that Paul might notice, got up to dance with him.

"I saw you sitting there alone," said the captain, "and I seized the precise opportunity I have been awaiting all evening."

"Excellent military tactics," said Margaret, wondering if these remarks had not been made a thousand times before, at a thousand different balls.

"I could be a splendid tactician," said the captain gallantly, as though carrying on his share of the echoing conversation, the words spoken under so many glittering chandeliers, "if my objective were always so agreeable to me."

"I saw you dancing with Carla," said Margaret.

"Carla," he said, and made a small gesture that somehow showed Carla as infinitely less than Margaret. Margaret knew that she had seen him make the same gesture to Carla, probably with reference to Margaret. She laughed.

"I forget what I'm supposed to say now," she told him.

"You're supposed to say," he told her seriously, " 'And do you really leave us so soon?' "

"And do you really leave us so soon?" said Margaret obediently.

"The sooner to return," he said, and tightened his arm around her waist. Margaret said, it being her turn, "We shall miss you very much."

"*I* shall miss *you*," he said, with a manly air of resignation.

They danced two waltzes, after which the captain escorted her handsomely back to the chair from which he had taken her, next to which Paul and the old lady continued in conversation, laughing and gesturing. The captain bowed to Margaret deeply, clicking his heels.

"May I leave you alone for a minute or so?" he asked. "I believe Carla is looking for me."

"I'm perfectly all right here," Margaret said. As the captain hurried away she turned to hear what Paul and the old lady were saying.

"I remember, I remember," said the old lady laughing, and she tapped Paul on the wrist with her fan. "I never imagined there would be a time when I should find it funny."

"But it *was* funny," said Paul.

"We were so young," the old lady said. "I can hardly remember."

She stood up abruptly, bowed to Margaret, and started back across the room among the dancers. Paul followed her as far as the doorway and then left her to come back to Margaret. When he sat down next to her he said, "So you met the old lady?"

"I went to the tower," Margaret said.

"She told me," he said absently, looking down at his gloves. "Well," he said finally, looking up with an air of cheerfulness. "Are they *never* going to play a waltz?"

Shortly before the sun came up over the river the next morning they sat at breakfast, Mr. and Mrs. Rhodes at the ends of the table, Carla and the captain, Margaret and Paul. The red roses in Carla's hair had faded and been thrown away, as had Margaret's yellow roses, but both Carla and Margaret still wore their ball gowns, which they had been wearing for so long that the soft richness of them seemed natural, as though they were to wear nothing else for an eternity in the house, and the gay confusion of helping one another dress, and admiring one another, and straightening the last folds to hang more gracefully, seemed all to have happened longer ago than memory, to be perhaps a dream that might never have happened at all, as perhaps the figures in the tapestries on the walls of the dining room might remember, secretly, an imagined process of dressing themselves and coming with laughter and light voices to sit on the lawn where they were woven. Margaret, looking at Carla, thought that she had never seen Carla so familiarly as in this soft white gown, with her hair dressed high on her head—had it really been curled and pinned that way? Or had it always, forever, been so?—and the fan in her hand—had she not always had that fan, held just so?—and when Carla turned her head slightly on her long neck she captured the air of one of the portraits in the long gallery. Paul and the captain were still somehow trim in their uniforms; they were leaving at sunrise.

"Must you really leave this morning?" Margaret whispered to Paul.

"You are all kind to stay up and say good-by," said the captain, and he leaned forward to look down the table at Margaret, as though it were particularly kind of her.

"Every time my son leaves me," said Mrs. Rhodes, "it is as though it were the first time."

Abruptly, the captain turned to Mrs. Rhodes and said, "I noticed this morning that there was a bare patch on the grass before the door. Can it be restored?"

"I had not known," Mrs. Rhodes said, and she looked nervously at Mr. Rhodes, who put his hand quietly on the table and said, "We hope to keep the house in good repair so long as we are able."

"But the broken statue by the lake?" said the captain. "And the tear in the tapestry behind your head?"

"It is wrong of you to notice these things," Mrs. Rhodes said, gently.

"What can I do?" he said to her. "It is impossible not to notice these things. The fish are dying, for instance. There are no grapes in the arbor this year. The carpet is worn to thread near your embroidery frame," he bowed to Mrs. Rhodes, "and in the house itself—" bowing to Mr. Rhodes "—there is a noticeable crack over the window of the conservatory, a crack in the solid stone. Can you repair that?"

Mr. Rhodes said weakly, "It is very wrong of you to notice these things. Have you neglected the sun, and the bright perfection of the drawing room? Have you been recently to the gallery of portraits? Have you walked on the green portions of the lawn, or only watched for the bare places?"

"The drawing room is shabby," said the captain softly. "The green brocade sofa is torn a little near the arm. The carpet has lost its luster. The gilt is chipped on four of the small chairs in the gold room, the silver paint scratched in the silver room. A tile is missing from the face of Margaret, who died for love, and in the great gallery the paint has faded slightly on the portrait of—" bowing again to Mr. Rhodes "—your great-great-great-grandfather, sir."

Mr. Rhodes and Mrs. Rhodes looked at one another, and then Mrs. Rhodes said, "Surely it is not necessary to reproach *us* for these things?"

The captain reddened and shook his head.

"My embroidery is very nearly finished," Mrs. Rhodes said. "I have only to put the figures into the foreground."

"*I* shall mend the brocade sofa," said Carla.

The captain glanced once around the table, and sighed. "I must pack," he said. "We cannot delay our duties even though we have offended lovely women." Mrs. Rhodes, turning coldly away from him, rose and left the table, with Carla and Margaret following.

Margaret went quickly to the tile room, where the white face of Margaret who died for love stared eternally into the sky beyond the broad window. There was indeed a tile missing from the wide white cheek, and the broken spot looked like a tear, Margaret thought; she kneeled down and touched the tile face quickly to be sure that it was not a tear.

Then she went slowly back through the lovely rooms, across the broad rose-and-white tiled hall, and into the drawing room, and stopped to close the tall doors behind her.

"There really is a tile missing," she said.

Paul turned and frowned; he was standing alone in the drawing room, tall and bright in his uniform, ready to leave. "You are mistaken," he said. "It is not possible that anything should be missing."

"I saw it."

"It is not *true*, you know," he said. He was walking quickly up and down the room, slapping his gloves on his wrist, glancing nervously, now and then, at the door, at the tall windows opening out onto the marble stairway. "The house is the same as ever," he said. "It does not change."

"But the worn carpet . . ." It was under his feet as he walked.

"Nonsense," he said violently. "Don't you think I'd know my own house? I care for it constantly, even when *they* forget; without this house I could not exist; do you think it would begin to crack while I am here?"

"How can you keep it from aging? Carpets *will* wear, you know, and unless they are replaced . . ."

"Replaced?" He stared as though she had said something evil. "What could replace anything in this house?" He touched Mrs. Rhodes's embroidery frame, softly. "All *we* can do is add to it."

There was a sound outside; it was the family coming down the great stairway to say good-by. He turned quickly and listened, and it seemed to be the sound he had been expecting. "I will always remember you," he said to Margaret, hastily, and turned again toward the tall windows. "Good-by."

"It is so dark," Margaret said, going beside him. "You will come back?"

"I will come back," he said sharply. "Good-by." He stepped across the sill of the window onto the marble stairway outside; he was black for a moment against the white marble, and Margaret stood still at the window watching him go down the steps and away through the gardens. "Lost, lost," she heard faintly, and, from far away, "All is lost."

She turned back to the room, and, avoiding the worn spot in the carpet and moving widely around Mrs. Rhodes's embroidery frame, she went to the great doors and opened them. Outside, in the hall with the rose-and-white tiled floor, Mr. and Mrs. Rhodes and Carla were standing with the captain.

"Son," Mrs. Rhodes was saying, "when will you be back?"

"Don't *fuss* at me," the captain said. "I'll be back when I can."

Carla stood silently, a little away. "Please be careful," she said, and, "Here's Margaret, come to say good-by to you, Brother."

"Don't linger, m'boy," said Mr. Rhodes. "Hard on the women."

"There are so many things Margaret and I planned for you while you were here," Carla said to her brother. "The time has been so short."

Margaret, standing beside Mrs. Rhodes, turned to Carla's brother (*and Paul; who was Paul?*) and said, "Good-by." He bowed to her and moved to go to the door with his father.

"It is hard to see him go," Mrs. Rhodes said. "And we do not know when he will come back." She put her hand gently on Margaret's shoulder. "We must show you more of the house," she said. "I saw you one day try the door of the ruined tower; have you seen the hall of flowers? Or the fountain room?"

"When my brother comes again," Carla said, "we shall have a musical evening, and perhaps he will take us boating on the river."

"And my visit?" said Margaret smiling. "Surely there will be an end to my visit?"

Mrs. Rhodes, with one last look at the door from which Mr. Rhodes and the captain had gone, dropped her hand from Margaret's shoulder and said, "I must go to my embroidery. I have neglected it while my son was with us."

"You will not leave us before my brother comes again?" Carla asked Margaret.

"I have only to put the figures into the foreground," Mrs. Rhodes said, hesitating on her way to the drawing room. "I shall have you exactly if you sit on the lawn near the river."

"We shall be models of stillness," said Carla, laughing. "Margaret, will you come and sit beside me on the lawn?"

[1950]

THE ROCK

Being on the water was not precisely a unique, but rather an unusual, experience for Paula Ellison, and for the first few minutes that she sat on the small seat almost too close to the front of the boat, she was perfectly still, afraid not so much of upsetting the boat as of being unprepared when it surely did upset. She had gotten in first, and sat with her back to the island where they were going, watching the young man in the oilskin jacket as he helped first her sister-in-law Virginia, and then her brother Charles, into the more comfortable seats in the center of the boat. Charles, Paula thought, looked tired, and she thought further that she did not grudge him the better seat, or the reassurance of sitting next to Virginia, because Charles had certainly been so very ill, and was still not well, and looked tired after their journey.

"I'm so *excited*," Virginia said, and bounced in the boat almost like a child. Then she added, in the gentle voice both she and Paula were now using toward Charles, "How do you feel, darling?"

"Very well indeed," Charles said. "Very much better."

"It looks so *exciting*," Virginia said. "Look at it, all dark and rocky against the sky and that *perfect* sunset."

"What is that picture?" Charles asked. "*You* know the one."

"Like a pirate stronghold," Virginia continued ecstatically, "or a prison or some—"

Paula said with amusement, "Charles, do you think it entirely wise to bring Virginia to a place where she can indulge her romantic temperament so fully?"

Charles, without hearing her, said to Virginia, "Actually,

I'm afraid it's only a rather ordinary summer resort." He smiled at his sister. "Do you think we might find one pirate for Virginia?"

Paula, without meaning to, looked over his head to the young man in the oilskin jacket who was running the boat, and found him at that moment looking at her, so that she turned quickly away and said, "It's cold."

"It *is* cold." Virginia pulled her coat closer around her.

"We're here so late in the year," Charles said.

Paula said immediately, "That's *much* better, you know; it means we'll be practically the only people and won't have to bother being sociable."

Virginia added, almost as quickly, "And I *always* think these early fall days are the best, after all. Relaxing," she added vaguely.

"Well, at least I didn't keep us from any vacation at all this year," Charles said.

"I never intended to take any vacation this year," Virginia said. "I *hate* going away in the summers, and the children are so much better off not going into public resorts."

"As you know," Paula said stiffly, "I rarely plan on a vacation at all. If it hadn't been for your insisting that you needed me—"

Charles laughed. "You worry too much," he said, turning from Virginia to Paula. "You don't have to fuss every time I mention being sick."

"You're not to think about it," Paula said.

"We all want to forget it," Virginia said.

"It's forgotten," Charles said. "How much longer will it take to reach the island?" From the inflection of his voice everyone immediately assumed that he was speaking to the young man in the oilskin jacket and did not know how otherwise to address him, whether as "driver" or "captain" or "ferryman" or perhaps "boy."

After a minute the young man said, "Nearly there."

"Does the island have a name?" Virginia asked.

"People round here call it mostly Rock Island," the young man said.

"Even *that* is exciting," Virginia said. She looked first at Charles and then at Paula. "Even that it should be named Rock Island. Like a stronghold, or a fort, or a—"

"Rock," Paula said.

"We land on the other side," the young man said, without being asked; it was as though every person whom he carried to the island asked the same series of questions, made the same comments, spoke of pirates and that picture, *you* know, and went on to ask how long now? and what was the name of the island, and as though the next question had to be "Where do we land?" or "Do we dock there?" or "How are you going to get the boat up onto those rocks?" and this time, for once, impatient and perhaps tired of ferrying, he answered the question before it could be asked. Paula, who thought that Virginia was again going to say "How exciting," said quickly, "Charles, are you tired?"

"No," he said, surprised. "Not tired at all; I'm feeling very well, really."

Although she had not intended to view this island, this site of her unexpected holiday, so soon, had meant ever since she stepped into the boat without being allowed a chance of turning around to keep her back steadfastly against the island and not turn, not turn, until she was close enough to touch it, Paula at last forgot her resolution and turned to look; she saw, looming impossibly large over her head and with the red sunset behind, a great black jagged rock, without signs of humanity or sympathy, with only dreadful reaching black rocks and sharp incredible outlines against the sunset and she said (thinking, I can always go back if it's *too* awful), "Charles, how do you feel?"

"I feel *fine*," he said sharply.

"It's just all *too* exciting," Virginia said.

As the boat came closer it appeared that the island was composed of a single rock instead of many; there were no pebbles or splinters of rock at the edges of the water in the little cove to which the young man guided the boat, and a series of steps leading up to the house above seemed to be carved out of the rock. The sun had gone by now and only a faint impression of the sunset lay in the sky; it had grown much colder and the coming darkness made the rock look blacker and the steps steep and wet.

"Can we get up there at all?" Paula said, leaning from the boat to look at the steps; realizing that she was expected to stand and move from the boat onto the steps she hesitated and then reflected that she could hardly stay on in the boat unless she chose to go back with the ferryman. I wish for once Virginia would move first, she thought, or Charles, and then rebuked herself with the recollection that after all Virginia could hardly climb over Paula in the end seat to get out, and Charles was ill. The young man stepped easily from the boat onto the rock and held out his hand to Paula, and she remembered that he had helped Virginia into the boat earlier, and took his hand and found herself with less grace than usual almost scrambling onto the rock steps. They were not wet, after all, or slippery, but seemed actually to press back against her feet as though holding firmly against her.

I like it here, she thought, surprising herself, and found the steps irresistible; before Virginia was even out of the boat Paula had turned and begun to climb. At first she only enjoyed the pressure of the steps under her feet, and then she raised her head and saw the house above her and she began to climb faster.

"Look at Paula, so far ahead," she heard Charles saying below her; he sounded cross, and she thought that perhaps he was annoyed with her for having spoken so much of his illness. Ahead of her the windows of the house showed light and then the door opened and someone came into the doorway, looking down and seeming to peer through the darkness.

"Who is it?" the woman in the doorway called.

Required to identify herself suddenly, Paula hesitated on the steps and then turned and looked behind her. Charles and Virginia were following her slowly, helping one another, and Paula felt first a small pang that she had not stayed with them, but had gone on so easily herself. Then, past the curve of the rock below her, she saw the boat going back, and was suddenly very frightened when she realized that the boat and the ferryman had never intended to stay with them; how will we ever get back? she wondered, and then smiled at herself, thinking that surely the ferryman must come back several times a day.

"Are you all right?" she called down to Charles and Virginia. "Shall I come back and help you?"

"We're all right," Virginia called up to her. "The steps are just a little steep for Charles."

Paula turned and climbed on up to the house while the woman in the doorway stood watching her. "So you've come," said the woman in the doorway when Paula was close enough for her to speak. "I'd almost given up expecting you."

Not a very gracious hostess, Paula thought. "We've been late for everything all day," she explained. "Trains, busses, meals, everything."

"You'll have to take what you can get here tonight," the woman said. "Dinner's been done with for an hour, and the dishes washed and put away."

"I'm sure we won't want much," Paula said. She was displeased, and as she came up onto the last, wider steps which led to the doorway she did not stop to look at the woman, but brushed past her and went inside. The room into which she came seemed to be made of the rock of the island, and for a minute she stood staring, forgetting the landlady behind her. A great fire burned on the far side of the huge room, and flickered against the walls in lines that might have been reflecting mica in rock, ran in light up and down the wide dark walls on which no pictures hung, and shattered itself oddly across and along the floor on which no rug lay. The furniture was huge and wooden, a great trestle table with benches on either side, and a long wooden bench with back and arms which brought the word "settle" to Paula's mind, and huge square wooden chairs, worn and smooth with use. There were no ornaments of any kind and no light except from the great fire.

Paula heard the landlady, still behind her in the doorway, calling down to Charles and Virginia that it was only a bit more to come, and then the landlady added very quietly, "You'll want to put in curtains and such, I daresay."

"Were you speaking to me?" Paula asked; there seemed no one else around.

"And flowers, I suppose."

Paula advanced to the fire and stood warming her hands. "It's a most unusual room," she said. She was trying to identify her own feelings; over and above everything else was a great despair and impulsive dislike of this house, this woman, this room; she tried to tell herself that it was the usual reaction to finishing a long journey and finding less comfort than she had been dreaming of since she left home. More than this, however, she was discouraged; this did not seem at all the sort of place in which to spend a belated vacation and she was anxious over how Charles and Virginia would feel about it. It'll be better in the morning when the sun is out, she told herself, and heard Charles and Virginia greeting the landlady.

"Did our suitcases come?" Charles was asking immediately; he had overseen their departure.

"This morning," said the landlady. "They're in your rooms."

"Splendid," said Charles. He came over to the fire and stood beside Paula. "Chill in the air," he said.

"It gets cold nights, this time of year," the landlady said.

"This is an extraordinary room," Virginia said. "It looks as though it's made out of rock."

"It *is* rock, as a matter of fact," said the landlady. "Most unusual. The greater part of the house is made of rock; I have a small booklet describing it for tourists, and I have put copies in your rooms. It is regarded as a most unusual house."

"It is *most* unusual," said Charles. "You are Mrs. Carter, of course?"

"Mrs. Carter," said the landlady, nodding. "Mr. and Mrs. Ellison."

"And Miss Ellison," said Charles, indicating Paula.

"Of course," said the landlady. "I have your rooms ready."

"Splendid," Charles said; he had taken command again now that there was no physical exertion required, and he looked patronizingly over Paula to say to the landlady, "Any chance of our having something to eat?"

The landlady waved her head back and forth sadly. "You

came so late, you know," she said. "I can give you cheese, and beer, and perhaps, if you wanted to wait for a broiled chicken . . ."

"Just some tea for me, thanks," said Virginia.

"I should like some tea," Paula said.

"Whatever you can find, then, in a minute or so," Charles said. "Nothing that means any trouble."

The landlady nodded politely and went out of the room, and Charles, looking around with an odd smile, said "Well."

"Isn't it wonderful?" said Virginia. "That marvelous old woman, and this house . . ." she gestured at the walls and then, remembering, laughed and turned to Paula. "You know what she said to me, that funny old woman?" she demanded. "When I was just coming in the door, she whispered to me, was the tall woman with our party?" She laughed again. "Meaning *you*," she said to Paula.

"She didn't seem to like me," Paula said.

"These women are unaccountable," Charles said. "Remember she lives practically alone on this island."

"In this *wonderful* house," Virginia said.

It was substantially better in the daylight. They had slept in rooms adjoining one another, Charles and Virginia in a huge fourposter bed with curtains, and Paula in a small room with windows overlooking the water almost directly, and in the morning, lying awake in her bed, Paula was for a minute surprised at the moving reflections on the ceiling of her room before she realized that it was only the reflection of the sun on the water, reflected again through her windows. She rose from the bed and went to look out on the water and was shocked to see the steep and immediate fall of the island below her; this was the side of the island away from the steps they had come up the night before, and all this part of the house almost hung over the water. Looking down, Paula thought how in many ways this might be extraordinarily good for Charles after his illness, and good for Virginia and Paula too, since the whole aspect of the island lacked that cloying servitude which they all three hated by now, Charles from receiving it for so long,

and she and Virginia from giving it; there was here no sense of
heavy luxury and overrich surroundings, but only a very clear
and distinct effect of an island out of sight of the mainland,
sharp and strong alone on the water, and nothing below but
solid rock and nothing more to do, perhaps, than endure the
constant and incessant triumphs of water over rock, rock over
water.

"I could spend all day," she thought, almost speaking aloud,
"just standing somewhere watching the horizon, or sitting on
a high rock, or walking down to the water and up again."

She put on a pair of heavy shoes, since if she were going to
climb rocks she must be protected against their animosity,
and went down the wide wooden stairs of the house into the
stone room, where already this morning a fire was burning and
the heavy furniture looked burnished in the sunlight through
the windows. A clean napkin lay on the long wooden table and
on it a heavy cup like the one she had had her tea from the
night before, and a wooden trencher. Paula went to the door
which she had learned led to the kitchen, opened it slightly,
and called "Good morning."

"Well, there," said the landlady from somewhere within.
"With us already?'

She swung the kitchen door wide and came into the stone
room with an earthenware jug which she set down on the
table. "Coffee," she said. "You'll have eggs, perhaps? And
bacon? Fresh-made rolls?"

"Thank you," Paula said. Even the landlady seemed more
cheerful this morning, and Paula thought that perhaps this
was because she herself was not so sullen. "I'll have anything I
may," she said, smiling. "I never dreamed I could be so hungry."

"It's being near the water," the landlady said profoundly.
"You'll always have good appetite here. I've known them eat a
whole chicken at a sitting."

"Tell me," Paula said, coming closer to look at the earthenware jug of coffee, "your dishes are so unusual, and so lovely.
Where did you ever find them?"

"They came with the house," the landlady said. "I keep
them because people seem to think they belong."

"They do, indeed," Paula said.

"Hard to wash clean," said the landlady, disappearing again into the kitchen.

This morning the moving lines of the firelight on the stone walls were caught and pursued by reflections of sunlight, and the broad windows overlooking the sea and the rock glittered until Paula wondered if the island could be seen from the mainland as a bright light on the horizon. She poured herself a cup of coffee from the earthenware jug, admiring its weight and solidity, and stood with her cup by the window, looking out. When the kitchen door opened she said without turning, "What is the rock the island is made of? I'd really swear it was black."

"Jet?" said the landlady's voice, musing, "malachite? I don't remember, but it's in the little book."

Paula came to the table and sat down, and served herself with eggs and bacon onto the wooden trencher. The landlady stood by, silently, and when Paula began to eat she said, "You'll see my other guest this morning."

"Another guest?" said Paula.

"You'll be wanting to meet him as soon as possible," said the landlady.

"Who is he?" said Paula, but the landlady was going into the kitchen. She finished her breakfast and lighted a cigarette, and came back to the window with her cigarette and her coffee cup, and pulled one of the great wooden chairs around to sit in, so that she was almost hidden by the back of it and was surprised for a minute by the landlady's scolding voice until she realized it could not possibly be addressed to her.

"She's been and gone, of course," said the landlady. "You ought to have come an hour ago." There was the dull sound of the wooden trenchers being stacked together and the landlady's voice went on, "I can't after all keep coming to look for you when I want you; there are people here needing food and bedding and attention, and where you've gone I can never tell."

Since she was eavesdropping, Paula thought that the only thing to do was stand up immediately and go to the table for more coffee as though she had not been listening at all, which turned out to be more difficult than she thought, when she saw the landlady's surprised face.

"She's here again, then," the landlady said. "This will be the other guest, Miss."

I hope she doesn't fall to addressing all her guests so impertinently, Paula thought, and turned to smile at the other guest; she felt an immediate shock of recognition, as though this were someone she had known all her life, and then realized that she had never seen him before. "How do you do," she said, and then stopped because she did not know his name.

"How do you do, Miss Ellison," he said courteously but in such a low voice that she was not completely sure if he had called her by name. He seemed so frightened of her that she refrained from asking his name, but only smiled again and said, "I was admiring the view of the water from the window."

"That's why I like an island," he said. His tone and his manner were precisely those of someone excruciatingly shy, who cannot always stop to frame sensible remarks. He was very small, and held his hands in front of him in an attitude of cringing, and the only fact against his being so terribly shy was that he did not avoid looking at her, as a shy person would, but kept his eyes fixed upon her in a sort of hypnotized stare, and, staring back rudely, Paula thought that his eyes must be almost the color and texture of the rock itself.

"I was waiting for your sister-in-law, actually," he said.

"She'll be down in a while," said Paula, trying not to smile. Virginia was small and lovely, and shy little men like this always found her reassuring. "She was very tired after our trip yesterday, and I expect she'll sleep late."

"You'll *do*, of course," he said ineptly.

"Thank you," Paula said with gravity. "Have you been here long?"

"Quite a while," said the little man vaguely. "A very long time, in fact."

"I understand that this is quite a popular spot earlier in the year."

"Moderately so. Never more than a few people, that is." He looked at her earnestly. "Not many people feel at *home* on an island," he said.

"I suppose only a certain sort of person would find this stimulating," Paula said. She glanced out the window again and down to the sea below. "It's an excellent place for my brother to be, right now; he's been very ill, and needed precisely this kind of lonely, stimulating spot."

"It will probably do him a great deal of good," said the little man politely.

"I hope so," said Paula. She was thinking of how such a concrete, limited world as an island and the sea might be extraordinarily helpful to Charles, since he would be given no choice except rock or water, and could not waste his mind in a thousand distractions; he might come to see everything, as she sternly hoped, in terms of solidity and fluidity, and learn that the rock was, as a place to live, far preferable to the sea. Perhaps, even, confining Charles to an island for a while would result in his taking an island away with him and being thus enabled to preserve for himself this kind of firm rock to live on always . . . The little man disturbed her by saying, "You mustn't be *entirely* sure of the rock, you know."

"I beg your pardon?"

"Well, it's been here for a number of years, of course . . . and rock is a hard thing to get rid of . . ."

"I don't understand."

"It doesn't matter at all," he said nervously. "Your brother's illness—it's given you a good deal of worry?"

"Of course," she said; she had mentioned Charles's illness originally as a sort of warning; it would be wisest, she felt, to let the other guest know immediately that Charles had been very ill indeed and must not be disturbed, and must not, indeed, be allowed to disturb others with vagaries left over from his illness. She had not expected, however, that the conversation might allow this little man to feel that he had any right to ask more personal questions; a polite murmur of sympathy was the most she had felt was required of him.

"It's been very difficult for you," he said.

"Do you expect to be here long?" She hoped she did not sound too emphatic; these little men were sometimes hard to discourage and yet, on the other hand, they might be so easily affronted.

"Not much longer now." He smiled at her, and again she thought that his eyes in the timid face were much like the rock under her feet. "I intend to walk up to the high rock this morning," he said. "The highest point on the island. You can't miss it."

"It must be very interesting," she said flatly.

"I shall be there all morning," he said. "Just follow the path that begins under your windows. Good-by."

As she stood staring at the doorway out of which he had gone so suddenly she heard footsteps on the stairs, and a moment later her sister-in-law came into the room.

"Charles is feeling very tired and plans to stay in bed," she said. "Good morning, Paula dear."

"Good morning, Virginia. I'm so sorry about Charles."

"Is this coffee?"

The landlady came in, bustling and fussing at Virginia; Virginia would have fresh-baked rolls and bacon, and perhaps a gently boiled egg? Would Virginia have peaches brought from the mainland this morning? And the poor sick gentleman; would he have a tray?

Paula stood at the window and watched Virginia breakfast; already the sharp air of the sea outside had made her impatient with being indoors, and she found herself unwilling to move into the room when Virginia invited her to sit at the table and take more coffee; the window was at present as close as she might reasonably go to the outdoors, and she must remain within sight of the sea.

"*Wonderful* coffee," said Virginia. "I'm so hungry."

The landlady came over to the window and leaned out, standing near Paula.

"He'll be up on the high rock," she said softly.

"I know, he—"

"Mrs. Carter," said Virginia, "might I possibly have another of your incredible muffins?"

The landlady hurried off and into the kitchen, and Virginia said, without turning around, "Isn't she unbelievable?"

"Would you like to go for a walk this morning?" Paula asked. "If Charles is resting, you and I could go exploring."

"*Love* to," said Virginia. "All over the island—I can't wait."

The kitchen door swung open and the landlady returned, saying as she came, "The tray has gone up to the poor gentleman, and I hope he feels the better for it."

"Mrs. Carter," said Paula deliberately, "will you tell me the name of your other guest?"

"You ladies will be wanting fresh coffee," said the landlady, peering into the coffee jug; "shame on me for letting you waste yourselves on this."

"What other guest?" said Virginia as the landlady hurried off again.

"An odd little man," Paula said.

"And the view," said the landlady, returning, "you'll be wanting to see the view."

"My sister and I thought we might walk over the island this morning," Paula said.

"Indeed you will," said the landlady, "and if the poor gentleman upstairs calls, I'll be right here."

"Where would you suggest we start?" Paula asked.

"Well," said the landlady. She stopped, thinking, her hands on her broad hips, and frowning slightly. "Most people," she said, "prefer the steps down to the sea and then the path around the seashore. Or if you turn to the right as you leave the front door, you will find a path that takes you through our garden. If it were earlier in the year I might suggest bathing in the cove, but delicate young ladies do not care for bathing when the weather is chilled. Or perhaps—"

"What about the path that starts under my window?"

"That of course," said the landlady, "takes you just back down to the seashore again. Only if you go so far away and the poor gentleman upstairs should happen to call . . ."

"We'd better stay near the house," Virginia said.

"You were asking about my kitchens," said the landlady to Virginia. "If the other lady chooses to go walking and yet you want to stay within hearing of the poor gentleman upstairs, I would account it a pleasure to show you my kitchens."

"I should love to see them," Virginia said. "Paula?"

"The other young lady is aching to be outside," the landlady said. "Some of us cannot resist the sea." She smiled politely at Paula and then turned again to Virginia. "If you are finished with your coffee," she said, "it might be as well to start before the day is much along." As Virginia rose, the landlady said over her shoulder to Paula, "We'll see you back, then, by lunchtime. Mind the slippery rocks."

"Ah—Johnson," said the little man. "Yes, Johnson."

"I'm Paula Ellison, Mr. Johnson."

"Yes, of course. It was Virginia Ellison I was—yes, of course."

"Marvelous view up here."

"Isn't it? You'll be tired of the sound of your brother's voice, I expect?"

"Why, I don't know that I am, particularly. Of course, he's been so very ill."

"Yes."

"It's been quite a strain on both of us."

"Both of us? Oh, yes, Virginia, I see."

"We've had to take *very* careful charge of him."

"Of course. It must have been most upsetting."

"Well—tiring."

"Your own brother. Yes, I quite understand. And his wife such a—may I say?—such a *dependent* person."

"She did as much as she was able."

"Of course. As much as she was able, yes."

"She is not strong. And she had the children."

"Let me confess—I *do* dislike children. You do too, I take it?"

"Well . . . not of course my own nieces."

"Of course not. Your own brother's children. But with the responsibility so much on you, and your sister-in-law so dependent, and the children too—it is not surprising you have been allowed to exhaust yourself."

"It has been very tiring, yes."

"And then of course in addition there would be the realization that there is actually no tie like that of flesh and blood. No love like that between brother and sister."

"We have always been very close, Mr. Johnson."

"Of course. Unusually so, I daresay."

"Perhaps we have. Too close, perhaps."

"Neither of you could do very well without the other, I suppose. And it is so hard when one is ill."

"Very hard."

"I suppose you have never been so ill?"

"Never."

"But I daresay if you *were*, your brother would care for you as attentively as you care for him."

"If he could, yes."

"He has so much more to worry about. His children, his wife."

"He would hardly have much time for *me*."

"His wife would need him. She is so dependent, she could hardly spare him to care for his sister. Only his sister, when his wife and children need him at home."

"I am sure she would be most concerned if anything happened to me."

"Most concerned, yes. She is really very fond of you, I suppose."

"We are very fond of each other. Quite companionable."

"Perhaps your mutual concern over your brother brought you even closer together. You share one dear object, after all."

"Charles is very dear to both of us."

"Of course. His wife is probably with him now."

"I ought to go back."

"Not at all. If she is there, you can hardly be needed."

"Now then," said the landlady heartily, "here you are, back again much before you're wanted. My little joke," she added, looking at Paula's frown. "I am indeed a great joker. And you didn't stay long. Nothing to worry about with your sister, neither. She's up with the poor gentleman has been so ill, and I daresay gives him better medicine than any of us could, with the smile on her sweet face. And so you met Mr. Arnold?"

"Arnold? He said his name was Johnson."

"And so it is, if he says so. I'll be calling you Arnold or Heathen or something, give me my head; I never could remember a name and that's the truth. So you met him, whatever he chooses to call himself?"

"I ran into him by accident."

"So you did, dear, so you did. And you'll be wanting to know now where you can meet him next?"

"Nothing of the sort," said Paula stiffly. "I was about to go up—"

"To the high rock again? He won't be *there* by now. Tomorrow maybe. Try late tonight in front of the great fire, after the rest of us are abed. *There* you will find him."

"Certainly not," said Paula.

"Well, then it'll take you a while," said the landlady. "And the things he can tell you and all. Solid rock," she continued smoothly as Virginia came into the room, "and standing here since no one knows when."

"How is Charles?" Paula asked Virginia.

"Feeling much better, thank you," Virginia said.

"I'll just go up for a minute."

"Please don't," said Virginia hastily. "I mean, he said he was going to try to sleep and it would be better not to disturb him."

"And then of course there's Virginia, so weak, and so safe."

"She's not entirely safe—"

"Not entirely. But for all you or I could do . . ."

"She's very fond of me."

"And very fond of Charles. But so dependent. So pretty, too, and so weak, and so fragile. Such a pretty girl."

"I have been very necessary to her."

"Of course now that Charles is better you will not be quite so necessary. They will have each other again."

"That is as it should be."

"As you say. That is as it should be. And you?"

"I shall go home again, I suppose."

"Home?"

"I have a small apartment. I left there of course while Charles was so very ill. It was necessary for me to stay with Virginia."

"But now you will go back?"

"I have not been asked to stay with Virginia."

"They have each other again. And the children, and their home. I suppose they will feel sorry for you?"

"Sorry for me?"

"That you have gone, I mean. Sorry to be without you."

"I suppose so."

"See how the fire shines on the walls. It is perfectly safe here in this room, of course. This room is solid rock. It is only in the rest of the house that fire might be a danger. The rest of the house is of wood."

"Virginia, will you come exploring with me *today*?" Paula stood by the window; it was her daily habit now to take her breakfast there, sitting in the great wooden chair, where she could keep sight of the sea. During the day she found the sound and the smell and the sight of the sea almost a necessity for her, and at night she either sat late in the rock room with the great fire roaring before her and the sound of the sea all outside, or lay straight and silent on her narrow bed with the windows open onto the cliffs below and the sea almost in her room. "We've been here almost a week, and I don't believe you've so much as stepped outdoors."

"It makes me nervous," said Virginia. She smiled across the coffee jug at Paula. "I think I'm beginning to feel caught in by the island. Almost homesick for land on all sides instead of sea."

"Charles likes it."

"Sometimes," said Virginia. "Sometimes he's as much afraid as I am."

"Afraid, Virginia?"

"*You* know," Virginia said, gesturing vaguely. "You get to

feeling so sort of cut off from everything. No way of escape. No way to get home again."

"I thought I'd run up and see Charles after breakfast," Paula said. "Is he sleeping?"

"Resting, anyway. Why don't you put it off until after lunch?"

"I will probably not be back. I intended to take a lunch with me and spend all day on the rocks."

"What can you find to *do* out there?"

"I find it stimulating, nothing but the sea and the rocks and nothing between them but me."

"And do you run across the other guest?" Virginia asked innocently.

"I sometimes gather shells, but there are no very interesting ones."

"You spoke once of another guest," Virginia said insistently. "Didn't you once mention an odd little man?"

"Suppose I just run up and say good morning to Charles, and spend just a minute trying to cheer him up?"

"He's cheerful enough. Why don't you wait till tonight?"

"I'd like to see him now, if you're sure you don't mind."

Silently, Virginia followed Paula upstairs and into the room Virginia and Charles shared. Paula had been here daily since they came, but Charles had not yet come downstairs, protesting that he was convalescing well enough in his bed, with the smell of the sea in his room and its sound in his ears always, and the landlady's good food brought to him regularly. He looked better, Paula thought; he had more color in his face—surprising, since he had not been outdoors or even had fresh air in the room—and he was astonishingly vigorous for someone who had been so very ill for such a long time.

"Good morning, Charles dear," she said as she entered. "And how well you look today!"

"I feel splendidly well," Charles said from the bed. He hoisted himself up slightly and turned his cheek for his sister's morning kiss. "*You* look well, Paula."

"I love it here. I'm afraid Virginia is bored, though."

"Is she?" Charles smiled over Paula's head at Virginia. "I don't think so," he said.

"You must try to get outdoors, Charles, and get nearer the sea. I can't tell you how invigorating I find it."

"Perhaps *you* do," Charles said. "Virginia and I prefer it indoors. We like our sea through windows."

"And *here*'s the poor gentleman's breakfast," said the landlady, bustling in with her tray. "Did he think I had forgotten him? When I was only waiting for hot corncakes from the oven? And see that you eat all of it, my poor Mr. Ellison, and we will have you well in no time at all."

"Will you have your breakfast, darling?" Virginia asked. She came closer to the bed. "Excuse me, Paula; let me come in here and see that his tray is right. Darling, are you hungry? I had such a wonderful breakfast downstairs."

"Good morning, Miss Ellison," said Mr. Johnson from the doorway. Paula looked up, over the heads of Charles and Virginia and the landlady and saw him, somehow taller, standing leaning against the doorway. "And how are *you* this morning?"

"I had eggs, and homemade sausage, just as you have, only I didn't have these wonderful corncakes. Just try one, darling. I believe Mrs. Carter made them especially for you."

"And how is your poor sick brother? *Is* he any better? And your sister-in-law, how is she?"

"Good morning, Mr. Johnson," Paula said.

"I beg your pardon, dear?" said Virginia, looking back at Paula over her shoulder. "Did you ask Charles something?"

"I doubt if she will bother with *me*, Miss Ellison. I doubt very much if she would ever be interested in me now."

Paula turned and stared, first at Charles and Virginia, who was bending over him laughing and feeding him, and then at the landlady, who was watching Paula silently and with an expression which might have been humorous.

"Mrs. Carter—" Paula said.

Mrs. Carter shrugged.

Mr. Johnson went on smoothly, "It had to be one or the other of you, you see; I told you I was waiting for your sister-in-law, but you *would* come first. It was your decision, you know; I would have been satisfied with either."

"Just don't try to answer him, dear," Mrs. Carter whispered. "There's no answer he'll take." She put a protective arm around Paula. "Try to hide behind me," she said very softly.

"No use, Mrs. Carter," he said, and smiled sadly. "No use at all, you know." He nodded at Paula. "*She* knows," he said, and went swiftly and silently away.

[c. 1951]

A DAY IN THE JUNGLE

The whole performance of the first two hours was so shock-
ingly, so abominably, easy, that her only vivid feeling about it
was surprise that the institution of marriage might pretend to
be stable upon such elusive foundations, as though the humili-
ation of the wedding and the bad dreams of the long nights
and the hideous unprivate months were an end and not a means,
as though two people sought one another out for no more than
this, this surprise that it should all be so easy to leave one
another. The other, fainter, emotion, hidden far beneath the
surprise, she refused to identify as any kind of fear, but called
it excitement instead.

It had been most pleasant packing her suitcase, consciously
choosing those clothes she would not ordinarily wear in the
middle of the week, the nice dresses and the good suit and—
with a distant humorous nod at the popular interpretation of
what her position was to be—her black evening dress, and the
few pieces of really good jewelry she owned, thinking that perhaps she might not have another chance at her clothes, that
they might be packed up and sent her, perhaps, or lumped in
with other possessions and sold (item: one blue-and-green
print house dress, coffee stain on right sleeve, two small safety
pins on lapel) and wondering, briefly, if the nicely chosen, not
expensive shoes and the hat so suitable for lunching with other
young matrons might, after all, suit her now, since they had so
obviously been bought from and for a married state. The suitcase had gone with her on her honeymoon and afterward on
the vacations and incidental week ends in the country and to
the hospital where she lost the baby, and had its accustomed

place, much more than she had herself, on the top closet shelf; taking it down was in itself an act of departure, dusting it, opening it to the scent of her traveling cologne, its reminiscence of trains, of hotel desks, of distant parts. She was able to get everything in, remembering handkerchiefs, toothbrush, stockings from the rack in the bathroom, which she had washed last night before it was clearly evident that she was leaving, and she had rinsed and hung them up innocently, as though she might never be going away again.

She had been very angry while she washed her stockings, and angry when she finished the dinner dishes and angry even before that, having her dinner alone, and the fact that he did not come home at all had not made her any the less angry, waiting there in her chair by the radio planning neat bitter things to say to him. ("Do you expect a wife to sit alone night after . . ." "If you prefer the company of your friends to . . ." "Before we were married you used to . . .") The phrasing of a note to him had been still another pleasure, since she knew by then that she was leaving and could say anything she pleased. She had written first, "Dear Don, I've decided I don't have to take this any more . . ." and had torn that one up, and had then written, "Don, I've had enough and I'm leaving," and had torn *that* one up, and had written, "I'm not going to stand for this any longer," and had of course torn *that* one up, and had finally written, "Dear Don, I know I'll be happier somewhere else," and had let that one do because already the enchantment of writing farewell notes was evaporating and she was restless to get on to something else. She had written "love, Elsa," very firmly at the foot of the note, set the note unfolded on his dresser and then on the table in the living room and finally on the telephone pad where they usually left messages for one another, and she carefully tore her previous notes into small pieces and put them into the garbage pail and emptied the coffee grounds onto them, so that Mrs. Hartford, coming in to clean this morning (for she had slept, finally, lying on the bed in her clothes next to the packed suitcase) might not be able to piece them together and know with relish that Mrs. Dayton had fumbled her farewell note before finally walking out on Mr. Dayton and no wonder, too. It was no more than Don deserved if Mrs. Hartford came before he came home and read the note on the telephone pad and met him at the door with knowing glances, watching with satisfaction from the corner of her eye while he in turn read the note, smiling to herself as he went bewildered from living room to bedroom, saw that the suitcase was certainly gone; she debated leaving her wedding ring on the dresser but decided at last that Mrs. Hartford was not trustworthy.

So it was ten o'clock in the morning, half an hour before Mrs. Hartford was due, when Elsa Dayton, leaving her husband as she had always suspected she might, went down the steps of her apartment house with her suitcase. She turned once and looked back up at the windows of what had been until now her home, and found them blank and unexciting as always, and thought, if living with Don had been a little bit more exciting . . .

Going to a hotel had always been part of leaving Don, because it was not necessary to explain to a hotel clerk, as it would be to a mother or a friend or an aunt, that she had left Don for once and all, and did not want to talk about it, and no, there was no particular reason, even his staying away so much, except that there had just come a point when she wanted to leave, and please, she did *not* want to talk about it.

She had almost no money. It occurred to her as she went to the corner to catch a taxi—something Don's true wife would not have done—that somehow with a crisis like this one ordinary problems were suspended, so that where yesterday she had not had enough money to do her week's shopping, and dared not charge more at the grocer's, she felt today that money was so small a worry, and no longer a concern of hers; Don must simply find a way of providing them both with money, and now that her interests no longer participated in his, she had abandoned the intention of making his meager funds go as far as possible. He was not a partner now, he was an opponent, and vulnerable here, and he could borrow money if he chose. Yesterday's inability to say to—for instance— Roger, in the office, "Can you let me borrow some money?"

would vanish under this new way of life; perhaps Don was not a better credit risk because his wife had left him, but she suspected that the deep sympathetic mutual feelings of men about their wives would promote a fund for Don as surely as if his house had been struck by lightning.

Thinking these things for lack of anything else to think about—this was, after all, a new world for her, with new standards and probably new laws, and entering upon it suddenly, equipped with no more than a few dollars and a black evening dress in a suitcase, was a thing to be done warily and without prepared courses of action—she sat in the taxi with her suitcase beside her on the seat, and looked with wonder and delight at the familiar streets which led her from Don's apartment to the hotel she had chosen because (she did not admit this to herself) it figured so prominently in the gossip columns which she read avidly every morning.

She was wearing a dark-red wool dress and her beaver coat and high-heeled black shoes and a black hat which she described to herself, without any deliberate meaning, as flirtatious. She came into the hotel carrying her suitcase and felt that no one observed that she was a local housewife dressed up at ten-thirty in the morning, rather than some freed creature from another town, who might have thought as she went across the lobby, "Right *now*, at home, they're polishing the silver and setting up the plates, and here *I* am in a hotel being waited on and not doing a thing!" She registered at the desk, the first time she had ever done such a thing alone, without betraying anything except that she intended to spend a day or two in the hotel. The facts that she was admitted without comment or even an appraising look, that her room was number 808, that the quarter she gave the bellboy was accepted with no more than a "Thank you, madam," could not communicate any awareness of the unbelievable daring of her position. She had even signed her name "Elsa Masters Dayton."

She was not quite, however, in the position of a visitor; she could not once in her room shower and change to another dress (she had only put this dress on half an hour before, after all, and had showered not ten minutes before *that*) and then go

out to visit points of interest about the town. She had no shopping to do, no important items which she could find nowhere
else but in town, and nothing she had been waiting and planning to do, no long-anticipated calls to pay. She did do, finally,
what she might have done at home; she took off her dress and
shoes and lay in her slip on the bed, reading a mystery story.

At one o'clock she dressed again and swung her coat over
her shoulders and went out of her room and locked the door
and went downstairs in the elevator, standing quietly without
interest in other people, with the weight of her coat pulling her
shoulders down. She walked into the cocktail lounge, stepping
quickly with her high heels across the quiet lobby; she was not
at all clear about what she intended to do, except that she
knew surely that a cocktail before lunch would not today give
her a headache. She chose a table, deliberately but with not
more than a swift casual glance around, in a corner and hard
against another table where a man (gray hair, she noticed in
her one quick look, gray suit) was sitting alone, and when she
sat down she thought, It's as though we were strangers at a
dinner party and had been seated next to one another and I
have only to speak to him as though our hostess had mumbled
both our names. She was acutely conscious of her pink nail
polish and wondered, as she might have during the first
uncomfortable minutes at a dinner table, if she might disgrace
herself by spilling something on him. He was compelled,
almost in self-defense, to help her with her coat when she
struggled to shift it from her shoulders to the back of her seat,
and she smiled at him and said kindly—perhaps he was shy—
"They put these tables so close together, don't they?"

He smiled back at her and said, "They certainly do," which,
if hardly a cosmopolitan answer, was at least civil and did not
sound as though he regularly met lovely women who had
nefarious designs upon him; he sounded, in fact, quite as
though she reminded him of the wife of one of his younger
friends, and she wondered briefly if she would have spoken to
him at all if he had been Don's age, or if she had been married
too long to know how to talk familiarly to younger men.

She told the waiter that she would like an old-fashioned, please, in the tone of one who regularly orders for herself and knows precisely what she wants, and then she turned to the man next to her and remarked, "I can never get used to this town for the first few days."

"*I* don't like it," he said immediately. "I'd be just as happy if I never had to *see* the place again."

"You're from the West, aren't you?"

"Chicago," he said. "And you?"

"Maine," she said; she *had* come from Maine originally.

"Nice country up there," he said. "Whereabouts in Maine?"

"A small town named Easton," she said. "Near Augusta."

"We drove through Maine one year," he said. "Spent three weeks."

"It's lovely country," she said.

"Beautiful," he said.

"Are you in town on business?"

"Only way they ever *get* me here," he said. "Give me Chicago every time."

"I've never been to Chicago," she said.

"Great town," he said.

It was the moment in the dinner-table conversation when she might properly have turned to the gentleman on her left and asked him where *he* was from, but failing that, she took up her cocktail and sipped at it, and accepted a cigarette and a light, and looked with interest around the room, and smiled at him because she could not think of anything to say. He seemed the very type of man she had expected to meet, without ever realizing it—middle-aged, and quiet, and respectable, a man for whom her black evening dress would be quite daring enough. Although her uneasiness in his presence had not quite worn off, and her larger, less-defined strange feeling (which she had called at various times since the night before, *anger*, and *excitement*, and *pleasure*) still remained at the back of her mind, hampering her free enjoyment of the moment, she leaned back against the soft leather of the chair and thought happily about the black evening dress.

"I'll be mighty glad to get home tomorrow," he said. ("At home, right now, they're all going out to lunch together from the office . . .")

"*I* wouldn't," she said. ("Mrs. Hartford had probably forgotten to do the kitchen shelves . . .") "I mean, I always hate to leave."

He hesitated, and she thought for a minute that he would say something indicating that perhaps he did *not* have to leave tomorrow, and then he said, "The town's all right if you just want to enjoy yourself. Shows, you know—nightclubs, and all that. No good for people like *me*, though."

"I don't believe *that*," she said, and thought, I am positively simpering.

"One thing you got to say for this town, though," he said, "people are always ready to help you. Taxi drivers and cops and even people on the street—always give you a hand. That way," he added, thinking deeply, "they're sort of like people out West. You know, out West everyone's more friendly, somehow."

"Perhaps I ought to go out West, then," she said.

"You'd like Chicago. Well," he said, and put out his cigarette, "time to get to work, I guess. I hate these late lunches—people here never seem to get around to eating till sometime in the afternoon. Home," he told her firmly, "we have our lunch at twelve sharp." He rose and half bowed to her. "Very pleasant," he said. "Hope you enjoy your stay."

"Thank you," she said. "And *you* have a nice trip home."

"Thank you," he said. "Good-by."

"Good-by," she said, and noticed that he had taken her check. She smiled deprecatingly at him and he waved gallantly, and she thought, at least he never dreamed I was anything but a nice lady, someone's wife on a vacation.

She lunched alone at the same table, although no one came to sit next to her. She had a second cocktail and although she felt that properly she might be eating strange sophisticated foods—subtle casseroles, spices, wine—she chose for herself a salad and coffee, and thought, at home I'd be having an egg. She lingered over her coffee, watching people come in and sit down, arrive late for appointments or early, drink or eat, speak to one another, laugh, apologize, greet acquaintances, go out again. No one bothered her; the waiter did not hover over her table indicating by his patient watchfulness that the management disapproved of attractive women sitting alone here for over an hour; her lunch, carefully chosen, would not cost more than she could pay, and she had a clear general impression of belonging in this scene of movement, of passage, that sitting here so quietly in the corner she had somehow achieved a status which enabled her to meet these moving creatures as equals.

This is what I have always wanted to do, she told herself with conscious satisfaction, this is the way I have been waiting to live, I have been intending to do this for a long time; right now at home Mrs. Hartford has finished eating whatever was in the refrigerator and is reading the paper, sitting at the kitchen table; perhaps Don is home already. This is where *I* belong, right here.

At about three o'clock she got up and took her coat; she had left enough of a tip for the waiter so that he came over quickly and pulled the table away and reached for her coat, but she shook her head and said, "I'll carry it, thanks, it's so warm," for some reason not wishing him to know that she had only come down from upstairs. She went through the restaurant, not knowing where she was going but feeling strongly that she must certainly seem like a happy woman who was going to keep an agreeable appointment; she felt this so strongly that she almost believed that somehow, perhaps in the next minute or so, she would find herself appointed, engaged, entreated, and she hesitated in the lobby, wandering over to look into the windows of the sleek jewelry shop, stopped by the florist's, and even spent a minute looking raptly at the hand-painted ties in the window of the men's furnishings shop.

After a few minutes she was no longer able to persuade herself that she was waiting for someone and so she went back to her room, liking the thought that she had a completely private place here, with her own suitcase set down next to the dresser and her own book on the arm of the chair. She sat by the window for a few minutes enjoying almost as a visitor might the sounds of the traffic below, and she thought complacently that she might shower now, and change her clothes, and in an hour or so go downstairs and perhaps out onto the street, and wander watching people until she chose to go into some other quiet shining place and have her dinner. She might go to a movie afterward, or come back to her room, she might fall into conversation with someone and come back to her room briefly, excited and laughing, to change hurriedly into the black evening dress, brushing her hair with little dancing motions, touching herself with more perfume.

The phone by the bed rang shortly, and then again, and at first she thought it was part of her new life which had suddenly become so real that it was perfectly possible for some vaguely glimpsed stranger to be telephoning her now to ask her to dine, to dance, to go off to Italy, and then she thought could it be that man from Chicago? and then that he did not know her name and could hardly have left his luncheon appointment to follow her, and then she knew of course it was Don. As the phone rang again sharply, almost in Don's angry tones, she lifted her hand from it and turned away, but the realization that he would have to give her some money in any case made her turn back and answer it. "Hello?" she said, hoping until she heard his voice.

"Elsa?"

"Of course, Don."

"For heaven's sake, what are you *doing*? I've called half the hotels in town and your sister's, and scared them half to death."

"You should have read my note." I want to wear pretty clothes all day long, she was thinking, remembering him as she heard his voice, I want to be beautiful and free and luxurious.

"I *read* your note—what on earth is the matter?"

"Well, if you read my note then you know I'm not coming back." I shouldn't have said that, she thought in panic; he didn't ask me if I *was* coming back; suppose he had accepted the fact that I wasn't coming back and now I've given him the idea that I might . . .

"Don?" she said.

"Look," he said, and his voice was subdued, but she knew so well all the tones of all his voices that these changes no longer meant anything now to her; if Don hoped to convince her at this late date that he could be reasonable after she had offended him so deeply, she would not be deceived. "Suppose you just forget this whole thing?" he said.

Trying to make it sound as though it's all *my* fault, she thought. "I like it here," she said.

"Elsa," he began, and then stopped. "We can't talk over the phone," he said. "If you won't come back now why not at least meet me somewhere and we can sit down and talk sensibly?"

"No," she said childishly, and then smiled to herself, thinking that after all he had been at one time an engaging companion and since she could now afford to choose her own friends he would have to be very entertaining indeed to hold her attention. "Maybe I will," she said.

"You sound funny," he said. "Are you all right?"

"Let me see," she said, one finger reflectively at her cheek, as though he could see her. "I can be at Henry's Restaurant at seven. You may take me to dinner."

There was a short silence, and then he said, "Right. I'll be there at seven." He sounded exactly like a man making a date; perhaps, she thought jubilantly, he perceives that I am to be pursued rather than commanded, and she had already begun to sketch out mentally a more flattering version of the conversation with the man from Chicago, to tell him about at dinner.

"Good-by," she said.

"Mrs. Hartford broke two of the blue cups, by the way," he said. "Good-by."

As she hung up she was wondering, most daringly, if she might just possibly wear the black evening gown, but she knew that she could not afford to expose herself to his ridicule, particularly since the black evening gown was as familiar to him

as it was to herself, and she decided reluctantly to put on
again the dark-red dress she had worn away from home that
morning.

She slept again, for an hour or so, and read her mystery
story, and did her nails in a new dark-red polish to match the
dress, and brushed her shoes. At five minutes to seven—it
would certainly do no harm to keep him waiting for a minute
or so—she slipped on her beaver coat and went out of the door
of her room; she left her housecoat thrown across the bed and
her slippers awry on the floor and powder on the glass top of
the dresser and a handkerchief on the chair; her mystery story
lay open across the arm of the chair and her used towel on the
bathroom floor; she turned as she went out and decided to
pick up everything when she came home.

She went down in the elevator as she had done before, very
conscious that she was a lady who had chosen to dine out with
a gentleman rather than having dinner sent up to her room,
very much aware of the fact that for the first time she moved
knowingly and of choice through a free world, that of all her
life this alone was the day when she had followed a path she
made alone; she walked across the lobby toward the outer
doors with the feeling suddenly very strong that if she desired
she might turn and without explanation to anyone leave the
hotel by another door, or go even back to her room and refuse
to answer the phone.

Free and at peace, she thought as the doorman held the door
open for her and she passed out onto the street with dignity
and a half-smile for the doorman's enforced kindness; free and
at peace and alone and no one to worry me; she had not gone
ten steps from the doorway when the nagging small feeling
which she knew clearly now as fear and which had been following her cautiously for hours, perhaps for weeks and years,
stepped up suddenly as though it had been waiting outside the
door for her, and walked along beside her. The loving concern
with which she put her feet down one after another on the
sidewalk became without perceptible change, terror—was the
cement secure? Down below, perhaps no more than two or
three feet below, was the devouring earth, unpredictable and

shifty. The sidewalk was set only upon earth, might move under her feet and sink, carrying her down and alone into the wet choking ground, and no one to catch her arm or a corner of her coat and hold her back.

Above her, the neon signs swung dangerously, dipping down almost to her head, bringing their live shattering wires so close that she almost put up an arm to protect herself, and then remembered that a mere arm was no protection against live wires or the weight of the falling signs—could she run? A sign shortly ahead of her, advertising a delicatessen (and one knew how badly these places were cared for, a hand-to-mouth existence and let the insurance take care of the emergencies) was swaying dangerously and obviously loosening; carefully she estimated the direction of its fall, not daring to slow her steps for fear some slight change in timing might mean disaster, not daring to run, with no one to hide behind, no one to say "Watch out, there!" If she could pass under without looking up she was perhaps safe—but beyond, the shuddering of the traffic had shaken a sign reading SHOE REPAIR; was that a wire swinging wild?

She pulled her coat tighter around her, looking from side to side. She was almost alone on this block, and she told herself that it was an hour when most people were at home or in restaurants or at least somewhere not on the streets, and then it came to her that it would be generally regarded as fortunate that only one woman was going down the street when the sign fell; suppose it had been during a heavy traffic hour, people would tell one another, shivering pleasantly and knowing that they rarely passed along this particular street, suppose it had been sometime when crowds of other people were near, suppose fifteen people had been under the sign when it fell instead of just that poor woman; well, they would say to one another wisely, lightning never strikes twice in the same place, at least *that* street is safe for a while.

She saw herself turning and going back to her hotel, explaining to the desk clerk and the elevator operator that she had changed her mind about going out, that it looked like rain or that she had sprained her ankle or that she felt a cold coming on? She turned once and saw with sinking horror the precarious rocking of the signs overhead, the dangerous slipping sideways of the upper stories of the buildings, the final and unutterable emptiness of the street; what can I do? she asked herself, who will help me? She could hear in her mind the proprietor of the delicatessen berating himself for not having taken care of his sign when he first noticed it was insecurely fastened, explaining to the police and the doctors and the faces in the crowd that he never dreamed it might fall, telling the strangers looking with grim curiosity at the poor woman that it had been there without falling for twelve, fifteen years, and it seemed to her that she could hear the strangers in the crowd telling one another, "Well, that's the way it goes—perfectly all right for fifteen years and then one day—it's all over. Who was she, do you know?"

What am I doing? she wondered abruptly; this is madness, this is idiotic; I am not supposed to be *afraid* of anything; I am a free person, and the path I have chosen for myself does not include fear. I am walking down the street because it is a pleasant walk to the restaurant where I am meeting a fascinating man for dinner. I have been down this street before and nothing happened to me or to anyone else, and if anything happens tonight it might just as well happen to the next person instead of me. How have I managed to stay safe this long? she wondered.

She was struck by the thought of how suddenly visible she was. An enemy, hidden in a second-floor room, peering out through the half-open window, could shoot her easily even with a small pistol and most probably escape and never be detected; not even an enemy, but a stranger, mistaking her for someone else, never knowing until later that she was the wrong one, the one who need not have been killed. Or, even worse, a madman, chuckling and raising the gun and estimating, telling himself he would shoot the tenth person who came, or the first woman who walked by wearing a fur coat, or anyone who glanced upward at his window where he waited unseen, shaken with silent laughter. Then a window ahead showed movement; was he there? Perhaps in the car turning into the street, the red car slowing down not for the corner, perhaps looking out the back window aiming carefully to compensate for the movement of the car, and he would be finished and away while the strangers passing a block away stopped and stared, and screamed, and then hurried, too late to be of any assistance.

What, on the other hand, was to prevent the red car, or any other, from driving up onto the sidewalk and crushing her against the side of the building? These things *did* happen, and perhaps the people they happened to had wondered, looking up, if the red car were not coming dangerously close to the curb, and then thought, that crazy driver ought to be arrested, and then, in the last second of sudden panic, tried to turn, seeing at the last the horrified face of the driver, pulling at the useless wheel and calling for help while the passers-by, useless against the weight of the car, watched in sickness, moving against one another and turning away their heads; or— suppose a pane of glass fell suddenly from a window and crashed shatteringly down onto her head without her ever seeing it fall? Or if she slipped suddenly while she was watching the red car and the buildings, turned her ankle in the high-heeled shoes and fell and smashed her face against the stone while people going by laughed for a minute before hesitating and then realizing . . .

Or, see, the trolley coming. It swayed dangerously from side to side; was it going to fall sideways, its steel and glass construction bending out of shape against the ground; that whole heavy weight would have to be moved before they could rescue anyone trapped beneath it, and people tomorrow might tell one another, "Lucky there was only this one woman going down the street—suppose there had been a crowd? They say she screamed for half an hour before . . ." Unidentified explosions had happened before, many times. People went quietly down a street, on their way to dinner, not expecting anything except possibly being late, and suddenly—it might be a gas stove left on, or just one of those incredible coincidences, of air

and pressure and a harmless household preparation left uncov-
ered, and of course the manufacturers could disclaim responsibility and deplore the tragedy—and the world buckled top
and bottom, there was only a convulsive, brain-splitting terror,
and there was the restaurant ahead, and there was no other way
to go except on and inside, hesitating only for a moment before
the heavy doors which could so easily slip their hinges and
instead of swinging docilely, fall flatly and with full weight . . .

Don was there, waving tentatively from across the room.
Suddenly the world fell into place outside, and she waved back;
he was so wonderfully safe and familiar in the worn gray suit
she had seen as many times as he had seen the red dress she
was wearing; she waved and smiled and thought, I have been
alone for so long.

[1952]

PAJAMA PARTY

It was planned by Jannie herself. I was won over reluctantly, by much teasing and promises of supernatural good behavior; as a matter of fact Jannie even went so far as to say that if she could have a pajama party she would keep her room picked up for one solid month, a promise so far beyond the realms of possibility that I could only believe that she wanted the pajama party more than anything else in the world. My husband thought it was a mistake. "You are making a terrible, an awful mistake," he said to me. "And don't try to say I didn't tell you so." My older son Laurie told me it was a mistake. "Man," he said, "*this* you will regret. For the rest of your life you will be saying to yourself 'Why did I let that dopey girl ever *ever* have a pajama party that night?' For the rest of your life. When you're an old lady you will be saying—"

"What can I do?" I said. "I promised." We were all at the breakfast table, and it was seven-thirty on the morning of Jannie's eleventh birthday. Jannie sat unhearing, her spoon poised blissfully over her cereal, her eyes dreamy with speculation over what was going to turn up in the packages to be presented that evening after dinner. Her list of wanted birthday presents had included a live pony, a pair of roller skates, high-heeled shoes of her very own, a make-up kit with real lipstick, a record player and records, and a dear little monkey to play with, and any or all of these things might be in the offing. She sighed, and set down her spoon, and sighed.

"You know of course," Laurie said to me, "I have the room right next to her? I'm going to be sleeping in there like I do every night? You know I'm going to be in my bed trying to

sleep?" He shuddered. "Giggle," he said. "Giggle, giggle, giggle, giggle, giggle, giggle. Two, three o'clock in the morning—
giggle giggle giggle. A human being can't bear it."

Jannie focused her eyes on him. "Why don't we burn up this
boy's birth certificate?" she asked.

"Giggle, giggle," Laurie said.

Barry spoke, waving his toast. "When Jannie gets her birthday presents can I play with it?" he asked. "If I am very very
careful can I please play with just the—"

Everyone began to talk at once to drown him out. "Giggle,
giggle," Laurie shouted. "Don't say I didn't warn you," my
husband said loudly. "Anyway I promised," I said. "Happy
birthday dear sister," Sally sang. Jannie giggled.

"There," Laurie said. "You hear her? All night long—five of
them." Shaking his head as one who has been telling them and
telling them and *telling* them not to bring that wooden horse
through the gates of Troy, he stamped off to get his school-
books and his trumpet. Jannie sighed happily. Barry opened
his mouth to speak and his father and Sally and I all said
"Shhh."

Jannie had to be excused from her cereal, because she was
too excited to eat. It was a cold frosty morning, and I forced
the girls into their winter coats and warm hats, and put Barry
into his snow suit. Laurie, who believes that he is impervious
to cold, came downstairs, said, "Mad, I tell you, mad," sympathetically to me, " 'By, cat," to his father, and went out the
back door toward his bike, ignoring my frantic insistence that
he put on some kind of a jacket or at least a sweater.

I checked that teeth had been brushed, hair combed, handkerchiefs secured, told the girls to hold Barry's hand crossing
the street, told Barry to hold the girls' hands crossing the
street, put Barry's mid-morning cookies into his jacket pocket,
reminded Jannie for the third time about her spelling book,
held the dogs so they could not get out when the door was
opened, told everyone good-by and happy birthday again to
Jannie, and watched from the kitchen window while they
made their haphazard way down the driveway, lingering, chat-
ting, stopping to point to things. I opened the door once more

to call to them to move along, they would be late for school, and they disregarded me. I called to hurry *up*, and for a minute they moved more quickly, hopping, and then came to the end of the driveway and onto the sidewalk where they merged at once into the general traffic going to school, the collection of red hoods and blue jackets and plaid caps that goes past every morning and comes past again at noontime and goes back after lunch and returns at last, lingering, at three o'clock. I came back to the table and sat down wearily, reaching for the coffeepot. "Five of them are too many," my husband explained. "One would have been quite enough."

"You can't have a pajama party with just one guest," I said sullenly. "And anyway no matter who she invited the other three would have been offended."

By lunchtime I had set up four cots, two of them borrowed from a neighbor who was flatly taken aback when she heard what I wanted them for. "I think you must be crazy," she said. Jannie's bedroom is actually two rooms, one small and one, which she calls her library because her bookcase is in there, much larger. I put one cot in her bedroom next to her bed, which left almost no room in there to move around. The other three cots I lined up in her library, making a kind of dormitory effect. Beyond Jannie's library is the guest room, and all the bedrooms except Laurie's are on the other side of the guest room. Laurie's room is separated by only the thinnest wall from Jannie's library. I used all my colored sheets and flowered pillowcases to make up the five beds, and every extra blanket in the house; I finally had to use the pillows from the couch.

When Jannie came home from school I made her lie down and rest, pointing out in one of the most poignant understatements of my life that she would probably be up late that night. In fifteen minutes she was downstairs asking if she could get dressed for her party. I said her party was not going to start until eight o'clock and to take an apple and go lie down again. In another ten minutes she was down to explain that she would probably be too excited to dress later and it would really be only common sense to put her party dress on now. I said if she came downstairs again before dinner was on the table I would personally call her four guests and cancel the pajama party. She finally rested for half an hour or so in the chair by the upstairs phone, talking to her friend Carole.

She was of course unable to eat her dinner, although she had chosen the menu. She nibbled at a piece of lamb, rearranged her mashed potatoes, and told her father and me that she could not understand how we had endured as many birthdays as we had. Her father said that he personally had gotten kind of used to them, and that as a matter of fact a certain quality of excitement did seem to go out of them after—say—thirty, and Jannie sighed unbelievingly.

"One more birthday like this would *kill* her," Laurie said. He groaned. "Carole," he said, as one telling over a fearful list, "Kate. Laura. Linda, Jannie. You must be *crazy*," he said to me.

"I suppose your friends are so much?" Jannie said. "I suppose Ernie didn't get sent down to Miss Corcoran's office six times today for throwing paper wads? I suppose Charlie—"

"You didn't seem to think Charlie was so bad, walking home from school," Laurie said. "I guess that wasn't *you* walking with—"

Jannie turned pink. "Does my own brother have any right to insult me on my own birthday?" she asked her father.

In honor of Jannie's birthday Sally helped me clear the table, and Jannie sat in state with her hands folded, waiting. When the table was cleared we left Jannie there alone, and assembled in the study. While my husband lighted the candles on the pink-and-white cake, Sally and Barry took from the back of the closet the gifts they had chosen themselves and lovingly wrapped. Barry's gift was clearly a leathercraft set, since his most careful wrapping had been unable to make the paper go right round the box, and the name showed clearly. Sally had three books. Laurie had an album of records he had chosen himself. ("This is for my *sister*," he had told the clerk in the music store, most earnestly, with an Elvis Presley record in each hand, "for my sister—not me, my *sister*.") Laurie also had to carry the little blue record player which my husband and I had decided was a more suitable gift for our elder daughter than a dear little monkey or even a pair of high-heeled shoes. I carried the boxes from the two sets of grandparents, one holding a flowered quilted skirt and a fancy blouse, and the other holding a stiff crinoline petticoat. With the cake leading, we filed into the dining room where Jannie sat. "Happy birthday to you," we sang, and Jannie looked once and then leaped past us to the phone. "Be there in a minute," she said, and then, "Carole? Carole, listen, I *got* it, the record player. 'By."

By a quarter to eight Jannie was dressed in the new blouse and skirt, over the petticoat, Barry was happily taking apart the leathercraft set, the record player had been plugged in and we had heard, more or less involuntarily, four sides of Elvis Presley. Laurie had shut himself in his room, dissociating himself utterly from the festivities. "I was willing to *buy* them," he explained, "I even spent good money out of the bank, but no one can make me *listen.*"

I took a card table up to Jannie's room and squeezed it in among the beds; on it I put a pretty cloth and a bowl of apples, a small dish of candy, a plate of decorated cupcakes, and an ice bucket in which were five bottles of grape soda imbedded in ice. Jannie brought her record player upstairs and put it on the table and Laurie plugged it in for her on condition that she would not turn it on until he was safely back in his room. With what Laurie felt indignantly was an absolute and complete disregard for the peace of mind and healthy sleep of a cherished older son I put a deck of fortunetelling cards on the table, and a book on the meaning of dreams.

Everything was ready, and Jannie and her father and I were sitting apprehensively in the living room when the first guest came. It was Laura. She was dressed in a blue party dress, and she brought Jannie a charm bracelet which Jannie put on. Then Carole and Linda arrived together, one wearing a green party dress and the other a fancy blouse and skirt, like Jannie. They all admired Jannie's new blouse and skirt, and one of them had brought her a book and the other had brought a dress and hat for her doll. Kate came almost immediately afterward. She was wearing a wide skirt like Jannie's, and she had a crinoline, too. She and Jannie compared crinolines, and each of them insisted that the other's was much, *much* prettier. Kate had brought Jannie a pocketbook with a penny inside for luck. All the girls carried overnight bags but Kate, who had a small suitcase. "You'll think I'm going to stay for a *month*, the stuff I brought," she said, and I felt my husband shudder.

Each of the girls complimented, individually, each item of apparel on each of the others. It was conceded that Jannie's skirt, which came from California, was of a much more advanced style than skirts obtainable in Vermont. The pocketbook was a most fortunate choice, they agreed, because it perfectly matched the little red flowers in Jannie's skirt. Laura's shoes were the prettiest anyone had *ever* seen. Linda's party dress was of orlon, which all of them simply *adored*. Linda said if she *did* say it herself, the ruffles never got limp. Carole was wearing a necklace which no one could *possibly* tell was not made of real pearls. Linda said that we had the *nicest* house, she was always telling her mother and father that she wished they had one just like it. My husband said we would sell any time. Kate said our dogs were just *darling*, and Laura said she *loved* that green chair. I said somewhat ungraciously that they had all of them spent a matter of thousands of hours in our house and the green chair was no newer or prettier than it had been the last time Laura was here, when she was bouncing up and down on the seat. Jannie said hastily that there were cupcakes and Elvis Presley records up in her room, and they were gone. They went up the back stairs like a troop of horses, saying "Cupcakes, cupcakes."

Sally and Barry were in bed, but permitted to stay awake because it was Friday night and Jannie's birthday. Barry had taken Jannie's leathercraft set up to his room, planning to make his dear sister a pair of moccasins. Because Sally and Barry were not invited to the party I took them each a tray with one cupcake, a glass of fruit juice, and three candies. Sally asked if she could play *her* phonograph while she read fairy tales and ate her cupcake and I said certainly, since in the general air of excitement prevailing I did not think that even Barry would fall asleep for a while yet. As I started downstairs

Barry called after me to ask if *he* could play *his* phonograph and of course I could hardly say no.

When I got downstairs my husband had settled down to reading freshman themes in the living room. "Everything seems . . ." he said; I believe he was going to finish "quiet," but Elvis Presley started then from Jannie's room. There was a howl of fury from Laurie's room, and then *his* phonograph started; to answer Elvis Presley he had chosen an old Louis Armstrong record, and he was holding his own. From the front of the house upstairs drifted down the opening announcement of "Peter and the Wolf," from Sally, and then, distantly, from Barry's room the crashing chords which heralded (blast off!) "Space Men on the Moon."

"What did you say?" I asked my husband.

"Oh, when the saints, come marching in . . ."

"I said it seemed quiet," my husband yelled.

"The cat, by a clarinet in a loooow register . . ."

"I want you, I need you . . ."

"Prepare for blast: five—four—three—two—"

"I want to be in their number . . ."

"It sure does," I yelled back.

"Boom." Barry's rocket was in space.

Barry took control for a minute, because he can sing every word of (blast off!) "Space Men on the Moon," but then the wolf came pacing up to Peter's gate, Jannie switched to "Blue Suede Shoes," and Laurie took out his trumpet. He played without a mute, ordinarily forbidden in the house, so for a few minutes he was definitely ascendant, even though a certain undeniable guitar beat intruded from Jannie, but then Jannie and her guests began to sing and Laurie faltered, lost the Saints, fell irresistibly into "Blue Suede Shoes," cursed, picked up the Saints, and finally conceded defeat in time for four—three—two—one—Boom. Peter's gay strain came through clearly for a minute and then Jannie finished changing records and our house rocked to its foundations with "Heartbreak Hotel."

"Mommy," Sally called down, "I can't even hear the hunters coming."

"Blast off!"

Laurie's door slammed and he came pounding down the back stairs and into the living room. He was carrying his record player and his trumpet. "Dad," he said pathetically.

His father nodded. "Play the loudest," he said.

"Got you, man." They finally decided on Duke Ellington, and I went to sit in the kitchen with all the doors shut so that all I could hear was a kind of steady combined beat which shivered the window frames and got the pots and pans crashing together softly where they hung on the wall. When it got close to nine-thirty I came out to check on Sally and Barry, and found that Sally, fading but grim, had taken off "Peter and the Wolf" and put on another record which featured a kind of laughing woodpecker, but she was getting sleepy. I told her good night, and went on to Barry's room, where Barry had fallen asleep in his space suit somewhere on the dim craters of the moon, fragments of leather all over his bed. I closed his phonograph, covered him, and by the time I came back to Sally she was asleep, with her fairy-tale book open on her stomach and her kitten next to her cheek on the pillow. I put away her book, and moved the kitten to the foot of the bed, where he waited until I was convincingly on the stairs going down again and then moved softly, tiptoeing, back onto Sally's pillow. Sally wiggled comfortably, the kitten purred, and I went on downstairs to find Laurie and my husband relaxing over "Take the A Train."

Laurie was about to change the record when he hesitated, lifted his head, listened, and looked at his father. His father was listening too. The phonograph upstairs had stopped, and Laurie shook his head gloomily. "Now it comes," he said.

He was right.

After about half an hour I went to the foot of the back stairs and tried to call up to the girls to be quiet, but they could not hear me. They were apparently using the fortunetelling cards, because I could hear someone calling on a tall dark man and someone else remarking bitterly upon jealousy from a friend. I went halfway up the stairs and shouted, but they still could not hear me. I went to the top and pounded on the door and I could have been banging my head against a stone wall. I could hear the name of a young gentleman of Laurie's acquaintance being bandied about lightly by the ladies inside, coupled—I think—with Laura's name and references to a certain cake-sharing incident at recess, and insane shrieks, presumably from the maligned Laura. Then Kate brought up another name, joining it with Linda's, and the voices rose, Linda disclaiming. I banged both fists on the door, and there was silence for a second until someone said, "Maybe it's your *brother*," and there was a great screaming of "Go away! Stay out! Don't come in!"

"Joanne," I said, and there was absolute silence.

"Yes, mother?" said Jannie at last.

"May I come in?" I asked gently.

"Oh, yes," said all the little girls.

I opened the door and went in. They were all sitting on the two beds in Jannie's room. The needle arm had been taken off the record, but I could see Elvis Presley going around and around. All the cupcakes were gone, and so was the candy. The fortunetelling cards were scattered over the two beds. Jannie was wearing her pink shortie pajamas, which were certainly too light for that cold night. Linda was wearing blue shortie pajamas. Kate was wearing college-girl-type ski pajamas. Laura was wearing a lace-trimmed nightgown, white, with pink roses. Carole was wearing yellow shortie pajamas. Their hair was mussed, their cheeks were pink, they were crammed uncomfortably together onto the two beds, and they were clearly awake long after their several bedtimes.

"Don't you think," I said, "that you had better get some sleep?"

"Oh, nooooo," they all said, and Jannie added, "The party's just *beginning*." They were like a pretty bouquet of femininity, and I said—with what I knew Laurie would find a deplorable lack of firmness—that they could stay up for just a few minutes more.

"Dickie," Kate whispered, clearly referring to some private joke, and all the little girls dissolved into helpless giggles, all except Carole, who cried out indignantly, "I did *not*, I never *did*, I *don't*."

Downstairs I said nostalgically to my husband and Laurie, "I can remember, when I was about Jannie's age—"

"I just hope the neighbors are all asleep," my husband said. "Or maybe they just won't know it's coming from here."

"Probably everyone in the neighborhood saw those characters coming in," Laurie said.

"Mommy," Jannie said urgently from the darkness of the dining room. Startled, I hurried in.

"Listen," she said, "something's gone *terribly* wrong."

"What's the matter?"

"Shh," Jannie said. "It's Kate and Linda. I thought they would both sleep in my library but now Kate isn't talking to Linda because Linda took her lunch box today in school and said she didn't and wouldn't give it back so now Kate won't sleep with Linda."

"Well, then, why not put Linda—"

"Well, you see, I was going to have Carole in with me because really only don't tell the others, but really she's my *best* friend of all of them only now I can't put Kate and Linda together and—"

"Why not put one of them in with you?"

"Well, I *can't* put Carole in with Laura."

"Why not?" I was getting tired of whispering.

"Well, because they *both* like Jimmy *Watson*."

"Oh," I said.

"And anyway Carole's wearing a shortie and Kate and Laura *aren't*."

"Look," I said, "how about I sneak up right now through the front hall and make up the guest-room bed? Then you can put someone in there. Jimmy Watson, maybe."

"*Mother*," Jannie turned bright red.

"Sorry," I said. "Take a pillow from one of the beds in your library. Put someone in the guest room. Keep them busy for a few minutes and I'll have it ready. I just hope I have two more sheets."

"Oh, *thank* you." Jannie turned, and then stopped. "Mother?" she said. "Don't think from what I said that *I* like Jimmy Watson."

"The thought never crossed my mind," I said.

I raced upstairs and found two sheets; they were smallish, and not colored, which meant that they were the very bottom of the pile, but as I closed the guest-room door behind me I thought optimistically that at least Jannie's problems were solved if I excepted Jimmy Watson and the dangerous rivalry of Carole, who is a natural platinum blonde.

Laurie played "Muskrat Ramble." Jannie came down to the dining room again in about fifteen minutes. "Shh," she said, when I came in to talk to her. "Kate and Linda want to sleep together in the guest room."

"But I thought you just said that Kate and Linda—"

"But they made up and Kate apologized for taking Linda's lunch box and Linda apologized for thinking she did, and they're all friends now except Laura is kind of mad because now Kate says she likes Harry Benson better."

"Better than Laura?" I asked stupidly.

"Oh, *Mother.* Better than Jimmy Watson, of course. Except *I* think Harry Benson is goony."

"If he was the one on patrol who let your brother Barry go across the street by himself he certainly *is* goony. As a matter of fact if there is one word I would automatically and instinctively apply to young Harry Benson it would surely be—"

"Oh, *Mother.* He is *not.*"

I had been kept up slightly past my own bedtime. "All right," I said. "Harry Benson is not goony and it is fine with me if Kate and Carole sleep in the guest room if they don't—"

"Kate and *Linda.*"

"Kate and Linda. If they don't, if they *only* don't giggle any more."

"*Thank* you. And may I sleep in the guest room too?"

"What?"

"It's a big bed. And we wanted to talk very quietly about—"

"Never mind," I said. "Sleep anywhere, but *sleep.*"

She was downstairs again about ten minutes later. Laurie and his father were eating crackers and cheese and discussing the probable derivation of "cool," as in "cool jazz."

"Listen," Jannie said in the dining room, "can Kate sleep in the guest room too?"

"But I thought Kate was already—"

"Well, she was, but they couldn't sleep, because Kate *did* take Linda's lunch box and she broke the Thermos and Carole saw her so Carole told Linda and then Kate wouldn't let Carole in the guest room but I can't leave Carole with Laura because Laura said Carole's shortie pajamas were goony and Linda went and told her."

"That was unkind of Linda," I said, floundering.

"So then Carole said Linda—"

"Never mind, I said. "Just tell me who is sleeping where."

"Well, Kate and I are sleeping in the guest room, because now everyone else is mad at Kate. And Carole is mad at Linda so Carole is sleeping in my room and Linda and Laura are sleeping in my library, except I just really don't know *what* will happen," she sighed, "if anyone tells Laura what Linda said about Jerry. Jerry Harper."

"But can't Carole change with Linda and sleep with Laura?"

"Oh, *Mother.* You *know* about Carole and Laura and Jimmy Watson."

"I guess I just forgot for a minute," I said.

"Well," Jannie said, "I just thought I'd let you know where everyone was."

About half-past one Laurie held up his hand and said, "Listen." I had been trying to identify the sensation, and thought it was like the sudden lull in a heavy wind which has been beating against the trees and the windows for hours, and then stops. "Can it be possible?" my husband said.

Laurie began to put his records away, moving very softly. I went up the back stairs in my stocking feet, not making a sound, and opened the door to Jannie's room, easing it to avoid the slightest squeak.

Jannie was peacefully asleep in her own bed. The other bed in her room and the three beds in her library were empty.

Reflecting upon the cataclysmic powers of Jimmy Watson's name, I found the four other girls all asleep on the guest-room bed. None of them was covered, but there was no way of putting a blanket over them without smothering somebody. I closed the window, and tiptoed away, and came downstairs to tell Laurie it was safe, he could go to bed now.

Then I got myself upstairs and fell into bed, and slept soundly until seventeen minutes past three by the bedroom clock, when I was awakened by Jannie.

"Kate feels sick," she said. "You've got to get up right away and take her home."

[1957]

LOUISA,
PLEASE COME HOME

"Louisa," my mother's voice came over the radio; it frightened me badly for a minute. "Louisa," she said, "please come home. It's been three long long years since we saw you last; Louisa, I promise you that everything will be all right. We all miss you so. We want you back again. Louisa, please come home."

Once a year. On the anniversary of the day I ran away. Each time I heard it I was frightened again, because between one year and the next I would forget what my mother's voice sounded like, so soft and yet strange with that pleading note. I listened every year. I read the stories in the newspapers—"Louisa Tether vanished one year ago"—or two years ago, or three; I used to wait for the twentieth of June as though it were my birthday. I kept all the clippings at first, but secretly; with my picture on all the front pages I would have looked kind of strange if anyone had seen me cutting it out. Chandler, where I was hiding, was close enough to my old home so that the papers made a big fuss about all of it, but of course the reason I picked Chandler in the first place was because it was a big enough city for me to hide in.

I didn't just up and leave on the spur of the moment, you know. I always knew that I was going to run away sooner or later, and I had made plans ahead of time, for whenever I decided to go. Everything had to go right the first time, because they don't usually give you a second chance on that kind of thing and anyway if it had gone wrong I would have looked like an awful fool, and my sister Carol was never one for letting people forget it when they made fools of themselves. I admit I planned it for the day before Carol's wedding on purpose, and for a long time afterward I used to try and imagine Carol's face when she finally realized that my running away was going to leave her one bridesmaid short. The papers said that the wedding went ahead as scheduled, though, and Carol told one newspaper reporter that her sister Louisa would have wanted it that way; "She would never have meant to spoil my wedding," Carol said, knowing perfectly well that that would be exactly what I'd meant. I'm pretty sure that the first thing Carol did when they knew I was missing was go and count the wedding presents to see what I'd taken with me.

Anyway, Carol's wedding may have been fouled up, but *my* plans went fine—better, as a matter of fact, than I had ever expected. Everyone was hurrying around the house putting up flowers and asking each other if the wedding gown had been delivered, and opening up cases of champagne and wondering what they were going to do if it rained and they couldn't use the garden, and I just closed the front door behind me and started off. There was only one bad minute when Paul saw me; Paul has always lived next door and Carol hates him worse than she does me. My mother always used to say that every time I did something to make the family ashamed of me Paul was sure to be in it somewhere. For a long time they thought he had something to do with my running away, even though he told over and over again how hard I tried to duck away from him that afternoon when he met me going down the driveway. The papers kept calling him "a close friend of the family," which must have overjoyed my mother, and saying that he was being questioned about possible clues to my whereabouts. Of course he never even knew that I was running away; I told him just what I told my mother before I left—that I was going to get away from all the confusion and excitement for a while; I was going downtown and would probably have a sandwich somewhere for supper and go to a movie. He bothered me for a minute there, because of course he wanted to come too. I hadn't meant to take the bus right there on the corner but with Paul tagging after me and wanting me to wait while he got the car so we could drive out and have dinner at the Inn, I had to get away fast on the first thing that came along, so I just ran for the bus and left Paul standing there; that was the only part of my plan I had to change.

I took the bus all the way downtown, although my first plan had been to walk. It turned out much better, actually, since it didn't matter at all if anyone saw me on the bus going downtown in my own home town, and I managed to get an earlier train out. I bought a round-trip ticket; that was important, because it would make them think I was coming back; that was always the way they thought about things. If you did something you had to have a reason for it, because my mother and my father and Carol never did anything unless *they* had a reason for it, so if I bought a round-trip ticket the only possible reason would be that I was coming back. Besides, if they thought I was coming back they would not be frightened so quickly and I might have more time to hide before they came looking for me. As it happened, Carol found out I was gone that same night when she couldn't sleep and came into my room for some aspirin, so at the time I had less of a head start than I thought.

I knew that they would find out about my buying the ticket; I was not silly enough to suppose that I could steal off and not leave any traces. All my plans were based on the fact that the people who get caught are the ones who attract attention by doing something strange or noticeable, and what I intended all along was to fade into some background where they would never see me. I knew they would find out about the round-trip ticket, because it was an odd thing to do in a town where you've lived all your life, but it was the last unusual thing I did. I thought when I bought it that knowing about that round-trip ticket would be some consolation to my mother and father. They would know that no matter how long I stayed away at least I always had a ticket home. I did keep the return-trip ticket quite a while, as a matter of fact. I used to carry it in my wallet as a kind of lucky charm.

I followed everything in the papers. Mrs. Peacock and I used to read them at the breakfast table over our second cup of coffee before I went off to work.

"What do you think about this girl disappeared over in

Rockville?" Mrs. Peacock would say to me, and I'd shake my head sorrowfully and say that a girl must be really crazy to leave a handsome, luxurious home like that, or that I had kind of a notion that maybe she didn't leave at all—maybe the family had her locked up somewhere because she was a homicidal maniac. Mrs. Peacock always loved anything about homicidal maniacs.

Once I picked up the paper and looked hard at the picture. "Do you think she looks something like me?" I asked Mrs. Peacock, and Mrs. Peacock leaned back and looked at me and then at the picture and then at me again and finally she shook her head and said, "No. If you wore your hair longer, and curlier, and your face was maybe a little fuller, there might be a little resemblance, but then if you looked like a homicidal maniac I wouldn't ever of let you in my house."

"I think she kind of looks like me," I said.

"You get along to work and stop being vain," Mrs. Peacock told me.

Of course when I got on the train with my round-trip ticket I had no idea how soon they'd be following me, and I suppose it was just as well, because it might have made me nervous and I might have done something wrong and spoiled everything. I knew that as soon as they gave up the notion that I was coming back to Rockville with my round-trip ticket they would think of Crain, which is the largest city that train went to, so I only stayed in Crain part of one day. I went to a big department store where they were having a store-wide sale; I figured that would land me in a crowd of shoppers and I was right; for a while there was a good chance that I'd never get any farther away from home than the ground floor of that department store in Crain. I had to fight my way through the crowd until I found the counter where they were having a sale of raincoats, and then I had to push and elbow down the counter and finally grab the raincoat I wanted right out of the hands of some old monster who couldn't have used it anyway because she was much too fat. You would have thought she had already paid for it, the way she howled. I was smart enough to have the exact change, all six dollars and eighty-nine cents, right in my hand, and I gave it to the salesgirl, grabbed the raincoat and the bag she wanted to put it in, and fought my way out again before I got crushed to death.

That raincoat was worth every cent of the six dollars and eighty-nine cents; I wore it right through until winter that year and not even a button ever came off it. I finally lost it the next spring when I left it somewhere and never got it back. It was tan, and the minute I put it on in the ladies' room of the store I began thinking of it as my "old" raincoat; that was good. I had never before owned a raincoat like that and my mother would have fainted dead away. One thing I did that I thought was kind of clever. I had left home wearing a light short coat; almost a jacket, and when I put on the raincoat of course I took off my light coat. Then all I had to do was empty the pockets of the light coat into the raincoat and carry the light coat casually over to a counter where they were having a sale of jackets and drop it on the counter as though I'd taken it off a little way to look at it and had decided against it. As far as I ever knew no one paid the slightest attention to me, and before I left the counter I saw a woman pick up my jacket and look it over; I could have told her she was getting a bargain for three ninety-eight.

It made me feel good to know that I had gotten rid of the light coat. My mother picked it out for me and even though I liked it and it was expensive it was also recognizable and I had to change it somehow. I was sure that if I put it in a bag and dropped it into a river or into a garbage truck of something like that sooner or later it would be found and even if no one saw me doing it, it would almost certainly be found, and then they would know I had changed my clothes in Crain.

That light coat never turned up. The last they ever found of me was someone in Rockville who caught a glimpse of me in the train station in Crain, and she recognized me by the light coat. They never found out where I went after that; it was partly luck and partly my clever planning. Two or three days later the papers were still reporting that I was in Crain; people thought they saw me on the streets and one girl who went into a store to buy a dress was picked up by the police and held until she could get someone to identify her. They were really looking, but they were looking for Louisa Tether, and I had stopped being Louisa Tether the minute I got rid of that light coat my mother bought me.

One thing I was relying on: there must be thousands of girls in the country on any given day who are nineteen years old, fair-haired, five feet four inches tall, and weighing one hundred and twenty-six pounds. And if there are thousands of girls like that, there must be, among those thousands, a good number who are wearing shapeless tan raincoats; I started counting tan raincoats in Crain after I left the department store and I passed four in one block, so I felt well hidden. After that I made myself even more invisible by doing just what I told my mother I was going to—I stopped in and had a sandwich in a little coffee shop, and then I went to a movie. I wasn't in any hurry at all, and rather than try to find a place to sleep that night I thought I would sleep on the train.

It's funny how no one pays any attention to you at all. There were hundreds of people who saw me that day, and even a sailor who tried to pick me up in the movie, and yet no one really *saw* me. If I had tried to check into a hotel the desk clerk might have noticed me, or if I had tried to get dinner in some fancy restaurant in that cheap raincoat I would have been conspicuous, but I was doing what any other girl looking like me and dressed like me might be doing that day. The only person who might be apt to remember me would be the man selling tickets in the railroad station, because girls looking like me in old raincoats didn't buy train tickets, usually, at eleven at night, but I had thought of that, too, of course; I bought a ticket to Amityville, sixty miles away, and what made Amityville a perfectly reasonable disguise is that at Amityville there is a college, not a little fancy place like the one I had left so recently with nobody's blessing, but a big sprawling friendly affair, where my raincoat would look perfectly at home. I told myself I was a student coming back to the college after a week end at home. We got to Amityville after midnight, but it still didn't look odd when I left the train and went into the station, because while I was in the station, having a cup of coffee and killing time, seven other girls—I counted—wearing raincoats like mine came in or went out, not seeming to think it the least bit odd to be getting on or off trains at that hour of the night. Some of them had suitcases, and I wished that I had had some way of getting a suitcase in Crain, but it would have made me noticeable in the movie, and college girls going home for week ends often don't bother; they have pajamas and an extra pair of stockings at home, and they drop a toothbrush into one of the pockets of those invaluable raincoats. So I didn't worry about the suitcase then, although I knew I would need one soon. While I was having my coffee I made my own mind change from the idea that I was a college girl coming back after a week end at home to the idea that I was a college girl who was on her way home for a few days; all the time I tried to think as much as possible like what I was pretending to be, and after all, I *had* been a college girl for a while. I was thinking that even now the letter was in the mail, traveling as fast as the U.S. Government could make it go, right to my father to tell him why I wasn't a college student any more; I suppose that was what finally decided me to run away, the thought of what my father would think and say and do when he got that letter from the college.

That was in the paper, too. They decided that the college business was the reason for my running away, but if that had been all, I don't think I would have left. No, I had been wanting to leave for so long, ever since I can remember, making plans till I was sure they were foolproof, and that's the way they turned out to be.

Sitting there in the station at Amityville, I tried to think myself into a good reason why I was leaving college to go home on a Monday night late, when I would hardly be going home for the week end. As I say, I always tried to think as hard as I could the way that suited whatever I wanted to be, and I liked to have a good reason for what I was doing. Nobody ever asked me, but it was good to know that I could answer them if they did. I finally decided that my sister was getting married the next day and I was going home at the beginning of the week to be one of her bridesmaids. I thought that was funny. I

didn't want to be going home for any sad or frightening reason, like my mother being sick, or my father being hurt in a
car accident, because I would have to look sad, and that might
attract attention. So I was going home for my sister's wedding.
I wandered around the station as though I had nothing to do,
and just happened to pass the door when another girl was
going out; she had on a raincoat just like mine and anyone
who happened to notice would have thought that it was me
who went out. Before I bought my ticket I went into the ladies'
room and got another twenty dollars out of my shoe. I had
nearly three hundred dollars left of the money I had taken
from my father's desk and I had most of it in my shoes because
I honestly couldn't think of another safe place to carry it. All I
kept in my pocketbook was just enough for whatever I had to
spend next. It's uncomfortable walking around all day on a
wad of bills in your shoe, but they were good solid shoes, the
kind of comfortable old shoes you wear whenever you don't
really care how you look, and I had put new shoelaces in them
before I left home so I could tie them good and tight. You can
see, I planned pretty carefully, and no little detail got left out.
If they had let me plan my sister's wedding there would have
been a lot less of that running around and screaming and
hysterics.

I bought a ticket to Chandler, which is the biggest city in
this part of the state, and the place I'd been heading for all
along. It was a good place to hide because people from Rockville tended to bypass it unless they had some special reason
for going there—if they couldn't find the doctors or orthodon-
tists or psychoanalysts or dress material they wanted in Rockville or Crain, they went directly to one of the really big cities,
like the state capital; Chandler was big enough to hide in, but
not big enough to look like a metropolis to people from Rockville. The ticket seller in the Amityville station must have seen
a good many college girls buying tickets for Chandler at all
hours of the day or night because he took my money and
shoved the ticket at me without even looking up.

Funny. They must have come looking for me in Chandler at
some time or other, because it's not likely they would have

neglected any possible place I might be, but maybe Rockville people never seriously believed that anyone would go to Chandler from choice, because I never felt for a minute that anyone was looking for me there. My picture was in the Chandler papers, of course, but as far as I ever knew no one ever looked at me twice, and I got up every morning and went to work and went shopping in the stores and went to movies with Mrs. Peacock and went out to the beach all that summer without ever being afraid of being recognized. I behaved just like everyone else, and dressed just like everyone else, and even *thought* just like everyone else, and the only person I ever saw from Rockville in three years was a friend of my mother's, and I knew *she* only came to Chandler to get her poodle bred at the kennels there. She didn't look as if she was in a state to recognize anybody but another poodle-fancier, anyway, and all I had to do was step into a doorway as she went by, and she never looked at me.

Two other college girls got on the train to Chandler when I did; maybe both of them were going home for their sisters' weddings. Neither of them was wearing a tan raincoat, but one of them had on an old blue jacket that gave the same general effect. I fell asleep as soon as the train started, and once I woke up and for a minute I wondered where I was and then I realized that I was doing it, I was actually carrying out my careful plan and had gotten better than halfway with it, and I almost laughed, there in the train with everyone asleep around me. Then I went back to sleep and didn't wake up until we got into Chandler about seven in the morning.

So there I was. I had left home just after lunch the day before, and now at seven in the morning of my sister's wedding day I was so far away, in every sense, that I *knew* they would never find me. I had all day to get myself settled in Chandler, so I started off by having breakfast in a restaurant near the station, and then went off to find a place to live, and a job. The first thing I did was buy a suitcase, and it's funny how people don't really notice you if you're buying a suitcase near a railroad station. Suitcases look *natural* near railroad stations, and I picked out one of those stores that sell a little bit of everything, and bought a cheap suitcase and a pair of stockings and some handkerchiefs and a little traveling clock, and I put everything into the suitcase and carried that. Nothing is hard to do unless you get upset or excited about it.

Later on, when Mrs. Peacock and I used to read in the papers about my disappearing, I asked her once if she thought that Louisa Tether had gotten as far as Chandler and she didn't.

"They're saying now she was kidnapped," Mrs. Peacock told me, "and that's what *I* think happened. Kidnapped, and murdered, and they do *terrible* things to young girls they kidnap."

"But the papers say there wasn't any ransom note."

"That's what they *say*." Mrs. Peacock shook her head at me. "How do we know what the family is keeping secret? Or if she was kidnapped by a homicidal maniac, why should *he* send a ransom note? Young girls like you don't know a lot of the things that go on, *I* can tell you."

"I feel kind of sorry for the girl," I said.

"You can't ever tell," Mrs. Peacock said. "Maybe she went with him willingly."

I didn't know, that first morning in Chandler, that Mrs. Peacock was going to turn up that first day, the luckiest thing that ever happened to me. I decided while I was having breakfast that I was going to be a nineteen-year-old girl from upstate with a nice family and a good background who had been saving money to come to Chandler and take a secretarial course in the business school there. I was going to have to find some kind of a job to keep on earning money while I went to school; courses at the business school wouldn't start until fall, so I would have the summer to work and save money and decide if I really wanted to take secretarial training. If I decided not to stay in Chandler I could easily go somewhere else after the fuss about my running away had died down. The raincoat looked wrong for the kind of conscientious young girl I was going to be, so I took it off and carried it over my arm. I think I did a pretty good job on my clothes, altogether. Before I left home I decided that I would have to wear a suit, as quiet and unobtrusive as I could find, and I picked out a gray suit, with a white blouse, so with just one or two small changes like a different blouse or some kind of a pin on the lapel, I could look like whoever I decided to be. Now the suit looked absolutely right for a young girl planning to take a secretarial course, and I looked like a thousand other people when I walked down the street carrying my suitcase and my raincoat over my arm; people get off trains every minute looking just like that. I bought a morning paper and stopped in a drugstore for a cup of coffee and a look to see the rooms for rent. It was all so usual— suitcase, coat, rooms for rent—that when I asked the soda clerk how to get to Primrose Street he never even looked at me. He certainly didn't care whether I ever got to Primrose Street or not, but he told me very politely where it was and what bus to take. I didn't really need to take the bus for economy, but it would have looked funny for a girl who was saving money to arrive in a taxi.

"I'll never forget how you looked that first morning," Mrs. Peacock told me once, much later. "I knew right away you were the kind of girl I like to rent rooms to—quiet, and well-mannered. But you looked almighty scared of the big city."

"I wasn't scared," I said. "I was worried about finding a nice room. My mother told me so many things to be careful about I was afraid I'd never find anything to suit her."

"*Any*body's mother could come into my house at any time and know that her daughter was in good hands," Mrs. Peacock said, a little huffy.

But it was true. When I walked into Mrs. Peacock's rooming house on Primrose Street, and met Mrs. Peacock, I knew that I couldn't have done this part better if I'd been able to plan it. The house was old, and comfortable, and my room was nice, and Mrs. Peacock and I hit it off right away. She was very pleased with me when she heard that my mother had told me to be sure the room I found was clean and that the neighborhood was good, with no chance of rowdies following a girl if she came home after dark, and she was even more pleased when she heard that I wanted to save money and take a secretarial course so I could get a really good job and earn enough to be able to send a little home every week; Mrs. Peacock believed that children owed it to their parents to pay back some of what had been spent on them while they were growing up. By the time I had been in the house an hour Mrs. Peacock knew all about my imaginary family upstate: my mother, who was a widow, and my sister, who had just gotten married and still lived at my mother's home with her husband, and my young brother Paul, who worried my mother a good deal because he didn't seem to want to settle down. My name was Lois Taylor, I told her. By that time, I think I could have told her my real name and she would never have connected it with the girl in the paper, because by then she was feeling that she almost knew my family, and she wanted me to be sure and tell my mother when I wrote home that Mrs. Peacock would make herself personally responsible for me while I was in the city and take as good care of me as my own mother would. On top of everything else, she told me that a stationery store in the neighborhood was looking for a girl assistant, and there I was. Before I had been away from home for twenty-four hours I was an entirely new person. I was a girl named Lois Taylor who lived on Primrose Street and worked down at the stationery store.

I read in the papers one day about how a famous fortune-teller wrote to my father offering to find me and said that astral signs had convinced him that I would be found near flowers. That gave me a jolt, because of Primrose Street, but my father and Mrs. Peacock and the rest of the world thought that it meant that my body was buried somewhere. They dug up a vacant lot near the railroad station where I was last seen, and Mrs. Peacock was very disappointed when nothing turned up. Mrs. Peacock and I could not decide whether I had run away with a gangster to be a gun moll, or whether my body had been cut up and sent somewhere in a trunk. After a while they stopped looking for me, except for an occasional false clue that would turn up in a small story on the back pages of the paper, and Mrs. Peacock and I got interested in the stories about a daring daylight bank robbery in Chicago. When the anniversary of my running away came around, and I realized that I had really been gone for a year, I treated myself to a new

hat and dinner downtown, and came home just in time for the
evening news broadcast and my mother's voice over the radio.

"Louisa," she was saying, "please come home."

"That poor poor woman," Mrs. Peacock said. "Imagine
how she must feel. They say she's never given up hope of finding her little girl alive someday."

"Do you like my new hat?" I asked her.

I had given up all idea of the secretarial course because the
stationery store had decided to expand and include a lending
library and a gift shop, and I was now the manager of the gift
shop and if things kept on well would someday be running the
whole thing; Mrs. Peacock and I talked it over, just as if she
had been my mother, and we decided that I would be foolish
to leave a good job to start over somewhere else. The money
that I had been saving was in the bank, and Mrs. Peacock and
I thought that one of these days we might pool our savings and
buy a little car, or go on a trip somewhere, or even a cruise.

What I am saying is that I was free, and getting along fine,
with never a thought that I knew about ever going back. It was
just plain rotten bad luck that I had to meet Paul. I had gotten
so I hardly ever thought about any of them any more, and
never wondered what they were doing unless I happened to see
some item in the papers, but there must have been something
in the back of my mind remembering them all the time because
I never even stopped to think; I just stood there on the street
with my mouth open, and said *"Paul!"* He turned around and
then of course I realized what I had done, but it was too late.
He stared at me for a minute, and then frowned, and then
looked puzzled; I could see him first trying to remember, and
then trying to believe what he remembered; at last he said, "Is
it possible?"

He said I had to go back. He said if I didn't go back he
would tell them where to come and get me. He also patted me
on the head and told me that there was still a reward waiting
there in the bank for anyone who turned up with conclusive
news of me, and he said that after he had collected the reward
I was perfectly welcome to run away again, as far and as often
as I liked.

Maybe I did want to go home. Maybe all that time I had been secretly waiting for a chance to get back; maybe that's why I recognized Paul on the street, in a coincidence that wouldn't have happened once in a million years—he had never even *been* to Chandler before, and was only there for a few minutes between trains; he had stepped out of the station for a minute, and found me. If I had not been passing at that minute, if he had stayed in the station where he belonged, I would never have gone back. I told Mrs. Peacock I was going home to visit my family upstate. I thought that was funny.

Paul sent a telegram to my mother and father, saying that he had found me, and we took a plane back; Paul said he was still afraid that I'd try to get away again and the safest place for me was high up in the air where he knew I couldn't get off and run.

I began to get nervous, looking out the taxi window on the way from the Rockville airport; I would have sworn that for three years I hadn't given a thought to that town, to those streets and stores and houses I used to know so well, but here I found that I remembered it all, as though I hadn't ever seen Chandler and *its* houses and streets; it was almost as though I had never been away at all. When the taxi finally turned the corner into my own street, and I saw the big old white house again, I almost cried.

"Of course I wanted to come back," I said, and Paul laughed. I thought of the return-trip ticket I had kept as a lucky charm for so long, and how I had thrown it away one day when I was emptying my pocketbook; I wondered when I threw it away whether I would ever want to go back and regret throwing away my ticket. "Everything looks just the same," I said. "I caught the bus right there on the corner; I came down the driveway that day and met you."

"If I had managed to stop you that day," Paul said, "you would probably never have tried again."

Then the taxi stopped in front of the house and my knees were shaking when I got out. I grabbed Paul's arm and said, "Paul . . . wait a minute," and he gave me a look I used to know very well, a look that said "If you back out on me now I'll see that you never forget it," and put his arm around me because I was shivering and we went up the walk to the front door.

I wondered if they were watching us from the window. It was hard for me to imagine how my mother and father would behave in a situation like this, because they always made such a point of being quiet and dignified and proper; I thought that Mrs. Peacock would have been halfway down the walk to meet us, but here the front door ahead was still tight shut. I wondered if we would have to ring the doorbell; I had never had to ring this doorbell before. I was still wondering when Carol opened the door for us. "Carol!" I said. I was shocked because she looked so old, and then I thought that of course it had been three years since I had seen her and she probably thought that *I* looked older, too. "Carol," I said, "Oh, Carol!" I was honestly glad to see her.

She looked at me hard and then stepped back and my mother and father were standing there, waiting for me to come in. If I had not stopped to think I would have run to them, but I hesitated, not quite sure what to do, or whether they were angry with me, or hurt, or only just happy that I was back, and of course once I stopped to think about it all I could find to do was just stand there and say "Mother?" kind of uncertainly.

She came over to me and put her hands on my shoulders and looked into my face for a long time. There were tears running down her cheeks and I thought that before, when it didn't matter, I had been ready enough to cry, but now, when crying would make me look better, all I wanted to do was giggle. She looked old, and sad, and I felt simply foolish. Then she turned to Paul and said, "Oh, *Paul*—how can you do this to me again?"

Paul was frightened; I could see it. "Mrs. Tether—" he said.

"What is your name, dear?" my mother asked me.

"Louisa Tether," I said stupidly.

"No, dear," she said, very gently, "your *real* name?"

Now I could cry, but now I did not think it was going to help matters any. "Louisa Tether," I said. "That's my name."

"Why don't you people leave us alone?" Carol said; she was white, and shaking, and almost screaming because she was so angry. "We've spent years and years trying to find my lost sister and all people like you see in it is a chance to cheat us out of the reward—doesn't it mean *any*thing to you that *you* may think you have a chance for some easy money, but *we* just get hurt and heartbroken all over again? Why don't you leave us *alone*?"

"Carol," my father said, "you're frightening the poor child. Young lady," he said to me, "I honestly believe that you did not realize the cruelty of what you tried to do. You look like a nice girl; try to imagine your own mother—"

I tried to imagine my own mother; I looked straight at her.

"—if someone took advantage of her like this. I am sure you were not told that twice before, this young man—" I stopped looking at my mother and looked at Paul—"has brought us young girls who pretended to be our lost daughter; each time he protested that he had been genuinely deceived and had no thought of profit, and each time we hoped desperately that it would be the right girl. The first time we were taken in for several days. The girl *looked* like our Louisa, she *acted* like our Louisa, she knew all kinds of small family jokes and happenings it seemed impossible that anyone *but* Louisa could know, and yet she was an imposter. And the girl's mother—my wife—has suffered more each time her hopes have been raised." He put his arm around my mother—his wife—and with Carol they stood all together looking at me.

"Look," Paul said wildly, "give her a *chance*—she *knows* she's Louisa. At least give her a chance to *prove* it."

"How?" Carol asked. "I'm sure if I asked her something like—well—like what was the color of the dress she was supposed to wear at my wedding—"

"It was pink," I said. "I wanted blue but you said it had to be pink."

"I'm sure she'd know the answer," Carol went on as though I hadn't said anything. "The other girls you brought here, Paul—*they* both knew."

It wasn't going to be any good. I ought to have known it. Maybe they were so used to looking for me by now that they would rather keep on looking than have me home; maybe once

my mother had looked in my face and seen there nothing of
Louisa, but only the long careful concentration I had put into
being Lois Taylor, there was never any chance of my looking
like Louisa again.

I felt kind of sorry for Paul; he had never understood them
as well as I did and he clearly felt there was still some chance
of talking them into opening their arms and crying out "Louisa! Our long-lost daughter!" and then turning around and
handing him the reward; after that, we could all live happily
ever after. While Paul was still trying to argue with my father
I walked over a little way and looked into the living room
again; I figured I wasn't going to have much time to look around
and I wanted one last glimpse to take away with me; sister
Carol kept a good eye on me all the time, too. I wondered
what the two girls before me had tried to steal, and I wanted
to tell her that if I ever planned to steal anything from that
house I was three years too late; I could have taken whatever I
wanted when I left the first time. There was nothing there I
could take now, any more than there had been before. I realized that all I wanted was to stay—I wanted to stay so much
that I felt like hanging onto the stair rail and screaming, but
even though a temper tantrum might bring them some fleeting
recollection of their dear lost Louisa I hardly thought it would
persuade them to invite me to stay. I could just picture myself
being dragged kicking and screaming out of my own house.

"Such a lovely old house," I said politely to my sister Carol,
who was hovering around me.

"Our family has lived here for generations," she said, just as
politely.

"Such beautiful furniture," I said.

"My mother is fond of antiques."

"Fingerprints," Paul was shouting. We were going to get a
lawyer, I gathered, or at least Paul thought we were going to
get a lawyer and I wondered how he was going to feel when he
found out that we weren't. I couldn't imagine any lawyer in
the world who could get my mother and my father and my sister Carol to take me back when they had made up their minds

that I was not Louisa; could the law make my mother look into my face and recognize me?

I thought that there ought to be some way I could make Paul see that there was nothing we could do, and I came over and stood next to him. "Paul," I said, "can't you see that you're only making Mr. Tether angry?"

"Correct, young woman," my father said, and nodded at me to show that he thought I was being a sensible creature. "He's not doing himself any good by threatening me."

"Paul," I said, "these people don't want us here."

Paul started to say something and then for the first time in his life thought better of it and stamped off toward the door. When I turned to follow him—thinking that we'd never gotten past the front hall in my great homecoming—my father—excuse me, Mr. Tether—came up behind me and took my hand. "My daughter was younger than you are," he said to me very kindly, "but I'm sure you have a family somewhere who love you and want you to be happy. Go back to them, young lady. Let me advise you as though I were really your father—stay away from that fellow, he's wicked and he's worthless. Go back home where you belong."

"We know what it's like for a family to worry and wonder about a daughter," my mother said. "Go back to the people who love you."

That meant Mrs. Peacock, I guess.

"Just to make sure you get there," my father said, "let us help toward your fare." I tried to take my hand away, but he put a folded bill into it and I had to take it. "I hope someday," he said, "that someone will do as much for our Louisa."

"Good-by, my dear," my mother said, and she reached up and patted my cheek. "Very good luck to you."

"I hope your daughter comes back someday," I told them. "Good-by."

The bill was a twenty, and I gave it to Paul. It seemed little enough for all the trouble he had taken and, after all, I could go back to my job in the stationery store. My mother still talks

to me on the radio, once a year, on the anniversary of the day
I ran away.

"Louisa," she says, "Please come home. We all want our
dear girl back, and we need you and miss you so much. Your
mother and father love you and will never forget you. Louisa,
please come home."

[1960]

THE LITTLE HOUSE

I'll have to get some decent lights, was her first thought, and her second: *and* a dog or something, or at least a bird, anything *alive*. She stood in the little hall beside her suitcase, in a little house that belonged to her, her first home. She held the front-door key in her hand, and she knew, remembering her aunt, that the back-door key hung, labeled, from a hook beside the back door, and the side-door key hung from a hook beside the side door, and the porch-door key hung from a hook beside the porch door, and the cellar-door key hung from a hook beside the cellar-door, and perhaps when she slammed the front door behind her all the keys swung gently, once, back and forth. Anything that can move and make some kind of a friendly noise, she thought, maybe a monkey or a cat or anything not stuffed—as she realized that she was staring, hypnotized, at the moose head over the hall mirror.

Wanting to make some kind of a noise in the silence, she coughed, and the small sound moved dustily into the darkness of the house. Well, I'm here, she told herself, and it belongs to me and I can do anything I want here and no one can ever make me leave, because it's mine. She moved to touch the carved newel post at the foot of the narrow stairway—it was hers, it belonged to her—and felt a sudden joy at the tangible reality of the little house; this is really something to own, she thought, thank you, Aunt. And my goodness, she thought, brushing her hand, couldn't my very own house do with a little dusting; she smiled to herself at the prospect of the very pleasant work she would do tomorrow and the day after, and for all the days after that, living in her house and keeping it clean and fresh.

Wanting to whistle, to do something to bring noise and movement into the house, she turned and opened the door on her right and stepped into the dim crowded parlor. I wish I didn't have to see it first at dusk, she thought, Aunt certainly didn't believe in bright light; I wonder how she ever found her way around this room. A dim shape on a low table beside the door resolved itself into a squat lamp; when she pressed the switch a low radiance came into the room and she was able to leave the spot by the door and venture into what had clearly been her aunt's favorite room. The parlor had certainly not been touched, or even opened or lighted, since her aunt's death; a tea towel, half-hemmed, lay on the arm of a chair, and she felt a sudden tenderness and a half-shame at the thought of the numbers of tea towels, hemmed, which had come to her at birthdays and Christmases over the years and now lay still in their tissue paper, at the bottom of her trunk still at the railroad station. At least I'll use her towels now, in her own house, she thought, and then: but it's my house now. She would stack the tea towels neatly in the linen closet, she might even finish hemming this one, and she took it up and folded it neatly, leaving the needle still tucked in where her aunt had left it, to await the time when she should sit quietly in her chair, in her parlor in her house, and take up her sewing. Her aunt's glasses lay on the table; had her aunt put down her sewing and taken off her glasses at the very end? Prepared, neatly, to die?

Don't think about it, she told herself sternly, she's gone now, and soon the house will be busy again; I'll clear away tomorrow, when it's not so dark; how did she ever manage to sew in here with this light? She put the half-hemmed towel over the glasses to hide them, and took up a little picture in a silver frame; her aunt, she recognized, and some smiling woman friend, standing together under trees; this must have been important to Aunt, she thought, I'll put it away safely somewhere. The house was distantly familiar to her; she had come here sometimes as a child, but that was long ago, and the

memories of the house and her aunt were overlaid with cyni-
cism and melancholy and the wearying disappointments of
many years; perhaps it was the longing to return to the laughter of childhood which had brought her here so eagerly to take
up her inheritance. The music box was in the corner where it
had always been and, touching it gently, she brought from it
one remote, faintly sweet, jangle of a note. Tomorrow I'll play
the music box, she promised herself, with the windows wide
open and the good fresh air blowing through and all the
bric-a-brac safely stowed away in the attic; this could be such
a pretty room—and she turned, her head to one side,
considering—once I take out the junk and the clutter. I can
keep the old couch and maybe have it recovered in something
colorful, and the big chair can stay, and perhaps one or two of
these tiny tables; the mantel is fine, and I'll keep a bowl of
flowers there, flowers from my own garden. I'll have a great
fire in the fireplace and I'll sit here with my dog and my
needlework—and two or three good floor lamps; I'll get those
tomorrow—and never be unhappy again. Tomorrow, lamps,
and air the room, and play the music box.

Leaving a dim trail of lighted lamps behind her, she went
from the parlor through a little sunporch where a magazine
lay open on the table; Aunt never finished the story she was
reading, she thought, and closed the magazine quickly and set
it in order on the pile on the table; I'll subscribe to magazines,
she thought, and the local newspaper, and take books from
the village library. From the sunporch she went into the kitchen
and remembered to turn on the light by pulling the cord hanging from the middle of the ceiling; her aunt had left a tomato
ripening on the window sill, and it scented the kitchen with a
strong air of decay. She shivered, and realized that the back
door was standing open, and remembered her aunt saying, as
clearly as though she heard it now, "Darn that door, I wish I
could remember to get that latch looked at."

And now I have to do it for her, she thought; I'll get a man
in the morning. She found a paper bag in the pantry drawer
where paper bags had always been kept, and scraped the rotten

tomato from the window sill and carried the bag to the garbage pail by the back steps. When she came back she slammed the back door correctly and the latch caught; the key was hanging where she knew it had been, beside the door, and she took it down and locked the door; I'm alone in the house, after all, she thought with a little chill touching the back of her neck.

The cup from which her aunt had drunk her last cup of tea lay, washed and long since drained dry, beside the sink; perhaps she put her sewing down, she thought, and came to the kitchen to make a cup of tea before going to bed; I wonder where they found her; she always had a cup of tea at night, all alone; I wish I had come to see her at least once. The lovely old dishes are mine now, she thought, the family dishes and the cut glass and the silver tea service. Her aunt's sweater hung from the knob of the cellar door, as though she had only just this minute taken it off, and her apron hung from a hook beside the sink. Aunt always put things away, she thought, and she never came back for her sweater. She remembered dainty little hand-embroidered aprons in the hall chest, and thought of herself, aproned, serving a charming tea from the old tea service, using the thin painted cups, perhaps to neighbors who had come to see her delightful, open, light, little house; I must have a cocktail party too, she thought; I'll bet there's nothing in the house but dandelion wine.

It would seem strange at first, coming downstairs in the morning to make herself breakfast in her aunt's kitchen, and she suddenly remembered herself, very small, eating oatmeal at the kitchen table; it would seem strange to be using her aunt's dishes, and the big old coffeepot—although perhaps not the coffeepot, she thought; it had the look of something crotchety and temperamental, not willing to submit docilely to a strange hand; I'll have tea tomorrow morning, and get a new little coffeepot just for me. Lamps, coffeepot, man to fix the latch.

After a moment's thought she took her aunt's sweater and apron and bundled them together and carried them out to the garbage pail. It isn't as though they were any good to anyone, she told herself reassuringly; *all* her clothes will have to be thrown away, and she pictured herself standing in her bright parlor in her smart city clothes telling her laughing friends about the little house; "Well, you should have seen it when I came," she would tell them, "you should have seen the place the first night I walked in. Murky little lamps, and the place simply crawling with bric-a-brac, and a stuffed moose head— *really*, a stuffed moose head, I mean it—and Aunt's sewing on the table, and what was positively her last cup in the sink." Will I tell them, she wondered, about how Aunt set her sewing down when she was ready to die? And never finished her magazine, and hung up her sweater, and felt her heart go? "You should have seen it when I came," she would tell them, sipping from her glass, "dark, and dismal; I used to come here when I was a child, but I honestly never remembered it as such a mess. It couldn't have come as more of a surprise, her leaving me the house, I never dreamed of having it."

Suddenly guilty, she touched the cold coffeepot with a gentle finger. I'll clean you tomorrow, she thought; I'm sorry I never got to the funeral, I should have tried to come. Tomorrow I'll start cleaning. Then she whirled, startled, at the knock at the back door; I hadn't realized it was so quiet here, she thought, and breathed again and moved quickly to the door. "Who is it?" she said. "Just a minute." Her hands shaking, she unlocked and opened the door. "Who is it?" she said into the darkness, and then smiled timidly at the two old faces regarding her. "Oh," she said, "how do you do?"

"You'll be the niece? Miss Elizabeth?"

"Yes." Two old pussycats, she thought, wearing hats with flowers, couldn't wait to get a look at me. "Hello," she said, thinking, I'm the charming niece Elizabeth, and this is my house now.

"We are the Dolson sisters. I am Miss Amanda Dolson. This is my sister Miss Caroline Dolson."

"We're your nearest neighbors." Miss Caroline put a thin brown hand on Elizabeth's sleeve. "We live down the lane. We were your poor poor aunt's nearest neighbors. But we didn't hear anything."

Miss Amanda moved a little forward and Elizabeth stepped

back. "Won't you come in?" Elizabeth asked, remembering her manners. "Come into the parlor. I was just looking at the house. I only just got here," she said, moving backward, "I was just turning on some lights."

"We saw the lights." Miss Amanda went unerringly toward the little parlor. "This is not our formal call, you understand; we pay our calls by day. But I confess we wondered at the lights."

"We thought *he* had come back." Miss Caroline's hand was on Elizabeth's sleeve again, as though she were leading Elizabeth to the parlor. "They say they do, you know."

Miss Amanda seated herself, as though by right of long acquaintance, on the soft chair by the low table, and Miss Caroline took the only other comfortable chair; my own house indeed, Elizabeth thought, and sat down uneasily on a stiff chair near the door; I must get lamps first thing tomorrow, she thought, the better to see people with.

"Have you lived here long?" she asked foolishly.

"I hope you don't plan to change things," Miss Amanda said. "Aunt loved her little house, you know."

"I haven't had much time to plan."

"You'll find everything just the way she left it. I myself took her pocketbook upstairs and put it into the drawer of the commode. Otherwise nothing has been touched. Except the body, of course."

Oh, that's not still here? she wanted to ask, but said instead, "I used to come here when I was a child."

"So he wasn't after her money," Miss Caroline said. "Sister took her pocketbook off the kitchen table; I saw her do it. She took it upstairs and nothing was missing."

Miss Amanda leaned a little forward. "You'll be bringing in television sets? From the city? Radios?"

"I hadn't thought much about it yet."

"We'll be able to hear your television set, no doubt. We are your closest neighbors and we see your lights; no doubt your television set will be very loud."

"We would have heard if she had screamed," Miss Caroline said, lifting her thin hand in emphasis. "They say she must have recognized him, and indeed it is my belief that Sheriff

Knowlton has a very shrewd notion who he is. It is my belief that we all have our suspicions."

"Sister, this is gossip. Miss Elizabeth detests gossip."

"We were here the first thing in the morning, Miss Elizabeth, and I spoke to the Sheriff myself."

"Sister, Miss Elizabeth does not trouble her mind with wild stories. Let Miss Elizabeth remember Aunt as happy."

"I don't understand." Elizabeth looked from one of the tight old faces to the other; the two old bats, she thought, and said, "My aunt died of a heart attack, they said."

"It is *my* belief—"

"My sister is fond of gossip, Miss Elizabeth. I suppose you'll be packing away all of Aunt's pretty things?"

Elizabeth glanced at the table near her. A pink china box, a glass paperweight, a crocheted doily on which rested a set of blue porcelain kittens. "Some of them," she said.

"To make room for the television set. Poor Aunt; she thought a good deal of her small possessions." She frowned. "You won't find an ash tray in here."

Elizabeth put her cigarette down defiantly on the lid of the small pink box.

"Sister," Miss Amanda said, "bring Miss Elizabeth a saucer from the kitchen, from the daily china. Not the floral set."

Miss Caroline, looking shocked, hurried from the room, holding her heavy skirt away from the tables and Elizabeth's cigarette. Miss Amanda leaned forward again. "I do not permit my sister to gossip, Miss Elizabeth. You are wrong to encourage her."

"But what is she trying to say about my aunt?"

"Aunt has been dead and buried for two months. You were not, I think, at the funeral?"

"I couldn't get away."

"From the city. Exactly. I daresay you were delighted to have the house."

"Indeed I was."

"I suppose Aunt could hardly have done otherwise. Sister, give Miss Elizabeth the saucer. Quickly, before the room catches fire."

"Thank you." Elizabeth took the chipped saucer from Miss Caroline and put out her cigarette; ash trays, she thought, lamps, ash trays, coffeepot.

"Her apron is gone," Miss Caroline told her sister.

"Already?" Miss Amanda turned to look fully at Elizabeth. "I am afraid we will see many changes, Sister. And now Miss Elizabeth is waiting for us to leave. Miss Elizabeth is determined to begin her packing tonight."

"Really," Elizabeth said helplessly, gesturing, "really—"

"All of Aunt's pretty things. This is not our formal call, Miss Elizabeth." Miss Amanda rose grandly, and Miss Caroline followed. "You will see us within three days. Poor Aunt."

Elizabeth followed them back to the kitchen. "Really," she said again, and "Please don't leave," but Miss Amanda overrode her.

"This door does not latch properly," Miss Amanda said. "See that it is securely locked behind us."

"They say that's how he got in," Miss Caroline whispered. "Keep it locked *always*."

"Good night, Miss Elizabeth. I am happy to know that you plan to keep the house well lighted. We see your lights, you know, from our windows."

"Good night," Miss Caroline said, turning to put her hand once more on Elizabeth's arm. "Locked, *remember*."

"Good night," Elizabeth said, "good night." Old bats, she was thinking, old bats. Sooner or later I'm going to have words with them; they're probably the pests of the neighborhood. She watched as they went side by side down the path, their heads not yet turned to one another, their long skirts swinging. "Good night," she called once more, but neither of them turned. Old bats, she thought, and slammed the door correctly; the latch caught, and she took down the key and locked it. I'll give them the moose head, she thought, my aunt would have wanted them to have it. It's late, I've got to find myself a bed, I haven't even been upstairs yet. I'll give them each a piece of the junk; my very own, my pretty little house.

Humming happily, she turned back toward the parlor; I wonder where they found her? she thought suddenly; was it in the parlor? She stopped in the doorway, staring at the soft chair and wondering: did he come up behind her there? While she was sewing? And then pick up her glasses from the floor and set them on the table? Perhaps she was reading her magazine when he caught her, perhaps she had just washed her cup and saucer and was turning back to get her sweater; would it have been this quiet in the house? Is it always this quiet?

"No, no," she said aloud. "This is silly. Tomorrow I'll get a dog."

Pressing her lips together firmly, she walked across the room and turned off the light, then came back and turned off the lamp beside the door, and the soft darkness fell around her; did they find her here? she wondered as she went through the sunporch, and then said aloud "This is silly," and turned off the light. With the darkness following close behind her she came back to the kitchen and checked that the back door was securely locked. He won't get in *here* again, she thought, and shivered.

There was no light on the stairs. I can leave the kitchen light on all night, she thought, but no; they'll see it from their windows; did he wait for her on the stairs? Pressing against the wall, the kitchen light still burning dimly behind her, she went up the stairs, staring into the darkness, feeling her way with her feet. At the top was only darkness, and she put out her hands blindly; there was a wall, and then a door, and she ran her hand down the side of the door until she had the doorknob in her fingers.

What's waiting behind the door? she thought, and turned and fled wildly down the stairs and into the lighted kitchen with the locked back door. "Don't leave me here alone," she said, turning to look behind her, "please don't leave me here alone."

Miss Amanda and Miss Caroline cuddled on either side of their warm little stove. Miss Amanda had a piece of fruitcake and a cup of tea and Miss Caroline had a piece of marshmallow cake and a cup of tea. "Just the same," Miss Caroline was saying, "she should have served something."

"City ways."

"She could have offered some of the city cake she brought with her. The coffeepot was right there in the kitchen. It's not polite to wait until the company goes and then eat by yourself."

"It's city ways, Sister. I doubt she'll be a good neighbor for us."

"Her aunt would not have done it."

"When I think of her searching that little house for valuables I feel very sorry for Aunt."

Miss Caroline set down her plate, and nodded to herself. "She might not like it here," she said. "Perhaps she won't stay."

[1962]

THE BUS

Old Miss Harper was going home, although the night was wet and nasty. Miss Harper disliked traveling at any time, and she particularly disliked traveling on this dirty small bus which was her only way of getting home; she had frequently complained to the bus company about their service because it seemed that no matter where she wanted to go, they had no respectable bus to carry her. Getting away from home was bad enough—Miss Harper was fond of pointing out to the bus company—but getting home always seemed very close to impossible. Tonight Miss Harper had no choice: if she did not go home by this particular bus she could not go for another day. Annoyed, tired, depressed, she tapped irritably on the counter of the little tobacco store which served also as the bus station. Sir, she was thinking, beginning her letter of complaint, although I am an elderly lady of modest circumstances and must curtail my fondness for travel, let me point out that your bus service falls far below . . .

Outside, the bus stirred noisily, clearly not anxious to be moving; Miss Harper thought she could already hear the weary sound of its springs sinking out of shape. I just can't make this trip again, Miss Harper thought, even seeing Stephanie isn't worth it, they really go out of their way to make you uncomfortable. "Can I get my ticket, please?" she said sharply, and the old man at the other end of the counter put down his paper and gave her a look of hatred.

Miss Harper ordered her ticket, deploring her own cross voice, and the old man slapped it down on the counter in front of her and said, "You got three minutes before the bus leaves."

He'd love to tell me I missed it, Miss Harper thought, and made a point of counting her change.

The rain was beating down, and Miss Harper hurried the few exposed steps to the door of the bus. The driver was slow in opening the door and as Miss Harper climbed in she was thinking, Sir, I shall never travel with your company again. Your ticket salesmen are ugly, your drivers are surly, your vehicles indescribably filthy . . .

There were already several people sitting in the bus, and Miss Harper wondered where they could possibly be going; were there really this many small towns served only by this bus? Were there really other people who would endure this kind of trip to get somewhere, even home? I'm very out of sorts, Miss Harper thought, very out of sorts; it's too strenuous a visit for a woman of my age; I need to get home. She thought of a hot bath and a cup of tea and her own bed, and sighed. No one offered to help her put her suitcase on the rack, and she glanced over her shoulder at the driver sitting with his back turned and thought, he'd probably rather put me off the bus than help me, and then, perceiving her own ill nature, smiled. The bus company might write a letter of complaint about *me*, she told herself and felt better. She had providentially taken a sleeping pill before leaving for the bus station, hoping to sleep through as much of the trip as possible, and at last, sitting near the back, she promised herself that it would not be unbearably long before she had a bath and a cup of tea, and tried to compose the bus company's letter of complaint. Madam, a lady of your experience and advanced age ought surely to be aware of the problems confronting a poor but honest little company which wants only . . .

She was aware that the bus had started, because she was rocked and bounced in her seat, and the feeling of rattling and throbbing beneath the soles of her shoes stayed with her even when she slept at last. She lay back uneasily, her head resting on the seat back, moving back and forth with the motion of the bus, and around her other people slept, or spoke softly, or stared blankly out the windows at the passing lights and the rain.

Sometime during her sleep Miss Harper was jostled by

someone moving into the seat behind her, her head was pushed
and her hat disarranged; for a minute, bewildered by sleep,
Miss Harper clutched at her hat, and said vaguely, "Who?"

"Go back to sleep," a young voice said, and giggled. "I'm
just running away from home, that's all."

Miss Harper was not awake, but she opened her eyes a little
and looked up to the ceiling of the bus. "That's wrong," Miss
Harper said as clearly as she could. "That's wrong. Go back."

There was another giggle. "Too late," the voice said. "Go
back to sleep."

Miss Harper did. She slept uncomfortably and awkwardly,
her mouth a little open. Sometime, perhaps an hour later, her
head was jostled again and the voice said, "I think I'm going
to get off here. 'By now."

"You'll be sorry," Miss Harper said, asleep. "Go back."

Then, still later, the bus driver was shaking her. "Look,
lady," he was saying, "I'm not an alarm clock. Wake up and
get off the bus."

"What?" Miss Harper stirred, opened her eyes, felt for her
pocketbook.

"I'm not an alarm clock," the driver said. His voice was
harsh and tired. "I'm not an alarm clock. Get off the bus."

"What?" said Miss Harper again.

"This is as far as you go. You got a ticket to here. You've
arrived. And I am not an alarm clock waking up people to tell
them when it's time to get off; you got here, lady, and it's not
part of my job to carry you off the bus. I'm not—"

"I intend to report you," Miss Harper said, awake. She felt
for her pocketbook and found it in her lap, moved her feet,
straightened her hat. She was stiff and moving was difficult.

"Report me. But from somewhere else. I got a bus to run.
Now will you please get off so I can go on my way?"

His voice was loud, and Miss Harper was sickeningly aware
of faces turned toward her from along the bus, grins, amused
comments. The driver turned and stamped off down the bus
to his seat, saying, "She thinks I'm an alarm clock," and Miss
Harper, without assistance and moving clumsily, took down
her suitcase and struggled with it down the aisle. Her suitcase

banged against seats, and she knew that people were staring at her; she was terribly afraid that she might stumble and fall.

"I'll certainly report you," she said to the driver, who shrugged.

"Come on, lady," he said. "It's the middle of the night and I got a bus to run."

"You ought to be *ashamed* of yourself," Miss Harper said wildly, wanting to cry.

"Lady," the driver said with elaborate patience, "please get off my bus."

The door was open, and Miss Harper eased herself and her suitcase onto the steep step. "She thinks everyone's an alarm clock, got to see she gets off the bus," the driver said behind her, and Miss Harper stepped onto the ground. Suitcase, pocketbook, gloves, hat; she had them all. She had barely taken stock when the bus started with a jerk, almost throwing her backward, and Miss Harper, for the first time in her life, wanted to run and shake her fist at someone. I'll report him, she thought, I'll see that he loses his job, and then she realized that she was in the wrong place.

Standing quite still in the rain and the darkness Miss Harper became aware that she was not at the bus corner of her town where the bus should have left her. She was on an empty crossroads in the rain. There were no stores, no lights, no taxis, no people. There was nothing, in fact, but a wet dirt road under her feet and a signpost where two roads came together. Don't panic, Miss Harper told herself, almost whispering, don't panic; it's all right, it's all right, you'll see that it's all right, don't be frightened.

She took a few steps in the direction the bus had gone, but it was out of sight and when Miss Harper called falteringly, "Come back," and, "Help," there was no answer to the shocking sound of her own voice out loud except the steady drive of the rain. I sound old, she thought, but I will not panic. She turned in a circle, her suitcase in her hand, and told herself, don't panic, it's all right.

There was no shelter in sight, but the signpost said RICKET'S LANDING; so that's where I am, Miss Harper thought, I've come to Ricket's Landing and I don't like it here. She set her suitcase down next to the signpost and tried to see down the road; perhaps there might be a house, or even some kind of a barn or shed where she could get out of the rain. She was crying a little, and lost and hopeless, saying Please, won't someone come? when she saw headlights far off down the road and realized that someone was really coming to help her. She ran to the middle of the road and stood waving, her gloves wet and her pocketbook draggled. "Here," she called, "here I am, please come and help me."

Through the sound of the rain she could hear the motor, and then the headlights caught her and, suddenly embarrassed, she put her pocketbook in front of her face while the lights were on her. The lights belonged to a small truck, and it came to an abrupt stop beside her and the window near her was rolled down and a man's voice said furiously, "You want to get killed? You trying to get killed or something? What you doing in the middle of the road, trying to get killed?" The young man turned and spoke to the driver. "It's some dame. Running out in the road like that."

"Please," Miss Harper said, as he seemed almost about to close the window again, "please help me. The bus put me off here when it wasn't my stop and I'm lost."

"Lost?" The young man laughed richly. "First I ever heard anyone getting lost in Ricket's Landing. Mostly they have trouble *finding* it." He laughed again, and the driver, leaning forward over the steering wheel to look curiously at Miss Harper, laughed too. Miss Harper put on a willing smile, and said, "Can you take me somewhere? Perhaps a bus station?"

"No bus station." The young man shook his head profoundly. "Bus comes through here every night, stops if he's got any passengers."

"Well," Miss Harper's voice rose in spite of herself; she was suddenly afraid of antagonizing these young men; perhaps they might even leave her here where they found her, in the wet and dark. "Please," she said, "can I get in with you, out of the rain?"

The two young men looked at each other. "Take her down to the old lady's," one of them said.

"She's pretty wet to get in the truck," the other one said.

"Please," Miss Harper said, "I'll be glad to pay you what I can."

"We'll take you to the old lady," the driver said. "Come on, move over," he said to the other young man.

"Wait, my suitcase." Miss Harper ran back to the signpost, no longer caring how she must look, stumbling about in the rain, and brought her suitcase over to the truck.

"That's awful wet," the young man said. He opened the door and took the suitcase from Miss Harper. "I'll just throw it in the back," he said, and turned and tossed the suitcase into the back of the truck; Miss Harper heard the sodden thud of its landing, and wondered what things would look like when she unpacked; my bottle of cologne, she thought despairingly. "Get *in*," the young man said, and, "My God, you're wet."

Miss Harper had never climbed up into a truck before, and her skirt was tight and her gloves slippery from the rain. Without help from the young man she put one knee on the high step and somehow hoisted herself in; this cannot be happening to me, she thought clearly. The young man pulled away fastidiously as Miss Harper slid onto the seat next to him.

"You are pretty wet," the driver said, leaning over the wheel to look around at Miss Harper. "Why were you out in the rain like that?"

"The bus driver." Miss Harper began to peel off her gloves; somehow she had to make an attempt to dry herself. "He told me it was my stop."

"That would be Johnny Talbot," the driver said to the other young man. "He drives that bus."

"Well, I'm going to report him," Miss Harper said. There was a little silence in the truck, and then the driver said, "Johnny's a good guy. He means all right."

"He's a bad bus driver," Miss Harper said sharply.

The truck did not move. "You don't want to report old Johnny," the driver said.

"I most certainly—" Miss Harper began, and then stopped. Where am I? she thought, what is happening to me? "No," she said at last, "I won't report old Johnny."

The driver started the truck, and they moved slowly down the road, through the mud and the rain. The windshield wipers swept back and forth hypnotically, there was a narrow line of light ahead from their headlights, and Miss Harper thought, what is happening to me? She stirred, and the young man next to her caught his breath irritably and drew back. "She's soaking wet," he said to the driver. "I'm wet already."

"We're going down to the old lady's," the driver said. "She'll know what to do."

"What old lady?" Miss Harper did not dare to move, even turn her head. "Is there any kind of a bus station? Or even a taxi?"

"You could," the driver said consideringly, "you could wait and catch that same bus tomorrow night when it goes through. Johnny'll be driving her."

"I just want to get home as soon as possible," Miss Harper said. The truck seat was dreadfully uncomfortable, she felt steamy and sticky and chilled through, and home seemed so far away that perhaps it did not exist at all.

"Just down the road a mile or so," the driver said reassuringly.

"I've never heard of Ricket's Landing," Miss Harper said. "I can't imagine how he came to put me off there."

"Maybe somebody else was supposed to get off there and he thought it was you by mistake." This deduction seemed to tax the young man's mind to the utmost, because he said, "See, someone else might of been supposed to get off instead of you."

"Then *he's* still on the bus," said the driver, and they were both silent, appalled.

Ahead of them a light flickered, showing dimly through the rain, and the driver pointed and said, "There, that's where we're going." As they came closer Miss Harper was aware of a growing dismay. The light belonged to what seemed to be a roadhouse, and Miss Harper had never been inside a roadhouse in her life. The house itself was only a dim shape looming in the darkness, and the light, over the side door, illuminated only a sign, hanging crooked, which read BEER *Bar & Grill*.

"Is there anywhere else I could go?" Miss Harper asked

timidly, clutching her pocketbook. "I'm not at all sure, you know, that I ought—"

"Not many people here tonight," the driver said, turning the truck into the driveway and pulling up in the parking lot which had once, Miss Harper was sad to see, been a garden. "Rain, probably."

Peering through the window and the rain, Miss Harper felt, suddenly, a warm stir of recognition, of welcome; it's the house, she thought, why, of course, the house is lovely. It had clearly been an old mansion once, solidly and handsomely built, with the balance and style that belonged to a good house of an older time. "Why?" Miss Harper asked, wanting to know why such a good house should have a light tacked on over the side door, and a sign hanging crooked but saying BEER *Bar & Grill;* "Why?" asked Miss Harper, but the driver said, "This is where you wanted to go. Get her suitcase," he told the other young man.

"In here?" asked Miss Harper, feeling a kind of indignation on behalf of the fine old house, "into this saloon?" Why, I used to live in a house like this, she thought, what are they doing to our old houses?

The driver laughed. "You'll be safe," he said.

Carrying her suitcase and her pocketbook Miss Harper followed the two young men to the lighted door and passed under the crooked sign. Shameful, she thought, they haven't even bothered to take care of the place; it needs paint and tightening all around and probably a new roof, and then the driver said, "Come on, come on," and pushed open the heavy door.

"I used to live in a house like this," Miss Harper said, and the young men laughed.

"I bet you did," one of them said, and Miss Harper stopped in the doorway, staring, and realized how strange she must have sounded. Where there had certainly once been comfortable rooms, high-ceilinged and square, with tall doors and polished floors, there was now one large dirty room, with a counter running along one side and half a dozen battered tables; there was a jukebox in a corner and torn linoleum on the floor. "Oh, no," Miss Harper said. The room smelled unpleasant, and the rain slapped against the bare windows.

Sitting around the tables and standing around the jukebox were perhaps a dozen young people, resembling the two who had brought Miss Harper here, all looking oddly alike, all talking and laughing flatly. Miss Harper leaned back against the door; for a minute she thought they were laughing about her. She was wet and disheartened and these noisy people did not belong at all in the old house. Then the driver turned and gestured to her. "Come and meet the old lady," he said, and then, to the room at large, "Look, we brought company."

"Please," Miss Harper said, but no one had given her more than a glance. With her suitcase and her pocketbook she followed the two young men across to the counter; her suitcase bumped against her legs and she thought, I must not fall down.

"Belle, Belle," the driver said, "look at the stray cat we found."

An enormous woman swung around in her seat at the end of the counter, and looked at Miss Harper; looking up and down, looking at the suitcase and Miss Harper's wet hat and wet shoes, looking at Miss Harper's pocketbook and gloves squeezed in her hand, the woman seemed hardly to move her eyes; it was almost as though she absorbed Miss Harper without any particular effort. "Hell you say," the woman said at last. Her voice was surprisingly soft. "Hell you say."

"She's wet," the second young man said; the two young men stood one on either side of Miss Harper, presenting her, and the enormous woman looked her up and down. "Please," Miss Harper said; here was a woman at least, someone who might understand and sympathize, "please, they put me off my bus at the wrong stop and I can't seem to find my way home. Please."

"Hell you say," the woman said, and laughed, a gentle laugh. "She sure is wet," she said.

"Please," Miss Harper said.

"You'll take care of her?" the driver asked. He turned and smiled down at Miss Harper, obviously waiting, and, remembering, Miss Harper fumbled in her pocketbook for her wallet. How much, she was wondering, not wanting to ask, it was

SHIRLEY JACKSON

such a short ride, but if they hadn't come I might have gotten
pneumonia, and paid all those doctor's bills; I have caught
cold, she thought with great clarity, and chose two five-dollar
bills from her wallet. They can't argue over five dollars each,
she thought, and sneezed. The two young men and the large
woman were watching her with great interest, and all of them
saw that after Miss Harper took out the two five-dollar bills
there were a single and two tens left in the wallet. The money
was not wet. I suppose I should be grateful for that, Miss
Harper thought, moving slowly. She handed a five-dollar bill
to each young man and felt that they glanced at one another
over her head.

"Thanks," the driver said; I could have gotten away with a
dollar each, Miss Harper thought. "Thanks," the driver said
again, and the other young man said, "Say, thanks."

"Thank *you*," Miss Harper said formally.

"I'll put you up for the night," the woman said. "You can
sleep here. Go tomorrow." She looked Miss Harper up and
down again. "Dry off a little," she said.

"Is there anywhere else?" Then, afraid that this might seem
ungracious, Miss Harper said, "I mean, is there any way of
going on tonight? I don't want to impose."

"We got rooms for rent." The woman half turned back to
the counter. "Cost you ten for the night."

She's leaving me bus fare home, Miss Harper thought; I suppose I should be grateful. "I'd better, I guess," she said, taking
out her wallet again. "I mean, thank you."

The woman accepted the bill and half turned back to the
counter. "Upstairs," she said. "Take your choice. No one's
around." She glanced sideways at Miss Harper. "I'll see you
get a cup of coffee in the morning. I wouldn't turn a dog out
without a cup of coffee."

"Thank you." Miss Harper knew where the staircase would
be, and she turned and, carrying her suitcase and her pocketbook, went to what had once been the front hall and there was
the staircase, so lovely in its still proportions that she caught
her breath. She turned back and saw the large woman staring
at her, and said, "I used to live in a house like this. Built about

the same time, I guess. One of those good old houses that were made to stand forever, and where people—"

"Hell you say," the woman said, and turned back to the counter.

The young people scattered around the big room were talking; in one corner a group surrounded the two who had brought Miss Harper and now and then they laughed. Miss Harper was touched with a little sadness now, looking at them, so at home in the big ugly room which had once been so beautiful. It would be nice, she thought, to speak to these young people, perhaps even become their friend, talk and laugh with them; perhaps they might like to know that this spot where they came together had been a lady's drawing room. Hesitating a little, Miss Harper wondered if she might call "Good night," or "Thank you" again, or even "God bless you all." Then, since no one looked at her, she started up the stairs. Halfway there was a landing with a stained-glass window, and Miss Harper stopped, holding her breath. When she had been a child the stained-glass window on the stair landing in her house had caught the sunlight, and scattered it on the stairs in a hundred colors. Fairyland colors, Miss Harper thought, remembering; I wonder why we don't live in these houses now. I'm lonely, Miss Harper thought, and then she thought, but I must get out of these wet clothes; I really am catching cold.

Without thinking she turned at the top of the stairs and went to the front room on the left; that had always been her room. The door was open and she glanced in; this was clearly a bedroom for rent, and it was ugly and drab and cheap. The light turned on with a cord hanging beside the door, and Miss Harper stood in the doorway, saddened by the peeling wallpaper and the sagging floor; what have they done to the house, she thought; how can I sleep here tonight?

At last she moved to cross the room and set her suitcase on the bed. I must get dry, she told herself, I must make the best of things. The bed was correctly placed, between the two front windows, but the mattress was stiff and lumpy, and Miss Harper was frightened at the faint smell of dark couplings and a remote echo in the springs; I will not think about such things, Miss Harper thought, I will not let myself dwell on any such thing; this might be the room where I slept as a girl. The windows were almost right—two across the front, two at the side—and the door was placed correctly; how they did build these old places to a square-cut pattern, Miss Harper thought, how they did put them together; there must be a thousand houses all over the country built exactly like this. The closet, however, was on the wrong side. Some oddness of construction had set the closet to Miss Harper's right as she sat on the bed, when it ought really to have been on her left; when she was a girl the big closet had been her playhouse and her hiding place, but it had been on the left.

The bathroom was wrong, too, but that was less important. Miss Harper had thought wistfully of a hot tub before she slept, but a glance at the bathtub discouraged her; she could simply wait until she got home. She washed her face and hands, and the warm water comforted her. She was further comforted to find that her bottle of cologne had not broken in her suitcase and that nothing inside had gotten wet. At least she could sleep in a dry nightgown, although in a cold bed.

She shivered once in the cold sheets, remembering a child's bed. She lay in the darkness with her eyes open, wondering at last where she was and how she had gotten here: first the bus and then the truck, and now she lay in the darkness and no one knew where she was or what was to become of her. She had only her suitcase and a little money in her pocketbook; she did not know where she was. She was very tired and she thought that perhaps the sleeping pill she had taken much earlier had still not quite worn off; perhaps the sleeping pill had been affecting all her actions, since she had been following docilely, bemused, wherever she was taken; in the morning, she told herself sleepily, I'll show them I can make decisions for myself.

The noise downstairs which had been a jukebox and adolescent laughter faded softly into a distant melody; my mother is singing in the drawing room, Miss Harper thought, and the company is sitting on the stiff little chairs listening; my father is playing the piano. She could not quite distinguish the song, but it was one she had heard her mother sing many times; I could creep out to the top of the stairs and listen, she thought, and then became aware that there was a rustling in the closet, but the closet was on the wrong side, on the right instead of the left. It is more a rattling than rustling, Miss Harper thought, wanting to listen to her mother singing, it is as though something wooden were being shaken around. Shall I get out of bed and quiet it so I can hear the singing? Am I too warm and comfortable, am I too sleepy?

The closet was on the wrong side, but the rattling continued, just loud enough to be irritating, and at last, knowing she would never sleep until it stopped, Miss Harper swung her legs over the side of the bed and, sleepily, padded barefoot over to the closet door, reminding herself to go to the right instead of the left.

"What are you doing in there?" she asked aloud, and opened the door. There was just enough light for her to see that it was a wooden snake, head lifted, stirring and rattling itself against the other toys. Miss Harper laughed. "It's my snake," she said aloud, "it's my old snake, and it's come alive." In the back of the closet she could see her old toy clown, bright and cheerful, and as she watched, enchanted, the toy clown flopped languidly forward and back, coming alive. At Miss Harper's feet the snake moved blindly, clattering against a doll house where the tiny people inside stirred, and against a set of blocks, which fell and crashed. Then Miss Harper saw the big beautiful doll sitting on a small chair, the doll with long golden curls and wide-lashed blue eyes and a stiff organdy party dress; as Miss Harper held out her hands in joy the doll opened her eyes and stood up.

"Rosabelle," Miss Harper cried out, "Rosabelle, it's me."

The doll turned, looking widely at her, smile painted on. The red lips opened and the doll quacked, outrageously, a flat slapping voice coming out of that fair mouth. "Go away, old lady," the doll said, "go away, old lady, go away."

Miss Harper backed away, staring. The clown tumbled and danced, mouthing at Miss Harper, the snake flung its eyeless head viciously at her ankles, and the doll turned, holding her skirts, and her mouth opened and shut. "Go away," she quacked, "go away, old lady, go away."

The inside of the closet was all alive; a small doll ran madly from side to side, the animals paraded solemnly down the gangplank of Noah's ark, a stuffed bear wheezed asthmatically. The noise was louder and louder, and then Miss Harper realized that they were all looking at her hatefully and moving toward her. The doll said "Old lady, old lady," and stepped forward; Miss Harper slammed the closet door and leaned against it. Behind her the snake crashed against the door and the doll's voice went on and on. Crying out, Miss Harper turned and fled, but the closet was on the wrong side and she turned the wrong way and found herself cowering against the far wall with the door impossibly far away while the closet door slowly opened and the doll's face, smiling, looked for her.

Miss Harper fled. Without stopping to look behind she flung herself across the room and through the door, down the hall and on down the wide lovely stairway. "Mommy," she screamed, "Mommy, Mommy."

Screaming, she fled out the door. "Mommy," she cried, and fell, going down and down into darkness, turning, trying to catch onto something solid and real, crying.

"Look, lady," the bus driver said. "I'm not an alarm clock. Wake up and get off the bus."

"You'll be sorry," Miss Harper said distinctly.

"Wake up," he said, "wake up and get off the bus."

"I intend to report you," Miss Harper said. Pocketbook, gloves, hat, suitcase.

"I'll certainly report you," she said, almost crying.

"This is as far as you go," the driver said.

The bus lurched, moved, and Miss Harper almost stumbled in the driving rain, her suitcase at her feet, under the sign reading RICKET'S LANDING.

[1965]

THREE LECTURES,
WITH TWO STORIES

EXPERIENCE AND FICTION

It is most agreeable to be a writer of fiction for several reasons—one of the most important being, of course, that you can persuade people that it is really work if you look haggard enough—but perhaps the most useful thing about being a writer of fiction is that nothing is ever wasted; all experience is good for something; you tend to see everything as a potential structure of words. One of my daughters made this abruptly clear to me when she came not long ago into the kitchen where I was trying to get the door of our terrible old refrigerator open; it always stuck when the weather was wet, and one of the delights of a cold rainy day was opening the refrigerator door. My daughter watched me wrestling with it for a minute and then she said that I was foolish to bang on the refrigerator door like that; why not use magic to open it? I thought about this. I poured myself another cup of coffee and lighted a cigarette and sat down for a while and thought about it; and then decided that she was right. I left the refrigerator where it was and went in to my typewriter and wrote a story about not being able to open the refrigerator door and getting the children to open it with magic. When a magazine bought the story I bought a new refrigerator. That is what I would like to talk about now—the practical application of magic, or where do stories come from?

People are always asking me—and every other writer I know—where story ideas come from. Where *do* you get your ideas, they ask; how do you ever manage to think them up? It's certainly the hardest question in the world to answer, since stories originate in everyday happenings and emotions, and any writer who tried to answer such a question would find himself telling over, in some detail, the story of his life. Fiction uses so many small items, so many little gestures and remembered incidents and unforgettable faces, that trying to isolate any one inspiration for any one story is incredibly difficult, but basically, of course, the genesis of any fictional work has to be human experience. This translation of experience into fiction is not a mystic one. It is, I think, part recognition and part analysis. A bald description of an incident is hardly fiction, but the same incident, carefully taken apart, examined as to emotional and balanced structure, and then as carefully reassembled in the most effective form, slanted and polished and weighed, may very well be a short story. Let me try an example.

I have lifted this from a story written several years ago by a college student I knew; it has always stayed in my mind as the most perfect nonstory I ever read. This is how the plot goes: In a small town the people are having a church fair, the high point of which is the raffling off of a particularly beautiful quilt made by one of the local ladies; the quilt has been the talk of the town for weeks, and the admiration and envy of all the women; all of them want it badly. The raffle is held, and the quilt is won by a summer visitor, a wealthy woman who has no use for the quilt and no desire for it. She sends her chauffeur over to the platform to pick up the quilt and bring it back to her car.

Now, this story written straight, as I just read it, is almost meaningless. It is a simple anecdote, and carries only the statement that the women in the small town resent the summer visitor, and dislike having her win the quilt; its only actual impact is the ironic point that the quilt should have been won by the only woman attending the raffle who really did not want it. Now, suppose this were taken apart and reassembled. We would then have to examine more particularly four or five people most concerned—the summer visitor, the chauffeur, the woman who made the quilt, the minister who raffled it off, and perhaps the one village woman—I believe there always *is* one—who was most open and loud in her disapproval; as things stand now, these people have no faces, only parts to play. Suppose we were to give them personalities, sketch in people, lightly at first, experimentally; suppose the summer visitor is actually a shy, friendly person who very much wants to be liked, and thinks that accepting the quilt will endear her to the villagers; suppose she is foolish enough to try to give the quilt back again afterward? Suppose the minister had intended this church fair as an attempt to make peace among the quarreling women in the village, and now sees their quarrels ended when they unite in hatred of the outsider? Then consider the chauffeur; as the story stands now he has the most agonizing two or three minutes of all—the walk from the car, through the people of the village, to the platform to take up the quilt and carry it back; if the chauffeur came from a small town himself, and knew what such people were like, how would he feel during those few minutes? Suppose the chauffeur were a boy from that town, hired for the summer to drive the wealthy visitor's car? And, beyond all else, how do the *men* in the village feel at the feuding over the quilt?

If the story is going to be a short one, it is of course only necessary to focus on one of these characters—I like the chauffeur, myself—and follow this character from beginning to end; in a short story the time would of course be limited to the actual moments of the raffle, with the background sketched in through conversation and small incidents—the way the village women look at the fancy car, perhaps, or the minister's nervousness when he comes to draw the number; the point of the story might be indicated early, telegraphed, as it were, if the story opened with the summer visitor buying a cake at one of the stands, while the village women watch her and make their private comments; I keep calling them "village women," by the way; I do not mean by that that they are primitive, or uneducated, or unsophisticated; I think of them only as a tightly knit group, interested in their own concerns, and as resentful of outsiders as any of us.

If it were going to be a longer story, these people would be examined in more detail, and there would have to be more incidents, all paralleling the final one, the characters would have to be more firmly drawn, and the scene of the fair made

more vivid as a background. The longer story might open with
the village ladies decorating the fair grounds in the morning,
with their bickering and arguing over whose booth was going
to have the best location, and the woman who made the quilt
would have to be there, set in with a definite character—
perhaps they all hate her, but will defend her and her quilt
because the summer visitor is the outsider?

It is almost silly to say that no one will read a story which
does not interest him. Yet many writers forget it. They write a
story which interests *them*, forgetting that the particular emotional investment they brought to the incident had never been
communicated to the reader because, writing the story, they
wrote down only what happened and not what was felt. In our
story of the quilt, the girl who orginally wrote it had been, as
a daughter of the woman who made the quilt, very much
involved in both the excitement and the indignation, but there
was nothing of that in the story. She only wrote down what
happened when an outsider won a quilt at a church fair. She
said she didn't want the story to be autobiographical, and so
she had kept herself entirely out of it. She had kept herself out
of it so successfully, in fact, that the story was hopelessly dull;
it had nothing in it except its one small ironic point; the rest of
the story was waste, and padding. The village ladies were
named Mrs. Smith and Mrs. Jones and it was not possible to
tell one from another. Even the minister merged into the general flat landscape, recognizable only by his name. She pointed
out that these were real people, and if she described them any
more clearly they might read the story and be offended. And
she couldn't change any of it because that was the way it had
really *happened*. What was the purpose, she thought, of
changing the events when this ironic little incident *had* really
happened, she had been there and seen it, and had always
wanted, she said, to write it down because it seemed just perfect material for a story.

Now there are three elements here, three mistaken concep-
tions, which would keep this anecdote from ever turning into
a story. I think it cannot be too firmly emphasized that in the
writing of any kind of fiction no scene and no character can be

allowed to wander off by itself; there must be some furthering of the story in every sentence, and even the most fleeting background characters must partake of the story in some way; they must be characters peculiar to *this* story and no other. A boy who climbs an apple tree to watch the raffling off of the quilt only wastes time and attention if that is *all* he does; the reader's mind is taken away from the story while he watches that boy climb the tree directly over the visitor's fancy car, and amuses himself by dropping green apples down onto the roof of the car and snickering, he is still a background character but he has added to the story by reinforcing the village attitude toward the outsider. The reader has, presumably, seen small boys climb apple trees before, but this boy exists nowhere else in the world than in this story and this village, and it must be made clear that that is where he belongs.

The second point I want to emphasize is that people in stories are called characters because that is what they are. They are not real people. It is, of course, possible to choose a character and describe him so completely that the reader sees him as a whole personality, rounded and recognizable. The only trouble with that is that it takes several thousand pages of solid description, including a lot of very dull reading. Most of us have enough trouble understanding ourselves and our families and friends without wanting to know *everything* about a fictional character. A person in a story is identified through small things—little gestures, turns of speech, automatic reactions; suppose one of the women in our quilt story is excessively and foolishly modest; suppose that when someone praises her cakes she answers that they're really not very good, actually; she made *much* better cakes for the church fair last year; she just wishes that no one would even *taste* a piece of this year's cake, because it's really not any good at all; or if someone else remarks on how delicate her embroidery is, she will say that it's really nowhere near as good as everyone else's, and she could do much better if she had more time, although of *course* nothing she ever made could *begin* to be as good as Mrs. Smith's, although of course if she had as much time to spend doing embroidery as Mrs. Smith she might be able to do

even *half* as well. That woman is identified for the reader per-
manently. If the reader comes to a conversation later, and he
reads the remark: "Oh, it's not really anything good at *all*;
anyone could have done better, really; I just get embarrassed if
anyone even *looks* at my poor work"—he knows at once who
is talking. It is not necessary to describe the woman any further; everyone has heard people who talk like that, and any
reader will know at once exactly what she is like. Any minor
character may be spotlighted in the background in this manner, and major characters will of course take on new depths of
personality by being so clearly identified; suppose the minister
in our story has a nervous or tired gesture that he makes over
and over without thinking—suppose he covers his eyes wearily with his hand when he is worried—a small gesture like
that will do more to describe him than a biography.

Further, let me stop briefly to quarrel with the statement
that this event cannot be improved upon because that is the
way it really happened. The only way to turn something that
really happened into something that happens on paper is to
attack it in the beginning the way a puppy attacks an old shoe.
Shake it, snarl at it, sneak up on it from various angles. Perhaps the simple little incident you are dying to turn into fiction
may carry a wholly new punch if you wrote it upside down or
inside out or starting at the end; many stories that just won't
work out as straightforward accounts go smoothly and neatly
if you start from the end; I mean, tell the ending first and then
let the story unfold, giving the explanations which make the
story plausible. In our quilt story, of course, the entire setup
would fall apart if we tried writing it from the end—unless the
end is really the girl who wrote the story in the first place, and
would not put in real people because she was one of them. See
what happens to the story then; it becomes a story about con-
flicting loyalties, the story of a girl who loves her home town
and yet, having left it behind, finds also in herself a certain
sympathy with the outsider, the wistful woman who does not
belong anywhere. If we do what I call turning the story inside
out, we can abandon the church fair and the raffle temporarily, give the summer visitor two small children, put the two

small children on the outskirts of the crowd—say down by the brook, playing with some of the village children, and let their amiable play stand in the foreground against the raffle in the background, contrasting the children playing with the suspicion and hatred building up among the grownups. Or suppose we want to turn the story outside in—how about making the summer visitor a fairly stupid woman, who is determined to win the quilt, and puts through some highhanded maneuvering to make sure she wins it? By changing the emphasis and angle on this little plot we can make it say almost anything we like. There is certainly no need to worry about whether any of this is true, or actually happened; it is as true as you make it. The important thing is that it be true in the story, and actually happen *there*.

I can, in the last analysis, talk only about my own work; it is not that I am so entirely vain, but because there is really one writer I know well enough to say these things about; I would not dare discuss intimately anyone else. So I would like to show you a little of how my own fiction comes directly from experience.

I have recently finished a novel about a haunted house. I was [working] on a novel about a haunted house because I happened by chance, to read a book about a group of people, nineteenth-century psychic researchers, who rented a haunted house and recorded their impressions of the things they saw and heard and felt in order to contribute a learned paper to the Society for Psychic Research. They thought that they were being terribly scientific and proving all kinds of things, and yet the story that kept coming through their dry reports was not at all the story of a haunted house, it was the story of several earnest, I believe misguided, certainly determined people, with their differing motivations and backgrounds. I found it so exciting that I wanted more than anything else to set up my own haunted house, and put my own people in it, and see what *I* could make happen. As so often happens, the minute I started thinking about ghosts and haunted houses, all kinds of things turned up to enforce my intentions, or perhaps I was thinking so entirely about my new book that everything I saw turned to it; I can't say, although I *can* say that I could do without some of the manifestations I have met. The first thing that happened was in New York City; we—my husband and I—were on the train which stops briefly at the 125th Street station, and just outside the station, dim and horrible in the dusk, I saw a building so disagreeable that I could not stop looking at it; it was tall and black and as I looked at it when the train began to move again it faded away and disappeared. That night in our hotel room I woke up with nightmares, the kind where you have to get up and turn on the light and walk around for a few minutes just to make sure that there is a real world and this one is it, not the one you have been dreaming about; my nightmares had somehow settled around the building I had seen from the train. From that time on I completely ruined my whole vacation in New York City by dreading the moment when we would have to take the train back and pass that building again. Let me just point out right here and now that my unconscious mind has *been* unconscious for a number of years now and it is my firm intention to keep it that way. When I have nightmares about a horrid building it is the horrid building I am having nightmares about, and no one is going to talk me out of it; that is final. Anyway, my nervousness was so extreme, finally, that we changed our plans and took a night train home, so that I would not be able to see the building when we went past, but even after we were home it bothered me still, coloring all my recollections of a pleasant visit to the city, and at last I wrote to a friend at Columbia University and asked him to locate the building and find out, if he could, why it looked so terrifying. When we got his answer I had one important item for my book. He wrote that he had had trouble finding the building, since it only existed from that one particular point of the 125th Street station; from any other angle it was not recognizable as a building at all. Some seven months before it had been almost entirely burned in a disastrous fire which killed nine people. What was left of the building, from the other three sides, was a shell. The children in the neighborhood knew that it was haunted.

I do not think that the Society for Psychic Research would accept me as a qualified observer; I think, in fact, that they would bounce me right out the door, but it seemed clear to me that what I had felt about that horrid building was an excellent beginning for learning how people feel when they encounter the supernatural. I have always been interested in witchcraft and superstition, but have never had much traffic with ghosts, so I began asking people everywhere what they thought about such things, and I began to find out that there was one common factor—most people have never seen a ghost, and never want or expect to, but almost everyone will admit that some-times they have a sneaking feeling that they just possibly *could* meet a ghost if they weren't careful—if they were to turn a corner too suddenly, perhaps, or open their eyes too soon when they wake up at night, or go into a dark room without hesitating first. . . .

Well, as I say, fiction comes from experience. I had not the remotest desire to see a ghost. I was absolutely willing to go on the rest of my life without ever seeing even the slightest super-natural manifestation. I wanted to write a book about ghosts, but I was perfectly prepared—I cannot emphasize this too strongly—I was perfectly prepared to keep those ghosts wholly imaginary. I was already doing a lot of splendid research read-ing all the books about ghosts I could get hold of, and particu-larly true ghost stories—so much so that it became necessary for me to read a chapter of *Little Women* every night before I turned out the light—and at the same time I was collecting pictures of houses, particularly odd houses, to see what I could find to make into a suitable haunted house. I read books of architecture and clipped pictures out of magazines and news-papers and learned about cornices and secret stairways and valances and turrets and flying buttresses and gargoyles and all kinds of things that people have done to inoffensive houses, and then I came across a picture in a magazine which really looked right. It was the picture of a house which reminded me vividly of the hideous building in New York; it had the same air of disease and decay, and if ever a house looked like a can-didate for a ghost, it was this one. All that I had to identify it was the name of a California town, so I wrote to my mother, who has lived in California all her life, and sent her the picture, asking if she had any idea where I could get information about this ugly house. She wrote back in some surprise. Yes, she knew about the house, although she had not supposed that there were any pictures of it still around. My great-grandfather built it. It had stood empty and deserted for some years before it finally caught fire, and it was generally believed that that was because the people of the town got together one night and burned it down.

By then it was abundantly clear to me that I had no choice; the ghosts were after me. In case I *had* any doubts, however, I came downstairs a few mornings later and found a sheet of copy paper moved to the center of my desk, set neatly away from the general clutter. On the sheet of paper was written DEAD DEAD in my own handwriting. I am accustomed to making notes for books, but not in my sleep; I decided that I had better write the book awake, which I got to work and did.

It is much easier, I find, to write a story than to cope competently with the millions of daily trials and irritations that turn up in an ordinary house, and it helps a good deal—particularly with children around—if you can see them through a flattering veil of fiction. It has always been a comfort to me to make stories out of things that happen, things like moving, and kittens, and Christmas concerts at the grade school, and broken bicycles; it is easier, as Sally said, to magic the refrigerator than it is to wrench at the door. And it is certainly easier to sit there taking notes while everyone else is running around packing the suitcases and giving last-minute instructions to the moving men. I remember that once the income-tax people were making one of their spot checks in our locality, and, to our intense dismay, one of the spots they decided to check was us. Nothing can protect you at a time like that; no matter how conscientious you have been about your income tax, guilt overwhelms you when that man walks in. He was only at our house for about an hour, and all the time he was in the study with my husband, studying canceled checks and mortgage receipts, and I could hear my husband yelling "Depreciation,

depreciation," I was in the dining room with my typewriter, defending myself. I had started to compose an impassioned letter to the United States Government about unjustifiable tyranny over honest law-abiding citizens, but I could not resist a few words of description of the way our family had received the news that the man was coming, and by the time the conference in the study was over I was well along in a story about a quietly lunatic tax investigation—and guess who was going to be the villain. When the income-tax man was ready to leave he came through the dining room with my husband and stopped to say, oh yes; he gathered that I was a writer. Say, he went on, he had often wondered—where did writing people get the ideas for the stuff they wrote? Huh? He picked up one page of my manuscript and I barely got it away from him in time. I really don't know what would have happened to our tax returns if he had read it.

I would like, if I may, to finish with a story which is the most direct translation of experience into fiction that I have ever done. For one thing, I had a high fever the whole time I was writing it. For another thing, I was interrupted constantly with requests to take upstairs trays of orange juice or chicken soup or aspirin or ginger ale or dry sheets or boxes of crayons. For another thing, while I was writing it, my husband was lying on the couch with a hot-water bottle saying that writing stories was all very well, but suppose he died right then and there—was there anyone to care? I may even have whined a little myself, carrying trays and getting hotter hot-water bottles and telling everyone that they were just pretty lucky that they had me at least, to wait on them and take care of them in spite of the fact that I was every bit as sick as they were, and only the purest spirit of self-sacrifice kept me going at all, and they should be grateful. Actually, my husband and two of our children had the grippe, and I was only just catching it; only the fact that I had to finish the story kept me from abandoning them and going someplace quiet to lie down. We had only three children then, by the way—we didn't know when we were well off—and the one referred to variously as Sally, or Baby, is now of an age to read, and repudiate, an accurate accounting of her own behavior. The story was published as "The Night We All Had Grippe," and I got a letter about it from a lady in Indiana. I would like to make a little extra money writing, she wrote to me in this letter. Tell me, where do you get ideas for stories? I can never make up anything good.

[1958]

THE NIGHT WE ALL
HAD GRIPPE

We are all of us, in our family, very fond of puzzles. I do Double-Crostics and read mystery stories, my husband does baseball box scores and figures out batting averages, our son Laurie is addicted to the kind of puzzle which begins, "There are fifty-four items in this picture beginning with the letter C," our older daughter Jannie does children's jigsaws, and Sally, the baby, can put together an intricate little arrangement of rings and bars which has had the rest of us stopped for two months. We are none of us, however, capable of solving the puzzles we work up for ourselves in the oddly diffuse patterns of our several lives (who is, now I think of it?); and along with such family brain-teasers as, "Why is there a pair of roller skates in Mommy's desk?" and, "What is *really* in the back of Laurie's closet?" and, "Why doesn't Daddy wear the nice shirts Jannie picked out for Father's Day?" we are all of us still wondering nervously about what might be called The Great Grippe Mystery. As a matter of fact, I should be extremely grateful if anyone could solve it for us, because we are certainly very short of blankets, and it's annoying not to have *any* kind of answer. Here, in rough outline, is our puzzle:

Our house is large, and the second floor has four bedrooms and a bathroom, all opening out onto a long narrow hall which we have made even narrower by lining it with bookcases so that every inch of hall which is not doorway is books. As is the case with most houses, both the front door and the back door are downstairs on the first floor. The front bedroom, which is my husband's and mine, is the largest and lightest, and has a double bed. The room next down the hall belongs to the girls, and contains a crib and a single, short bed. Laurie's room, across the hall, has a double-decker bed and he sleeps on the top half. The guest room, at the end of the hall, has a double bed. The double bed in our room is made up with white sheets and cases, the baby's crib has pink linen, and Jannie's bed has yellow. Laurie's bed has green linen and the guest room has blue. The bottom half of Laurie's bed is never made up, unless company is going to use it immediately, because the dog, whose name is Toby, traditionally spends a large part of his time there and regards it as his bed. There is no bed table on the distaff side of the double bed in our room. One side of the bed in the guest room is pushed against the wall. No one can fit into the baby's crib except the baby; the ladder to the top half of Laurie's double-decker is very shaky and stands in a corner of the room; the children reach the top half of the bed by climbing up over the footboard. All three of the children are accustomed to having a glass of apple juice, to which they are addicted, by their bedsides at night. My husband invariably keeps a glass of water by *his* bedside. Laurie uses a green glass, Jannie uses a red glass, the baby uses one of those little flowered cheese glasses, and my husband uses a tin glass because he has broken so many ordinary glasses trying to find them in the dark.

I do not take cough drops or cough medicine in any form.

The baby customarily sleeps with half a dozen cloth books, an armless doll, and a small cardboard suitcase which holds the remnants of half a dozen decks of cards. Jannie is very partial to a pink baby blanket, which has shrunk from many washings. The girls' room is very warm, the guest room moderately so; our room is chilly, and Laurie's room is quite cold. We are all of us, including the dog, notoriously easy and heavy sleepers; my husband never eats coffeecake.

My husband caught the grippe first, on a Friday, and snarled and shivered and complained until I prevailed upon him to go to bed. By Friday night both Laurie and the baby were feverish, and on Saturday Jannie and I began to cough and sniffle. In our family we take ill in different manners; my husband is extremely annoyed at the whole procedure, and is convinced that his being sick is somebody else's fault, Laurie tends to become a little lightheaded and strew handkerchiefs around his room, Jannie coughs and coughs and coughs, the baby turns bright red, and I suffer in stoical silence, so long as everyone knows clearly that I am sick. We are each of us privately convinced that our own ailment is far more severe than anyone else's. At any rate, on Saturday night I put all the children into their beds, gave each of them half an aspirin and the usual fruit juice, covered them warmly, and then settled my husband down for the night with his glass of water and his cigarettes and matches and ash tray; he had decided to sleep in the guest room because it was warmer. At about ten o'clock I checked to see that all the children were covered and asleep and that Toby was in his place on the bottom half of the double-decker. I then took two sleeping pills and went to sleep in my own bed in my own room. Because my husband was in the guest room I slept on his side of the bed, next to the bed table. I put my cigarettes and matches on the end table next to the ash tray, along with a small glass of brandy, which I find more efficacious than cough medicine.

I woke up some time later to find Jannie standing beside the bed. "Can't sleep," she said. "Want to come in *your* bed."

"Come along," I said. "Bring your own pillow."

She went and got her pillow and her small pink blanket and her glass of fruit juice, which she put on the floor next to the bed, since she had gotten the side without any end table. She put her pillow down, rolled herself in her pink blanket, and fell asleep. I went back to sleep, but some time later the baby came in, asking sleepily, "Where's Jannie?"

"She's here," I said. "Are you coming in bed with us?"

"Yes," said the baby.

"Go and get your pillow, then," I said. She returned with her pillow, her books, her doll, her suitcase, and her fruit juice, which she put on the floor next to Jannie's. Then she crowded in comfortably next to Jannie and fell asleep. Eventually the pressure of the two of them began to force me uneasily toward the edge of the bed, so I rolled out wearily, took my pillow and my small glass of brandy and my cigarettes and matches and my ash tray and went into the guest room, where my husband was asleep. I pushed at him and he snarled, but finally moved over to the side next to the wall, and I put my cigarettes and matches and my brandy and my ash tray on the end table next to *his* cigarettes and matches and ash tray and tin glass of water and put my pillow on the bed and fell asleep. Shortly after this he woke me and asked me to let him get out of the bed, since it was too hot in that room to sleep and he was going back to his own bed.

He took his pillow and his cigarettes and matches and his ash tray and his tin glass of water and went padding off down the hall. In a few minutes Laurie came into the guest room where I had just fallen asleep again; he was carrying his pillow and his glass of fruit juice. "Too cold in my room," he said, and I moved out of the way and let him get into the bed on the side next to the wall. After a few minutes the dog came in, whining nervously, and came up onto the bed and curled himself up around Laurie, and I had to get out or be smothered. I gathered together what of my possessions I could, and made my way into my own room, where my husband was asleep with Jannie on one side and the baby on the other. Jannie woke up when I came in and said, "Own bed," so I helped her carry her pillow and her fruit juice and her pink blanket back to her own bed.

The minute Jannie got out of our bed the baby rolled over and turned sideways, so there was no room for me. I could not get into the crib and I could not climb into the top half of the double-decker so since the dog was in the guest room I went and took the blanket off the crib and got into the bottom half of the double-decker, setting my brandy and my cigarettes and matches and my ash tray on the floor next to the bed. Shortly after that Jannie, who apparently felt left out, came in with her pillow and her pink blanket and her fruit juice and got up into the top half of the double-decker, leaving her fruit juice on the floor next to my brandy.

At about six in the morning the dog wanted to get out, or else he wanted his bed back, because he came and stood next to me and howled. I got up and went downstairs, sneezing, and let him out, and then decided that since it had been so cold anyway in the bottom half of the double-decker I might as well stay downstairs and heat up some coffee and have that much warmth, at least. While I was waiting for the coffee to heat, Jannie came to the top of the stairs and asked if I would bring *her* something hot, and I heard Laurie stirring in the guest room, so I heated some milk and put it into a jug and decided that while I was at it I might just as well give everybody something hot, so I set out enough cups for everyone and brought out a coffeecake and put it on the tray and added some onion rolls for my husband, who does not eat coffeecake. When I brought the tray upstairs Laurie and Jannie were both in the guest room, giggling, so I put the tray down in there and heard Baby waking from our room in the front. I went to get her and she was sitting up in the bed talking to her father, who was only very slightly awake. "Play card?" she was asking brightly, and she opened her suitcase and dealt him onto the pillow next to his nose four diamonds to the ace jack and the seven of clubs.

I asked my husband if he would like some coffee and he said it was terribly cold. I suggested that he come down into the guest room, where it was warmer. He and the baby followed me down to the guest room and my husband and Laurie got into the bed and the rest of us sat on the foot of the bed and I poured the coffee and the hot milk and gave the children coffeecake and my husband the onion rolls. Jannie decided to take her milk and coffeecake back into her own bed and since she had mislaid her pillow she took one from the guest room bed. Baby of course followed her, going first back into our room to pick up *her* pillow. My husband fell asleep again while I was pouring his coffee, and Laurie set his hot milk precariously on the headboard of the bed and asked me to get his pillow from wherever it was, so I went into the double-decker and got him the pillow from the top, which turned out to be Jannie's, and her pink blanket was with it.

I took my coffeecake and my coffee into my own bed and had just settled down when Laurie came in to say cloudily that Daddy had kicked him out of bed and could he stay in here? I said of course and he said he would get a pillow and he came back in a minute with the one from the bottom half of the double-decker, which was mine. He went to sleep right away, and then the baby came in to get her books and her suitcase and decided to stay with her milk and her coffeecake so I left and went into the guest room and made my husband move over and sat *there* and had my coffee. Meanwhile Jannie had moved into the top half of the double-decker, looking for her pillow, and had taken instead the pillow from baby's bed and my glass of brandy and had settled down there to listen to Laurie's radio. I went downstairs to let the dog in and he came upstairs and got into his bed on the bottom half of the double-decker and while I was gone my husband had moved back over onto the accessible side of the guest-room bed so I went into Jannie's bed, which is rather too short, and I brought a pillow from the guest room, and my coffee.

At about nine o'clock the Sunday papers came and I went down to get them, and at about nine-thirty everyone woke up. My husband had moved back into his own bed when Laurie and Baby vacated it for their own beds, Laurie driving Jannie into the guest room when he took back the top half of the double-decker, and my husband woke up at nine-thirty and found himself wrapped in Jannie's pink blanket, sleeping on Laurie's green pillow and with a piece of coffeecake and Baby's fruit-juice glass, not to mention the four diamonds to the ace jack and the seven of clubs. Laurie in the top half of the double-decker had my glass of brandy and my cigarettes and matches and the baby's pink pillow. The dog had my white pillow and my ash tray. Jannie in the guest room had one white pillow and one blue pillow and two glasses of fruit juice and my husband's cigarettes and matches and ash tray and Laurie's hot milk, besides her own hot milk and coffeecake and her father's onion rolls. The baby in her crib had her father's tin glass of water and her suitcase and books and doll and a blue pillow from the guest room, but no blanket.

The puzzle, is, of course, what became of the blanket from Baby's bed? I took it off her crib and put it on the bottom half of the double-decker, but the dog did not have it when he woke up, and neither did any of the other beds. It was a blue-patterned patchwork blanket, and has not been seen since, and I would most particularly like to know where it got to. As I say, we are very short of blankets.

[1952]

BIOGRAPHY OF A STORY

On the morning of June 28, 1948, I walked down to the post office in our little Vermont town to pick up the mail. I was quite casual about it, as I recall—I opened the box, took out a couple of bills and a letter or two, talked to the postmaster for a few minutes, and left, never supposing that it was the last time for months that I was to pick up the mail without an active feeling of panic. By the next week I had had to change my mailbox to the largest one in the post office, and casual conversation with the postmaster was out of the question, because he wasn't speaking to me. June 28, 1948 was the day *The New Yorker* came out with a story of mine in it. It was not my first published story, nor my last, but I have been assured over and over that if it had been the only story I ever wrote or published, there would be people who would not forget my name.

I had written the story three weeks before, on a bright June morning when summer seemed to have come at last, with blue skies and warm sun and no heavenly signs to warn me that my morning's work was anything but just another story. The idea had come to me while I was pushing my daughter up the hill in her stroller—it was, as I say, a warm morning, and the hill was steep, and beside my daughter the stroller held the day's groceries—and perhaps the effort of that last fifty yards up the hill put an edge to the story; at any rate, I had the idea fairly clearly in my mind when I put my daughter in her playpen and the frozen vegetables in the refrigerator, and, writing the story, I found that it went quickly and easily, moving from beginning to end without pause. As a matter of fact, when I read it over later I decided that except for one or two minor corrections, it needed no changes, and the story I finally typed up and sent off to my agent the next day was almost word for word the original draft. This, as any writer of stories can tell you, is not a usual thing. All I know is that when I came to read the story over I felt strongly that I didn't want to fuss with it. I didn't think it was perfect, but I didn't want to fuss with it. It was, I thought, a serious, straightforward story, and I was pleased and a little surprised at the ease with which it had been written; I was reasonably proud of it, and hoped that my agent would sell it to some magazine and I would have the gratification of seeing it in print.

My agent did not care for the story, but—as she said in her note at the time—her job was to sell it, not to like it. She sent it at once to *The New Yorker*, and about a week after the story had been written I received a telephone call from the fiction editor of *The New Yorker*; it was quite clear that he did not really care for the story, either, but *The New Yorker* was going to buy it. He asked for one change—that the date mentioned in the story be changed to coincide with the date of the issue of the magazine in which the story would appear, and I said of course. He then asked, hesitantly, if I had any particular interpretation of my own for the story; Mr. Harold Ross, then the editor of *The New Yorker*, was not altogether sure that he understood the story, and wondered if I cared to enlarge upon its meaning. I said no. Mr. Ross, he said, thought that the story might be puzzling to some people, and in case anyone telephoned the magazine, as sometimes happened, or wrote in asking about the story, was there anything in particular I wanted them to say? No, I said, nothing in particular; it was just a story I wrote.

I had no more preparation than that. I went on picking up the mail every morning, pushing my daughter up and down the hill in her stroller, anticipating pleasurably the check from *The New Yorker*, and shopping for groceries. The weather stayed nice and it looked as though it was going to be a good summer. Then, on June 28, *The New Yorker* came out with my story.

Things began mildly enough with a note from a friend at *The New Yorker*: "Your story has kicked up quite a fuss around the office," he wrote. I was flattered; it's nice to think that your friends notice what you write. Later that day there was a call from one of the magazine's editors; they had had a couple of people phone in about my story, he said, and was there anything I particularly wanted him to say if there were any more calls? No, I said, nothing particular; anything he chose to say was perfectly all right with me; it was just a story.

I was further puzzled by a cryptic note from another friend: "Heard a man talking about a story of yours on the bus this morning," she wrote. "Very exciting. I wanted to tell him I knew the author, but after I heard what he was saying I decided I'd better not."

One of the most terrifying aspects of publishing stories and books is the realization that they are going to be read, and read by strangers. I had never fully realized this before, although I had of course in my imagination dwelt lovingly upon the thought of the millions and millions of people who were going to be uplifted and enriched and delighted by the stories I wrote. It had simply never occurred to me that these millions and millions of people might be so far from being uplifted that they would sit down and write me letters I was downright scared to open; of the three-hundred-odd letters that I received that summer I can count only thirteen that spoke kindly to me, and they were mostly from friends. Even my mother scolded me: "Dad and I did not care at all for your story in *The New Yorker*," she wrote sternly; "it does seem, dear, that this gloomy kind of story is what all you young people think about these days. Why don't you write something to cheer people up?"

By mid-July I had begun to perceive that I was very lucky indeed to be safely in Vermont, where no one in our small town had ever heard of *The New Yorker*, much less read my story. Millions of people, and my mother, had taken a pronounced dislike to me.

The magazine kept no track of telephone calls, but all letters addressed to me care of the magazine were forwarded directly

to me for answering, and all letters addressed to the magazine—
some of them addressed to Harold Ross personally; these were
the most vehement—were answered at the magazine and then
the letters were sent me in great batches, along with carbons of
the answers written at the magazine. I have all the letters still,
and if they could be considered to give any accurate cross section
of the reading public, or the reading public of *The New Yorker*,
or even the reading public of one issue of *The New Yorker*, I
would stop writing now.

Judging from these letters, people who read stories are gullible, rude, frequently illiterate, and horribly afraid of being
laughed at. Many of the writers were positive that *The New
Yorker* was going to ridicule them in print, and the most cau-
tious letters were headed, in capital letters: NOT FOR PUBLICA-
TION or PLEASE DO NOT PRINT THIS LETTER, or, at best, THIS
LETTER MAY BE PUBLISHED AT YOUR USUAL RATES OF PAY-
MENT. Anonymous letters, of which there were a few, were
destroyed. *The New Yorker* never published any comment of
any kind about the story in the magazine, but did issue one
publicity release saying that the story had received more mail
than any piece of fiction they had ever published; this was
after the newspapers had gotten into the act, in midsummer,
with a front-page story in the San Francisco *Chronicle* begging to know what the story meant, and a series of columns in
New York and Chicago papers pointing out that *New Yorker*
subscriptions were being canceled right and left.

Curiously, there are three main themes which dominate
the letters of that first summer—three themes which might
be identified as bewilderment, speculation, and plain old-
fashioned abuse. In the years since then, during which the story
has been anthologized, dramatized, televised, and even—in one
completely mystifying transformation—made into a ballet, the
tenor of letters I receive has changed. I am addressed more
politely, as a rule, and the letters largely confine themselves to
questions like what does this story mean? The general tone of
the early letters, however, was a kind of wide-eyed, shocked
innocence. People at first were not so much concerned with
what the story meant; what they wanted to know was where

these lotteries were held, and whether they could go there and watch. Listen to these quotations:

(Kansas)   Will you please tell me the locale and the year of the custom?

(Oregon)   Where in heaven's name does there exist such barbarity as described in the story?

(New York)   Do such tribunal rituals still exist and if so where?

(New York)   To a reader who has only a fleeting knowledge of traditional rites in various parts of the country (I presume the plot was laid in the United States) I found the cruelty of the ceremony outrageous, if not unbelievable. It may be just a custom or ritual which I am not familiar with.

(New York)   Would you please explain whether such improbable rituals occur in our Middle Western states, and what their origin and purpose are?

(Nevada)   Although we recognize the story to be fiction is it possible that it is based on fact?

(Maryland)   Please let me know if the custom of which you wrote actually exists.

(New York)   To satisfy my curiousity would you please tell me if such rites are still practiced and if so where?

(California)   If it is based on fact would you please tell me the date and place of its origin?

(Texas)   What I would like to know, if you don't mind enlightening me, is in what part of the United States this organized, apparently legal lynching is practiced? Could it be that in New England or in equally enlightened regions, mass sadism is still part and parcel of the ordinary citizen's life?

(Georgia)   I'm hoping you'll find time to give me further details about the bizarre custom the story describes, where it occurs, who practices it, and why.

(Brooklyn, N.Y.)   I am interested in learning if there is any particular source or group of sources of fact or legend on which and from which the story is based? This story has caused me to be particularly disturbed by my lack of knowledge of such rites or lotteries in the United States.

(California)   If it actually occurred, it should be documented.

(New York)   We have not read about it in *In Fact*.

(New York)   Is it based on reality? Do these practices still continue in back-country England, the human sacrifice for the rich harvest? It's a frightening thought.

(Ohio)   I think your story is based on fact. Am I right? As a psychiatrist I am fascinated by the psychodynamic possibilities suggested by this anachronistic ritual.

(Mississippi)   You seem to describe a custom of which I am totally ignorant.

(California)   It seems like I remember reading somewhere a long time ago that that was the custom in a certain part of France some time ago. However I have never heard of it being practiced here in the United States. However would you please inform me where you got your information and whether or not anything of this nature has been perpetrated in modern times?

(Pennsylvania)   Are you describing a current custom?

(New York)   Is there some timeless community existing in New England where human sacrifices are made for the fertility of the crops?

(Boston)   Apparently this tale involves an English custom or tradition of which we in this country know nothing.

(Canada)   Can the lottery be some barbaric event, a hangover from the Middle Ages perhaps, which is still carried on in the States? In what part of the country does it take place?

(Los Angeles)   I have read of some queer cults in my time, but this one bothers me.

(Texas)   Was this group of people perhaps a settlement descended from early English colonists? And were they continuing a Druid rite to assure good crops?

(Quebec)   Is this a custom which is carried on somewhere in America?

(A London psychologist)   I have received requests for elucidation from English friends and patients. They would like to know if the barbarity of stoning still exists in the U.S.A. and in general what the tale is all about and where does the action take place.

(Oregon)   Is there a witchcraft hangover somewhere in these United States that we Far Westerners have missed?

(Madras, India)   We have been wondering whether the story was based on fact and if so whether the custom described therein of selecting one family by lot jointly to be stoned by the remainder of the villagers still persists anywhere in the United States. *The New Yorker* is read here in our United States information library and while we have had no inquiries about this particular article as yet, it is possible we shall have and I would be glad to be in a position to answer them.

(England)   I am sorry that I cannot find out the state in which this piece of annual propitiatory sacrifice takes place. Now I just frankly don't believe that even in the United States such things happen—at least not without being sponsored by Lynching Inc. or the All-American Morticians Group or some such high-powered organization. I was once offered a baby by a primitive tribe in the center of Laos (Indochina) which my interpreter (Chinese) informed me I had to kill so that my blood lust was satiated and I would leave the rest of the tribe alone. But NOT in the United States, PLEASE.

(Connecticut)   Other strange old things happen in the Appalachian mountain villages, I'm told.

As I say, if I thought this was a valid cross section of the reading public, I would give up writing. During this time, when I was carrying home some ten or twelve letters a day, and receiving a weekly package from *The New Yorker*, I got one letter which troubled me a good deal. It was from California, short, pleasant, and very informal. The man who wrote it clearly expected that I would recognize his name and his reputation, which I didn't. I puzzled over this letter for a day or two before I answered it, because of course it is always irritating to be on the edge of recognizing a name and have it escape you. I was pretty sure that it was someone who had written a book I had read or a book whose review I had read or a story in a recent magazine or possibly even—since I come originally from California—someone with whom I had gone to high school. Finally, since I had to answer the letter, I decided that something carefully complimentary and noncommittal would be best. One day, after I had mailed him my letter, some friends also from California stopped in and asked—as everyone was asking then—what new letters had come. I showed them the letter from my mysterious not-quite-remembered correspondent. Good heavens, they said, was this really a letter from *him*? Tell me who he is, I said desperately, just tell me who he is. Why, how could anyone forget? It had been all over the California papers for weeks, and in the New York papers, too; he had just been barely acquitted of murdering his wife with an ax. With a kind of awful realization creeping over me I went and looked up the carbon of the letter I had written him, my noncommittal letter. "Thank you very much for your kind letter about my story," I had written. "I admire *your* work, too."

The second major theme which dominates the letters is what I call speculation. These letters were from the people who sat down and figured out a meaning for the story, or a reason for writing it, and wrote in proudly to explain, or else wrote in to explain why they could not possibly believe the story had any meaning at all.

(New Jersey) Surely it is only a bad dream the author had?

(New York) Was it meant to be taken seriously?

(New York) Was the sole purpose just to give the reader a nasty impact?

(California) The main idea which has been evolved is that the author has tried to challenge the logic of our society's releasing its aggressions through the channel of minority prejudice by presenting an equally logical (or possibility more logical) method of selecting a scapegoat. The complete horror of the cold-blooded method of choosing a victim parallels our own culture's devices for handling deep-seated hostilities.

(Virginia) I would list my questions about the story but it would be like trying to talk in an unknown language so far as I am concerned. The only thing that occurs to me is that perhaps

the author meant we should not be too hard on our presidential
nominees.

(Connecticut)   Is *The New Yorker* only maintaining further its
policy of intellectual leg-pulling?

(New York)   Is it a publicity stunt?

(New Orleans)   I wish Mrs. Hutchinson had been queen for a
day or something nice like that before they stoned the poor frightened creature.

(New York)   Anyone who seeks to communicate with the public should be at least lucid.

(New Jersey)   Please tell me if the feeling I have of having dreamed it once is just part of the hypnotic effect of the
story.

(Massachusetts)   I earnestly grabbed my young nephew's ency-
clopedia and searched under "stoning" or "punishment" for some
key to the mystery; to no avail.

(California)   Is it just a story? Why was it published? Is it a para-
ble? Have you received other letters asking for some explanation?

(Illinois)   If it is simply a fictitious example of man's innate cruelty, it isn't a very good one. Man, stupid and cruel as he is, has
always had sense enough to imagine or invent a charge against
the objects of his persecution: the Christian martyrs, the New
England witches, the Jews and Negroes. But nobody had anything against Mrs. Hutchinson, and they only wanted to get
through quickly so they could go home for lunch.

(California)   Is it an allegory?

(California)   Please tell us it was all in fun.

(Los Angeles *Daily News*)   Was Tessie a witch? No, witches
weren't selected by lottery. Anyway, these are present-day people. Is it the post-atomic age, in which there is insufficient food
to sustain the population and one person is eliminated each
year? Hardly. Is it just an old custom, difficult to break? Probably. But there is also the uncomfortable feeling that maybe the
story wasn't supposed to make sense. The magazines have been
straining in this direction for some time and *The New Yorker*,
which we like very much, seems to have made it.

(Missouri)   In this story you show the perversion of democracy.

(California)   It seems obscure.

(California)   I caught myself dreaming about what I would do if my wife and I were in such a predicament. I think I would back out.

(Illinois)   A symbol of how village gossip destroys a victim?

(Puerto Rico)   You people print any story you get, just throwing the last paragraph into the wastebasket before it appears in the magazine.

(New York)   Were you saying that people will accept any evil as long as it doesn't touch them personally?

(Massachusetts)   I am approaching middle age; has senility set in at this rather early age, or is it that I am not so acute mentally as I have had reason to assume?

(Canada)   My only comment is what the hell?

(Maine)   I suppose that about once every so often a magazine may decide to print something that hasn't any point just to get people talking.

(California)   I don't know how there could be any confusion in anyone's mind as to what you were saying; nothing could possibly be clearer.

(Switzerland)   What does it mean? Does it hide some subtle allegory?

(Indiana)   What happened to the paragraph that tells what the devil is going on?

(California)   I missed something here. Perhaps there was some facet of the victim's character which made her unpopular with the other villagers. I expected the people to evince a feeling of dread and terror, or else sadistic pleasure, but perhaps they were laconic, unemotional New Englanders.

(Ohio)   A friend darkly suspects you people of having turned a bright editorial red, and that is how he construed the story. Please give me something to go on when I next try to placate my friend, who is now certain that you are tools of Stalin. If you *are* subversive, for goodness sake I don't blame you for not wanting to discuss the matter and of course you have every constitutional right in back of you. But at least please explain that damned story.

(Venezuela)   I have read the story twice and from what I can gather all a man gets for his winnings are rocks in his head, which seems rather futile.

(Virginia)   The printers left out three lines of type somewhere.
(Missouri)   You printed it. Now give with the explanations.
(New York)   To several of us there seemed to be a rather sinister symbolism in the cruelty of the people.
(Indiana)   When I first read the story in my issue, I felt that there was no moral significance present, that the story was just terrifying, and that was all. However, there has to be a reason why it is so alarming to so many people. I feel that the only solution, the only reason it bothered so many people is that it shows the power of society over the individual. We saw the ease with which society can crush any single one of us. At the same time, we saw that society need have no rational reason for crushing the one, or the few, or sometimes the many.
(Connecticut)   I thought that it might have been a small-scale representation of the sort of thing involved in the lottery which started the functioning of the selective-service system at the start of the last war.

Far and away the most emphatic letter writers were those who took this opportunity of indulging themselves in good old-fashioned name-calling. Since I am making no attempt whatsoever to interpret the motives of my correspondents, and would not if I could, I will not try now to say what I think of people who write nasty letters to other people who just write stories. I will only read some of their comments.

(Canada)   Tell Miss Jackson to stay out of Canada.
(New York)   I expect a personal apology from the author.
(Massachusetts)   I think I had better switch to the *Saturday Evening Post*.
(Massachusetts)   I will never buy *The New Yorker* again. I resent being tricked into reading perverted stories like "The Lottery."
(Connecticut)   Who is Shirley Jackson? Cannot decide whether she is a genius or a female and more subtle version of Orson Welles.
(New York)   We are fairly well educated and sophisticated people, but we feel that we have lost all faith in the truth of literature.

(Minnesota)   Never in the world did I think I'd protest a story in *The New Yorker*, but really, gentlemen, "The Lottery" seems to me to be in incredibly bad taste. I read it while soaking in the tub and was tempted to put my head under water and end it all.

(California; this from a world-famous anthropologist)   If the author's intent was to symbolize into complete mystification and at the same time be gratuitously disagreeable, she certainly succeeded.

(Georgia)   Couldn't the story have been a trifle esoteric, even for *The New Yorker* circulation?

(California)   "The Lottery" interested some of us and made the rest plain mad.

(Michigan)   It certainly is modern.

(California)   I am glad that your magazine does not have the popular and foreign-language circulation of the *Reader's Digest*. Such a story might make German, Russian, and Japanese realists feel lily-white in comparison with the American. The old saying about washing dirty linen in public has gone out of fashion with us. At any rate this story has reconciled me to not receiving your magazine next year.

(Illinois)   Even to be polite I can't say that I liked "The Lottery."

(Missouri)   When the author sent in this story, she undoubtedly included some explanation of place or some evidence that such a situation could exist. Then isn't the reader entitled to some such evidence? Otherwise the reader has a right to indict you as editor of willfully misrepresenting the human race. Perhaps you as editor are proud of publishing a story that reached a new low in human viciousness. The burden of proof is up to you when your own preoccupation with evil leads you into such evil ways. A few more such stories and you will alienate your most devoted readers, in which class I—until now—have been included.

(New Hampshire)   It was with great disappointment that I read the story "The Lottery." Stories such as this belong to *Esquire*, etc., but most assuredly not to *The New Yorker*.

(Massachusetts)   The ending of this story came as quite a jolt to my wife and, as a matter of fact, she was very upset by the whole thing for a day or two after.

(New York) I read the story quite thoroughly and confess that I could make neither head nor tail out of it. The story was so horrible and gruesome in its effect that I could hardly see the point of your publishing it.

Now, a complete letter, from Illinois.

EDITOR:

Never has it been my lot to read so cunningly vicious a story as that published in your last issue for June. I tremble to think of the fate of American letters if that piece indicated the taste of the editors of a magazine I had considered distinguished. It has made me wonder what you had in mind when accepting it for publication. Certainly not the entertainment of the reader and if not entertainment, what? The strokes of genius were of course apparent in the story mentioned, but of a perverted genius whose efforts achieved a terrible malformation. You have betrayed a trust with your readers by giving them such a bestial selection. Unaware, the reader was led into a casual tale of the village folk, becoming conscious only gradually of the rising tension, till the shock of the unwholesome conclusion, skillful though it was wrought, left him with total disgust for the story and with disillusionment in the magazine publishing it.

I speak of my own reaction. If that is not the reaction of the majority of your readers I miss my guess. Ethics and uplift are apparently not in your repertoire, nor are they expected, but as editors it is your responsibility to have a sounder and saner criterion for stories than the one which passed on "The Lottery."

Heretofore mine has been almost a stockholder's pride in *The New Yorker*. I shared my copy with my friends as I do the other possessions which I most enjoy. When your latest issue arrived, my new distaste kept me from removing the brown paper wrapping, and into the wastebasket it went. Since I can't conceive that I'll develop interest in it again, save the results of your efforts that indignity every week and cancel my subscription immediately.

Another letter, this one from Indiana.

SIR:

Thanks for letting us take a look at the nauseating and
fiction-less bit of print which appeared in a recent issue. I gather
that we read the literal translation.

The process of moving set us back a few weeks, but unfortu-
nately your magazine and Miss Jackson's consistently correct
spelling and punctuation caught up with us.

We are pleased to think that perhaps her story recalled happier days for you; days when you were able to hurl flat skipping
stones at your aged grandmother. Not for any particular reason,
of course, but because the village postmaster good-naturedly
placed them in your hands, or because your chubby fingers felt
good as they gripped the stone.

Our quarrel is not with Miss Jackson's amazingly clear style
or reportorial observation. It is not with the strong motives
exhibited by the native stone-throwers, or with the undertones
and overtones which apparently we missed along the way.

It is simply that we read the piece before and not after supper. We are hammering together a few paragraphs on running the head of our kindly neighbor through the electric
eggbeater, and will mail same when we have untangled her top-
piece. This should give your many readers a low chuckle or at
least provide the sophisticates with an inner glow. Also it might
interest you to know that my wife and I are gathering up the
smoothest, roundest stones in our yard and piling them up on
the corner in small, neat pyramids. We're sentimentalists
that way.

I have frequently wondered if this last letter is a practical joke;
it is certainly not impossible, although I hope not, because it is
quite my favorite letter of all "Lottery" correspondence. It was
mailed to *The New Yorker*, from Los Angeles, of course, and
written in pencil, on a sheet of lined paper torn from a pad;
the spelling is atrocious.

DEAR SIR:

The June 26 copy of your magazine fell into my hands in the Los Angeles railroad station yesterday. Although I donnot read your magazine very often I took this copy home to my folks and they had to agree with me that you speak straitforward to your readers.

My Aunt Ellise before she became priestess of the Exalted Rollers used to tell us a story just like "The Lottery" by Shirley Jackson. I don't know if Miss Jackson is a member of the Exhalted Rollers but with her round stones sure ought to be. There is a few points in her prophecy on which Aunt Ellise and me don't agree.

The Exalted Rollers donnot believe in the ballot box but believe that the true gospel of the redeeming light will become accepted by all when the prophecy comes true. It does seem likely to me that our sins will bring us punishment though a great scouraging war with the devil's toy (the atomic bomb). I don't think we will have to sacrifice humin beings fore atonement.

Our brothers feel that Miss Jackson is a true prophet and disciple of the true gospel of the redeeming light. When will the next revelations be published?

Yours in the spirit.

Of all the questions ever asked me about "Lottery," I feel that there is only one which I can answer fearlessly and honestly, and that is the question which closes this gentleman's letter. When will the next revelations be published, he wants to know, and I answer roundly, never. I am out of the lottery business for good.

[1960]

THE LOTTERY

The morning of June 27th was clear and sunny, with the fresh warmth of a full-summer day; the flowers were blossoming profusely and the grass was richly green. The people of the village began to gather in the square, between the post office and the bank, around ten o'clock; in some towns there were so many people that the lottery took two days and had to be started on June 26th, but in this village, where there were only about three hundred people, the whole lottery took less than two hours, so it could begin at ten o'clock in the morning and still be through in time to allow the villagers to get home for noon dinner.

The children assembled first, of course. School was recently over for the summer, and the feeling of liberty sat uneasily on most of them; they tended to gather together quietly for a while before they broke into boisterous play, and their talk was still of the classroom and the teacher, of books and reprimands. Bobby Martin had already stuffed his pockets full of stones, and the other boys soon followed his example, selecting the smoothest and roundest stones; Bobby and Harry Jones and Dickie Delacroix—the villagers pronounced this name "Dellacroy"—eventually made a great pile of stones in one corner of the square and guarded it against the raids of the other boys. The girls stood aside, talking among themselves, looking over their shoulders at the boys, and the very small children rolled in the dust or clung to the hands of their older brothers or sisters.

Soon the men began to gather, surveying their own children, speaking of planting and rain, tractors and taxes. They

stood together, away from the pile of stones in the corner, and
their jokes were quiet and they smiled rather than laughed.
The women, wearing faded house dresses and sweaters, came
shortly after their menfolk. They greeted one another and
exchanged bits of gossip as they went to join their husbands.
Soon the women, standing by their husbands, began to call to
their children, and the children came reluctantly, having to be
called four or five times. Bobby Martin ducked under his
mother's grasping hand and ran, laughing, back to the pile of
stones. His father spoke up sharply, and Bobby came quickly
and took his place between his father and his oldest brother.

The lottery was conducted—as were the square dances, the
teen-age club, the Halloween program—by Mr. Summers,
who had time and energy to devote to civic activities. He was
a round-faced, jovial man and he ran the coal business, and
people were sorry for him, because he had no children and his
wife was a scold. When he arrived in the square, carrying the
black wooden box, there was a murmur of conversation among
the villagers, and he waved and called, "Little late today,
folks." The postmaster, Mr. Graves, followed him, carrying a
three-legged stool, and the stool was put in the center of the
square and Mr. Summers set the black box down on it. The
villagers kept their distance, leaving a space between themselves
and the stool, and when Mr. Summers said, "Some of you fellows want to give me a hand?" there was a hesitation before
two men, Mr. Martin and his oldest son, Baxter, came forward
to hold the box steady on the stool while Mr. Summers stirred
up the papers inside it.

The original paraphernalia for the lottery had been lost long
ago, and the black box now resting on the stool had been put
into use even before Old Man Warner, the oldest man in town,
was born. Mr. Summers spoke frequently to the villagers about
making a new box, but no one liked to upset even as much tradition as was represented by the black box. There was a story
that the present box had been made with some pieces of the
box that had preceded it, the one that had been constructed
when the first people settled down to make a village here.
Every year, after the lottery, Mr. Summers began talking again

about a new box, but every year the subject was allowed to fade off without anything's being done. The black box grew shabbier each year; by now it was no longer completely black but splintered badly along one side to show the original wood color, and in some places faded or stained.

Mr. Martin and his oldest son, Baxter, held the black box securely on the stool until Mr. Summers had stirred the papers thoroughly with his hand. Because so much of the ritual had been forgotten or discarded, Mr. Summers had been successful in having slips of paper substituted for the chips of wood that had been used for generations. Chips of wood, Mr. Summers had argued, had been all very well when the village was tiny, but now that the population was more than three hundred and likely to keep on growing, it was necessary to use something that would fit more easily into the black box. The night before the lottery, Mr. Summers and Mr. Graves made up the slips of paper and put them in the box, and it was then taken to the safe of Mr. Summers's coal company and locked up until Mr. Summers was ready to take it to the square next morning. The rest of the year, the box was put away, sometimes one place, sometimes another; it had spent one year in Mr. Graves's barn and another year underfoot in the post office, and sometimes it was set on a shelf in the Martin grocery and left there.

There was a great deal of fussing to be done before Mr. Summers declared the lottery open. There were the lists to make up—of heads of families, heads of households in each family, members of each household in each family. There was the proper swearing-in of Mr. Summers by the postmaster, as the official of the lottery; at one time, some people remembered, there had been a recital of some sort, performed by the official of the lottery, a perfunctory, tuneless chant that had been rattled off duly each year; some people believed that the official of the lottery used to stand just so when he said or sang it, others believed that he was supposed to walk among the people, but years and years ago this part of the ritual had been allowed to lapse. There had been, also, a ritual salute, which the official of the lottery had had to use in addressing each person who came up to draw from the box, but this also had changed with time, until now it was felt necessary only for the official to speak to each person approaching. Mr. Summers was very good at all this; in his clean white shirt and blue jeans, with one hand resting carelessly on the black box, he seemed very proper and important as he talked interminably to Mr. Graves and the Martins.

Just as Mr. Summers finally left off talking and turned to the assembled villagers, Mrs. Hutchinson came hurriedly along the path to the square, her sweater thrown over her shoulders, and slid into place in the back of the crowd. "Clean forgot what day it was," she said to Mrs. Delacroix, who stood next to her, and they both laughed softly. "Thought my old man was out back stacking wood," Mrs. Hutchinson went on, "and then I looked out the window and the kids was gone, and then I remembered it was the twenty-seventh and came a-running." She dried her hands on her apron, and Mrs. Delacroix said "You're in time, though. They're still talking away up there."

Mrs. Hutchinson craned her neck to see through the crowd and found her husband and children standing near the front. She tapped Mrs. Delacroix on the arm as a farewell and began to make her way through the crowd. The people separated good-humoredly to let her through; two or three people said, in voices just loud enough to be heard across the crowd, "Here comes your Missus, Hutchinson," and "Bill, she made it after all." Mrs. Hutchinson reached her husband, and Mr. Summers, who had been waiting, said cheerfully, "Thought we were going to have to get on without you, Tessie." Mrs. Hutchinson said, grinning, "Wouldn't have me leave m'dishes in the sink, now, would you, Joe?" and soft laughter ran through the crowd as the people stirred back into position after Mrs. Hutchinson's arrival.

"Well, now," Mr. Summers said soberly, "guess we better get started, get this over with, so's we can go back to work. Anybody ain't here?"

"Dunbar," several people said. "Dunbar, Dunbar."

Mr. Summers consulted his list. "Clyde Dunbar," he said.

"That's right. He's broke his leg, hasn't he? Who's drawing for him?"

"Me, I guess," a woman said, and Mr. Summers turned to look at her. "Wife draws for her husband," Mr. Summers said. "Don't you have a grown boy to do it for you, Janey?" Although Mr. Summers and everyone else in the village knew the answer perfectly well, it was the business of the official of the lottery to ask such questions formally. Mr. Summers waited with an expression of polite interest while Mrs. Dunbar answered.

"Horace's not but sixteen yet," Mrs. Dunbar said regretfully. "Guess I gotta fill in for the old man this year."

"Right," Mr. Summers said. He made a note on the list he was holding. Then he asked, "Watson boy drawing this year?"

A tall boy in the crowd raised his hand. "Here," he said. "I'm drawing for m'mother and me." He blinked his eyes nervously and ducked his head as several voices in the crowd said things like "Good fellow, Jack," and "Glad to see your mother's got a man to do it."

"Well," Mr. Summers said, "guess that's everyone. Old Man Warner make it?"

"Here," a voice said, and Mr. Summers nodded.

A sudden hush fell on the crowd as Mr. Summers cleared his throat and looked at the list. "All ready?" he called. "Now, I'll read the names—heads of families first—and the men come up and take a paper out of the box. Keep the paper folded in your hand without looking at it until everyone has had a turn. Everything clear?"

The people had done it so many times that they only half listened to the directions; most of them were quiet, wetting their lips, not looking around. Then Mr. Summers raised one hand high and said, "Adams." A man disengaged himself from the crowd and came forward. "Hi, Steve," Mr. Summers said, and Mr. Adams said, "Hi, Joe." They grinned at one another humorlessly and nervously. Then Mr. Adams reached into the black box and took out a folded paper. He held it firmly by one corner as he turned and went hastily back to his place in the crowd, where he stood a little apart from his family, not looking down at his hand.

"Allen," Mr. Summers said. "Anderson. . . . Bentham."

"Seems like there's no time at all between lotteries any more," Mrs. Delacroix said to Mrs. Graves in the back row. "Seems like we got through with the last one only last week."

"Time sure goes fast," Mrs. Graves said.

"Clark. . . . Delacroix."

"There goes my old man," Mrs. Delacroix said. She held her breath while her husband went forward.

"Dunbar," Mr. Summers said, and Mrs. Dunbar went steadily to the box while one of the women said, "Go on, Janey," and another said, "There she goes."

"We're next," Mrs. Graves said. She watched while Mr. Graves came around from the side of the box, greeted Mr. Summers gravely, and selected a slip of paper from the box. By now, all through the crowd there were men holding the small folded papers in their large hands, turning them over and over nervously. Mrs. Dunbar and her two sons stood together, Mrs. Dunbar holding the slip of paper.

"Harburt. . . . Hutchinson."

"Get up there, Bill," Mrs. Hutchinson said, and the people near her laughed.

"Jones."

"They do say," Mr. Adams said to Old Man Warner, who stood next to him, "that over in the north village they're talking of giving up the lottery."

Old Man Warner snorted. "Pack of crazy fools," he said. "Listening to the young folks, nothing's good enough for *them*. Next thing you know, they'll be wanting to go back to living in caves, nobody work any more, live *that* way for a while. Used to be a saying about 'Lottery in June, corn be heavy soon.' First thing you know, we'd all be eating stewed chickweed and acorns. There's *always* been a lottery," he added petulantly. "Bad enough to see young Joe Summers up there joking with everybody."

"Some places have already quit lotteries," Mrs. Adams said.

"Nothing but trouble in *that*," Old Man Warner said stoutly. "Pack of young fools."

"Martin." And Bobby Martin watched his father go forward. "Overdyke. . . . Percy."

"I wish they'd hurry," Mrs. Dunbar said to her older son. "I wish they'd hurry."

"They're almost through," her son said.

"You get ready to run tell Dad," Mrs. Dunbar said.

Mr. Summers called his own name and then stepped forward precisely and selected a slip from the box. Then he called, "Warner."

"Seventy-seventh year I been in the lottery," Old Man Warner said as he went through the crowd. "Seventy-seventh time."

"Watson." The tall boy came awkwardly through the crowd. Someone said, "Don't be nervous, Jack," and Mr. Summers said, "Take your time, son."

"Zanini."

After that, there was a long pause, a breathless pause, until Mr. Summers, holding his slip of paper in the air, said, "All right, fellows." For a minute, no one moved, and then all the slips of paper were opened. Suddenly, all the women began to speak at once, saying, "Who is it?" "Who's got it?" "Is it the Dunbars?" "Is it the Watsons?" Then the voices began to say, "It's Hutchinson. It's Bill," "Bill Hutchinson's got it."

"Go tell your father," Mrs. Dunbar said to her older son.

People began to look around to see the Hutchinsons. Bill Hutchinson was standing quiet, staring down at the paper in his hand. Suddenly, Tessie Hutchinson shouted to Mr. Summers, "You didn't give him time enough to take any paper he wanted. I saw you. It wasn't fair!"

"Be a good sport, Tessie," Mrs. Delacroix called, and Mrs. Graves said, "All of us took the same chance."

"Shut up, Tessie," Bill Hutchinson said.

"Well, everyone," Mr. Summers said, "that was done pretty fast, and now we've got to be hurrying a little more to get done in time." He consulted his next list. "Bill," he said, "you draw for the Hutchinson family. You got any other households in the Hutchinsons?"

"There's Don and Eva," Mrs. Hutchinson yelled. "Make *them* take their chance!"

"Daughters draw with their husbands' families, Tessie," Mr. Summers said gently. "You know that as well as anyone else."

"It wasn't *fair*," Tessie said.

"I guess not, Joe," Bill Hutchinson said regretfully. "My daughter draws with her husband's family, that's only fair. And I've got no other family except the kids."

"Then, as far as drawing for families is concerned, it's you," Mr. Summers said in explanation, "and as far as drawing for households is concerned, that's you, too. Right?"

"Right," Bill Hutchinson said.

"How many kids, Bill?" Mr. Summers asked formally.

"Three," Bill Hutchinson said. "There's Bill, Jr., and Nancy, and little Dave. And Tessie and me."

"All right, then," Mr. Summers said. "Harry, you got their tickets back?"

Mr. Graves nodded and held up the slips of paper. "Put them in the box, then," Mr. Summers directed. "Take Bill's and put it in."

"I think we ought to start over," Mrs. Hutchinson said, as quietly as she could. "I tell you it wasn't *fair*. You didn't give him time enough to choose. *Every*body saw that."

Mr. Graves had selected the five slips and put them in the box, and he dropped all the papers but those onto the ground, where the breeze caught them and lifted them off.

"Listen, everybody," Mrs. Hutchinson was saying to the people around her.

"Ready, Bill?" Mr. Summers asked, and Bill Hutchinson, with one quick glance around at his wife and children, nodded.

"Remember," Mr. Summers said, "take the slips and keep them folded until each person has taken one. Harry, you help little Dave." Mr. Graves took the hand of the little boy, who came willingly with him up to the box. "Take a paper out of the box, Davy," Mr. Summers said. Davy put his hand into the box and laughed. "Take just *one* paper," Mr. Summers said.

"Harry, you hold it for him." Mr. Graves took the child's hand and removed the folded paper from the tight fist and held it while little Dave stood next to him and looked up at him wonderingly.

"Nancy next," Mr. Summers said. Nancy was twelve, and her school friends breathed heavily as she went forward, switching her skirt, and took a slip daintily from the box. "Bill, Jr.," Mr. Summers said, and Billy, his face red and his feet overlarge, nearly knocked the box over as he got a paper out. "Tessie," Mr. Summers said. She hesitated for a minute, looking around defiantly, and then set her lips and went up to the box. She snatched a paper out and held it behind her.

"Bill," Mr. Summers said, and Bill Hutchinson reached into the box and felt around, bringing his hand out at last with the slip of paper in it.

The crowd was quiet. A girl whispered, "I hope it's not Nancy," and the sound of the whisper reached the edges of the crowd.

"It's not the way it used to be," Old Man Warner said clearly. "People ain't the way they used to be."

"All right," Mr. Summers said. "Open the papers. Harry, you open little Dave's."

Mr. Graves opened the slip of paper and there was a general sigh through the crowd as he held it up and everyone could see that it was blank. Nancy and Bill, Jr., opened theirs at the same time, and both beamed and laughed, turning around to the crowd and holding their slips of paper above their heads.

"Tessie," Mr. Summers said. There was a pause, and then Mr. Summers looked at Bill Hutchinson, and Bill unfolded his paper and showed it. It was blank.

"It's Tessie," Mr. Summers said, and his voiced was hushed. "Show us her paper, Bill."

Bill Hutchinson went over to his wife and forced the slip of paper out of her hand. It had a black spot on it, the black spot Mr. Summers had made the night before with the heavy pencil in the coal-company office. Bill Hutchinson held it up, and there was a stir in the crowd.

"All right, folks," Mr. Summers said. "Let's finish quickly."

Although the villagers had forgotten the ritual and lost the original black box, they still remembered to use stones. The pile of stones the boys had made earlier was ready; there were stones on the ground with the blowing scraps of paper that had come out of the box. Mrs. Delacroix selected a stone so large she had to pick it up with both hands and turned to Mrs. Dunbar. "Come on," she said. "Hurry up."

Mrs. Dunbar had small stones in both hands, and she said, gasping for breath, "I can't run at all. You'll have to go ahead and I'll catch up with you."

The children had stones already, and someone gave little Davy Hutchinson a few pebbles.

Tessie Hutchinson was in the center of a cleared space by now, and she held her hands out desperately as the villagers moved in on her. "It isn't fair," she said. A stone hit her on the side of the head.

Old Man Warner was saying, "Come on, come on, everyone." Steve Adams was in the front of the crowd of villagers, with Mrs. Graves beside him.

"It isn't fair, it isn't right," Mrs. Hutchinson screamed, and then they were upon her.

[1948]

NOTES FOR
A YOUNG WRITER

These are some notes, not necessarily complete, on the writing of short stories; they were originally written as a stimulus to my daughter Sally, who wants to be a writer.

In the country of the story the writer is king. He makes all the rules, with only the reservation that he must not ask more than a reader can reasonably grant. Remember, the reader is a very tough customer indeed, stubborn, dragging his feet, easily irritated. He will willingly agree to suspend disbelief for a time: he will go along with you if it is necessary for your story that you both assume temporarily that there really is a Land of Oz, but he will not suspend reason, he will not agree, for any story ever written, that he can see the Land of Oz from his window. As a matter of fact, you would do well to picture your typical reader as someone lying in a hammock on a soft summer day, with children playing loudly near by, a television set and a radio both going at once, a sound truck blaring past in the street, birds singing and dogs barking; this fellow has a cool drink and a pillow for his head, and all you have to do with your story is catch his attention and hold it. Remember, your story is an uneasy bargain with your reader. Your end of the bargain is to play fair, and keep him interested, his end of the bargain is to keep reading. It is just terribly terribly easy to put a story down half-read and go off and do something else. Nevertheless, for as long as the story does go on you are the boss. You have the right to assume that the reader will accept the story on your own terms. You have the right to assume that the reader, however lazy, will exert some small intelligence while he is reading. Suppose you are writing a story

about a castle. You do not need to describe every tower, every
man at arms, every stone; your reader must bring his own
complement of men at arms and towers; you need only describe
one gardener to imply that the castle is well stocked with servants. In your stories, then, set your own landscape with its
own horizons, put your characters in where you think they
belong, and move them as you please.

Your story must have a surface tension, which can be considerably stretched but not shattered; you cannot break your
story into pieces with jagged odds and ends that do not belong.
You cannot begin a story in one time and place, say, and then
intrude a major flashback or a little sermon or a shift in
emphasis to another scene or another character, without seriously marring the story, and turning the reader dizzy with trying to keep up. Consider simple movement from one place to
another; if some movement is necessary and inevitable—as of
course it is in most stories—then let the reader come along
with you; do not jolt him abruptly from one place to another;
in other words, let your story move as naturally and easily as
possible, without side trips into unnecessary spots of beauty.
Suppose you are writing a story about a boy and a girl meeting
on a corner; your reader wants to go to that very corner and
listen in; if, instead, you start your boy and girl toward the
corner and then go off into a long description of the streetcar
tracks and a little discussion of the background of these two
characters and perhaps a paragraph or so about the town
improvement which is going to remove the streetcar tracks
they are crossing, and the girl's father's long-time aversion to
any form of wheeled traffic—you will lose your reader and
your story will fall apart. Always, always, make the duller
parts of your story work *for* you; the necessary passage of
time, the necessary movement must not stop the story dead,
but must push it forward.

Avoid small graceless movements. As much as possible free
yourself from useless and clumsy statements about action.
"They got in the car and drove home" is surely too much
ground to cover in one short simple sentence; assuming that
your characters did get into the car and did have to drive

home, you have just the same wasted a point where your action might work for your story; let the process of their getting home be an unobtrusive factor in another, more important action: "On their way home in the car they saw that the boy and the girl were still standing talking earnestly on the corner." Let each such potentially awkward spot contribute to your total action. In almost every story you will face some unwanted element, something your characters *have* to do to keep the story going at all; people have to get from one place to another, or get dressed, or eat their dinners, before the story can continue; try always to make these actions positive. For instance: "She dealt the cards; her fingers clung to each card as though unwilling to let go of anything they had once touched," or, "During all of dinner the singing went on upstairs, and no one said a word." (I would like to see someone write that story.) Or, "It was only one block to walk, so she counted her footsteps anxiously." Does your unfortunate heroine have to do the dishes before she can go out and meet her hero in the rose garden? "She washed and dried the dishes with extreme care, wondering all the time if she dared to smash a cup against the wall."

All of this has applied to necessary but essentially uninteresting action. The same thing is true of description and some conversation; certainly in every story there comes a time when you have to give in and let your reader know what something looks like, or that your hero and heroine said good-morning-how-are-you-today-isn't-the-weather-lovely-how's-your-mother before they got on to the most important business of the story, or to the rose garden. Try to remember with description that you must never just let it lie there; nothing in your story should ever be static unless you have a very good reason indeed for keeping your reader still; the essence of the story is motion. Do not let your chair be "a straight chair, with no arms and a hard wooden seat." Let your heroine go over and take a firm hold of the back of a straight wooden chair, because at the moment it is stronger than she. Naturally it is assumed that you are not going to try to describe anything you don't need to describe. If it is a sunny day let the sun make a pattern through the fence rail; if you don't care what the weather is don't bother your reader with it. Inanimate objects are best described in use or motion: "Because his cigarette lighter was platinum he had taken to smoking far too much." "The battered chimney seemed eager to hurl down bricks on anyone passing." Also, if your heroine's hair is golden, call it yellow.

Conversation is clearly one of the most difficult parts of the story. It is not enough to let your characters talk as people usually talk because the way people usually talk is extremely dull. Your characters are not going to stammer, or fumble for words, or forget what they are saying, or stop to clear their throats, at least not unless you want them to. Your problem is to make your characters sound as though they were real people talking (or, more accurately, that this is "real" conversation being read by a reader; look at some written conversation that seems perfectly smooth and plausible and natural on the page, and then try reading it aloud; what looks right on the page frequently sounds very literary indeed when read aloud; remember that you are writing to be read silently). Now the sounds and cadences of spoken speech are perfectly familiar to you; you have been talking and listening all your life. You know, for instance that most people speak in short sentences, tending to overuse certain words. You know that whenever anyone gets the floor and a chance to tell a story or describe an incident he will almost always speak in a series of short sentences joined by "and"; this is of course a device to insure that his audience will have no chance to break in before he has finished his story. You know that in a conversation people do say the same things over and over; there is very little economy in spoken speech. There is a great deal of economy in written speech. Your characters will use short sentences, and will tell long stories only under exceptional circumstances, and even then only in the most carefully stylized and rhythmic language; nothing can dissolve a short story quite so effectively as some bore who takes up the middle of it with a long account of something that amuses him and no one else. A bore is a bore, on the page or off it.

Listen always to people talking. Listen to patterns of talking. Listen to patterns of thinking displayed in talking. Think about this: if a husband comes home at night and says to his wife, "What do you think happened to me? When I got onto the bus tonight I sat down next to a girl and when the conductor came along he had a live penguin riding on his head, a live penguin, can you imagine? And when I looked at it, it turned out it was a talking penguin and it said 'Tickets, please,' and there was this guy across the aisle and you really won't believe this but it turned out *he* had a parrot in his pocket and the parrot put out his head and he and the penguin got to talking and I never heard anything like it in my life," don't you know that after the husband has said all this his wife is going to say, "What did the girl look like?" Your characters will make their remarks only once unless there is a good reason for repeating them; people hear better in stories than in real life. Your characters will start all their conversations in the middle unless you have a very good reason for their telling each other good morning and how are you. Remember the importance of the pattern, as important on paper as in real life; a character who says habitually, with one of those silly little laughs, "Well, that's the story of my life," is not ever going to turn around and say, with a silly little laugh, "Well, that's my life story."

Now look at this device: " 'I hate fresh asparagus,' she said to her kitchen clock, and found herself saying it again ten minutes later to Mrs. Butler in the grocery; 'I hate fresh asparagus,' she said, 'it always takes so long to cook.' " You are, at this moment, well into a conversation with Mrs. Butler; your reader, being a common-sense type, no doubt assumes that before the remark about asparagus your heroine and Mrs. Butler said good morning my aren't you out early and isn't that a charming hat. Your reader may also assume, if he is perceptive, that your heroine in some fashion turned away from her kitchen clock, got her hat and coat on, picked up her pocketbook, forgot her shopping list, and in some fashion either walked or drove or bicycled to the store. She is there, she is in the middle of a conversation with Mrs. Butler; not ten words ago she was at home talking to the clock. The transition has been relatively painless; your reader has been required to read only one sentence and get around one semicolon, and the asparagus remark has been repeated simply to tie together the two halves of the sentence.

Your characters in the story, surely, are going to be separate and widely differing people, even though they are not necessarily described to the reader. You yourself have some idea of what they are like and how they differ; there is, for instance, in almost everyone's mind, an essential difference between the hero and the heroine. They don't look alike, even if you are the only one who knows it; your reader will assume it; after all, he has seen people before. They don't dress alike, they don't sound alike. They have small individualities of speech, arising naturally out of their actions and their personalities and their work in the story. Suppose you are using three little girls talking together; you *could* distinguish them by saying that one wore a blue dress, the second had curly hair, and the third was on roller skates, but wouldn't it be simply better writing to identify them by their positions in the group of three; that is, making their actions and their conversations more meaningful because the girls are related to one another at once? They form a hierarchy: first there is a leader who does most of the talking, makes the plans, and provokes the action. The second must be subordinate, but not too much so; she does not initiate, but by following the leader encourages the leader into further action; she will disagree and perhaps even rebel up to a point. The third is of course the tag-along, the one left out when three is a crowd, and her actions and conversation are echoing and imitative of the other two, particularly the leader. The third character will throw her support to whichever of the other two seems stronger at the moment, and can thus, although a very minor character indeed, bring force to bear and influence action. Once three such characters are determined, the entire course of their conversation, no matter how trivial it might be in the story, is predetermined and strong. Once again: people in stories tend to talk in patterns. If your heroine is prepared to be so violent about fresh asparagus it would be reasonable to suppose that her conversation and opinions would generally be a little more emphatic than another character's. She would "adore that silly hat," for instance, or "die if that noise doesn't stop." She will carry out this positive manner in her actions; she will put out a cigarette, for instance, with forceful little poundings, she will set the table carelessly and noisily, but quickly, there will be no nonsense about her likes and dislikes. You might oppose to her a character who is uncertain, who lets cigarettes burn out in the ash tray, who rarely finishes a sentence or who will substitute a phrase like "*you* know" for a finished thought: "I usually carry an umbrella but sometimes . . . *you* know." "I guess it's time I left. I guess you're pretty busy?" Your character, remember, must not talk one way and act another, and can only outrage this consistency for a reason; a character who breaks out of a pattern is shocking and generally insane.

Use all your seasoning sparingly. Do not worry about making your characters shout, intone, exclaim, remark, shriek, reason, holler, or any such thing, unless they are doing it for a reason. All remarks can be *said*. Every time you use a fancy word your reader is going to turn his head to look at it going by and sometimes he may not turn his head back again. My own name for this kind of overexcited talking is the-other-responded. As in this example: "'Then I'm for a swim,'" cried Jack, a gallant flush mantling his cheek. "'And I am with you!' the other responded."

Your coloring words, particularly adjectives and adverbs, must be used where they will do the most good. Not every action needs a qualifying adverb, not every object needs a qualifying adjective. Your reader probably has a perfectly serviceable mental picture of a lion; when a lion comes into your story you need not burden him with adjectives unless it is necessary, for instance, to point out that he is a green lion, something of which your reader might not have a very vivid mental picture.

Use all the tools at your disposal. The language is infinitely flexible, and your use of it should be completely deliberate. Never forget the grotesque effect of the absolutely wrong words: "He swept her into his arms; 'I will always love you,' he giggled." "Top the finished cake with a smear of whipped cream." "'I am not afraid of anything in the world,' he said thinly."

Remember, too, that words on a page have several dimensions: they are seen, they are partially heard, particularly if they seem to suggest a sound, and they have a kind of tangible quality—think of the depressing sight of a whole great paragraph ahead of you, solidly black with huge heavy-sounding words. Moreover, some words seem soft and some hard, some liquid, some warm, some cold; your reader will respond to "soft laughter" but not to "striped laughter"; he will respond more readily to "soft laughter" than to "sweet laughter," because he can hear it more easily. There are also words like "itchy" and "greasy" and "smelly" and "scratchy" that evoke an almost physical response in the reader; use these only if you need them. Exclamation points, italics, capitals, and, most particularly, dialect, should all be used with extreme caution. Consider them as like garlic, and use them accordingly.

Do not try to puzzle your reader unnecessarily; a puzzled reader is an antagonistic reader. Do not expect him to guess why a character does something or how it happens that some remark is made; it may be that you want him to stop and wonder for a minute; if so, make it perfectly clear that everything is going to be all right later on. If you want the reader to be troubled by a nagging question, and go through a part of your story with a kind of expectancy, let one of your characters do something outrageous—turn, perhaps, and throw an apple core through an open window. But then be sure that before your story is finished you explain in some manner that inside the open window lives the character's great-uncle, who keeps a monkey who devours apple cores and catches them on the fly as they come through the window. The reader brings with him a great body of knowledge which you may assume, but he must rely on you for all information necessary to the understanding of this story which, after all, you have written.

Someone—I forget who—once referred to the easier sections of his work as "benches for the reader to sit down upon," meaning, of course, that the poor reader who had struggled through the complex maze of ideas for several pages could rest gratefully at last on a simple clear paragraph. Provide *your* reader with such assistance. If you would like him to rest for a minute so you can sneak up behind him and sandbag him, let him have a little peaceful description, or perhaps a little something funny to smile over, or a little moment of superiority. If you want him to stop dead and think, do something that will make him stop dead; use a wholly inappropriate word, or a startling phrase— "pretty as a skunk"—or an odd juxtaposition: "Her hair was curly and red and she had great big feet," or something that will make him think back: "Fresh asparagus is most significant symbolically." Give him something to worry about: "Although the bank had stood on that corner for fifty years it had never been robbed." Or something to figure out: "If John had not had all that tooth trouble there would never have been any question about the rabbits." In all this, though, don't let the reader stop for more than a second or he might get away. Catch him fast with your next sentence and send him reeling along.

And if you want your reader to go faster and faster make your writing go faster and faster. "The room was dark. The windows were shaded, the furniture invisible. The door was shut and yet from somewhere, some small hidden precious casket of light buried deep in the darkness of the room, a spark came, moving in mad colored circles up and down, around and in and out and over and under and lighting everything it saw." (Those adjectives are unspeakable in every sense of the word, and wholly unnecessary; this is an example, not a model.) If you want your reader to go slower and slower make your writing go slower and slower: "After a wild rush of water and noise the fountain was at last turned off and the water was gone. Only one drop hung poised and then fell, and fell with a small musical touch. Now, it rang. Now."

Now I want to say something about words artificially weighted; you can, and frequently must, make a word carry several meanings or messages in your story if you use the word right. This is a kind of shorthand. I once had occasion to send a heroine on a long journey during which she expressed her loneliness and lack of a home by imagining dream lives in various places she passed; this daydream is climaxed when at lunch she hears a little girl at a near by table ask for her milk in a cup of stars; the lonely girl thinks that what she too is asking for is a cup of stars, and when she finally finds her home she will drink from a cup of stars. Later, when other characters are talking of their own comfort and security the lonely girl announces proudly that *she* has a cup of stars; this is by then not only recognizable as an outright lie, but a pathetic attempt to pretend that she is neither lonely nor defenseless. "Cup of stars" has become a shorthand phrase for all her daydreams. Notice, however, that once such a word or phrase has been given a weighting you cannot afford to use the word or phrase *without* the weighting; my lonely girl cannot refer idly to cups of stars anywhere else, because those words are carrying an extra meaning which must not be dissipated.

If you announce early in your story that your lady with the aversion to asparagus is wearing a diamond-and-ruby wrist watch your reader will be intrigued: here is a detail apparently not essential to the story and yet you thought it worthwhile to put it in; the reader will be watching to see what you are going to do with it. If you then turn up another character who is wearing a solid-gold wrist watch your reader will begin to wonder whether you are just queer for watches or whether this is going to amount to something in the story. You must satisfy his curiosity. If you then remark that the diamond-and-ruby wrist watch was a gift from an old boy friend of the lady's, the watch is then carrying something extra, and when at the end of the story she throws the watch at her husband's head she is throwing her old boy friend too. The reader is also going to have to know who gave the other fellow the solid-gold wrist watch and whose head *that* one is going to hit; nothing can be left suspended in mid-air, abandoned. If you start your story on a small boy going home to pick up his football so he can get into the game in the corner lot, and then let him fall into one adventure after another until the end of the story, your reader is going to come out of that story fighting mad unless he is told whether or not the boy got his football and whether he ever got back to the game.

Now about this business of the beginning implying the ending, something which all the textbooks insist upon. You will actually find that if you keep your story tight, with no swerving from the proper path, it will curl up quite naturally at the end, provided you stop when you have finished what you have to say. One device, of course, is beginning and ending on what is essentially the same image, so that a story beginning, say, "It was a beautiful sunny day," might end, "The sun continued to beat down on the empty street." This is not a bad policy, although it can be limiting. There is no question but that the taut stretched quality of the good short story is pulled even tighter by such a construction. You can tie your story together, however, with similar devices—how about a story which opens on a lady feeding her cat, and ends on a family sitting down to dinner? Or a story which opens on your heroine crying and closes on her laughing? The beginning and ending should of course belong together; the ending must be implicit in the beginning, although there have been stories which were defeated because the author thought of a wonderful last line and then tried to write a story to go with it; this is not wrong, just almost impossible. I am not going to try to tell you how to set up a plot. Just remember that primarily, in the story and out of it, you are living in a world of people. A story must have characters in it; work with concrete rather than abstract nouns, and always dress your ideas immediately. Suppose you want to write a story about what you might vaguely think of as "magic." You will be hopelessly lost, wandering around formlessly in notions of magic and incantations; you will never make any forward progress at all until you turn your idea, "magic," into a person, someone who wants to do or make or change or act in some way. Once you have your first character you will of course need another to put into opposition, a person in some sense "anti-magic"; when both are working at their separate intentions, dragging in other characters as needed, you are well into your story. All you have to do then is write it, paying attention, please, to grammar and punctuation.

[1962]

AVAILABLE FROM PENGUIN CLASSICS

The Haunting of Hill House

Introduction by Laura Miller

Four spirit seekers arrive at a notoriously unfriendly heap called Hill House. At first, their stay seems destined to be merely a spooky encounter with inexplicable phenomena. But Hill House is gathering its powers—and soon it will choose one of them to make its own.

ISBN 978-0-14-303998-3

We Have Always Lived in the Castle

Introduction by Jonathan Lethem

Taking readers deep into a labyrinth of dark neurosis, *We Have Always Lived in the Castle* is a deliciously unsettling novel about a perverse, isolated, and possibly murderous family and the struggle that ensues when a cousin arrives at their estate.

ISBN 978-0-14-303997-6

AVAILABLE FROM PENGUIN

Life Among the Savages

Shirley Jackson was known for her terse, haunting prose. But the writer possessed another side, one which is delightfully exposed in this hilariously charming memoir of her family's life in rural Vermont.

ISBN 978-0-14-026767-9

Printed in the United States
by Baker & Taylor Publisher Services